DARK
GODS

ABOUT THE TYPE

This book was set in Caslon, a typeface first designed in 1722 by William Caslon (1692–1766). Its widespread use by most English printers in the early eighteenth century soon supplanted the Dutch typefaces that had formerly prevailed. The roman is considered a "workhorse" typeface due to its pleasant, open appearance, while the italic is exceedingly decorative.

DARK
GODS

T.E.D.
KLEIN

DIP

Published in November 2021 by Drugstore Indian Press by arrangement
with the author. All rights reserved by the author. The right of
T.E.D. Klein to be identified as Author of this Work has been asserted
by him in accordance with the Copyright, Designs and Patents Act 1988.

Three of the stories in this collection first appeared in the following anthologies:
"Children of the Kingdom" in *Dark Forces*, Viking, 1980; "Petey" in *Shadows* 2,
Doubleday, 1979; "Black Man with a Horn" in *New Tales of the Cthulhu Mythos*,
Arkham House, 1980. "Nadelman's God" first appeared in *Dark Gods*, Viking, 1985.

All four stories have been slightly revised for this edition.

2 4 6 8 10 9 7 5 3 1

ISBN
978-1-78636-821-8 (trade paperback)
978-1-78636-820-1 (slipcased hardback)

Design and layout by Alligator Tree Graphics.
Printed in England by T. J. Books Limited.

Drugstore Indian Press / Grosvenor House /
1 New Road / Hornsea, HU18 1PG / England

editor@pspublishing.co.uk / www.pspublishing.co.uk

CONTENTS

AUTHOR'S NOTE   vii

CHILDREN OF THE KINGDOM   I

PETEY   73

BLACK MAN WITH A HORN   131

NADELMAN'S GOD   177

AUTHOR'S NOTE

Many years ago, a married couple I know from my Manhattan neighborhood flew 1,600 miles to the Yucatan for their vacation. Braving the tropical heat, they spent a day exploring the mysterious thousand-year-old Mayan ruins at Uxmal, having dutifully boned up beforehand on its ancient civilization, its pyramids and palaces, its ceremonies, its human sacrifice. Along with other tourists, they climbed to the top of a vine-covered pyramid and stood contemplating the vast unbroken green of the Mexican rain forest. At that moment, a woman nearby overheard them talking. Apparently recognizing them as fellow New Yorkers, she hurried over to them.

"Oh," she said, smiling brightly, "are you from the city?"

The city. That's how New Yorkers talk, and how New Yorkers think: that there's really only one city, after all. Friends who've moved to Boston and San Francisco have admitted that, after New York, these places feel like small towns. Saul Steinberg's famous *New Yorker* cover got it right, and so did John Updike: "The true New Yorker," he wrote, "secretly believes that people living anywhere else have to be, in some sense, kidding."

And hand in hand with this comes another belief—perhaps ignorant, no doubt arrogant—that the city is inherently interesting, even if you don't happen to live there. I certainly hope it is, since it's where three of the stories in this book are set (with the fourth an evening's drive away).

I've tinkered a bit with all four stories since their previous publication, sometimes merely tweaking a word here and there, sometimes more. I'm aware that one can overdo this—that students taking the SAT are advised to resist the urge to rethink their original answers, and that it's often wiser to stick with one's initial, more spontaneous response. But I don't know; sometimes things just need fixing. A popular writer known for his speed once got his knuckles rapped for having had a character "eating cold hamburgers with great relish"—a line that might have benefited from, as they say, another pass through the typewriter.

However, though they're all slightly revised, no attempt has been made to update these stories. Like it or not, for better or worse, they are of their time; and that time is the late '70s and early '80s. It's claimed—or I, at least, used to claim—that the nice thing about supernatural horror is that it doesn't date the way other genres do, and that it enjoys a unique longevity. In support of this, I would bring up writers like Robert Hichens, Robert W. Chambers, W. W. Jacobs, A. E. Coppard, Clemence Dane, Marjorie Bowen, Richard Marsh, even L. P. Hartley, popular and prolific authors in their day, whose only stories remaining in print and still anthologized, or at least that are still read, tend to be their supernatural tales.

But once again, I don't know; that now seems a bit too glib. Age matters. Everything dates. Just as one reads, appalled, of times before anesthesia, it's hard to read of a pre-wired world without feeling a certain comfortable distance from it, maybe even a certain degree of condescension. Imagine: they had to make do without laptops, and they cluttered up their shelves with vinyl records. Lacking the internet, researchers had to waste precious hours wandering around the library. Lacking GPS, travelers could still get lost. Those poor people!

Nonetheless, that's the world my characters inhabit. They may lack cell phones, but at least they still have phone booths (an amenity now extinct in New York); they've never worn masks, nor are they "woke" (and their author, as those quotes may suggest, isn't either). I hope you'll extend them your sympathy.

DARK
GODS

CHILDREN OF
THE KINGDOM

Mischief is their occupation, malice their habit, murder their sport, and blasphemy their delight.
—Maturin, *Melmoth the Wanderer*

They are everywhere, those creatures.
—Derleth, *The House on Curwen Street*

It taught me the foolishness of *not* being afraid.
—Rape victim, New York City

On a certain spring evening several years ago, after an unsuccessful interview in Boston for a job I'd thought was mine, I missed the last train back to New York and was forced to take the eleven-thirty bus. It proved to be a "local," wending its way through the shabby little cities of southern New England and pulling into a succession of dimly lit Greyhound stations far from the highway, usually in the older parts of town—the decaying ethnic neighborhoods, the inner-city slums, the ghettos. I had a bad headache, and soon fell asleep. When I awoke, I felt disoriented. All the other passengers were sleeping. I didn't know what time it was, but hesitated to turn on the light and look at my watch lest it disturb the man next to me. Instead, I looked out the window. We were passing through the heart of yet another shabby, nameless city, moving past the same gutted buildings I'd been seeing all night in my dreams, the same lines of cornices and rooftops, empty windows, gaping doorways. In the patches of darkness, familiar shapes seemed strange. Mailboxes and fire hydrants sprouted like tropical plants. Yet somehow it was stranger beneath the streetlights, where garbage cast long shadows on the sidewalk, and vacant lots hid glints of broken glass among the weeds. I remembered what I'd read of those great Mayan cities standing silent and abandoned in the Central American jungle, with no clue to where the inhabitants had gone. Through the window I could now see crumbling rows of tenements, an ugly red-brick housing project, some darkened and filthy-looking shops with alleys blocked by iron gates. Here and there a solitary figure would turn to watch the bus go by. Except for my reflection, I saw not one white face. A pair of little children threw stones at us from behind a fortress made of trash; a grown man stood pissing in the street like an animal

and watched us with amusement as we passed. I wanted to be out of
this benighted place and prayed that the driver would get us through
quickly. I longed to be back in New York. Then a street sign caught
my eye, and I realized that I'd already arrived. This was my own
neighborhood; my home was only three streets down and just across
the avenue. As the bus continued south, I caught a fleeting glimpse
of the apartment building where, less than half a block away, my wife
lay awaiting my return.

Less than half a block can make a difference in New York. Different
worlds can coexist side by side, scarcely intersecting. There are places
in Manhattan where you can see a modern high-rise, with its terraces and doormen and well-appointed lobby, towering white and
immaculate above some soot-stained little remnant of the city's
past—a tenement built during the Depression, lines of garbage cans
in front, or a nineteenth-century brownstone gone to seed, its brick-
work defaced by graffiti, its front door yawning open, its hallway
dark, narrow, and forbidding as a tomb. Perhaps the two buildings
will be separated by an alley; perhaps not even that. The taller one's
shadow may fall across the other, blotting out the sun; the other
may disturb the block with loud music, voices raised in argument,
the gnawing possibility of crime. Yet to all appearances the people
of each group will live their lives without acknowledging the other's
existence. The poor will keep their rats, like secrets, to themselves;
the cooking smells, the smells of poverty and sickness and backed-up
drains, will seldom pass beyond their windows. The sidewalk in front
may be lined with the idle and unshaven, men with T-shirts and dark
skins and a gaze as sharp as razors, singing, or trading punches, or
disputing, perhaps, in Spanish; or they may sit in stony silence on
the stoop, passing round a bottle in a paper bag. They are rough-
looking and impetuous, these men; but they will seldom leave their
kingdom for the alien world next door. And those who inhabit that
alien world will move with a certain wariness when they find themselves on the street, and will hurry past the others without meeting
their eyes.

My grandfather, Herman Lauterbach, was one of those people who could move in either world. Though his Brooklyn apartment had always seemed a haven of middle-class respectability, at least for as long as I knew him, whatever refinements it displayed were in fact the legacy of his second wife; Herman himself was more at home among the poor. He, too, had been poor for most of his life—a bit of a radical, I suspect—and always thought of my father, his son-in-law, as "nothing but a goddamn stuffshirt" simply because my father had an office job. (As his beloved daughter's only child I was spared such criticisms, although I'm sure he found my lackluster academic career a disappointment and my chosen field, the Puritan Heritage, a bore.) His attitudes never changed, even when, past seventy, having outlived two exasperated wives, he himself was forced to don a necktie and go to work for the brother of an old friend in a firm that manufactured watch casings. He had always been a comical, companionable man, fond of women, jokes, and holidays, but forty-hour weeks went hard with him and soured his temper. So did the death of my mother the following year. Afterward, things were not the same; he was no longer quite so endearing. One saw a more selfish side, a certain hardness, like that of a child who has grown up in the street. Yet one inevitably forgave him, if only because of his age and lack of consequence, and because there still hung about him a certain air of comedy, as if it was his doom to provide the material for other people's anecdotes. There was, for example, his violent altercation with the driver of a Gravesend Bay bus, which my grandfather had boarded in the belief that it went to Bay Ridge; and then there was the episode in Marinaro's bar, where jokes about the Mafia were not taken lightly. Several weeks later came a highly injudicious argument with the boss's son, less than half his age, over the recent hike in transit fares for senior citizens, and whether this entitled my grandfather to a corresponding increase in pay. Finally, when the two of them nearly came to blows over an equally minor disagreement—whether or not the city's impending bankruptcy was the fault of Mayor Beame, whom my grandfather somewhat resembled—everyone agreed that it was time for the old man to retire.

For the next three years he managed to get by on his modest savings, augmented by Social Security and regular checks from my father, now remarried and living in New Jersey. Then, suddenly, his age caught up with him: on May 4, 1977, while seated in his kitchen watching the first of the Frost-Nixon interviews (and no doubt shaking his fist at the television set), he suffered a minor stroke, toppled backward from his chair, and had to be hospitalized for nearly a month. He was, at this time, eighty-three years old.

Or at least that was what he admitted to. We could never actually be sure, for in the past he'd been known to subtract as much as a decade when applying for a job, and to add it back, with interest, when applying for golden-age discounts at a local movie house. Whatever the case, during his convalescence it became clear that he was in no shape to return to Brooklyn, where he'd been living on the third floor of a building without elevators. Besides, like his once-robust constitution, the neighborhood had deteriorated over the years; gangs of black and Puerto Rican youths preyed on the elderly of all races, especially those living alone, and an ailing old widower was fair game. On the other hand, he was not yet a candidate for a nursing home, at least not the elaborate kind with oxygen tents and cardiac units attached. What he needed was a rest home. As his doctor explained in private to my wife and me on our second visit, my grandfather was by no means permanently incapacitated; why, just look at Pasteur, who after a series of fifty-eight strokes had gone on to make some of his greatest discoveries. ("And who knows?" the doctor said. "Maybe your granddad'll make a few discoveries of his own.") According to the prognosis, he was expected to be on his feet within a week or two. Perhaps before that time he would have another stroke; likely, though, it would come later; more than likely it would kill him. Until then, however, he'd be alert and responsive and sufficiently ambulant to care for himself; he would not be walking with his usual speed, perhaps, but he'd be walking.

My grandfather put it more succinctly. "What the hell you think I am," he said, voice gravelly with age, when the question of a rest home was raised, "some vegetable in a wheelchair?" Struggling to sit up in bed, he launched into an extended monologue about how he'd rather die alone and forgotten on Skid Row than in a "home"; but for all its Sturm und Drang the speech sounded curiously insincere, and I had the impression that he'd been rehearsing it for years. No doubt his pride was at stake; when I assured him that what we had in mind was not some thinly disguised terminal ward, nor anything like a day-care center for the senile and decrepit, but rather a sort of boardinghouse where he could live in safety among people his own age, people as active as he was, he calmed down at once. I could see that the idea appealed to him; he had always thrived on conversation, even aimless chatter, and the prospect of some company—especially that of fellow retirees with time on their hands—was an inviting one. The truth is, he'd been lonely out in Brooklyn, though of course he would never have admitted it. For my part I was feeling rather guilty; I hadn't come to see him as often as I should have. From now on, I told him, things would be different: I would find him a place in Manhattan, a place where I could visit him once or twice a week. I'd even take him out to dinner, when I got the chance.

He appeared to think it over. Then—for my sake, I think (and somehow I found this horribly depressing)—he screwed his face into a roguish grin, like a small boy boasting to an adult. "Make sure there are plenty of good-looking dames around," he said, "and you got yourself a deal."

The following weekend, with this qualified blessing in mind, Karen and I set about looking for a place. The press had recently brought to light a series of scandals involving various institutions for the aged, and we were particularly anxious to find a reputable one. By Saturday afternoon we'd discovered that many of the private homes were more expensive than we'd counted on—as much as two or three hundred dollars a week—and that in most of them the supervision was too strict; they resembled nothing so much as tiny smiling prisons. Grandfather would never stand for being cooped up inside all day; he liked to wander. Another, run by nuns, was comfortable, clean, and open to non-Catholics, but its residents were in no condition to feed themselves, much less join in human conversation. These were the unreclaimables, lapsed into senescence; my grandfather would have seemed positively vigorous beside them.

Finally, early Sunday evening, on the recommendation of a friend, we visited a place on West Eighty-First Street, scarcely a dozen blocks from where we lived. It was called, somewhat optimistically, the Park West Manor for Adults, even though it was rather less than a manor house and nowhere near the park. The owner was a certain Mr. Fetterman, whom we never actually met; we later learned that he was a bit of a crook, though never in ways that directly affected us. I gathered from my wife, who, as accountant for a publishing firm, has always had a better head for business, that the home was part of some statewide franchise operation with vague ties to local government. According to the agreement—common, she informed me—my grandfather's rent was to be paid for out of his now-meager savings; when they were depleted (as indeed they would be in a year or so), the cost would be borne by Medicaid for the rest of his life.

The building itself, a dirty red ornamental brick, occupied the south side of the street between Broadway and Amsterdam Avenue, a block and a half from the Museum of Natural History. It consisted of two wings, each nine stories tall, connected by a narrow recessed entranceway several steps down from the sidewalk. The place seemed respectable enough, though at first sight it was not particularly impressive, especially at the end of the day, with the sun sinking behind the Hudson and long shadows darkening the block. The pavement in front of the building had recently been torn up for some kind of sewer work, and huge brown metal pipes lay stacked on either side like ammunition. My wife and I had to step across a series of planks to reach the front door. Inside it, just before the lobby, was an alcove with a battered wooden desk, behind which, seemingly stupefied with boredom, sat a wrinkled old black man in a guard's uniform—the sort of man one sees at banks these days, ineffectually directing people to the appropriate tellers. He nodded and let us pass through. No doubt he thought he recognized us; it's said that, to whites, all blacks look alike, and years in various city classrooms have convinced me that the reverse is true as well.

The lobby wasn't much of an improvement. Like most lobbies, it was dim, depressing, and cold. The rear wall was lined by a mirror, so that on entering, my wife and I found ourselves confronted by a rather discouraged-looking little couple approaching from across the room, the woman frowning at the man, no doubt for some trifling thing he had just said, the man glancing with increasing frequency at his watch. To the couple's left ran a long, ornate mantelpiece overhanging a blank expanse of wall where a fireplace should have been. Grouped around this nonexistent fireplace were half a dozen caved-in leather chairs and a pair of dusty rubber plants sagging wearily in their pots, their leaves reflected in the mirror and, on a smaller scale, in the painting hanging just above the mantel: a framed reproduction of Rousseau's *Children of the Kingdom,* the primitive figures peering out at us like a ring of ghosts, their faces pale and impassive against the violets, reds, and greens of the surrounding jungle. The colors were faded, as if from having been stared at by generations of residents.

It was the dinner hour. The lobby was deserted; from somewhere to the right came the sound of voices and the clank of pots and plates, accompanied by a scraping of chairs and the smell of boiled meat. We moved toward it, following the right-hand corridor past a series of turns until we came to a pair of wooden doors with windows in the top. Karen, emboldened by fatigue, pushed her way through. Before us stretched the dining room, barely more than half filled, the diners grouped around tables of various shapes and designs. It reminded me of the mess hall at summer camp, as if my fellow campers had aged and withered right there in their seats without ever having gained appreciably in size. Even the waiters looked old: a few, hurrying up the aisles, still sported oily black pompadours, but most looked as if they could easily have traded places with the people they served. White hair was the rule here, with pink skull showing through. This was as true for the women as the men, for by this age the sexes had once more begun to merge; like babies, the individuals in the room were hard to tell apart. Nor were they any more inclined than children to disguise their curiosity; dozens of old pink heads swiveled in our direction as we stood there in the doorway. We were intruders; I felt as if we'd blundered into a different world. Then I saw the expectation in their faces and felt doubly bad: each of them had probably been hoping for a visitor, a son or daughter or grandchild, and must have been keenly disappointed by every new arrival that was not the one awaited.

A small, harried-looking man approached us and identified himself as the assistant manager. He looked as if he was about to scold us for having arrived during dinner—he, too, probably assumed we were there to visit someone—but he brightened immediately when we explained why we'd come. "Follow me," he said, moving off at a kind of dogtrot. "I'll show you the place from top to bottom." In the noise and hubbub of the dining room I hadn't caught his name, but as soon as he started toward the nearest exit, my wife and me in tow, a plaintive chorus of "Mr. Calzone" arose behind us. He ignored it and pushed on through the door; I suppose he was glad of the diversion.

We found ourselves in the kitchen, all iron pots and steam, with cooks in white T-shirts and white-jacketed waiters shouting at one another in Spanish. "This used to be kosher," yelled Calzone, "but they cut all that out." I assured him that my grandfather liked his bacon as well as the next man. "Oh, we don't give 'em bacon too often," he said, taking me literally, "but they really go for the pork chops." My wife seemed satisfied, and nodded at the dishwashers and the ranks of aluminum cabinets. As for me, I wasn't sure just what to look for, but am happy to report I saw no worm eggs and not one dead cat.

Calzone was as good as his word. From the kitchen he conducted us "up top" to the ninth floor via a clanging old elevator of the self-service type, with the numbers beside the buttons printed so large—in raised numerals nearly an inch high—that even a blind man could have run it. (Its speed was such that, had one of the home's frailer residents preferred to take the stairs, she would probably have arrived in time to meet us.) The rooms on the ninth floor, most of them unoccupied, were shabby but clean, with private bathrooms and plenty of closet space. Grandfather would have nothing to complain about. In fact, with its boarders all downstairs at dinner, the place seemed more a college dormitory than an old-folks' home. Aside from the oversized elevator panel and the shiny new aluminum railings we'd noticed everywhere—in easy reach of stairways, tubs, and toilets—the only concession to age appeared to be a sign-up sheet my wife came across on a bulletin board in the second-floor "game room," for those who wished to make an appointment at some community medical center over on Columbus Avenue.

Our tour ended with the laundry room in the basement. It was hot and uncomfortable and throbbed with the echoes of heavy machinery, like the engine room of a freighter; you could almost feel the weight of the building pressing down on you. The air seemed thick, as if clogged with soapsuds, and moisture dripped from a network of flaking steam pipes suspended from the ceiling. Against one side stood four coin-operated dryers, staring balefully at four squat Maytag washers ranged along the opposite wall. One of the washers, in the farthest corner, appeared to be having a breakdown. It was heaving back and forth on its base like something frantic to escape, a pair of red lights blinking in alarm above the row of switches. From somewhere in its belly came a frenzied churning sound, as if the thing were delivering itself of a parasite, or perhaps just giving birth. A man in a sweat-stained T-shirt was on his knees before it, scowling at an exposed bit of circuitry where a panel had been removed. Beside him stood an open tool kit, its contents scattered here and there across the concrete floor. He was introduced to us as Reynaldo "Frito" Ley, the building's superintendent, but he barely had time to look up, and when he did the scowl stayed on his face.

"She acting up again," he told the assistant manager, in a thick Hispanic accent. "I think somebody messing with the 'lectric wire." Reaching around back to the wall, he yanked out the plug, and the machine ground noisily to a halt.

"Maybe it's rats," I said, feeling somewhat left out. He looked at me indignantly, and I smiled to show that I'd been joking.

But Calzone was taking no chances. "Believe me," he said quickly, "that's one thing they don't complain about." He ran a hand through his thinning hair. "Sure, I know this building ain't exactly new, and okay, maybe we'll get a little bitty roach now and then, that's only natural. I mean, you're not gonna find a single building in the whole damned city that hasn't got one or two of them babies, am I right? But rats, never. We run a clean place."

"Rats not gonna bother my machines," added the superintendent. "They got no business here. Me, I think it was *los niños*. Kids."

"Kids?" said my wife and I in unison, with Calzone half a beat behind.

"You mean children from the neighborhood?" asked Karen. The *Times* had just run a series about the revival of youth gangs on the West Side, after more than a decade of peace. "What would they want in a place like this? How could they get in?"

He shrugged. "I don' know, lady. I don' see them. I only know is hard to keep them out. They all the time looking for money. Come down here, try to get the quarters from machines. No good, so they got to go break something—cut up hoses in the back, pull the plug . . . That kind, they do anything."

Calzone stepped between them. "Don't worry, Mrs. Klein. It's not what you're thinking. What Frito means is, on weekends like this you get people coming in to visit relatives, and sometimes they bring the kids along. And before you know it the kids are getting bored, and they're running up and down the halls or playing in the elevator. We're trying to put a stop to it, but it's nothing serious. Just pranks, that's all." Moving to the door, he opened it and ushered us outside. Behind us the superintendent frowned and shook his head, but when my wife looked back questioningly he turned away. We left him sulking in front of his machine.

"Craziest thing I ever heard of," muttered Calzone, as he led us back to the elevator. "The kids in this neighborhood may cause a bit of trouble now and then, but they sure as hell ain't causing it in here!" The elevator door slid shut with a clang. "Look, I'm not gonna lie to you. We've had our share of problems. I mean, who hasn't, right? But if we've had any break-ins here, it's the first time I've ever heard of it. Fact is, we've just beefed up our security, and there's no way anyone from outside's getting in. Believe me, your granddad's gonna be as safe here as anywhere else in the city."

Since that very morning's paper had carried the story of a wealthy widow and her maid found strangled in their East Sixty-Second Street townhouse, these words were hardly reassuring.

Nor was my wife's expression when we got out of the elevator. She nudged me with her elbow. "I'd hate to think what the security was like before they beefed it up," she said. Calzone pretended not to hear.

The first battalions of old men and women were marching unsteadily from the dining room as the two of us bid him goodbye. "Come back again and I'll show you our new TV lounge," he called after us, retiring to his little office just beyond the stairs. As soon as he'd closed the door, I approached a pair of well-fed-looking old women who were shuffling arm-in-arm across the lobby. The stouter one had hair as blue as the veins that lined her forehead. Gazing up at me, she broke into a slightly bewildered smile.

I cleared my throat. "Pardon me, but would you two ladies say this is a safe place to live? I mean, from the standpoint of the neighborhood?"

Silence. The smile, the gaze, never wavered.

"Mrs. Hirschfeld doesn't hear so good," explained the other, tightening her grip on the woman's arm. "Even with the new battery, you have to shout a little." She spoke with her eyes cast demurely downward, avoiding mine. Her hair was tied in a coquettish little bun. Who knows, I thought, Grandfather might like her. She told me her name was Mrs. Rosenzweig. She and Mrs. Hirschfeld were roommates. "Elsie's very happy here," she said, "and me, I can't complain. Three years already we've been here, and never any trouble." The lashes fluttered. "But of course, we never go outside." They moved off together toward the elevator, leaning on each other for support.

"Well, what do you think?" I asked my wife, as we headed for the exit in front.

She shrugged. "He's your grandfather."

Emerging from the lobby, we found ourselves once more in the presence of the guard, slumped glassy-eyed behind his desk. Here he is in the flesh, I thought, Calzone's beefed-up security. He nodded sleepily to us as we passed.

Outside, dusk had fallen on the block. To the west lay the familiar trees and benches of Broadway, with TV showrooms, banks, and Chinese restaurants. Copperware and cappuccino-makers gleamed in Zabar's window; Sunday browsers chatted by a bookstall on the corner. "Anyway," I said, "it's better than Brooklyn."

But when we turned east I wasn't so sure. The building next door was a six-story tenement ribbed with fire escapes and a crumbling succession of ledges. On the front stoop, beneath a rust-stained NO LOITERING sign, sat a conclave of bored-looking young men, one with a gold earring, one fiddling with the dial of a radio as big as an attaché case. I wished we didn't have to walk past them.

"They look like they're posing for a group photo," I said hopefully, taking my wife's hand.

"Yeah—Attica, Class of 1980."

We moved by them silently, drawing hostile glares. Behind us, with a blare of trumpets, the radio exploded into "Soul Soldier." Another group of teenagers was gathered in front of a closed-up shop on the corner of Eighty-First and Amsterdam. CHECKS CASHED, a corrugated metal sign proclaimed, and below it, on a faded piece of cardboard taped inside the window, *Food Stamps Welcome.* The place was dark and empty, the window grey with dust.

Snap out of it, I told myself, the neighborhood's not so bad. Just another culture or two, that's all it was, and no worse here than where I lived, half a mile farther uptown. I noted the ancient public library, a shoe-repair shop, a pawnshop with guitars and watches in the window, a place where Haitian magazines were sold, a Puerto Rican social club, a shop whose sign read BARBER on one side and BARBERÍA on the other. Several *botanicas,* shut for the day behind steel gates, displayed windows full of painted plaster figures: Jesus and Mary, a bearded black man brandishing a snake, an angel with a dagger in his hand. All wore haloes.

Still, the people in the neighborhood did not. The crime rate, in fact, had been climbing that year, and while Park West Manor seemed as good a place as any for my grandfather, I had doubts about the safety of the block. As my wife and I walked home that night, heading up Columbus with the lights of Sunday traffic in our eyes, I thought of the old brick building receding behind us into

the shadows of West Eighty-First, and of the doorways, stoops, and
street corners surrounding it, where unsmiling black youths waited
like a threat. I worried about whether they might somehow sneak
inside, and about all the damage they might cause—although in
view of what actually occurred, these fears now seem, to say the least,
rather ironic.

Wednesday, June 8, 1977

If heaven is really populated by the souls of the dead, with their
earthly personalities and intellect surviving intact, then the place
must be almost as depressing as an old-folks' home. The angels may
handle their new wings with a certain finesse, and their haloes may
glow bright as gold, but the heads beneath them must be pretty
near as empty as the ones I saw the first time I visited my grandfather at Park West Manor. Around me, in the game room, old men
and women played leisurely hands of canasta or poker or gin, or sat
watching in silence as two of their number shuffled round a pool
table, its worn and faded surface just above the spectators' sight. One
old man stood talking to himself in the corner; others merely dozed.
Contrary to my expectations, there were no twinkle-eyed old Yankee
types gathered over a checkerboard puffing corncob pipes, and I
looked in vain for bearded Jewish patriarchs immersed in games of
chess. No one even had a book. Most of those in the room that day
were simply propped up in the lounge chairs like a row of dolls,
staring straight ahead as if watching a playback of their lives. My
grandfather wasn't among them.

If I sound less than reverent toward my elders, there's a good
reason: I am. No doubt I'll be joining their ranks someday myself
(unless I'm already food for worms, knocked down by an addict or a
bus), and I'll probably spend my time blinking and daydreaming like
everyone else. Meanwhile, though, I find it hard to summon up the
respect one's supposed to feel for age. In fact, old people have always
struck me as rather childish. Despite their reputation, they've never
seemed particularly wise.

Perhaps I just tend to look for wisdom in the wrong places. I remember a faculty party where I introduced myself to a celebrated visiting theologian and asked him a lot of earnest questions, only to discover that he was more interested in making passes at me. I once eavesdropped on the conversation of two well-known writers on the occult who turned out to be engaged in a passionate argument over whether a Thunderbird got better mileage than a Porsche. I bought the book by Dr. Kübler-Ross, the one in which she interviews patients with terminal cancer, and I found, sadly, that the dying have no more insight into life, or death, than the rest of us.

But old people have been the biggest disappointment of all; I've yet to hear a one of them say anything profound. They're like that ninety-two-year-old Oxford don who, when asked by some def-erential young man what wisdom he had to impart after nearly a century of living, ruminated a moment and replied, "Always check your footnotes." Old people have never told me anything I didn't know already. But Father Pistachio . . . Well, maybe he was different. Maybe he was on to something after all.

At first, though, he seemed no more than an agreeable old humbug. I met him on June 8, when I went to visit Grandfather. It was the spring of '77, with the semester just ending; I had Wednesday after-noons free and had told Grandfather to expect me. We had installed him in Park West the previous weekend, after collecting some things from his Brooklyn apartment and disposing of the rest. At one-thirty today, unable to find him in his bedroom on the ninth floor, I'd tried the TV lounge and the game room, both in vain, and had finally gone downstairs to ask Miss Pascua, a little Filipino woman who worked as the administrative secretary.

"Mr. Lauterbach likes to spend his time outdoors," she said, a hint of disapproval in her voice. "We let them do what they want here, you know. We don't like to interfere."

"I understand."

"He's doing very well, though," she went on. "He's already made a lot of friends. We're very fond of him."

"Glad to hear it. Any idea where he might be?"

"Well, he seems to have hit it off with some of the local people.

They sit out there and talk all day." For a moment I pictured him in dignified conversation with some cronies on a sunny Broadway bench, but then she added: "I'd try looking for him one block down, on the other side of Amsterdam. He's usually on a stoop out there, sitting with a bunch of . . . " She chose her words with care. " . . . people from the neighborhood."

I walked out frowning. I should have known that's what he'd do. When you gave him a choice between the jungle to the east—with its fire escapes, its alleyways, its rat-infested basements—and the tamer pastures of Broadway, Broadway didn't stand a chance.

The spot he'd picked was a particularly disagreeable one. It was just up the block from an evil-looking bar called Davey's (since closed down by the police), a little bit of Harlem on the West Side: the sort of place where you expect a shoot-out every Saturday night. The buildings beside it were ancient with grime; even the bricks seemed moist, and the concrete foundations were riddled with some-thing curiously like wormholes. I passed a doorway full of teenaged boys who should have been in school. They were hunched furtively against the wall, lighting something out of sight, while others shot craps on the sidewalk, striking poses out of Damon Runyon. In the dim light of an open first-floor window, heavy shapes moved back and forth. A man in dark glasses hurried toward me, angrily dragging a child by the arm. The child said something—he couldn't have been more than five—and as the man passed by he scowled and muttered back, "Don't tell me 'bout your mother, your mother's a goddamn whore!" Already I was beginning to feel depressed. I was glad Karen hadn't come.

My grandfather was three stoops in from the corner, seated beside a large black woman easily twice his weight. On the railing to his right, perched above his shoulder like a raven, sat another old man, with skin like aged parchment and a halo of white hair. He was dressed in black trousers and a black short-sleeve shirt, with the white square of a priest's collar peeking out above it like a window. His mouth was half concealed behind a shaggy white moustache, and the sole incongruous touch was the unnatural redness of his lips, almost as if he were wearing lipstick. On his lap lay a white paper bag.

Grandfather smiled when he saw me and got to his feet. "Where's that pretty wife of yours?" he asked. I reminded him that Karen was at work. He looked puzzled. "What, today?"

"It's Wednesday, remember?"

"My God, you're right!" He broke into astonished laughter. "It feels just like a Sunday!"

I alluded to the trouble I'd had finding him. Here he was, hiding in the shadows, when only one block over—east to the museum, west to Broadway—there were plenty of comfortable benches in the sun.

"Benches are for women," he replied, with a conviction that allowed of no argument—just as, in some long-vanished luncheon-ette of my childhood, he'd told me, "Straws are for girls." (What does it say about him that he believed this? And what does it say about me that, since that time, I've never used a straw?)

"Besides," he said, "I wanted you to meet my friends. We get together here because the Father lives upstairs." He nodded toward the old man but introduced the woman to me first. Her name was Coralette. She was one of those wide, imperturbable creatures who take up two seats or more on the subway. It was impossible to guess her age, but I could hear, each time she spoke, the echoes of a girl-hood in the South.

The man was introduced as "Father Pistachio." This was not his name, but it was close enough. My grandfather never got his names or facts exactly right. Perhaps this had something to do with his general rebelliousness. It was certainly not a product of his age, for this imprecision had existed as long as I'd known him; half the time, in fact, he confused me with my father. Yet the names he thought up for most people were insidiously appropriate, and often stuck. Father Pistachio was one; I never saw the man without a white paper bag in his hand or, as it was now, crumpled in his lap—a bag that had been filled with those obscene-looking little red nuts, whose dye so stained his lips that he might have passed for some inhabitant of Transylvania.

But he wasn't Transylvanian; nor was he, despite my grandfather's introduction, a Puerto Rican. "No, no," he said quickly, looking somewhat pained, "you no understand, my friend, I say Costa Rica my home. Paraíso, Costa Rica. City of Paradise."

My grandfather shrugged. "So if it was paradise, what are you doing up here with an *alter kocker* like me?"

Coralette seemed to find this irresistibly funny, though I suspect the Yiddish escaped her. Pistachio smiled, too.

"My dear Herman," he said, "one is not permitted to stay forever in Eden." He winked at me, and added: "Besides, Paraíso just a name. Paradise here, in front of your face."

I nodded dutifully, but could not help noticing the darkened corridor behind him, the graffiti on the crumbling bricks, and, just above his head, a filthy window box from which a dead brown ivy plant and two long snakelike tendrils drooped. I wished he'd picked a more convincing spot.

But he was already quoting the authorities for support. "Buddha, he say, 'Every day is a good day.' Jesus Christ say, '*El Reino del Padre*—the Kingdom of the Father—is spread upon the earth, but men are blind and do not see it.'"

"Yeah, where he say that?" asked Coralette. "Ain't in no Bible I ever read."

"Is in the one I read," said Pistachio. "The Gospel According to Thomas."

My grandfather chuckled and shook his head. "Thomas," he said, "always this Thomas! That's all you ever talk about."

I knew that Bible talk had always bored my grandfather to tears—he'd said so more than once—but this rudeness seemed uncharacteristic of him, especially to a man he'd known so short a time. Seating myself against the opposite railing, facing the old priest, I searched my mind for more congenial subjects. I forget exactly what we talked of first—the unseasonably warm weather, perhaps—but I do recall that twice again there were references to some private dispute between the two of them.

The first time, I believe, we'd been talking of the news—of the start of Queen Elizabeth's Silver Jubilee, in fact, which my wife and I had watched on TV the night before. Coralette appeared uninterested in the story, but it brought a curious response from Father

Pistachio—"I could tell you of another queen"—and an immediate dismissal from my grandfather: "Oh, stop already with your queen!" The second time came much later, and only after the conversation had taken a number of circuitous turns, but once again the starting point was an item from the previous night's news: in this case the repeal of Miami's gay rights ordinance (*"Faygelehs,"* my grandfather snapped, "they oughta send 'em back where they came from!"), which had led to a discussion of Florida in general. Pistachio expressed an interest in settling there eventually—somehow he was under the impression that more than half its citizens spoke Spanish—but my grandfather had had a grudge against the place ever since, during the '20s, he'd made the mistake of investing in some real estate "just off the Everglades" and had lost his shirt. "Hell," he fumed, "they were selling land down there that was still underground!"

I let that one go by; I could never have touched it. But it did bring a kind of response: Coralette, who read the *Enquirer* each week as religiously as she read the Bible, reported that a colony of derelicts had been discovered living "unnergroun'" in the catacombs below Grand Central Station. (Six months later the story would resurface in the *Times*.) There were as many as forty of these derelicts, pale, frightened, and skinny, subsisting on garbage and handouts from people in the street but spending most of their time down below, amid the steam pipes and the darkness. "Now some folks be wantin' the city to clear 'em outa there," she said, "but it don't make no difference to me. Fact is, I feels kinda sorry for 'em. They just a bunch o' poor homeless men."

Pistachio sighed, stirred once again by some private memory. "All men are homeless," he said. "We have journeyed for so many years that—"

"Enough with the journey!" said my grandfather. "Can't we ever talk about anything else?"

Hoping to forestall an argument, I tried to change the subject yet again. I had noticed a fat little paperback protruding from Pistachio's back pocket, with *Diccionario* printed at the top. "I see you like to come prepared," I said, pointing to the title.

He gave a shrug both courtly and ambiguous, in true Old World style. "Is for my book," he said. His voice was modest, but there'd been a hint of capitals in it: My Book.

"You're writing something?" I asked.

He smiled. "Is already written. More than forty years ago I finish it. Then I write it over in Latin, then in *Portugués*. Now I am retired, write in English."

So that was why he'd come up north—to work on a translation of his book. It had already been published (at his own expense, he admitted) in Costa Rica and Brazil. The English title, itself the work of almost three days, was to be "A New and Universal Commentary on the Gospel According to Thomas, Revised in Light of Certain Excavations."

"I write it just before I leave the Order," he explained. "It say all I ever want to say. If I live long enough, *si Dios quiere,* I pray that I may see my book in the seven major languages of the world."

This struck me as a shade optimistic, but I didn't want to risk insulting him. He was obviously an extreme case of the proverbial one-book author.

"Who knows," he added, with a nod to my grandfather, "maybe we even do the book in Yiddish."

Grandfather raised his eyebrows and pointedly looked away. I could see that he had heard all this before.

"I gather that it's some sort of religious tract," I said, trying to sound interested. "The Puritans used to go in for that sort of thing. Treatises on doctrine, damnation, the Nativity—"

He shrugged. "Is about a *natividad,* but not the one you think. Is about *natividad* of man."

"Ain't no big mystery in that," said Coralette. "Ain't none of us so different from the monkeys and the lizards and the worms. Lawd done made us outa earth, just like the Bible say. Made each and ever' one of us the same." Reaching back, she took Father Pistachio's dictionary and worked a finger back and forth against the glossy surface of its cover. Soon a little roll of dirt and rubbed-off skin, grey-black in color, had accumulated beneath it; whereupon, taking my own hand between her two much broader ones, she rubbed my fingertip against the same surface. The same material appeared, the same color.

"See?" she said triumphantly. "We's all of us God's clay."

I never got to ask Father Pistachio his own views on the subject, because by this time three o'clock had passed and the older children of the neighborhood, released from school, were accumulating on the sidewalk before us like Coralette's grey-black matter. My grandfather got unsteadily to his feet just as a trio of teenaged girls swept up the steps, followed by a boy with a pirate's bandana and the straggly beginnings of a moustache. Not one of them was carrying a schoolbook. For a moment Coralette remained where she'd been sitting, blocking half the entranceway, but then she, too, sighed heavily and made as if to stand. I gathered that this was the usual hour for the group to break up.

"I say farewell for now," said Father Pistachio. "Is time for me to go upstairs to sleep. Tonight I work a little on my book." I helped him down from his perch, amazed at how small and fragile he seemed; his feet had barely reached the landing.

"Come on," I said to Grandfather, "I'll walk you back." I told the others that I hoped to see them again. I half believe I meant it.

My grandfather appeared to be in a good mood as we headed up Eighty-First. I, too, was feeling good, if only from relief that he'd adjusted so readily to his new situation. "This life seems to be agreeing with you," I said.

"Yeah, things are always easier when you got a few friends around. That colored girl is good as gold, and so's the Father. He may not speak good English, but I'm telling you, he's one smart cookie. I almost wonder what he sees in me."

I had to admit it seemed an unlikely friendship: a self-professed scholar—a man of the cloth—keeping company with someone, in Whittier's phrase, "innocent of books" and of religion, the one equipped with little English, the other with no Spanish at all. What queer conversations those two old-timers must have had!

"You'll have to come by more often," Grandfather was saying. "I could tell he took to you right away. And he's dying to meet Karen."

"Oh? Why's that?"

"I don't know, he said she sounded interesting."

"That's funny, I wonder why he'd . . . " I paused; I had a sudden suspicion. "Hey, did you by any chance happen to mention where she works?"

"Sure. She's with that big publishing outfit, isn't she? Something to do with books."

"That's right. *Account* books! She's in the billing department, remember?"

He shrugged. "Books are books."

"I suppose so," I said, and let the matter drop. Inside, though, I was wincing. Poor old Pistachio! No wonder he'd taken such an interest in us: the old fellow probably thought we'd help him sell his book! The truth was, of course, that using Karen as an "in" to the publishing world was like trying to break into Hollywood by dating an usher. But I saw no reason to tell this to Pistachio; he would find out soon enough. Meanwhile, he'd be a good friend for my grandfather.

"'Course, he does go on a bit about that book of his," Grandfather was saying. "He'll talk your ear off if you let him. Some of the theories he's got . . . " He shook his head and laughed. "Know what he told me? That the Indians are a long-lost tribe of Israel!"

I was disappointed; I had heard that long-lost tribe routine too many times before. It had become something of a joke, in fact, like the Hollow Earth theory and Bigfoot. I didn't mind Pistachio's having a few crackpot notions—at his age he was entitled to believe what he pleased—but couldn't he have been just a bit more original? Even my grandfather seemed to regard it as a joke.

But typically, he'd gotten it all wrong.

Saturday, June 11

"Is no one safe today," said Father Pistachio. It was a statement, not a question. "Is the same even for an old man like me. Two nights ago I am followed home by six, seven boys. Maybe, in the dark, they do not see I wear the collar of a priest. I think they are getting ready to push me down, but I am lucky. God, He watches. Just as I am asking

myself if it is wise to call for help, a car of the police comes slowly up
the street, and when I turn around, the boys are gone."

"*Po*-lice," sniffed Coralette. "Don't have no use for them *po*-lice.
Kids ain't scared o' them no more, and the law don't mean a thing.
Station's sittin' right up there in the middle of Eighty-Second Street,
just a block away, and you ever see the house right next door to it?
Hmmph! Wouldn't want no daughter o' *mine* livin' there—not these
days. Blocks 'round here ain't fit for walkin' down."

"Aw, come on," said my grandfather, "that's no way to talk. Brooklyn's ten times worse than this, believe me. The way I see it, if you're
gonna sit inside all day, you may as well be dead."

At this moment we, too, were sitting inside, round a greasy
little table at Irv's Snack Bar near the corner of Eighty-First and
Amsterdam, sipping our afternoon coffee and talking crime, New
York's favorite subject. Irv and his wife would let the old folks sit
for hours, so Grandfather's friends came here often, especially on
weekends, when the stoop of Pistachio's building was occupied by
teenagers. Occasionally the blare of their radios penetrated the snack
bar's thin walls, along with the pounding rhythms of soul music from
the jukebox inside Davey's, just across the street. Saturday nights
began early around here, at least when the weather was warm; even at
noontime the noise was almost incessant, and it continued through
the weekend. I don't know how anyone could stand it.

"My cousin's step-sister up on Ninety-Seventh, she say things
just as bad up there. Say they's a prowler in the neighborhood."
The metal chair sagged noticeably as Coralette shifted her weight.
"Some kinda pervert, she say. Lady downstairs from her—Mrs.
Jackson, down in 1-B—she hear her little girl just a cryin' out the
other night and see the light go on. Real late it was, and the chile
only seven years old. She get up and go into the chile's room to
see what happen. Window's wide open to let in the breeze, but she
ain't worried, 'cause they's bars across it, like you got to have when
you's on the groun' floor. But that chile, she shakin' fit to die.
Say she wake up and they's a boy standin' right by her bed, just a
lookin' down at her and doin' somethin' evil to hisself. She give a
holler and reach for the light, and he take off. Wiggle hisself right

out the window, she say. Mrs. Jackson, she look, but she don't see nothin', and she think the chile be havin' bad dreams, 'cause ain't nobody slippery enough to get through them bars . . . But then she look at the wall above the window, and they's some kinda picture drew up there, higher than the little girl could reach. So Mrs. Jackson know that what the chile say is true. Chile say she seen that boy standin' there, even in the dark. Say it was a *white* boy, that's what she say, and mother-naked, too, 'cept for somethin' he had on over his head, somethin' real ugly like. I tell you, from now on that chile gwin' be sleepin' wid the light on!"

"You mean to say steel bars aren't enough these days?" I laughed, but I'm not sure why; we, too, lived on the ground floor, and not so far from there. "That's all Karen has to hear. She'll be after me again about moving to a more expensive place." I turned to Grandfather. "Do me a favor, don't mention this to her, okay?"

"Of course," he said. "You don't want to go around scaring women."

Father Pistachio cleared his throat. "I would like very much to meet this Karen someday . . . "

"Absolutely," I assured him. "We're going to get the two of you together real soon. Not today, though. Today she's busy painting."

My grandfather squinted at his watch, a souvenir of his years with the watch-casing firm. "Uh-oh, speak of the devil, I have to get back. She's probably up there already."

My wife had gotten permission to repaint part of Grandfather's bedroom wall, as well as a few pieces of furniture salvaged from his former apartment. She was convinced she did such things better without my help and that I would only get in the way—a belief which I'd encouraged, as I was in no hurry to join the two of them. I much preferred to sit here in the snack bar, eating jelly doughnuts and tracing patterns in the sugar on the table. Besides, there were some questions I wanted to ask Father Pistachio. Later, Karen and I were taking Grandfather out to eat, to celebrate his first successful week at the Manor. He'd told us it would be a welcome change.

"I'm looking forward to a decent meal tonight," he was saying as he got up from his chair. He placed an unsteady hand on my shoulder. "These grandchildren of mine really know how to treat an old man!"

Making his way to the counter, he insisted on paying for my doughnuts and coffee, as well as for the Sanka he'd been restricted to since his stroke. "And give me some quarters, will you, Irv?" he asked, laying down another dollar. "I gotta do some wash, spruce up my wardrobe. My grandchildren are taking me out tonight—someplace swanky." Suddenly a doubt arose; he looked back at me. "Hey, I'm not going to have to wear a tie, am I?"

I shook my head. "It's not going to be *that* swanky!"

"Good," he said. "Just the same, I think I'll wear the socks with the monograms on 'em, the ones your mother gave me. You never can tell who you may be sitting next to." He bid the three of us goodbye, nodded to the counterman—"Take care, Irv, say hello to Mrs. Snackbaum for me"—and shuffled out the door.

Irv scratched his head. "I keep tellin' him, my name's Shapiro!"

Across the street the music had grown louder. I could feel the throb of the bass line through the soles of my shoes, and the air rang with grunting and screeching. I was glad I'd stayed inside.

Until now I'd avoided bringing up Pistachio's book. With Grandfather gone it was easier. "I understand," I said, "that you have some rather novel theories about the Indians and the Jews."

His face wrinkled into a grin. "Indian, Jew, Chinese, Turk—is all come from the same place."

"Yes, I remember. You said that's what you deal with in your 'Commentary.'"

"*Exactamente.* Is all there in the Gospel, for those who understand. Thomas, he is very clear, tell you all you want to know. Is through him I discover where man come from."

"Okay, I'll bite. Where *does* he come from?"

"Costa Rica."

The grin remained, but the eyes were absolutely earnest. I waited in vain for a punch line. Beside him Coralette nodded sagely, as if she'd heard all this before and was convinced it was true.

"That sounds just a little unlikely," I said at last. "Man first walked erect somewhere in East Africa, at least that's what I've always read.

They've got it all mapped out. Asia and Europe were next, and then across the Bering Strait and down into America. That was where the Indians came from: they kept on spreading southward till they'd covered the New World."

Pistachio had been listening patiently, mumbling, "Yes . . . yes . . . " to himself as he searched his pockets for nuts. Finding one, he split it apart and studied it with the quiet satisfaction of a man contemplating a good cigar. At last he looked up. "Yes," he said, "all this I too have heard, from the time I am *estudiante*. But is all wrong. Is—how you say?—backward. Truth, she is far more strange."

The old man had gotten a faraway look in his eyes. Coralette pushed heavily to her feet and, mumbling excuses, waddled off upon some errand. I could see that it was lecture time.

For the next half hour or so, as I sipped at still another cup of coffee, while the music from across the street grew steadily more primitive and the afternoon sunlight crept by inches up the wall, Pistachio gave me a short course in human history. It was an idiosyncratic one, to say the least, based as it was on certain Indian myth patterns and a highly selective reading of some fossil remains. According to his theory, the first men had evolved in the warm volcanic uplands of Central America, somewhere in the vicinity of Paraíso, Costa Rica— which was, by sheer coincidence, his own hometown. For aeons they had dwelled there in a city now gone but for the legends, one great happy tribe beneath a wise and all-powerful queen. Then, hundreds of millennia ago, threatened by invaders from the surrounding jungle—apparently some rival tribe, though I found his account here confusing—they had suddenly abandoned their city and fled northward. What's more, they hadn't paused for rest; as if still in the grip of some feverish need to escape, the tribe had kept on moving, streaming up through the Nicaraguan rain forests, spreading eastward as the land widened before them, but also pressing northward, ever northward, through what was now the United States, Canada, and Alaska, until the more adventurous pushed past the edge of the continent, crossing into Asia and beyond.

I listened to all this in silence, trying to decide just how seriously to take it. The whole thing sounded quite implausible to me, an old man's harmless fantasy, yet like a Velikovsky or a von Däniken he was able to buttress his argument with a wide array of figures, facts, and names—names such as the Ameghino brothers, a pair of prominent nineteenth-century archaeologists who'd advanced a theory similar to his, but with their own home, Argentina, as the birthplace of mankind. I looked them up the following Monday in the school library and discovered that they'd actually existed, though their theories had reportedly been "held in disrepute" since the late 1880s.

The name that came up most often, however, was that of Saint Thomas himself. I looked him up as well. His "Gospel" isn't found in standard Bibles, but it's featured in the ancient Gnostic version (an English translation of which, published here in 1959, is on the desk beside me as I write). I should add, by way of a footnote, that Thomas has a special link with America: when the Spaniards first arrived on these shores in the sixteenth century, they were shocked to find the Aztecs and other tribes practicing something that looked rather like Christianity, complete with hellfire, resurrections, virgin births, and magic crosses. Rather than admit that their own faith was far from unique, they theorized that Saint Thomas must have journeyed to the New World fifteen hundred years before, and that the Indians were merely practicing a debased form of the religion he had preached.

Somehow Pistachio had managed to scrape together all these queer old theories, folk tales, and fancies into a full-blown expla-nation of the human race—or at least that's what he claimed. He assured me that none of it conflicted with present-day Catholic doctrine, but then, I doubt he cared a fig for Catholic doctrine; he was obviously no normal priest. It was clear that, like a certain James character, he had "followed strange paths and worshipped strange gods." I wish now that I'd asked him what order he was from. I wonder if he'd left it voluntarily.

Yet at the time, despite my skepticism, I found the old man's sin-cerity persuasive. Moved by his description of the vast antediluvian city with its pyramids, towers, and domes, and carried along by the sound of his voice as he traced man's hasty march across the planet, I could almost picture the course of events as if it were a series of tableaux. It had, I must admit, a certain grandeur: the idyllic tropical beginnings, a civilization sleeping through the centuries of peace, and then, all at once, the panicky flight from an army of invaders and the sudden dramatic surge northward—the first step in a global migration which would see that great primitive tribe break up, branching into other tribes that spread throughout the continent, wave upon wave, to become the Mochicas, the Chibchas, and the Changos; the Paniquitas, Yuncas, and Quechuas; the Aymaras and Atacamenos, the Puquinas and Paezes, the Coconucas, Barbacoas, and Antioquias; the Nicaraguan Zambos and Mosquitos, the Chontals of Honduras, the Maya and the Trahumare of Guatemala and Mexico; the Pueblo and the Navaho, the Paiute and the Crow, the Chinook and the Nootka and the Eskimo . . .

"Let me get one thing straight," I said. "You're telling me that this accounts for all the races of mankind? Even the Jews?"

He nodded. "They are just another tribe."

So Grandfather had gotten it backward. According to Pistachio, the Israelites were merely a long-lost tribe of Costa Rican Indians!

"But how about family records?" I persisted. "Train tickets, steamship passages, immigration forms? I know for a fact that my family came over here from Eastern Europe."

The old man smiled and patted me on the shoulder. "Then, my son, you have made a circle of the world. Welcome home!"

The elevator shuddered to a halt, and I stepped out onto the ninth floor. There was an odor of paint in the hall outside Grandfather's door. I knocked, but no one answered. When there was no response the second time, I pushed my way inside. None of the residents' doors were ever locked, old people being notoriously prone to heart attacks and fainting spells, strokes, broken hips, and other dislocations requiring immediate assistance. Though the supervision here was generally lax, absence from a meal without prior notice brought a visit from the staff. The previous summer, in a locked apartment in the middle of the Bronx, the body of an old man had lain alone and undiscovered for months until, riddled with maggots and swollen to four times its size, it had literally seeped through the floor and into the apartment below. That fate, at least, my grandfather would be spared.

His room, at the moment, was empty, but a radio whispered softly in the corner, tuned to some news station, and I saw my wife's handiwork in the freshly painted nightstand and armoire. I was admiring the job she'd done on the molding round the window when the two of them walked in, looking somewhat out of sorts. I asked them what was the matter.

"It's that laundry room," said Karen. "Only three of the washers are working, and we had a few slowpokes ahead of us. And of course your gallant old grandpa insisted that some women behind us go first, and we ended up waiting till everybody else was done. We just got the clothes in the dryer five minutes ago."

"Now, now," said Grandfather, "it'll just be a few minutes more, and then we can get this show on the road." He turned up the radio, an ancient white plastic Motorola, and for the next half hour we listened to reports of Mrs. Carter's South American tour, South Moluccan terrorists in Holland, and increasingly hot weather in New York. Soon he stretched and began fiddling sleepily with his pipe, which, as long as I'd known him, he'd never been able to keep lit. My wife saw some spots she'd missed beneath the window. I picked up the laundry bag and headed down the hall, attempting to look useful. When the elevator arrived, I pressed the lowest button, marked by a "B" as big as my thumb.

Minutes later, when the door slid open once again, I felt momentarily disoriented. Outside the world still lay in daylight; down here, now that the machines were not in use, the corridor was gloomy and silent. It reminded me of a hospital at midnight, tiled walls receding into the distance while, down the middle of the ceiling, a line of dim, caged safety-bulbs made spots of illumination separated by areas of shadow.

The door to the laundry room would normally have stood within the light, but the bulb just above it was missing, leaving that section of the hall somewhat darker than the rest. Opening the door, I reached inside and groped for the light switch while my face was bathed by waves of steamy air. The superintendent's office must have been just beyond the farther wall, because I could hear, very faintly, the drumbeat of some mambo music. Then the fluorescent lights winked on, one after the other, with a loud insect-like buzzing, but beneath it I could still make out the beat.

I recognized the broken washer at once. It was the unit in the corner at the back, the one that had been out of order weeks ago. Its electrical wire, coiled beside it, had been messily severed near the end, while another length still dangled from the socket in the wall. Evidently Frito had already attempted some repairs, for the unit had been pushed out of line, nearly two feet toward the center of the room. Beneath it, now exposed to view, lay a wide semicircular drainage hole that extended, from the look of it, hundreds of feet down to some place Coleridge might have dreamed of, where waters flowed in everlasting night. No doubt the machines emptied into an underground spring, or one of those rivers that are said to run beneath Manhattan; only last winter the *Times* had written up a Mercer Street man who fished through a hole in his basement, pulling up eyeless white eels from a subterranean stream.

Leaning over, I caught a whiff of sewage and could see, very dimly, the swirl of blackish current down below. Within it, outlined against the overhead lights, floated the reflection of my own familiar face, distorted by the movement of the water. It brought back memories of my honeymoon at a Catskill resort where, near the woods, an abandoned well lay covered by a moss-grown granite slab. When workmen lifted it aside, my wife and I had peered into the hole and, for an instant, had seen, there in the water, a pair of enormous frogs staring back at us, their pale bodies bloated like balloons. Suddenly they'd blinked, turned their bottoms up, and disappeared into the inky depths.

The dryer regarded me silently with its great cyclopean eye. The fluorescent lights buzzed louder. On the wall someone had scratched a crude five-pointed shape halfway between a holly leaf and a hand. I stuffed Grandfather's laundry into the bag and hurried from the room, happy to get out of there. Before closing the door, I switched the lights off. In the darkness, more clearly now, I heard the drumming. Where was Frito, anyway? He should have been spending less time on the mambo and more on the machines.

Grandfather appeared to be dozing when I got back to his room, but as soon as I stepped inside he looked up, seized the laundry bag, and dumped it on his bed. "Got to have my lucky socks!" he said, searching through a collection of the rattiest-looking underwear I'd ever seen.

"Where's my skirt?" asked Karen, peering over his shoulder.

"You're wearing it," I said.

"No, I mean the one I had on first—that old summer thing I use for painting. It got filthy, so I stuck it in with Grandfather's stuff."

I knew the one she meant—a dowdy old green rag she'd had since college. "I must have left it in the dryer," I said, and walked wearily back down the hall. The elevator hadn't moved since I'd left it.

Yet someone had gotten to the laundry room ahead of me; I saw light streaming under the door, and heard the distant music and a stream of Spanish curses. Inside I found Frito, shoulders heaving as he strained to push the broken washer back against the wall. He looked very angry.

He turned when I came in, and nodded once in greeting. "You give me hand with this, yes? This thing, she weigh six hundred pound."

"How'd you manage to move it out here in the first place?" I asked, eyeing the squat metal body. Six hundred seemed a conservative guess.

"Me?" he said. "I didn't move it." His eyes narrowed. "Did you?"

"Of course not. I just thought—"

"Why I do this for, huh? Is no reason. Must have been *los niños*. They do anything."

I pointed to the severed wire. "And kids did that? Looks more like rats to me. I mean, look at it! It's all chewed up."

"No," he said, "I tell you once already, rats not gonna bother my machine. They try and eat through this stuff, they break their fuckin' teeth. Same with the cement." He stamped vehemently upon the floor; it sounded sturdy enough. " 'Leven year I'm in this place, and never any trouble till a couple weeks ago. I want to buy a lock, but Calzone says—"

But my eye had just been caught by a blob of faded green lying crumpled in the shadow of the dryer by the wall. It was Karen's skirt. Leaving the superintendent to his fulminations, I went to pick it up. I grasped the edge of the cloth—and dropped it with a cry of disgust. The thing was soaking wet, and, as I now saw, it had been lying in a puddle of milky white fluid whose origin seemed all too apparent. About it hung the sour odor I'd smelled before.

"Ugh!" I said. I made a face. I wasn't going to take this back upstairs. Let Karen believe it was lost. Gingerly I prodded it across the floor with my foot and kicked it down the drainage hole. It flashed green for a moment, spreading as it fell, and then was lost from sight in the blackness. I thought I saw the oily waters stir.

Frito shook his head. *"Los niños,"* he said. "They getting in here."

My eye followed the glistening trail that led from the dryer to the hole. "That's not kids," I said. "That's a grown man living in the building. Come on, let's get this covered up before somebody falls through." Bracing myself, I put my shoulder to the machine and pushed. Even when the superintendent joined me, it was difficult to budge; it felt like it was bolted to the floor. At last, as metal scraped on concrete with an ugly grating sound, we got the thing back into line.

Just before leaving the room, I looked back to see Frito crouched by the coils of electric cord, glumly poking at the strands of wire that twisted like claws from the end. I sensed that there was something missing but couldn't decide what it was. With a final wave I stepped into the hall, my mind already on dinner. Behind me, aside from the buzzing of the lights, the place was absolutely silent.

Wednesday, June 15

My grandfather was long overdue for a haircut; he'd last had one in April, well before his stroke, and his hair was beginning to creep over the back of his collar, giving him the appearance of an aged poet or, as he maintained, "an old bum." I'd have thought that he'd be pleased to get it trimmed and to idle away an afternoon at the barber's, but when I arrived to pick him up in the lobby of the Manor, he looked weary and morose.

"Everything's slowing down," he said. "I guess I must be feeling my age. I looked at my face in the mirror when I got up this morning, and it was the face of an old man." He ran his fingers through his hair, which had long ago receded past the top of his head. "Even my hair's slowing down," he said. "Damned stuff doesn't grow half as fast as it used to. I remember how my first wife—your grandmother— used to say I looked distinguished because my hair was prematurely grey." He shook his head. "Well, it's still grey, what's left of it, but it sure as hell ain't premature."

Maybe he was depressed because, after a lifetime of near perfect health, he'd finally encountered something he couldn't shake off; though the doctor considered him recovered, the stroke had left him weak, uncoordinated, and increasingly impatient with himself. Or maybe it was just the weather. It was one of those heavy, overcast spring days that threaten rain before nightfall and, in the coming weeks, a deadly summer. As we strolled outside, the air was humid, the sky dark as slate. Beneath it, earthly objects—the tropical plants for sale outside a florist's shop, an infant in red shorts and halter with her ears already pierced, the gaudy yellow signboard of La Concha Superette—stood out with unnatural clarity, as if imbued with a ter- rible significance.

"My legs feel like they're ready for the junk heap," said Grand- father. "My mind'll probably go next, and then where will I be?"

He was, in fact, walking even more slowly than usual—he'd stum- bled on the planks across the sewage ditch in front of the Manor, and I'd had to shorten my steps in order to stay by his side—but I assured him that he had a few good decades left. "If worst comes to worst," I said, "you've still got your looks."

This brought a snort of derision, but I noticed that he stood a little straighter. Screwing up his face, he thrust his hands into his pockets like some actor in a 1930s Warner Bros. movie. "Nobody wants a man with a mug like mine," he said, "except maybe somebody like Mrs. Rosenzweig."

"Well, there you are." I remembered the little old woman with the deaf roommate. "See? There's someone for everyone." He shook his head and muttered something about its not being right. "Not right?" I said. "What's the matter? Saving yourself for some pretty little blonde?"

He laughed. "There aren't any blondes where I live. They're all old and grey like me."

"So we'll get you someone from the neighborhood."

"Stop already with the dreaming! The closest thing you'll find around here is some colored girl with dyed blonde hair."

"Here's one that looks white enough," I said, tapping on the glass. We had reached the Barbería/Barbershop, where an advertising placard in the window, faded by the sun, showed a beefy Mark Spitz lookalike, hair aglisten with Vitalis, attempting to guess the identity of a sinuous young woman who had just crept up behind him. Covering his eyes with two pale, finely manicured hands, she was whispering, "Guess who?" That unwarranted question mark annoyed me.

The shop's front door was open to let in a nonexistent breeze, and the smell of rose water, hair tonic, and sweat hung nostalgically in the doorway. There was only one barber inside, fluttering over a burly Latino who sat glowering into the mirror, somehow retaining his dignity despite the clumps of shiny black hair that covered his shoulders like fur. Portraits of Kennedy, Pope John, and some unidentified salsa king beamed down at us through a talcum-powder haze. Seating himself by the magazine rack, my grandfather reached instinctively for the *Daily News*, realized he'd already seen it, and passed it on to me. Bored, I scanned the headlines—Spain holding its first free elections in forty-one years, James Earl Ray returned to prison following an escape, two derelicts found dead and blinded in a men's room at Grand Central Station—while Grandfather stared doubtfully at a pile of Spanish-language magazines on the lower shelf. Moments later I saw him frown, lean forward, and extract from beneath the pile a tattered, thumb-stained *Hustler,* which he opened near the middle. His expression changed, more in shock than delight. "Mmmph," he said, "they never had stuff like this back in Brooklyn." Suddenly remembering himself, he shut the magazine. I could see he was embarrassed. "You know," he said, "it's silly for you to sit around here all afternoon. I'll be okay on my own."

"Fine," I said. "We can meet later for coffee." Karen wouldn't be home till after her Wednesday evening class, and I had plenty of errands to do.

Outside, the sky had grown even darker. As I started up Amsterdam, I could see shopkeepers rolling up their awnings. Davey's Tavern, on the corner ahead, was already noisy with patrons, while soul music, drunks, and broken beer bottles spilled out upon the pavement in front. An overturned garbage can disgorged its contents into the gutter; a few feet past it, the opening to a sewer was clogged with bread crusts, wormy lettuce leaves, and pools of curdled cream. "Peewee, huh?" a man on the sidewalk was shouting. He wore greasy overalls and a sleeveless T-shirt dark with perspiration. "Hey, nigger, why they callin' you Peewee for? You needs some o' what I got?" He began digging drunkenly at his fly while the small goateed man he'd been shouting at hurried toward a nearby car, muttering threats to "get me somethin' an' bust that nigger's ass."

I was just crossing the street to avoid the inevitable fight when I heard my name called. It was Father Pistachio, lounging calmly on his stoop just around the corner from the scene of action and grinning at me beneath his halo of white hair. In truth I'd been hoping to avoid him as well: I just didn't have the time today for another history lesson. Resolving that our meeting would be brief, I waved and circled warily in his direction. He seemed to be alone.

"Where's your friend?" I asked, declining his invitation to sit down.

"Coralette? She call me up this morning, so very *dolorosa,* tell me she have trouble in the building where she live. Something about Last Rites. I tell her I am a priest, I can give Last Rites, but she say is no need, she going to be asking her minister. Then someone else is having to use the telephone—Coralette, you know, she live in a hotel, is not a nice place at all—and so there is no more time for talking. She tell me she will come by later. Maybe you will still be here, yes?"

"I doubt it," I said. "I really can't stay. I've got to join my grandfather in a little while."

"Ah, yes." The old man smiled. "Herman, he say he gain twenty pound Saturday night at the restaurant. Say he have the best time of his life. And I am thinking to myself, is good to know that some young people today still have respect for the old."

I nodded uneasily, hoping he wasn't leading up to another request to meet Karen. I hated to keep putting him off.

"Maybe soon you and your wife will be my guests for dinner," he went on. "Real Costa Rican food. How you like that?"

I sighed and said I'd like it very much.

"Good, good." He was visibly pleased. "I am just upstairs. And after I make the dinner, I show you what is to be in my book. Charts, maps, pictures—you understand? *Las ilustraciones.* Some I have already in the first edition, published in Paraíso. I bring it for you next time, yes?"

I said that would be fine.

All this time we had been hearing music from around the corner. Now, suddenly, came the sounds of a scuffle: a taunt, a scream, sporadic bursts of laughter from the crowd.

Pistachio shook his head. "Is a shame. Men, they just want to fight."

"Some men," I said. "Though our great-great-granddaddies don't seem to have gone in for it much, at least according to you. They sound pretty cowardly, in fact—pulling up stakes when another tribe showed up, running off like a bunch of kids, leaving the city behind . . . Sounds to me like they gave up without a fight."

I suppose I was needling him a bit, but it didn't seem to faze him.

"I think you do not understand," he said. "I never say it is another tribe. Is another *raza,* maybe, another people. One cannot be sure. No one knows where they are from. No one knows their name. Maybe they are things God make before He make a man. Legend say that they are soft, like God's first clay, but that they love to fight.

Quick like the piranha, impossible to kill. No use to hit them in the head."

"And why's that?"

"Is hard to say. Many different stories. In one the Chibcha tell, is because they have something on the face. Flat places, ridges, things like little hooks. Back of head, she is like the front; all look much the same. Me, I think this mean they wear a special thing to cover the head in war." He made a kind of helmet with his hands. "See? This way you cannot hurt them, cannot keep them out. They go where they want, take what they want. Break into the city, steal the food, carry many captives to their king. The lucky ones they kill."

"They sound pretty unpleasant."

He gave a short unmerry laugh. "Some Indians say that they are devils. Chibcha say they are the children of God, but children He make wrong. Is no pity inside them, no love for God or man. When God see how they will not change, He try to get rid of them. They are so strong He have to try one, two, three times! Chibcha call them *Xo Tl'mi-go*, 'the Thrice Accursed.'"

I'm quoting here from memory and my spelling is approximate at best; whatever it was that he actually said, it was unpronounceable. My eyes were held by his plump little red-stained lips, which worked up and down when he talked, and which continued to do so as he paused to stuff another nut between them. The fight noise down the block had momentarily subsided, but then I heard the jangle of breaking glass—for me, even at a distance, the most unnerving and ugly of sounds—and I realized that the battle was still very much in progress. I'd swear that at one point I could hear the echoes of a faraway war cry; but maybe it was just the effect of the story.

The story—an Indian legend, he claimed—seemed to have been cooked up by a committee of primitive tribesmen sitting round a fire trying to scare themselves. It told of the invaders—clearly a bad bunch, given to all manner of atrocities—and of God's repeated attempts to exterminate them.

"First, they say, God curse the women, make them all *estériles*, barren. But is no good; is not enough. The men, they leave the jungle, raid the city, carry off its women from their bed. As long as they find women, they are still breeding."

"So then God curses the men, right?"

"*Exactamente!*" Raising a finger dramatically, he leaned toward me and lowered his voice, though there was no one else around. "God, He make their *penes* drop off. Their manhood. But again it is no good. Even this is not enough. The fighting, the raiding, she goes on as before. The women, they are taken from the city and—" Here a disapproving little clucking sound. "—just as before."

"But how could they keep on breeding without their, uh . . . "

He gave another one of those all-purpose Latin shrugs, which seemed terribly enigmatic but may just have been embarrassed. "Oh," he said vaguely, "they find a way." He picked a sliver of pistachio from his teeth and stared at it a moment. "But is hard to guess what is truth here, what is *fábula.* Is not history, you know. Is only a story the Indians tell. *Un cuento de hadas.*"

A fairy tale—yes, that's exactly what it was. A prehistoric fairy tale.

"Well," I said, "I guess you can't blame our ancestors for running away. Those Xotls don't sound like you'd want to meet them. What happened, they take over when the others moved out?"

The old man nodded. "City, she is theirs now. Belong to them. For sport they pull her down—every temple, every tower, every brick. Soon they are making ready to go after the others; is time to breed again, time to bring back food, women, captives for the sacrifice. And now, just before they leave, God make His final curse: He seal their eyes close, every one, forever. No more can they follow the tribe of our fathers. For them, is no more sunlight, no more day. One by one they crawl back to the jungle. One by one they are lost. All of them are dead now, dead and in the earth for two hundred thousand year. Paraíso, she is built upon the place where bodies lie. Farmers turn their bones up with the plow, grind them up for meal. All are *cenizas* now—dust and ashes."

That certainly sounded final enough, I thought. *Exeunt the enemy.* At least the fairy tale had a happy ending . . .

"But hold on," I said, "what if these fellows survived even a third curse? I mean, the first two didn't even slow them down, they adapted right away. And it's not as if losing your sight were a sentence of death. Who's to say they didn't stick around? Their children could be down there in the jungle right this minute, trying to figure out where all the women went!"

"You think perhaps they are going to make a new raid on Paraíso?" The old priest smiled wanly. "No, my friend. The last of them die off down there two hundred thousand year ago. Their story, she is over. *Se termino.*" He clapped his hands. "Now the tribes of man, they are far more interesting. My book tells how they learn to read the stars, build ships, make fire . . . "

But I wasn't listening. I was thinking once again of those great Mayan cities, Tikal and Copán and the rest, standing silent and deserted in the middle of the jungle—as if, without warning, one afternoon or in the dead of night, all of their inhabitants had simply disappeared, or walked away, or fled.

I wasn't sure just where those cities lay, but I knew they were nowhere near Paraíso.

My grandfather sat waiting for me in the snack bar, lacquered and perfumed and shorn. "You shoulda seen the fight," he said as I settled into my chair. "Those colored boys can really take a beating. Damn thing would still be going on if it wasn't for the weather." He nodded toward the window, against which heavy drops of rain were splattering like gunfire.

For the next few minutes he regaled me with a description of the fight, which he'd viewed from the doorway of the barbershop. The shop itself had disappointed him—"four seventy-five," he said ruefully, "I could've cut my own hair for less than that!"—but its magazines had been a revelation. "It's unbelievable," he said, "they're showing everything nowadays. And you could see their faces!"

Maybe I hadn't heard right. "You spent your time looking at their faces—"

"No, no, I didn't mean that! What the hell you take me for?" He leaned forward and lowered his voice. "What I'm saying is, you could tell who these gals *were*. You'd recognize 'em if you saw 'em on the street. In my day, if some floozy took her clothes off in a magazine, they made damn sure they blocked her eyes out first. Or maybe they'd show you the back of her head. But you hardly ever got to see the face."

I was going to ask him where he'd been living the past twenty years, but he was staring behind me and beginning to get up. I turned to see Coralette squeezing through the door. She saw us and moved ponderously toward our table, shaking rain from her umbrella as she came. "Lawd," she said, "if this ain't just the worst day I ever see!" Heaving herself into a seat, she sighed and shook her head, bursting with tragedies to impart. "Trouble, jus' no end o' trouble."

Coralette, it turned out, was a resident of the Notre Dame Hotel, which stood beside a drug rehabilitation center on West Eightieth Street. I had passed beneath its awning several times; it was a shabby little place, notable only for the grandiosity of its name and for a Coke machine that all but filled its lobby. Coralette's room was on the second floor, by the rear landing. Across the hall lived a tall, ungainly young black girl, a former addict who'd been enrolled in one of the programs at the building next door. The girl was severely retarded, with impaired speech and a pronounced mongoloid cast to her features, yet according to the scandalized Coralette she spent most of her time with a succession of men—criminals and fellow addicts, to judge by their appearance—from the s.r.o. hotels uptown. Occasionally she would bring one of these men back with her; more often she was out all night and would return home in the morning barely able to report where she had been.

This spring had seen a change in her. She had stopped going out and had taken to spending nights in her room, although it was several weeks before the older woman had realized it. "She been in there all the time," said Coralette, "only I figured she away, 'cause I don't never see no light under the door. Then one night I's on the way to the bafroom and hears her voice, but she ain't sayin' nothin' . . . First I think maybe she sick, or cryin' out in her sleep. But then I hears this movin' around, and I know she got somebody in there with her. I hears the two of 'em again on my way back. They makin' a lot o' noise, but they ain't talkin', if you know what I mean."

The noise had been repeated on succeeding nights, and once Coralette had walked by when the visitor apparently was sleeping, "snorin' fit to kill." A few weeks later she had heard somebody coming up the stairs, followed by the closing of the door across the hall. "Now I ain't nosy," she declared, "but I did take me a peek through the keyhole when he pass. Didn't see much, 'cause the light out in the hall and it was dark as sin, but look to me like he didn't have no trousers on."

One night in April she'd encountered the girl outside the bathroom. "She lookin' sorta sick—say she think she got some sorta worm in her—so I asks her to come on in and rest herself. I got me a hot plate, so I cooks up a can o' black bean soup. Poor chile don't even know enough to say thank you, but she drink it all right down. 'Fore she go I asks her how she feelin', and she say she a whole lot better now. Say she think she gwin' be my frien'. Got herself a bran' new boyfrien', too. Sound like she real proud of herself."

For the past two weeks no one had seen her, though from time to time Coralette had heard her moving about in the room. "Sound like she alone now," Coralette recalled. "I figured she was finally settlin' down, takin' that treatment like she s'posed to. But then today the lady from the center come and say that girl ain't showed up for a month."

They had tried her door and found it locked. Knocking had brought no response; neither had an appeal from Coralette. Several other tenants had grown nervous. Finally the manager had been summoned; his pass key had opened the door.

The room, said Coralette, had been a shambles. "They was some kinda mess high up on the walls, and you got to hold your nose when you go in." The girl had been found near the center of the room, hanging naked from the light fixture with a noose around her neck. Oddly, her feet had still been resting on the floor; she must have kept her legs drawn up while dying.

"I guess that boy of hers done left her all alone." Coralette shook her head sorrowfully. "Seems a shame when you think of it, leavin' her like that, 'specially 'cause I recollect how proud she been. Say he was the first white boyfrien' she ever had."

Wednesday, June 29

As one who believes that mornings are for sleeping, I've always tried, both as a student and a teacher, to schedule my classes for later in the day. The earliest I ever ride the subway is ten or ten-thirty a.m., with the executives, the shoppers, and the drones. One morning just before my marriage, however, returning home from Karen's house downtown, I found myself on the subway at half past seven. Immediately I knew that I was among a different class of people, virtually a different tribe; I could see it in their work clothes, in the absence of neckties, and in the brown bags and lunch pails that they carried in place of briefcases. But it took me several minutes to discern a more subtle difference: that, instead of the *Times,* the people around me were reading (and now and then moving their lips to) the *Daily News.*

This, as it happens, was my grandfather's favorite—nay, only—reading matter, aside from an occasional racing form. "You see the story on page nine?" he demanded, waving the paper in my face. On an afternoon as hot as this, I was grateful for the breeze. We were seated like three wise men, he, Father Pistachio, and I, on the stoop of Pistachio's building. I had joined them only a moment before and was sweating from my walk. Somehow these old men didn't mind the heat as much as I did; I couldn't wait to get back to my air conditioner.

"Recognize this?" said my grandfather, pointing to a photo sandwiched between a paean to the threatened B-1 bomber and a piece on Mayor Beame. "See? Bet you won't find this in your fancy-schmancy *Times!*"

I squinted at the photo. It was dark and rather smudged, but I recognized the awning of the Notre Dame Hotel.

"Wow," I said, "we'll have to send this down to Coralette." Last week, totally without warning, she had packed her bags and gone to stay with a sister in South Carolina, crossing herself and mumbling about "white boys" who were smashing the lights in her hall. I'd had to get the details from Grandfather, as my wife and I had been upstate last week. I hadn't even had a chance to say goodbye.

"I don't know," said Grandfather, "I'm not so sure she'd want to read this."

The article—WATERY GRAVE FOR INFANT QUINTS—was little more than an extended caption. It spoke of the "five tiny bodies . . . shrunken and foul-smelling" that had been discovered in a flooded area of the hotel basement by Con Ed men investigating a broken power line. All five had displayed the same evidence of "albinism and massive birth defects," giving the *News* the opportunity to refer to them as "the doomed quintuplets" and to speculate about the cause of death; "organic causes" seemed likely, but drowning and even strangulation had not been ruled out. "Owing to decomposition," the article noted, "it has not been possible to determine the infants' age at the time of death, nor whether they were male or female. Caseworkers in the NYPD's newly revamped Child Welfare Bureau say that despite recent budget cutbacks they are tracking down several leads."

"Pretty horrible," I said, handing the paper back to my grandfather. "I'm just glad Karen doesn't read things like this."

"But I have brought for you a thing she may like." Father Pistachio was holding up a slim orange book bound in some sort of shiny imitation cloth. It had one of those crude British-type spines that stick out past the edges of the cover: obviously a foreign job, or else vanity press. This book, as it happened, was both. It was the Costa Rican edition of his "Commentary on Saint Thomas."

"Is a present," he said, placing it reverently in my hand. "For you, also for your wife. I inscribe it to you both."

On the flyleaf, in trembly old-fashioned script, he had written, *"To my dear American friends: With your help I will spread the truth to all readers of your country,"* and, beneath it, *"'We wander blind as children through a cave; yet though the way be lost, we journey from the darkness to the light.'—Thomas xv:i."*

I read it out loud to Karen after dinner that night while she was in the kitchen washing up. "Gee," she said, "he's really got his heart set on getting that thing published. Sounds to me like a bit of a fanatic."

"He's just old." I flipped through the pages, searching for illustrations, since my Spanish was rusty and I didn't feel like struggling through the text. Two Aztecs with a cornstalk flashed past me, then drawings of an arrowhead, a woolly mammoth, and a thing that resembled a swim-fin. *"El guante de un usurpador,"* the latter's caption said. The glove of a usurper. It looked somehow familiar; maybe I'd seen one at the YMCA pool. I turned past it and came to a map. "See this?" I said, holding up the book. "A map of where your ancestors came from. Right on up through Nicaragua."

"Mmm."

"And here's a map of that long-lost city—"

"Looks like something out of Flash Gordon." She went back to the dishes.

"—and a cutaway view of the main temple."

She peered at it skeptically. "Honey, are you sure that old man's not putting you on? I'd swear that's nothing but a blueprint of the Pyramid at Giza. You can find it in any history book, I've seen it dozens of times. He must have gotten hold of a Xerox machine and—Good God, what's that?"

She was pointing toward a small line drawing on the opposite page. I puzzled out the caption. "That's, um, let me see, *'La cabeza de un usurpador,'* the head of a usurper . . . Oh, I know, it must be one of the helmets the invaders wore. A sort of battle mask, I guess."

"Really? Looks more like the head of a tapeworm. I'll bet he cribbed it from an old biology text."

"Oh, don't be silly. He wouldn't stoop to that." Frowning, I drifted back to the living room, still staring at the page. From the page the thing stared blankly back. She was right, I had to admit. It certainly didn't look like any helmet I'd ever seen: the alien proportions of the face, with great blank indentations where the eyes should be (unless those two tiny spots were meant for eyes), the round, puckered "mouth" area with rows of hook-like "teeth" . . .

Shutting the book, I strolled to the window and gazed out through the latticework of bars. Darkness had fallen on the street only half an hour before, yet already the world out there seemed totally transformed.

By day the neighborhood was pleasant enough; we had what was considered a "nice" building, fairly well maintained, and a "nice" block, at least our half of it. The sidewalk lay just outside our windows, level with the floor on which I stood. Living on the bottom meant a savings on the rent, and over the years I'd come to know the area rather well. I knew where the garbage cans were grouped like sentries at the curbside, and how the large brass knocker gleamed on the reconverted brownstone across the street. I knew which of the spindly little sidewalk trees had failed to bud this spring, and where an old Cadillac was regularly parked, and what the people looked like in the windows facing mine.

But it suddenly occurred to me, as I stood there watching the night, that a neighborhood can change in half an hour as assuredly as it can change in half a block. After dark it becomes a different place: another neighborhood entirely, coexisting with the first and separated by only a few minutes in time, the first a place where everything is known, the other a place of uncertainty; the first a place of safety, the other—

It was time to draw the curtains, but for some reason I hesitated. Instead, I reached over and switched off the noisy little air conditioner, which had been rattling metallically in the next window. As it ground into silence, the noise outside seemed to rise and fill the room. I could hear crickets, and traffic, and the throb of distant drums. Somewhere out there in the darkness they were snapping their fingers, bobbing their heads, maybe even dancing; yet for all that, the sound felt ominous. My eyes kept darting back and forth, from the shadows of the lampposts to the line of strange dark trees— and to that menacing stretch of unfamiliar sidewalk down which, at any moment, anything might walk on any errand.

Stepping back to adjust the curtains, I was startled by the movement of my own pale reflection in the glass, and I had a sudden vision, decidedly unscientific, no doubt inspired by that picture in the book: a vision of a band of huge white tapeworms, with bodies big as men, inching blindly northward toward New York.

———

Wednesday, July 6

"It was awful. *Awful.*"

"You're telling me! Musta been a real nightmare."

I folded my paper and sat up in the chair, straining to hear above the hum of the fan. The lobby was momentarily deserted, except for an old man dozing in the corner and two old women leafing through a magazine; a third sat numbly by their side, as if waiting for a bus. In the mirror I could see Miss Pascua and Mr. Calzone talking in the office just behind me. They were keeping their voices low.

"You've heard the, uh, details?"

"Nope. Just what I read in yesterday's *Post.* Oh, sure, they're all talking about it back in the kitchen. You know how the guys are. Most of 'em got interviewed by the police, and they think they're on *Kojak.* But nobody knows much. I ain't seen Mrs. Hirschfeld all week."

"Her daughter came and took her Monday morning. I doubt if she'll be coming back."

I'd had the same impulse myself last night, when I'd first heard of the incident. I had telephoned my grandfather and asked him if he wanted to move out. He'd sounded angry and upset, but he'd expressed no desire to leave. The Manor, he'd decided, was as safe as anywhere else. A new guard had been hired for the entranceway, keys had been distributed, and tenants had been told to lock their doors.

"They haven't finished with the room yet," Miss Pascua was saying. "They keep marching through here with their bags and equipment and things. Plus we've got the Con Ed men downstairs. It's a real madhouse."

"And Mrs. Rosenzweig?"

"Ah, the poor thing's still at Saint Luke's. I was the one who telephoned the police. I heard the whole thing."

"Yeah? Bad, huh?" He sounded eager.

"Absolutely awful. She said she was fast asleep, and then something woke her up. I guess it must've been pretty loud, because you know what a racket the air conditioner makes."

"Well, don't forget, *she's* not the one who's got problems there. Her hearing's pretty sharp."

"I guess it must be. She said she could hear somebody snoring. At first, though, she didn't think anything of it. She figured it was just Mrs. Hirschfeld in the next room, so she tries to get back to sleep. But then she hears the snoring getting louder, and it seems to be coming closer. She calls out, 'Elsie, is that you?' I mean, she was confused, she didn't know what was going on, she thought maybe Mrs. Hirschfeld was walking in her sleep. But the snoring doesn't stop, it just keeps getting closer to the bed . . . "

Across the lobby the elevator door slid open with an echoing of metal; several old men and women emerged. I was about to stand, until I saw that Grandfather wasn't among them. He had never been on time in his life.

"That's when she starts getting scared—"

Miss Pascua leaned forward. Above the mantel to my left, the figures in the painting were frozen gravely at attention, as if listening.

"—because all of a sudden she realizes that the sound's coming from *more than one place*. It's all around her now, like there are dozens of sleepwalkers in her room. She puts out her hand, and she feels a face right next to hers. And the mouth is open—her fingers slide all the way in. She said it was like sticking your hand inside a tin can: all wet and round, with little teeth around the edge."

"Jesus."

"And she couldn't scream, because one of them got his hand over her face and held it there. She said it smelled like something you'd find in the gutter. God knows where he'd been or what he'd been doing . . . "

My eyebrows rose skyward; I'm sure I must have started from my chair. If what Miss Pascua said was true, I knew exactly where the culprit had been and what he'd been doing. I almost turned around and called out to the two of them, but instead I remained silent. There'd be time enough to tell someone later; I would go to the authorities this very afternoon. I sat back, feeling well pleased with myself, and listened to Miss Pascua's voice grow more and more excited.

"I guess she must've thrashed around a lot, because somehow she got free and yelled for Mrs. Hirschfeld to come help her. She's screaming, 'Elsie! Elsie!'"

"A lot of good that'll do her! The old broad's deaf as a post."

"Sure, she'd sleep through anything. Right there in the next room, too. But poor old Mrs. Rosenzweig, she must've got them mad with all her yelling, because they hit her—hard. Oh, you should've seen her face, it's swollen up like a melon. And they wrapped their arms around her neck and, do you know, they almost strangled her. She was just lying there, trying to breathe, and then she felt some others yank the sheet and blanket down, then they turned her on her stomach and pushed her face into the pillow, and she could feel their hands on her ankles, hauling her legs apart—the nightgown was actually ripped right up the side—and then another one of them pulled it up over her waist . . ."

Miss Pascua paused for breath. "Jesus," said Calzone, "don't it make you just want to—" He shook his head. "It musta been the blacks. No one else coulda done a thing like that. I mean, to them one woman's the same as any other, they don't care how old she is, or if she's maybe got a handicap or something, just so long as she's white. You know, they caught this guy over on Seventy-Sixth Street, in one of them welfare hotels, he was going around with a stocking over his head—"

The elevator door slid open and my grandfather stepped out. He waved and started across the lobby. Behind me Miss Pascua had interrupted the other's story and was plunging breathlessly on, as if impatient to reach the climax of her own.

"And then, she says, there was this soft scratching sound, real close to her ear. She says it was like someone rubbing his hands together from the cold. That's when—well, it sure doesn't sound like any rape I ever heard of. All she'd keep saying was it felt like getting slapped. I mean, that's just what she said."

My grandfather had reached me in time to overhear this. "God," he whispered, shaking his head, "it's absolutely unbelievable, isn't it? A woman that age—a poor defenseless blind woman . . ."

"And the most horrible thing of all," Miss Pascua was saying, "she told me that the whole time, with all the things they did to her, they never spoke a single word."

Age-yellowed eyes opened infinitesimally wider. Wrinkled heads turned slowly as I passed. The second floor was crowded that day. I felt as if I were striding through a world of garden gnomes: old folks on the benches by the elevator, old folks standing motionless in the hall, old folks in listless conversation round the doorway to the game room. These were the same ones who congregated in the lobby each morning, waiting for the mailman to arrive, and who began gathering outside the dining room hours before mealtime. Now they had drifted up here, unmindful of the heat, to partake of what little drama yet remained from the events of Sunday night.

I was glad my grandfather wasn't one of them. At least he still got out. I'd said goodbye to him only a minute or two before, when, following the usual coffee and conversation with Pistachio, he'd retired upstairs for his afternoon nap. I hadn't told him about my suspicions, or what I intended to do. He would never have understood.

It wasn't hard to find where Mrs. Rosenzweig had been living; that end of the corridor had been screened off from the rest behind a folding canvas partition, the sort of thing hospitals use to shield the sick from one another and the dead from those alive. A small knot of residents stood chatting in front, as if waiting to see some performance inside. They regarded me with interest as I approached; I suppose that during the past few days they'd been treated to a stream of detectives and police photographers and took me for another.

"Have you caught them yet?" one of the ladies demanded.

"Not yet," I said, "but we may have a very good lead."

Indeed, I intended to supply it myself. I must have sounded confident, because they moved respectfully aside for me, and I heard them repeating to each other, "A good lead," "He says they have a good lead," as I made my way around the screen.

Mrs. Rosenzweig's door was ajar. Sunlight flooded the room through an open window. Inside, two beefy-looking men sat perspiring over a radio, listening to a Yankees game. Neither of them was in uniform—one wore a plaid short-sleeve shirt, the other just a T-shirt and shorts—but the former, the younger of the two, had a silver badge hanging from his shirt pocket. They had been laughing about some aspect of the game, but when they saw me in the doorway, their smiles disappeared.

"You got a reason to be here, buddy?" asked the one with the badge. He got up from the windowsill where he'd been sitting.

"Well, it's nothing very important." I stepped into the room. "There's something I wanted to call to your attention, that's all. Just in case you haven't already considered it. I was downstairs earlier today, and I overheard a woman who works here saying that—"

"Whoa, whoa, hold it," he said. "Now just slow down a second. What's your interest in all this, anyway?"

Above the clamor of the radio (which neither of them made a move to turn down) I explained that I'd been visiting my grandfather, who lived here at the Manor. "I come by almost every week," I said. "In fact, I even had a slight acquaintance with Mrs. Rosenzweig and her roommate."

I saw the two cops exchange a quick glance—*Oh my God,* I thought, *what if these guys think I did it?*—but the attack of paranoia proved short-lived, for I watched their expressions change from wary to indifferent to downright impatient as I told them what Miss Pascua had said.

"She said something about a foul smell, a sort of 'gutter smell.' And so it just occurred to me—I don't know, maybe you've checked this out already—it occurred to me that the logical group of suspects might be right outside." I pointed through the open window, toward the gaping brown sewage ditch that stretched along the sidewalk like a wound. "See? They've been working down there for at least a month or so, and they probably had access to the building."

The man in the T-shirt had already turned back to the game. The other gave me a halfhearted nod. "Believe me, mister," he said, "we're checking out every possibility. We may not look like it to you, but we do a pretty thorough job."

"Fine, that's fine, just so long as you intend to talk to them—"

The man in the T-shirt looked up. "We *do,*" he said. "It's being done. Thank you very much for coming forward. Now why don't you just give my partner here your name, address, and phone number in case we have to contact you." He reached out and turned up the volume on the radio.

Laboriously the other one took down the information; he seemed far more concerned with getting the spelling of my name right than with anything else I'd had to say. While he wrote, I looked around the room—at the discolorations in the plaster, the faded yellow drapes, a lilac sachet on the bureau, a collection of music boxes on a shelf. It didn't look much like the scene of a crime, except for strips of black masking tape directing one's attention to certain parts of the walls and floor. Four strips framed the light switch, another four an overturned table lamp, presumably for guests. Beside it stood a clock with its dial exposed so that a blind person could read it. The bed, too, was bordered by tape, the sheet and blanket still in violent disarray. With sunlight streaming in, it was hard to imagine what had happened here: the old woman, the darkness, the sounds . . .

Snapping shut his notebook, the younger cop thanked me and walked me to the door. Beyond it stood the canvas screen, blocking out the view, though in the space between the canvas and the floor I could see a line of stubby little shoes and hear the shrill chatter of old ladies. Okay, I told myself, so maybe I didn't get to play Sherlock Holmes, but at least I've done my duty.

"We'll call you if there's anything we need," said the cop, practically shutting the door in my face. As it swung closed I saw, for the first time, that there were four strips of masking tape near the top, around a foot square, enclosing a familiar-looking shape.

"Wait a second," I said. "What's that?"

The door swung back. He saw where I was pointing. "Don't touch it," he said. "We found it there on the door. That tape's for the photo and fingerprint guys."

Standing on tiptoe, I took a closer look. Yes, I had seen it before—the outline of a crude five-pointed holly leaf scratched lightly into the wood. The scratch marks extended outward from the shape in messy profusion, but none penetrated inside.

"You know," I said, "I saw the same thing a few weeks ago on the wall of the laundry room."

"Yeah, the super already told us. Anything else?"

I shook my head. It wasn't till hours later, back in the solitude of my apartment, that I realized I had seen the shape in still another place.

They say the night remembers what the day forgets. Pulling out the crudely bound orange book, I opened it to one of the drawings. There it was, that shape again, in the outline of the flipper-like gauntlets which Pistachio claimed his *usurpadors* had worn.

I got up and made myself some tea, then returned to the living room. Karen was still at her Wednesday evening class and would not be back till nearly ten. For a long time I sat very still, with the book open on my lap, listening to the comforting rattle of the air conditioner as it shielded me against the night. One memory kept intruding: how, as a child, I liked to take a pencil and trace around the edges of my hand. This shape, I knew, is one that every child learns to draw.

I wondered what it would look like if the child's hands were webbed.

Wednesday, July 13

Certain things are not supposed to happen before midnight. There's a certain category of events—certain freak encounters and discoveries, certain crimes—for which mere nighttime doesn't seem quite dark enough. Only after midnight, after most of the world is asleep and the laws of the commonplace suspended, only then are we prepared for a touch, however brief, of the impossible.

But that night the impossible didn't wait.

The sun had been down for exactly an hour. It was twenty minutes after nine o'clock. My grandfather and I were sitting edgily in his room, listening to news on the radio and waiting for the weather report. The past three days had been exceptionally hot, but tonight there was a certain tension, that feeling of impending rain. In the window beside us churned an antiquated little Fedders, competing with the blare of soul and salsa from the street below. Occasionally we could see flashes of heat lightning far away to the north, lighting up the sky like distant bombs.

We were waiting for Father Pistachio, who was already several minutes late. I had promised to take both of them to an evening flute recital at Temple Ohav Sholom on Eighty-Fourth Street, on the other side of Broadway. There'd be a lot of old people in attendance, or so Grandfather believed. According to his calculations, the "boring part"—that is, the actual flute playing—would be over soon, and with a little luck the three of us would arrive just in time for the refreshments. I wondered if Pistachio was going to show up in his priest's collar, and what they'd make of it at the temple.

The radio announced the time. It was nine twenty-two.

"What the hell's keeping him?" said my grandfather. "We really ought to be getting over there. The ladies always leave early." He got up from the bed. "What do you think? This shirt look okay?"

"You're not wearing any socks."

"What?" He glared down at his feet. "*Oy gevalt,* it's a wonder I remember my own name!" Looking dejected, he sat back on the bed but immediately jumped up again. "I know where the damn things are. I stuck them in with Esther Feinbaum's wash." He began moving toward the door.

"Wait a second," I said. "Where are you going?"

"Downstairs. I'll be right back."

"But that's ridiculous! Why make a special trip?" I fought down my exasperation. "Look, you've got plenty of socks right there in your drawer. Karen just bought you some, remember? The others'll wait till tomorrow."

"They may not be there tomorrow. Old Esther leaves 'em hanging down by the dryers. She doesn't like to have men in her room!" He grinned. "Anyway, you don't understand. They're my lucky socks, the ones your mother made. I had 'em washed special for tonight, and I'm not going without 'em."

I watched him shuffle out the door. He seemed to be aging faster, and moving slower, with each passing week.

"The time," said the radio, "is nine twenty-five."

I went to the window and looked down. Plenty of people were out on the sidewalk, drinking or dancing or sitting on the stoop, but there was no sign of Pistachio. He had said something about bringing me some "new proof " of his theory, and I tried to imagine what it could be. A rabbi with a Costa Rican accent, perhaps, or a Xo Tl'mi-go skull. Or maybe just a photo of the back of his own head. I stood there while the wind from the air conditioner blew cold against my skin, watching heat lightning flash in the distance. Then I sat down and returned to the news. Karen would be on her way home, just about now, from her class up at Lehman in the Bronx. I wondered if it was raining up there. The radio didn't say.

Nine minutes later it happened. Suddenly the lights in Grandfather's room dimmed, flickered, and died. The radio fell silent. The air conditioner clattered to a halt.

I sat there in the darkness feeling faintly annoyed. The first thing that crossed my mind, I remember, was that somehow, perhaps in opening one of the dryers downstairs, Grandfather had inadvertently triggered a short circuit. Yes, I thought, that would be just like him!

In the unaccustomed silence I heard a frightened yell, then another, coming from the hall. They were joined, in a moment, by shouts from down in the street. Only then did I realize that more than just the building was affected. It was the whole city. We were having a blackout.

Still, even then, it seemed a minor annoyance. We'd had many such episodes before, in summers past, and I thought I knew what to expect. The city's overloaded current would dip momentarily; lights would flicker, clocks lose time, record players slow so that the voices turned to growls—and then, a few seconds later, the current would come back. Afterward we'd get the usual warnings about going easy on appliances, and everyone would turn his air conditioner down a degree or two. Perhaps this time the problem might be a little more severe, but it was still nothing to get excited about. Con Ed would fix things in a moment. They always did . . .

Already it had grown hot inside the room. I switched the lamp on and off, on and off, with that sense of incomprehension and resentment one feels when a familiar object, something that's supposed to work, suddenly and mysteriously does not. Well, well, I thought, The Machine Stops. I went to the window, opened it, and peered into the darkness. There were no streetlights to be seen, and the sidewalk below me was almost invisible; it was as if I were looking down upon a courtyard or a river, though I could hear a babble of excited voices down there, voices and pounding feet and slamming doors. Buildings could be seen a bit more clearly, and all of them looked dead—massive black monoliths against a black sky, with the moon just a sliver on the horizon. Across the water New Jersey was still lit, its brightness reflected in the Hudson, but here the only light came from the files of cars moving tentatively up Amsterdam and Broadway. In the glow of their headlights I could see faces at the windows of some of the other buildings, gazing out as I was, with varying degrees of wonder or curiosity or fear. From the street below came the sound of breaking glass.

It roused my sense of urgency, that sound. I wasn't worried about Karen—she'd get home okay—and no doubt old Pistachio, if he hadn't left yet, would have the sense to sit tight till the lights came on again.

But Grandfather was another story. For all I knew, the old fool was trapped down there in a pitch-black laundry room without a single sound or ray of light to guide him. Perhaps he was unable to locate the door; perhaps he was terrified. I had to get down there to him. Feeling my way to the night table, I pocketed a book of matches from beside his pipe rack and moved slowly toward the hall.

Outside I could hear the residents shouting to one another from their doorways, their voices querulous and frightened. "Frito!" they were shouting. "Where's Frito?" Blindly I continued toward the stairs, inching my way across the polished floor. "Frito? Is that Frito?" an old lady called out as I passed. She sounded on the edge of panic. Immediately others up and down the hall took up the cry. "Frito, is it a blackout?" "Frito, do you have a flashlight?" "Frito, I want to call my son!"

"Everybody, please, stop it!" I shouted. "I'm not Frito—see?" I lit a match in front of my face; it probably made me look like a cadaver.

"Just stay in your rooms and keep calm," I said. "We'll get the lights on for you as soon as we can."

I felt my way past the elevator, now useless, and went on until I'd reached the top of the stairs, where I lit another match. The first step lay just beneath my foot. Holding on to the metal railing, I started down.

As a boy I'd been afraid of the dark—or, more specifically, of monsters. I knew they only inhabited the world of movies, but sometimes in the dark it would occur to me that I, too, might be performing, all unwittingly, in a movie, perhaps even in the dread role of victim. There were two things movie victims never did, at least in my day: they never swore, and they never uttered brand names. Knowing this, I had hit upon an ingenious way to keep my courage up. Whenever I was forced to brave the darkness, whether in the cellar or the attic or even my own room, I'd chant the magic words *"Fuck"* and *"Pepsi-Cola"* and I knew that I'd be safe.

Somehow, though, I doubted that these words—or any words, in any tongue—would still be so effective. Magic wasn't what it used to be; I would simply have to put one foot in front of the other and take my chances.

Echoes of voices floated up the stairwell—cries for assistance, for candles, for news. Others were calling out to friends. At each floor the cries would get louder, diminishing again as I passed on toward the next. While I descended, I kept a tight grip on the railing, nervously feeling my way around the landings where the railing came to an end.

The eighth floor disappeared behind me, and the seventh; I counted them off in my head.

The sixth . . . The fifth . . .

Passing the fourth floor, I saw a moving light on the stairway beneath and heard footsteps advancing upward. Then the light veered through a doorway and was lost from sight.

One floor later I heard Calzone's voice and saw a flashlight beam receding down the hall.

"No, you can't go nowhere," he was shouting, "it's blacked out all the way to Westchester. Con Ed says they're working on it now.

They'll get it fixed up before too long." I hoped he was right.

As I passed the second floor, I began to hear a noise that, at the time, I couldn't identify: a hollow, rhythmic banging noise from down below, like someone hammering on a coffin. I couldn't even tell where it was coming from, unless from the wall itself, for the hammering became louder as I continued my descent, reaching its loudest point almost midway between the two floors—after which, unlike the voices, it began growing fainter again. By the time I reached the first floor it was lost amid the noises from the street.

They were having a festival out there, or a riot. I could hear shouts, laughter, and Latin music from some battery-driven tape deck. I also heard the shattering of glass and what I first mistook for gunshots, but which I later realized were only firecrackers left over from the Fourth. Despite the clamor outside, the lobby wore an air of desolation, like an abandoned palace in time of war. As I rounded the stairs, I caught a glimpse of its high mirrored wall and, in it, dim reflections of the rubber plants, the mantelpiece, the sagging empty chairs. The room was illuminated by a lantern that flickered in the alcove in front. Nearby stood the new security guard, talking to a group of shadowy figures in the doorway. I remember wondering whether he'd be called upon to keep the neighborhood at bay tonight, and whether he'd be able to do so.

But at the moment that didn't seem important. Finding the railing again, I continued downward. The lantern light vanished with a turn in the stairs, and I found myself once more in total darkness. Already the first floor's noise seemed far behind; my footsteps, deliberate as they were, echoed softly from the walls.

Seconds later I felt the railing end, and knew I'd reached the landing. Here I paused for breath, fingers pressed against the rough concrete. The air was suffocating; I felt as if I were chin-deep in warm water and that if I stepped forward, I would drown. Digging into my pocket, I found a match and, like a blind man, lit it. Walls leapt into view around me. I felt better now—though for a moment an old warning flashed through my mind about people smothering in locked vaults because they'd lit matches and burned up their oxygen.

Silly, I thought, *it's nothing but a basement*—and proceeded down the final flight of steps.

At last my feet touched bottom. I lit another match and saw, ahead of me, the narrow corridor stretching into darkness. As I followed it, I listened. There was no sound. The match burned my fingers and I dropped it.

"Grandfather?" I called, in the half-embarrassed voice of one not sure of a response. "Grandfather?" I thought I heard a stirring from farther down the hall, like something being scraped across a cement floor. "It's okay, I'm coming!"

Lighting still another match, I made my way toward the door to the laundry room. Even at this distance I could smell the moist, sweet laundry smell and, beneath it, something sour, like a backed-up drain. *Sewer men,* I thought, and shook my head.

When I was still a step or two away, the match went. Blindly I groped for the door. I could hear someone on the other side, scrabbling to get out. At last my fingers found the knob.

"It's okay," I said, turning it, "I'm here—"

The door exploded in my face. I went down beneath a mob of twisting bodies pouring through the doorway, tumbling out upon me like a wave. I was kicked, tripped over, stepped on; I struggled to rise and felt, in the darkness, the touch of naked limbs, smooth rubbery flesh, hands that scuttled over me like starfish. In seconds the mob had swept past me and was gone; I heard them padding lightly up the hall, heading toward the stairs.

Then silence.

I lay back on the floor, exhausted, unable to believe it was over. I knew that, in a little while, I would not be able to believe it had happened at all. Though they'd left the stench of sewage in my nostrils, the gang—whoever they were, wherever they had gone—already seemed a crazy dream born of the darkness and the heat.

But Grandfather was real. What had they done to him? Trembling, head spinning, I staggered to my feet and found the doorway to the laundry room. Inside, I lit one last match. The floor shone wet and slippery; the four washers lay scattered across it like children's discarded toys. There was no sign of my grandfather.

Hours later, when they pulled him from the elevator stalled midway between the first and second floors—Frito with his crowbar, Calzone holding the light—all my grandfather would say (feebly waving the two little pieces of dark cloth as if they were trophies) was, "I found my socks."

Karen, all this time, was fifty blocks uptown.

At nine-thirty she and her friend Marcia had been driving home in Marcia's little white Toyota, returning from their evening class at Lehman. There'd been an obstruction at 145th Street, and Marcia had turned south onto Lenox Avenue, past the Lenox Terrace project and the blocks of ancient brownstones. Though the traffic was heavy tonight, they were making good time; a mile ahead, at Central Park, they would be turning west. The air inside the car was hot and stuffy, but they kept the doors locked and the windows rolled up tight. This was, after all, the middle of Harlem.

Suddenly, as if some child had yanked the plug, the lights went out.

Marcia's foot went instinctively to the brakes; the car slowed to a crawl. So did the cars in front and behind. A few, elsewhere, did not. From somewhere up ahead came a grinding crash and the sound of tearing metal. Horns blared, bumpers smashed against bumpers, and the traffic rolled to a standstill. Beyond the unmoving line of headlights there was nothing but darkness.

But all at once the darkness was filled with moving shapes.

"Oh my God," said Marcia. "Look!"

Up and down the blackened street, hordes of figures were rushing from the houses, cheering, clapping, arms waving, as if they'd been waiting all their lives for this moment. It reminded the women of a prison break, an end of school, a day of liberation. They saw one tall, gangling figure burst through a doorway and dash into the street directly in front of them. Suddenly, in sheer exuberance, he bounded high into the air, feet kicking like a ballet dancer's, and sailed clear across the hood of the car, landing moments later on the other side and disappearing into the night. Karen never got to see his face, but there was one image she'd remember long afterward, whenever the blackout was discussed: the image of those two white sneakers dancing high above the beam of the headlights, six feet in the air, as if somehow released, not just from man's law, but from the law of gravity as well.

It was nearly one o'clock, and I still couldn't reach her.

I was sitting in Grandfather's room with the phone cradled in my lap. Beside me the old man lay snoring. I had put him to bed only a few minutes before, but he'd already fallen asleep, exhausted from his ordeal in the elevator. There would be no sleep for me, though: I was too worried about Karen, and events outside the window only made me worry more. I heard hoarse shouts, the shattering of glass, and gangs of youths passing unseen in the streets below, bragging to one another about the jewelry, clothes, and radios they'd robbed. On Amsterdam Avenue a crowd had formed in front of the pawnshop, and three dark burly men, naked to the waist, were struggling to tear down the metal security gate that stretched across the window and the door. Others, holding flashlights, were egging them on. There were distant fires to the north, and sirens, and the echoes of explosions. I was almost beginning to think of myself as a widower.

Suddenly, on my lap, the phone began to ring; telephones worked off a separate electrical system and had not been affected by the power failure. I snatched it to my ear before Grandfather awoke.

"Goddammit, Karen, where the hell were you all this time? I've been trying you for hours. Couldn't you at least have picked up a phone—"

"I couldn't," she said. "Honestly. I haven't been near a phone all night."

Her voice sounded far away. "Where are you now?" I said. "At Marcia's? I tried there, too."

"Believe it or not, I'm up here at the Cloisters."

"*What?*"

"It's true—the castle's right behind me, completely dark. I'm in a phone booth near the parking lot. There's a whole bunch of people up here, it's really beautiful. I can see stars I've never seen before."

For all her seeming rapture, I thought I detected a thin edge of hysteria in her voice—and when she told me what had happened, I understood why.

She and Marcia had spent the first part of the blackout sitting terrified in their car, watching things go to pieces around them. Store windows were being smashed, doors broken down; people were running past them waving torches. Others hurried back and forth along the avenue in a travesty of Christmas shopping, their arms weighed down with merchandise. Amid such activity those trapped within the cars had been ignored, but there'd been a few bad moments, and help had been slow to arrive. With stoplights out all over the city and traffic tied up everywhere at once, the accident had cost them over an hour.

Even when the line of cars began rolling again, they made little speed, creeping through the dark streets like a funeral cortege, their headlights providing the sole illumination—though here and there the eastern sky across the Harlem River seemed to glow with unseen fires. As they drew farther south, the crowds grew thicker, crowds who made no effort to move aside for them. More than once their way was blocked by piles of burning refuse; more than once a fist would pound against the car door and a black face would glare fiercely or gleefully through the window. Continuing in their present course seemed madness, and when some obstruction several blocks ahead seemed likely to halt them a second time, Marcia turned up the first wide thoroughfare they came to, 125th Street, and drove west in the direction of the Hudson, narrowly avoiding the bands of looters stockpiling food crates in the center of the street. At Riverside Drive, instead of resuming their way south, on impulse they had headed in the opposite direction, eager to get as far from the city as they could. They had driven all the way to Fort Tryon Park, at the northernmost tip of the island.

"We've both had a chance to calm down now," she added. "We're ready to start back. Marcia's getting tired, and both of us want to get home. We're going to take the West Side Highway all the way to Ninety-Sixth, so we shouldn't have any problems. But I swear the next rioter we see, I hope we hit him!"

I said I hoped that wouldn't be necessary and made her promise to call me as soon as she got home; I'd be spending the night here in Grandfather's room. I was careful to say nothing about my encounter in the basement. She had had enough youth gangs for one night.

After hanging up, I turned back to the action in the street below. Over on Amsterdam the crowd had succeeded in pulling down the pawnshop's metal gate. The large display window had already been stripped bare; glass littered the sidewalk. Now they were lined up in front of the shop like patrons at a movie theater, patiently awaiting their turn to file inside and take something. It was clear that the ones at the end of the line were not going to find much left. They passed the time by breaking the shards of glass into still smaller pieces. It was impossible not to hear, in that sound, echoes of *Kristallnacht*. It set my teeth on edge.

Suddenly there was a cry of *"Cuidado!"* and the crowd melted away. A minute passed, and then, like twin spaceships from another world, a pair of blue-and-white police cars rolled silently up the avenue, red lights whirling on their roofs. They paused, and from each car a searchlight beam swept dispassionately over the ruins of the shop. Then the searchlights were switched off and the cars moved on, unhurried and silent. The crowd returned moments later. The sound of breaking glass continued through the night.

There were thousands of similar stories that night. There was the story of the man who pulled up before an appliance store in a rented truck and carted off an entire shipment of refrigerators; and the story of the twelve-year-old boy who walked up to a white woman on the street and nearly strangled her when he tried to wrench a string of pearls from her neck; and the story, repeated many times, of mobs racing through the aisles of five-and-tens, stealing ribbons, erasers, spools of thread, shoes that didn't fit—anything they could lay their hands on, anything they saw. For months afterward the people of the poorer black sections of Brooklyn were forced to do their shopping miles from home because the stores in their own neighborhoods had been destroyed. By the time the blackout was over, nine million people had gone a day without electricity, three thousand had been arrested for looting, with thousands more unpunished, and a billion dollars had been lost in damages.

But amid the statistics and postmortems, the newspaper stories and police reports, there were other reports—"unsubstantiated rumors," the *Times* called them—of roaming whites glimpsed here and there in the darker corners of the city, whites dressed "oddly," or undressed, or "emaciated" looking, or "masked," terrorizing the women of the neighborhood and hiding from the light. A woman in Crown Heights said she'd come upon a "white boy" thrusting his hand between her infant daughter's legs, but that he'd run away before she got a look at him. A Hunts Point girl swore that, minutes after the blackout began, a pack of "skinny old men" had come swarming up from the basement of an abandoned building and had chased her up the block. At the Astoria Boulevard subway stop near Hell Gate, an electrical worker had heard someone—a woman or a child—sobbing on the tracks where, hours before, a stalled train had been evacuated, and had seen, in the flashlight's beam, a group of distant figures fleeing through the tunnel. Hours later a man with a Spanish accent had telephoned the police to complain, in broken English, that his wife had been molested by "kids" living in the subway. He had rung off without giving his name. A certain shopping-bag lady, subject of a humorous feature in the *Enquirer*, even claimed to have had sexual relations with a "Martian" who, after rubbing his naked groin, had groped blindly beneath her dress; she had a long history of alcoholism, though, and her account was treated as a joke. The following September the *News* and the *Post* ran indignant reports on the sudden hike in abortions among the city's poor—but then, such stories, like those of climbing birth rates nine months later, are part and parcel of every blackout.

If I seem to credit these stories unduly—to dwell on them, even— it's because of what had happened to me in the basement, at the start of the blackout, and because of another incident, far more terrible, which occurred later that night. Since then some years have elapsed; and now, with Karen's permission, I can speak of it.

The two of them had driven back without mishap. Marcia had left Karen off in front of our apartment and had waited till she got inside. After all they had been through that night, the neighborhood seemed an oasis of safety. There'd been stores broken into on Columbus, but our block, by this time, was relatively quiet. It was two-fifteen a.m.

Unlocking the door, Karen felt her way into the kitchen and, with some difficulty, located a dusty box of Sabbath candles, one of which she lit on the top burner of the stove. A thin white stream of candle wax ran wormlike down her hand; she stood the candle upon a saucer to protect the rug. Moving slowly so that the flame would not go out, she walked into the bedroom, pausing to open the window and let some air into the room. She noticed, with some irritation, that it was already halfway open; someone had been careless, and it wasn't her. She would have to remember to mention it to me when she called. The phone was there before her on the night table. Carefully, in the flickering light, she dialed Grandfather's number.

I had been nodding off, lulled by the rhythm of Grandfather's snoring, when the telephone jerked me awake. For a moment I forgot where I was, but then I heard Karen's voice.

"Well," she said, "here I am, safe and sound, and absolutely exhausted. One thing's a relief, at least I won't have to go to work tomorrow. I feel like I could use a good twelve hours' sleep, though it'll probably be pretty unbearable in here tonight without the air conditioner. There's a funny smell, too. I just took a peek in the refrigerator, and all that meat you bought's going to spoil unless— *Oh God, what's that?*"

I heard her scream. She screamed several times. Then there was a thud, and then a jarring succession of bangs as the phone was dropped and left dangling from the edge of the table.

And then, in the background, I heard it: a sound so similar to the one coming from the bed behind me that for one horrifying second I confused the two.

It was the sound of snoring.

Nine flights of stairs and a dozen blocks later I stumbled from the darkness into the darkness of our apartment. The police had not arrived yet, but Karen had already regained consciousness, and a candle burned once more upon the table. A two-inch purple welt just below her hairline showed where, in falling, she had hit the table's edge.

I was impressed by how well she was bearing up. Even though she'd awakened alone in the dark, she had managed to keep herself busy: after relighting the candle and replacing the telephone, she had methodically gone about locking all the windows and had carefully washed the stickiness from her legs. In fact, by the time I got there, she seemed remarkably composed, at least for the moment—composed enough to tell me, in a fairly level voice, about the thing she'd seen drop soundlessly into the room through the open window, just as another one leaped toward her from the hall and a third, crouched gaunt and pale behind the bed, rose up and, reaching forward, pinched the candle out.

Her composure slipped a bit—and so did mine—when the next morning's sunlight revealed a certain shape scratched like a marker in the brick outside our bedroom window.

Six weeks later, while we were still living at her mother's house in Westchester, the morning bouts of queasiness began. The tests came back negative, negative again, then positive. Whatever was inside her might well have been mine—we had, ironically, decided some time before to let nature take its course—but we took no chances. The abortion cost only $150, and we got a free lecture from a Right to Life group picketing in front. We never asked the doctor what the wretched little thing inside her looked like, and he never showed the least inclination to tell us.

Wednesday, February 14, 1979

"'Young men think that old men are fools,'" said Mrs. Rosenzweig, quoting with approval one of my grandfather's favorite sayings, "'but old men know that young men are fools.'" She pursed her lips doubtfully. "Of course," she added, "that wouldn't apply to you."

I laughed. "Of course not! Besides, I'm not so young anymore."

It had been exactly a year since I'd last seen her. Having arrived today with a big red box of Valentine's Day chocolates for her, I was glad to find her still alive—and still living at the Manor. Despite the night of terror she'd suffered back in '77, she had returned here as soon as she'd been discharged from the hospital, believing herself too old for a change of scene, too old to make new friends. The Manor was her home, and she was determined to stay.

Here, inside her own room, it was virtually impossible to tell that she was blind (just as I had been fooled the first time I'd met her); habit had taught her the location of every article, every piece of furniture. But elsewhere in the building, with her former roommate, Mrs. Hirschfeld, no longer there to lean on, she'd felt helpless and alone—until my grandfather had acted the gentleman. He'd befriended her, made her feel secure; they had walked along Broadway together, traded stories of the past, and kept each other company through the long summer afternoons. For a while, he had replaced Mrs. Hirschfeld in her life; she had replaced poor old Father Pistachio in his . . .

"Did I ever show you what Herman gave me?" Unerringly she picked a small round object from the shelf beside her and began winding a key in its base. It appeared to be a miniature globe of the world, with a decal on the base proclaiming *Souvenir of Hayden Planetarium.* When she set it back on the shelf, it played the opening bars of "Home Sweet Home."

"That's very nice."

The music ran on a few seconds more, then died in the air. The old woman sighed.

"It was nice of you to bring that chocolate. That's just the kind of thing your grandfather would have done. He was always very generous."

"Yes," I said, "he was. He never had much, but he was devoted to his friends."

The chocolate—in fact, the visit itself—had been my way of commemorating this day. It was the first anniversary of his death.

He had died following another stroke, just as the doctors had predicted—one of the few times in his life that he'd acted according to prediction. It had happened after dinner, while he'd been sitting in the game room with several of his cronies, laughing heartily at one of his own jokes. Laughter, Svevo tells us, is the only form of violent exercise old men are still permitted, but perhaps in this case the violence had been too much. Rushed to the hospital, he had lingered less than a week. I don't believe his end was a hard one. His last words are unrecorded, which is probably just as well—what are anyone's last words, after all, except a curse, a cry for help, or a string of nonsense?—but the last words I ever heard him say, and which have now become a family legend, were addressed to a young intern, fresh out of med school, who had come to take his blood pressure. During this process the old man had remained silent—speaking had become extremely difficult—and his eyes were closed; I assumed he was unconscious. But when the intern, putting away his instruments, happened to mention that he had a date waiting for him that night as soon as he got off work, my grandfather opened his eyes and said, in what was little more than a whisper, "Ask her if she's got a friend for me."

And Father Pistachio—he, too, is gone now, gone even before my grandfather. Although he has never been listed as such, he remains, as far as I'm concerned, one of the few likely fatalities of the Great 1977 Blackout. It appears that, at the moment the power failed, he'd been on his way to visit Grandfather and me in the Manor, a short walk up the street. Beyond that it's impossible to say, for no one saw what happened to him. Maybe, in the darkness, he got frightened and ran off; maybe he had a run-in with the same gang that attacked me; maybe he simply fell down a rabbit hole and disappeared. I have one or two suspicions of my own—suspicions about the blackout itself, in fact, and whether it was really Con Ed's fault—but such speculations only get my wife upset. All we really know is that the old man vanished without a trace, though Grandfather later claimed to have seen a white paper bag lying crumpled and torn near the stoop of Pistachio's house.

As for his effects, the contents of his room, I am not the one to ask—and the one to ask is dead. Grandfather was supposed to have gone over and inquired about them, but he told me he'd been "given the runaround" by the superintendent of the building, a gruff Dominican man who understood almost no English. The super had maintained that he'd given all Pistachio's belongings to the *"policía,"* but I wouldn't be surprised if, in fact, he'd kept for himself the things he thought of value and had thrown away the rest. Still, I like to pretend that somewhere, in a storeroom down the dusty corridors of some obscure city department, hidden away in some footlocker or cubbyhole or file shelf, there lies the old priest's great work—the notes and maps and photos, the pages of English translation—complete with all the "new material" he'd hinted at.

One thing, at least, has survived. The super, a religious man (or perhaps just superstitious), had held back one of Pistachio's books, believing it to be a Bible, and this he allowed my grandfather to take. In a sense, he was right; it was a Bible—the 1959 Harper & Row edition of *The Gospel According to Thomas,* which now stands on my desk looking very scholarly next to the cheap Spanish version of Pistachio's "Commentary." The Harper book holds little interest for me, nor is it particularly rare, but I find it makes an excellent memento of its former owner, thanks to the hundreds of annotations in Pistachio's crabbed hand: tiny comments scribbled in the margins, *"sí "* and *"indudable!"* and even one *"caramba!"* along with some more cryptic—*"Ync."* and *"Qch."* and *"XT"*—and pages and pages of underlinings. One passage, attributed to Christ himself, was actually circled in red ink:

Whoever feels the touch of my hand shall become as I am, and the hidden things shall be revealed to him . . . I am the All, and the All came forth from me. Cleave a piece of wood and you will find me; lift up a stone and I am there.

Beneath it he had written, *"Está hecho."* It is done.

I was feeling depressed as I said goodbye to Mrs. Rosenzweig. Though I agreed to visit her again soon, privately I doubted I'd be back before next year. Coming here aroused too many painful memories.

Outside, the world looked even bleaker. It was not yet five p.m. and already getting dark. We'd had below-freezing temperatures throughout the week, and the pavement was covered with patches of snow. Turning up my collar against the icy wind, I headed up the block.

Now, one of the hoariest clichés of a certain type of cheap fiction—along with the mind that "suddenly goes blank," and the fearful town where everyone "clams up" when a stranger arrives, and the victimized industrialist who won't go to the police because "I don't want the publicity," and the underworld informer who says "I know who did it, but I can't tell you over the phone"—along with these is the feeling of "being watched." One's flesh is supposed to creep, one's hair to stand on end; one is supposed to have an "indefinable sense" that one is under scrutiny. The truth is not so mystical. In the course of my life I have stared, and stared hard, at thousands of people who, were they the least bit sensitive to my gaze, would have shivered or turned or perhaps even leapt in the air. None has ever done so. For that matter, I've undoubtedly been glared at by hundreds of people in my time without ever realizing it.

This time was the same. I was standing on the corner of Eighty-First and Amsterdam, hunching my shoulders against the cold and waiting impatiently for the light to change. My mind was on the clean new restaurant across the street that advertised "Asian Fusion Cuisine," right where Davey's Tavern used to stand.

How nice, I said to myself. *Things are looking up.*

The light changed. I took one step off the curb and heard

something crackle underfoot. That was why I happened to look down. I saw that I had stepped upon a little mound of pistachio shells, red against the snow, piled by the opening to a sewer.

And I froze—for there was something in the opening, just beside my shoe: something watching intently, its face pressed up against the metal grating, its pale hands clinging tightly to the bars. I saw, dimly in the streetlight, the empty craters where its eyes had been—empty but for two red dots, like tiny beads—and the gaping red ring of its mouth, like the sucker of some undersea creature. The face was alien and cold, without human expression, yet I swear that those eyes regarded me with utter malevolence—and that they recognized me.

It must have realized that I'd seen it—surely it heard me cry out—for at that moment, like two exploding white stars, the hands flashed open and the figure dropped back into the earth, back to that kingdom, older than ours, that calls the dark its home.

PETEY

"*L*et's face it, Doctor, if an inmate's suicidal there ain't a hell of a lot you can do. Sure, you can take away his shoes so he don't strangle himself with the laces, and you take away his clothes for the same reason—I once seen a man hanging from the bars on his window by his T-shirt—and maybe just to be safe you take the cot out of his room, since last year we had a lady who slashed her wrists on the springs . . .

"But you can't do everything. I mean, if they want to kill themselves, they're gonna figure out a way to do it. We once had a guy who ran into the wall with his head. A nine-by-seven room, that's all it was, so he couldn't build up much speed . . . Still, he gave himself a pretty nice concussion. Put a nice dent in the plaster, too. Now, of course, we keep the place padded. And another one we had, I swear to God he just held his breath till he croaked. I mean it—if they've got the will, they can do it.

"Now the guy you're gonna see, he had us fooled. We thought we'd took every precaution with him, you know? But we should've used a straitjacket. Christ, the guy really tore the hell out of his throat. With his bare hands yet."

"George, I've got to admit it. I'm jealous, I really am. This place is fantastic." Lenny raised his glass. "Here's to you, you old son of a bitch! And to your new house."

He was about to down his scotch, but Ellie stayed his hand.

"Honey, wait. Let's get everybody in on it." She turned to the other guests, who were gathered in little clumps of conversation throughout the vast living room. "Hey, everybody! Can I have your attention, please? My husband has just proposed a toast to our charming host and hostess . . . " She waited for silence. "And to their bountiful kindness in letting us peasants—"

"Peons, Ellie, peons!" shouted Howard. Like the rest of them, he was already rather drunk.

"Yeah," echoed Milt, "us miserable peons!"

"Okay," Ellie laughed. "To their bountiful kindness in opening their new home—"

"Their *stately* new home."

"Their mansion!"

"For opening their mansion to us poor miserable downtrodden peons. And furthermore—"

"Hey," interrupted her husband, "I thought *I* was going to make the toast!" They all laughed. "I mean, I've been practicing for this all week!" He turned to the rest. "I tell you, the old lady doesn't let me get a word in edgewise anymore!"

"Yeah, come on, El," shouted Howard, "give the poor guy a chance, then you can put the muzzle back on!"

Everyone laughed except Howard's wife, Joyce, who whispered, "Really, honey, I sometimes think it's *you* that needs—"

"Ladies and gentlemen." Lenny spoke with mock gravity. "I hereby propose a toast to our esteemed host—"

All eyes turned toward George, who grinned and made a low bow.

"—and to Phyllis, our *equally* esteemed hostess—"

"Gee, Ellie, you've really got him trained, haven't you!"

"I freely admit it," said Lenny, placing the hand with the drink over his heart. "After twenty-eight years—"

"Twenty-seven."

"It just *feels* like twenty-eight!"

"Oh, Howard, hush up."

"After twenty-seven years of wedded bliss, she's finally done it. She's even got me making my own bed!" He paused for the cheers and the groans, then turned toward Phyllis. "But as I was saying, I would like to pay tribute to that gracious, charming, ravishingly beautiful—"

Phyllis tittered.

"—stunningly coiffed—"

Self-consciously she patted the streaks in her new feather cut.

"—and delightfully sexy woman he calls his wife."

"I'll drink to that!"

"Hear hear!"

"You're allowed to drink to that too, Phyllis."

"Yeah, somebody mix her a drink."

"Oh, that's silly!" squealed Phyllis. "I'm not supposed to drink to myself."

"Nonsense, my dear." George handed her a vodka and tonic, then seized his own.

"And finally," continued Lenny, raising his voice and his glass, "to the reason we're all gathered here tonight, the cause of all our celebration—"

"And jealousy," added his wife.

"To this beautiful house, this rustic retreat nestled amidst the wilds of Connecticut, this find of a lifetime, which makes our own split-levels look like something out of Levittown—"

"You're laying it on a bit thick," said George. He winked at the others. "I think Len missed his true calling. He should have been a poet, not a stockbroker."

"Or a salesman!" cried Howard.

Lenny continued undaunted. "This museum—"

"Museum?" George winced; all this congratulation embarrassed him. He could sense the envy in it, and the bitterness. "Mausoleum is more like it!"

"—containing, or so I've been informed, room after room of the rarest antiquities—"

"Junk! Nothing but junk!"

"—this magnificent Colonial mansion—"

"Aw, come on, Len! It's just an old *barn,* for Chrissake!"

"—in which George can play country squire and Phyllis lady of the manor to their hearts' content—"

George laughed. "I've still got to drive to work every day!"

"—this baronial hall, this playground of the landed gentry, this irrefutable testament to the smartest real estate finagling this side of Manhattan Island—"

George's smile faded.

"—this glorious old homestead, now a *new* home for George and Phyllis, in the hope that their years here are blessed with just as much luck as they've had in acquiring it."

There was a moment's uneasy silence.

"Are you done, Lenny?" said George.

"That's right, old buddy." Lenny downed his scotch. The others followed with a round of applause, but it was a feeble one; George's embarrassment embarrassed them all. Then Howard yelled out, "And in the hope you'll throw lots more parties like this one! How about next weekend, for starters?" And that relaxed them into laughter, though a little too loud, a little too long.

"When are you gonna show us the rest of this place?" cried Sidney Silber.

"Yeah, when do we get a tour of the estate? That's what we came for!"

"Come on, Phyllis, you promised."

"She's been talking about this place for months!"

"Yeah, you really had us drooling."

"So what does she do now? Keeps us cooped downstairs here like a bunch of kids!"

"How about it, Phyl? What're you ashamed of?"

Phyllis smiled. "The tour starts when everybody gets here."

"Isn't everybody here?"

"Who's missing?"

"Herb and Tammie Wagner haven't shown up yet," said George. "They told me they'd be able to make it . . . "

"I think they were having some trouble finding a sitter," said Doris, Sidney's wife. "I spoke to them this morning."

Milt made a face. "Aw, they're always late. It takes Tammie two hours to put on her makeup." He shuffled toward the alcove where the bar stood and poured himself another whiskey and soda. In the dining room beyond, a table still lay covered with platters of food—the remains of a roast, quiche, cold cuts, pumpkin pie—in case any guests had failed to stuff themselves.

"Let's start without 'em, then."

"Now, Sid, really," said Doris, taking him by the hand, "you know that wouldn't be fair. Come on, let's go over and look at these." She pulled him past a rustic brick-lined fireplace, newly cleaned and empty, toward a wall of bookshelves. "Maybe you can reach the ones on top. They're too high for me."

"Aw, gee, honey, they're just a lot of old books. Kid stuff, too, from the look of them. Fairy tales. Probably came with the house."

"But they look interesting, those big ones up there. Maybe they're worth a lot of money."

Grunting, he stood on tiptoe and removed one, a heavy volume shedding flakes of leather when he opened it, like a dead man's skin.

"Here, you take it. You know I can't read this." He handed the book to her and turned away, bored.

Squinting at the text, Doris frowned in disappointment. "Oh, damn," she muttered, "wouldn't you just know it?"

George left off talking business with Fred Weingast and ambled over, glass in hand. "Having trouble, Dorie?"

She grimaced. "This really makes me feel my age. I used to be so good in French—even knew some Provençal dialect—and now I'm so rusty."

"Never could stand it, myself. All that masculine-feminine stuff, and those goddamn accents . . . " He took a sip of vodka. "Actually, I'd toss all these old books out, only they're supposed to be a good investment."

Silber turned back to them. "Investment, did you say? You really think these are worth something?"

"Damn right. They're going up all the time." He nodded to the man who stood talking a few feet away. "Isn't that right, Fred?"

Weingast walked over, followed by Milt and another guest, Artie Faschman. "That's what people are saying. My accountant suggested getting into books, especially with the market the way it is. But you've gotta have the room for 'em." He shrugged. "Our apartment's much too small."

"Naw, that's not the problem," said Faschman. "The problem is keeping them cool and dry. Look at those things up there—they're probably full of mice and silverfish."

George smiled uneasily. "Oh, I doubt there's any mice. We had the place fumigated before moving in. *Really* fumigated!" He took a final swallow of his drink. "But you know, you're right, those damned things do decay something awful, and when summer comes I'll bet they begin to smell. To tell you the truth, I've been thinking of selling the lot of them to a place in New Haven. Maybe install a state-of-the-art video system, with one of those screens that come down from the ceiling."

"Now you're talking," said Faschman. "I've been thinking about getting one of those myself. And I'll tell you what you do then—you invest in stamps. They're a lot easier to keep."

Weingast nodded. "Stamps are okay," he said, "but my accountant says coins are even better. With gold going up again, they're a pretty safe bet."

When George left them, the men were deep into high finance. He returned to the bar and refilled his glass, heavy on the tonic.

Even with the Wagners' tardiness, and the absence of the Foglers and the Greens, and the fact that Bob Childs was sick and Evelyn Platt was away, it was a sizable housewarming party. The Bregmans were there, Len and Ellie, and the Silbers, Sid and Doris, and Art and Judy Faschman, and Fred and Laura Weingast, and the Stanleys just back from Miami, Dennis and Myra sporting their new suntans, and Milt and Florence Lazarus, and Roy Bullard, looking heavier than ever with his improbably tiny fiancée, whose name they all kept forgetting, and Phil and Mimi Stahl, and the Chasens, Chuck and Cindy, and the Stillmans, Howard and Joyce, and Ben and Janice Millhauser, and Jeff and Irene Crystal, and the Fitzgeralds and the Goodhues, and Alan Mendelson and Michael Cooper and poor Cissy Feinstock, who was so homely that Alan and Mike were paying her practically no attention, even though she was supposed to be fixed up with one of them.

Thirty-one guests gathered in the Kurtzes' living room; and with the Wagners arriving now, amid much hugging and handshaking and cries of "At last!" and "It's about time!" and the inevitable wolf whistles at Tammie Wagner's décolletage, that made thirty-three.

That was a lot of people, George conceded. Too many, really, when one considered how many of them weren't even close friends. Why, he and Phyllis barely saw the Millhausers from one year to the next. And as for the Goodhues, they didn't even know them; they'd been invited by the Fitzgeralds. Leaning back against the bar, George held the glass to his eye and surveyed his guests through a frost of vodka. At times like this it was hard to keep track of them: too many faces to smile at, too many names to remember. Sometimes they seemed almost interchangeable.

Still, it was nice to have a living room large enough to hold a crowd this size. And anyway, George reflected, he and Phyllis had vowed that as soon as they'd moved into the house, they'd become great entertainers. A party like this was the perfect way to establish their new identities.

"George!" Phyllis broke into his reverie. "Come over here and take Tammie's coat." She looked up at Herb. "And as for you, I think you're a big enough boy to hang your own coat up. It's very informal tonight, we haven't really settled in yet. And you'll have to mix yourselves drinks, we don't even have a bartender!" She laughed, as if to suggest that, in the future, in this fine new house, bartenders would be routine.

Tammie was talking about how hard it was to find a decent sitter these days. "And so finally we decided the hell with it and left her off till tomorrow at Herb's folks. They never go out anymore anyway." She smoothed her new dress.

"Lord, George, this place is swell!" said Herb, pumping George's hand. "I'm just sorry we didn't get here earlier, so we could see it by daylight. The trees must be beautiful this time of year. But God almighty, let me tell you, it's hard as hell to *find* this place!"

"Weren't Phyllis's directions good enough?"

"Oh sure, they were all right." Herb followed George to the coat closet. "But I mean, it gets so *dark* out here in the country. I'm just not used to it." He paused until George had found a spare hanger for Tammie's coat. "We took the Turnpike all the way up to New Haven—that part was fine, of course—and we got off at 81, just like we were supposed to, and then onto 501 . . . But once you're off that, the road gets pretty bad. It's like they suddenly turned out the lights!

No markers or anything." He shook his head. "You know people on the highway commission around here, don't you, George? I mean, you really ought to do something about it. It's a disgrace!"

"Yeah, the roads are a little tricky at night, till you get used to them."

"They're a lot worse than tricky, let me tell you. I damn near *hit* something! Honest to God, I think it was a bear."

"Oh, come on, Herb!" George slapped him on the back. "You've been living in Fort Lee too long. This is the country, sure, but it's not the middle of the *woods,* for Chrissake! You won't find bears in this part of the state."

"Well, whatever it was—"

"Probably some poor old sheep dog. All the farms around here have 'em."

"Okay, it was a sheep dog, then. Who knows? It was so dark . . . Anyway, I nearly hit the thing, and I would have if Tammie hadn't yelled. And then I got so rattled I missed the turnoff at, what is it, Death's Head?"

George laughed. "Brother, what an imagination! You Madison Avenue guys are all alike. The town's name is Beth Head, dummy! *Beth* Head."

Herb laughed too. "Anyway, I missed the place completely and ended up driving through the gates of some state park. Can you believe it? Tammie was having a fit! We're looking for your house and we end up in some damned *park!*"

"Yeah, that's Munson Hollow. I've done some fishing there with a few of the local bigwigs. Very nice area."

"It must be, during the day. But it's not the kind of place I like visiting at night. Tammie thought she saw a light in the ranger's cabin—you know, the one by the gates—and I got out to ask directions. I mean, we hadn't even brought along a goddamned map!"

George grinned from ear to ear. "Poor Herb! You weren't cut out to be a backwoodsman!"

"Now that's not fair!" Herb seemed genuinely stung. "Tammie was fussing about her goddamned *dress* so much she didn't even think to—Well, anyway, I'm walking up to this godforsaken little cabin, and immediately I see that Tammie was wrong, there's no light in it, the place is boarded up for the season . . . But just in case, I start pounding on the door, you know? And yelling for the ranger. I mean, we were really *lost!*" He lowered his voice. "Besides, I knew Tammie would squawk if I didn't make sure it was actually empty."

"And was it?"

"Of course it was! Who the hell would hang around a place like *that* all night?" He shook his head. "So there I am, pounding on this door and wondering if there's a pay phone around so maybe I could call you . . . when I hear something lumbering through the bushes."

"Probably the ranger."

"I didn't wait to find out. You should have seen how fast I got back in that car and took off! Believe me, I was ready to head right back to Jersey, but Tammie wanted to show off her new dress." He paused. "And of course, I wanted to see this place."

"You tell Tammie what you heard?"

"Are you kidding? I'd never hear the end of it. Listen, she thinks I'm a coward as it is. *She's* the tough one, she really is. I'd never have found your house if it weren't for her. She caught that last turnoff after I was half a mile past it. The damned thing's almost hidden by trees! You ought to cut a few of them down, for Chrissake!"

"I thought you were supposed to be the big conservationist."

Herb laughed. "Well, just because I send a few bucks to the Sierra Club doesn't mean I have to worship trees. I mean, someone's going to have an *accident* one of these days. Really, George, you ought to do something about it. Get them to put up some lights or something. You've got influence with the highway people, don't you?"

"Not as much as everyone seems to think."

"Well, anyway, it's a safety hazard. I mean, that winding road, so goddamned narrow that I had to go about twenty miles an hour . . . It's just a good thing there weren't any cars going the other way. As a matter of fact, there wasn't a single other car on the road. Pretty desolate for Connecticut."

"No pollution."

"Amen to that! Hey, I *mean* it, old buddy. I may not be a nature freak, but I think it's great out here. Like to live here myself."

"Why not move, then? There's plenty of homes for sale in these parts. I could even help you look. I mean, it gets a little lonely sometimes . . . "

"Hey, I thought you *liked* living way out here."

"Oh sure, of course I do. Wouldn't trade it for the world. I just mean, we don't have any friends in the area yet, and it'd be nice to have someone nearby."

"Aw, c'mon, George, you make friends pretty quick. Besides, I could never afford a place like this. I mean, all this land!"

"No, really, it wasn't so bad. Didn't cost much."

"So you claim. But I'll bet you've got room for a couple of good-sized golf courses out here. And that driveway of yours, it's as long as a country road. You could probably go hunting right on your own property. And probably get lost, too."

"Yeah, well, I guess we're really in the sticks."

"But that's the best part! I mean it, that's just great! That's the whole point of living out here, I can see that now. The seclusion, the solitude . . . Boy, could I do with some solitude these days!"

"Business pretty rough, huh?"

"Boy, you know it! We're all tightening the belt. How about you?"

"Oh, pretty much the same, I guess."

"Aw, now don't be modest, George. You're always selling yourself short. This place must have cost a pretty penny."

George paused and cleared his throat. "Well, to tell you the truth, it cost me almost nothing. Got it for a song. The owner went a little you-know-what." He tapped his head.

"Christ! Leave it to you to find the bargains!" They were back in the living room now. Through the doorway Herb could see his wife chatting with Phyllis and heaping a plate with food. He gazed around him, taking in the furnishings, the sheer size of the room, the familiar faces of the other guests. "Oh well, I suppose the rest of us will just have to get along with our little shacks in the suburbs!"

"Not me, man," Howard piped up. "I'm buying myself an estate just like this one." As the conversation paused, Howard grinned. "Just as soon as the market picks up!"

"You'd better watch out, Howard," called Florence. "Someday

somebody might take you seriously. You'll run into some shyster and wind up in the street, walking around in a barrel!"

Lenny moved toward them, staggering slightly, and put his arm around Howard's shoulder. He seemed drunk. "If you wanna buy some land, you don't hafta wait till the market's better," he said. "You just gotta know the right people. Right, George?"

Under the weight of their stares, George managed to maintain his smile, but it was an effort. "Oh, you need a little patience, that's all. And you have to wait till the right deal comes along. I was lucky, I admit." The look he gave Lenny was not pretty.

As if on cue, Phyllis emerged from the dining room and announced gaily, "Well, I don't know about you, but I'm just grateful to be living in a place like this. And now that everyone's finally here, I'd like to show you just how lucky we are."

"Well, it's about time," said Ellie. She turned to the rest. "She's been keeping us in suspense."

"You mean at long last we'll get to see it?" asked Florence.

"That's right," said Phyllis, all smiles. She fluttered her eyelids in parody of a grand duchess. "Madame Kurtz will now escort her guests around her palatial estate."

George managed an apologetic laugh. "It's just an old barn," he said. "Honest—nothing but a barn!"

"See, I got him trussed up pretty tight now. Won't catch me making the same mistake twice, no, sir!"

"Are you sure the straps aren't a little, um, too tight?"

"You kidding, Doc? If I loosened them, he'd rip the bandages off in two seconds flat. No, sir, nothing doing."

The doctor stepped into the room and looked down at the man on the cot. "Well, hello there," he said genially. "I'm sorry to find you like this. Hope you're not terribly uncomfortable. Just as soon as those lacerations heal, we'll remove those bandages . . . and then we'll see if we can't get you out of that jacket, okay? We believe in giving our patients here a second chance."

The man on the cot glared at him.

"And so I do hope that, um . . . " He turned to the orderly. "Can he hear what I'm saying?"

"Oh, yeah, he can hear you fine. But we think he must've done some-thing to his vocal cords, you know? 'Cause he don't seem to be able to speak." He smiled. "Just between you and me, I ain't so broken up about that. I mean, all that screaming, it was really getting to me. Always going on about feeding time . . . I mean, you'd think we never fed the guy!"

"It isn't fair. Honestly, it just isn't fair." Snapping on the light, Ellie entered the bedroom. "Just look at that. That's exactly the kind of bed frame Lenny and I have been looking all over the city for."

"I'll bet it's real brass, too," said Doris. "Hey, Florie," she called over her shoulder, "do you think that bed frame's real brass?"

Florence emerged from one of the hall bathrooms, Irene Crystal behind her. "It sure is," she said. "God, I'm absolutely green with envy." The bedroom was imposing in size, though the smallness of the curtained windows, four in a row, revealed the house's age. "And that quilt, did you ever *see* such a thing? It must have taken years! Don't you just love it?"

"Oh, I do," said Doris. "Such workmanship!" She ran her hand down one of the gleaming bedposts.

"It's criminal, that's what I think," said Ellie. "Here I spend my whole life dreaming of a house in the country with a greenhouse and a pantry and a kitchen big enough to walk around in—"

"And a real library," said Doris.

"That's right, an honest-to-God library, the kind they have in those Joan Fontaine movies, remember? With comfortable chairs and little tables next to them so you can sit and sip your sherry while you read . . . And who gets all this? The Kurtzes. I tell you, it's simply criminal. I mean, has anyone ever seen either of them so much as *open* a book?"

"Oh, George is a reader," said Florence. "I can tell."

"How?"

She grinned. "There's a pile of *Sports Illustrated*s in the bathroom!"

"And how about that nursery?" said Doris. She enjoyed baiting Ellie.

"Yes, can you *imagine?* A separate nursery, and their kid's away at school. It makes me so angry I could positively scream!"

"Oh, come on, El," said Florence, "don't get all worked up. Your two aren't exactly toddlers anymore. Your oldest is already out of *college,* for heaven's sake!"

"Still, all I can think of is how nice this place would have been when Lenny and I were just starting out. Honestly, going home to Long Island's going to be such a letdown."

"For sure," said Irene. "And the drive back's not going to be much fun either. Jeff's been grumbling about it all night. We figure if we leave here at ten—I mean, we've *got* to stay at least that late—we won't be home till way past midnight."

"Well, my husband had a brilliant idea," said Florence, pulling up a rocking chair as the others settled back on an old-fashioned couch along the wall. "He took one look at that guest room down at the other end, the one with all those antique toys, and decided he wanted to spend the night here. He says if we hang around long enough, they'll have to ask us to stay."

"Hey, you little schemers in there!" They all looked up guiltily, but it was only Roy Bullard looming large and portly in the doorway, his fiancée pressing behind him. "I heard all that. You can hatch all the plots you want about staying the night, but I warn you, Gail and I have dibs on this room." He strode inside with her in tow, the wide plank floorboards creaking beneath his weight.

"Sorry, Roy, I'm afraid you're out of luck," said Florence. "This one's the master bedroom. See? Two dressers, two mirrors, and matching night tables."

Bullard grinned. "But just one bed, huh?" Its springs groaned as he and Gail seated themselves heavily upon it. "Didn't think old George had it in him anymore."

Fred Weingast poked his head into the room; other voices came from the hall behind him. "Roy, I do declare, you're getting as catty as the girls." He leaned against the doorway, still holding his half-filled cocktail glass. "I don't know about you folks, but I'm not so sure I'd *want* to spend the night way out here. I'm a city boy. Places like this make me nervous."

"Aw, what's the matter?" said Bullard. "Can't fall asleep without the sound of traffic?"

"He'll miss the roaches," said Florence.

"Come on over and sit with us." Bullard patted the bed beside him; there was just enough room for one more person.

Weingast looked uncertain. "Well, I don't think old George would be too happy if his bed collapsed . . . Think I'll go take a look at the attic, if I can make it up those wooden steps. I hear it's really something. Anyway, kids, you'd all better mind your manners. Our esteemed hostess is on her way upstairs—" He glanced back over his shoulder. "—accompanied, I do believe, by her royal entourage."

As if caught in a transgression, the women got to their feet and filed hurriedly from the room, pushing past him into the hall and leaving Bullard and his fiancée on the bed. Meanwhile, the babble of voices grew louder; Phyllis was conducting her promised tour of the house.

Initially the company had trooped after her like a column of dutiful schoolchildren, gaping at the various rooms that formed the first floor: the parlor and the pantry, the library with its walls of closely packed bookshelves broken only by a set of windows and a fireplace, the kitchen with its original oaken beams and cast-iron meat hooks still hanging from them, the storerooms and the fragrant little potting shed that led into the greenhouse . . .

But thirty adults, inebriated at that, had proved difficult to keep together; they'd spilled over into the corridors, getting sidetracked over old framed prints and maps, exploring on their own or lagging behind and returning to the living room to refill their glasses. At last she'd simply given up and had encouraged them to wander wherever they pleased.

"Just make sure Howard doesn't trip down the stairs," she'd said, winking at him. "We can't afford a lawsuit! And oh, by the way, I know most of it's junk, but please try not to break anything at *this* early date. Wait till we've lived here a bit longer! Otherwise, you can have the run of the house and, I guess, the run of the grounds—if anyone feels like stepping outside in this weather." She glanced doubtfully toward the window.

"What's the matter," joked Milt, "don't the bathrooms work?"

Phyllis laughed. "I just mean if you're going to get sick, I'd rather you do it outside, over the dead leaves, than on my nice new carpet! We had it laid down only a few weeks ago."

Some of the women had drifted back to the kitchen to exclaim once again over the oak-top breakfast table and the old wrought-iron gas range with the extra-deep compartment for baking bread, which stood in quaint contrast to the newly installed dishwasher beside it. Others had gone ahead to the second floor, and a few of the men had made straight for the narrow stairway to the attic, vowing to "work from the top down."

Phyllis was now advancing along the upstairs hall, accompanied by the more faithful of her audience, including Cissy Feinstock, who followed her like a child afraid of getting lost.

"Wow," Cissy was saying, "the steps in these old houses are so *steep!*" She lingered near the top of the stairs, catching her breath. "How do you do it, Phyl?"

"Remember, I've been living here for a couple of months." She smiled down at the others still on the stairs. Janice Millhauser stood on the landing, panting softly and clutching the bannister for support. "Honestly, girls, it does wonders for the figure."

Janice glared at her with a touch of malevolence, then started up. "I had no idea how out of shape I was," she muttered. "I haven't been this winded since the elevator strike!"

But Phyllis was already walking down the hall to her bedroom, pointing out the wall hangings to Cissy and the others. "This one had to be repaired," she was saying. "See? Right here, this area at the bottom, and the border as well. We had a little shop in New Haven do the reweaving. They're very cheap."

"Gosh, what *is* it?" asked Cissy. "I guess this green part is meant to be leaves, but what's that group in the center? Faces?"

"Animal faces, yes. But they're so faded I'm afraid you can hardly see them. The man in the shop thought it might be a Middle Eastern design." Phyllis turned and addressed the group around her. "You know, there are two kinds of tapestries: grotesque and arabesque. Arabesque just has leaves and flowers, but this one's a grotesque—there are animals mixed in."

Ellie stood watching from further down the hall, then turned to Doris. "Honestly, did you *ever?*" she whispered. "Listen to her, parading around her new knowledge to impress the masses."

"It's like the book, then, isn't it?" Cissy was saying. *"Tales of the Grotesque and Arabesque."*

"Oh, really?" said Phyllis. She turned to the next tapestry; it had been hanging crookedly, and she adjusted it. "This one's in much better condition. See? It's a deer and a bear, I think. George is going to have it appraised."

Irene and Florence had joined the little group; the latter smiled ingratiatingly. "Where is he, by the way?"

"Oh, probably downstairs."

"I saw him duck into the loo at the other end of the hall," said Fred Weingast. He stepped heavily out of the bedroom, his drink sloshing in his glass. "The old boy looked a bit under the weather. Too much of this stuff." He held up his drink, then turned back to the couple in the room. "Anybody care to join me?"

"In the attic?" asked Roy Bullard, getting up from the bed with a groan and a little support from his fiancée. "Anything you say." Pulling her behind him, he followed Weingast into the hallway, pausing to explain to Phyllis, "Some of the guys are already up there prowling around, I think." Ahead of them, at a turn in the corridor, a large wooden door hung open, revealing the entrance to the attic. The three disappeared up the stairs.

"Don't stay long," Phyllis called after them. "It's cold up there."

Cissy, all this time, had not left her side. "Gosh, Phyl," she said, "you actually have three bathrooms on this floor?"

Phyllis nodded modestly. "And two downstairs."

From behind them came a gasp. "Oh, this stuff's *lovely!*" Janice had made it up the stairs and now stood examining the tiny figurines on a ledge in an alcove by the guest room. "The expressions on these little things' faces are so *precious!* Bone china, aren't they?"

"I think so. Have you seen the ones inside the doorway?"

The women followed her into the guest room. Against one wall stood a multi-shelved display case.

"Hey, this is some collection!"

Phyllis merely smiled.

"Good grief!" laughed Irene. "What do you call this stuff—knick-knacks, gewgaws . . . ?"

"Thingamajigs?"

"How about whatnots?"

"Plain old bric-a-brac's good enough for me."

"Gee, I haven't seen one of these in years." Florence picked up a small glass globe with a winter scene inside; when she shook it, snow swirled in a miniature blizzard. The globe beside it held a shiny black beetle, and the one next to that a tiny bouquet of dried flowers: chrysanthemums, black-eyed Susans, cornflowers, even a tiny thistle—all the colors of autumn.

The Stillmans strolled in, arm in arm. While Joyce examined the objects on the shelves, Howard leaned back against a wall and closed his eyes as if shutting out the room full of women. He'd had too much to drink.

"This stuff must be worth a fortune," said Joyce, examining the small figure of an elf carved in dark wood. "You just don't see things like this every day. And I'll bet the ones on the bottom—" She indicated a shelf of antique cast-iron banks: dogs and elephants, a hunter and a bear, a clown and hoop. "—would cost a couple of hundred dollars, at least in the city."

Phyllis shrugged. "Some of it may be valuable, all right, but a lot of it's just junk. George hasn't gotten around to throwing it out." She pushed aside two small sculptured heads and picked up a grey ceramic candle holder in the shape of a gargoyle, the black taper seeming to sprout from between the creature's wings. "This, for example. It looks old, doesn't it?"

"Medieval."

"Yes, but feel." She handed the thing to Joyce. "See? Light as a feather. It's just some cheap plaster-of-paris souvenir. From Paris, appropriately enough. We saw tons of them when we were over last year. They sell them at Notre Dame for seven or eight francs."

Cissy looked disappointed. "Well, maybe it's not all exactly *price-less,*" she said, "but you probably have enough here to open your own antique shop."

"Three antique shops!" said Florence.

Phyllis laughed. "This is nothing. You should see the attic—though I don't recommend it!"

"There's *more* up there? Where'd you acquire all this stuff?"

"Don't forget, it wasn't us who acquired it. It was the man George bought this place from. That lunatic."

"Well, he may have been a lunatic, but he certainly had interesting taste," remarked Janice, studying a group of prints on the wall by the window, a series of faded storybook engravings; below them a pen-and-ink sketch showed what looked like the Notre Dame gargoyle, though the wings had been replaced by things resembling ropes. "Eclectic, at least," she said. "What was he like?"

"I have no idea," said Phyllis. "I never met the man, thank God. George never wanted me to. I'm told he was highly unpleasant."

"What was his problem?" asked Florence. She was sliding open the drawer of a small end table; the inside was freshly dusted and empty. "He keep raving about little green men?"

"He may have. He may very well have. All I know is, he had very unclean habits. This place stank like a sewer when I first saw it. And it wasn't fixed up like this, believe me. It was a mess."

"What, the whole house?"

"You could barely push your way through, for the junk."

"No, I mean the smell. All over?"

Phyllis paused to draw the curtains, shutting out the night. "Every room. That's why we took so long to move in. First we tried to air the place out, but that didn't work, so then we had to have men in to fumigate. And believe me, those people charge an arm and a leg. George nearly had a fit."

"All I know is, it smells okay now," said Cissy earnestly. "Really, Phyl, you've done a marvelous job cleaning."

"Well, I don't deserve the credit. There are people you can hire for jobs like that. Those fireplaces were the hardest, I'm told. Filled with dirt and ashes. I'm glad we won't have to depend on them when winter comes. Imagine, one in every room!"

"Even in the kitchen," sighed Joyce. "Oh, Howard, if we could only have one built in our kitchen—even a fake one . . . Wouldn't that be nice?"

Her husband opened his eyes, which were bloodshot. "Totally," he said. "We'd be the rage of Scarsdale." He closed them again.

"Why don't you just settle for the hooks?" asked Florence.

"You mean those meat hooks on the ceiling?"

"Sure, they wouldn't cost much. And Howard could hang salami on them!"

"But we have no beams to hold them."

Phyllis intervened. "Obviously, then, the thing to do is to let George find you a house like this, beams and all."

"That's what I keep *tellin'* everybody," said Howard.

She ignored him. "Come on, let me show you our bedroom. There's some more junk in there."

They followed her down the hall, Howard shuffling after them, and all the women who hadn't already seen the brass bed frame made the appropriate gasps of delight.

"Oh, where'd you *get* it?" Janice wanted to know. "You don't mean to tell me this came with the house, too."

Phyllis looked pleased. "Where else?"

"Boy, the previous owner must have lived a pretty good life here. What happened, his wife die and he go to pieces?"

"I'm sure I don't know," said Phyllis. "I doubt he was even married."

Janice's eyes widened. "You mean he lived here all alone? In this huge house?"

Phyllis shrugged. "I told you he was crazy. He may have had a dog to keep him company, I'm not sure. George said something about a pet."

The springs groaned as Howard fell heavily onto the bed. He lay back full length, careful nonetheless to keep his shoes off the patchwork quilt. "Well, I'd say he was one guy who knew how to live." Giving an extended yawn, he stretched as if ready for sleep.

"I mean, this is a comf'table place. A li'l drafty, but comf'table. An' this is a comf'table bed." He closed his eyes and appeared to doze.

Joyce gave her hostess a stricken look. "God, I'm so sorry! He's had a hard week. Anyone want to help me drag him off?"

"No no no, leave him be. Let him take a little nap. Like he said, it's a comfortable bed." Phyllis prided herself on her tact. "The weird thing is, the man we bought the house from didn't even use it. Would you believe it, he slept on a mattress."

"You're kidding!"

"Nothing but a mattress?"

"That's all. I tell you, the way some bachelors live . . . " Phyllis shook her head. "George found this brass frame in the attic, underneath a pile of junk. We polished it up and bought new box springs for it. But it's still not in such good condition. See?" She pointed toward the metal legs; they looked slightly gnawed. "I'm afraid it got a bit battered up there."

From the hall came the sound of heavy footsteps and loud voices. Herb peered into the doorway, blinking at the light. "Excuse me, ladies. Is my wife in here?"

"Tammie's downstairs."

"Hey, Howard! Howard!" Milt Lazarus burst into the room, pushing the others out of the doorway. "Wake up, boy, you've got to come up and see the attic." He began tugging at Howard's ankles.

"Honey, come on, leave him alone. He's taking a little nap." Florence put her arm around Milt's waist. "Let's go back downstairs. I need some more Chardonnay."

"Is it really nice up there?" asked Cissy.

"It's great!" said Milt, disengaging himself from his wife's arm. "There's stacks of magazines, some crazy old almanacs and star charts, old knives, a barber chair, kids' toys . . . A lot of the stuff's pretty rusted, but you ought to see the magazines. Almost a hundred years old, some of them."

Phyllis frowned. "I nearly forgot about those things. When we cleaned this place out, we put off doing the attic. We just stuck all the junk up there, all the stuff we couldn't use. Someday we'll have to go over the whole place—just as soon as it gets warm. As it is, it's a firetrap, all that paper."

"Aw, don't throw those magazines away," said Milt. "They might be worth something. A few bucks, at least. Or donate 'em to a library for a tax write-off."

Phyllis shook her head. "It's a real rats' nest up there. Like something out of the Collyer brothers."

"No way!" said Milt.

Fred Weingast entered the room, his glass now empty. "Hey, that's a wild place you've got, Phyl. Weird stuff in those jars, and those old uniforms—Christ, I didn't think I'd ever see one of those army jackets again, the kind with the snaps on the pockets . . . There's even an old department store mannequin, way in the corner, pretty chewed up now but scary as hell." He laughed. "I mean, the thing was naked! Herb thought we'd found a body!"

"Come on, Florie, let's go up." Milt tugged at his wife's arm. "I want to show you some of the ads for women's clothes, they're really a scream."

"Aw, honey, I'm too tired, and those steps look so steep . . . Couldn't you just bring a few down?" She turned to Phyllis for help.

"It's really not worth going up," agreed Phyllis. "It isn't insulated up there, and the place really gets freezing this time of year. Especially at night."

"She's right, you know," said Weingast, shifting his empty glass from hand to hand. "You could see your breath, even. Think I'll head back down for something that'll warm me up." He turned to look down the hall. "Anyway, I think the wife's down there."

"There's a huge pot of coffee brewing in the kitchen," said Phyllis.

"Good," said Weingast, "I'll need it for the ride home."

Milt looked disappointed as the rest filed out behind Weingast. He glanced at his friend; Howard lay sprawled on the bed, snoring softly like some large hibernating animal. Milt gave him a few ineffectual nudges, then said, "Ah, hell," and followed the others downstairs.

George sat in the bathroom, crouching like some small hunted

creature. He was acutely conscious of the muffled voices that penetrated the bathroom door, punctuated now and again by more
boisterous ones when a couple strode past in the hall outside. He
leaned forward, waiting for the cramps to subside. If he held his
breath and strained to hear, he could pick out a few words. " . . .
may take the option on it, but they don't . . . " That would be Faschman and, most likely, Sid Silber.

Silence for a while. Footsteps creaked in the attic overhead. Then
whispered voices, women's. "No, wait, don't go in."

"I just—"

"No, I think someone's in there."

The voices moved on.

George sighed and stared down at the tiled floor, wishing he had
something to read. Against Phyllis's wishes he always left a few magazines in the bathroom near the stairs, but that had been occupied;
and this one, just off what had been the nursery, was still relatively
bare, save for the black plastic shelves and soap dish, all glossy and
sharp-edged, that his wife had placed there this morning. Already a
slab of soap lay melting like ice in a little puddle of greasy water. And
the little black guest towels, they were her idea, too, with stiff lace
trim, to be left sopping on the floor or stuck awkwardly back on the
rack. The house was not yet livable.

Yet any bareness was preferable to the squalor in which he'd found
it. Of course, it was what he should have expected, after seeing the
flecks of dried skin on the man's lips and the stain on those trousers. A
recluse, they'd called him, using the polite word. Eyes like a sorcerer,
they said. Possibly the locals had thought him merely eccentric. But
George still recalled the bags of blackened vegetables sprouting pale
tendrils, the deposits under the sink, and the stench of rotting meat.

And the threats . . .

He felt his intestines churn, and winced; when would it stop? The
floor tiles seemed to conform to some sort of pattern, but the pain
made him impatient. Red rectangle at the upper left of each square,
no, every other square, and in the next row the design was reversed,
so that . . . Yet over by the door the pattern changed. Automatically
he cursed the ancient, unknown builders of this house.

He and Phyllis had kept all the original fixtures; it added to the atmosphere. The bathtub even had legs, like in the old pictures, reminding him of animal claws, thick and stubby. One, two, three . . . He lost count and started over. Yes, there were five fingers on each claw. They didn't make bathtubs like that anymore. Big enough for a whole family—not that the original owner had ever needed one that size. He'd smelled as if he hadn't bathed in years.

A woman's laughter echoed in the hall, and then the low, eager voice of a man, perhaps recounting a joke. Damn it, he'd miss the whole party this way! Searching for something to pass the time, he tugged out his wallet and began leafing through it. I.D. cards told him he was George C. Kurtz, credit cards listed restrictions in tiny blue print . . . What a bore. He began counting his money.

"George?" Phyllis knocked on the door. "Are you in there?"

"Yeah," he grunted. "I'll be right out."

"Are you all right, honey?"

"Yeah, I'm okay. I'll be right out."

"Is there anything I can get you?"

"I said I was okay."

She seemed to go away for a moment, then returned; her voice came from just outside the door. "We're all going back downstairs. Howard's asleep on our bed, though. Don't wake him."

"Mmm."

"Did you say something, honey?" Holding his own breath, he could hear her breathing on the other side. She paused as if to say something else, then went away.

In the silence he wondered what was wrong with him. Something he'd eaten, perhaps. Those shrimp last night? But no, that had been two nights ago, and he'd barely had a thing all day. Maybe he could no longer hold his liquor.

Still, the ache felt like fear. He wondered what he was afraid of.

That was how it always worked: he'd feel tension in the pit of his stomach, and only then, examining one by one his inventory of fears, would he attempt to discover what had produced it. First the effect, then the cause—as if his mind held so many unexplored levels, mystery upon mystery, that he never knew the things it contained until his stomach told him.

Nerves, most likely, over the success of this party. The bane of all hosts, particularly at a big affair like this. Still, he hadn't realized he'd been so worried . . .

An unsatisfying explanation—but abruptly the pain left him. He made himself ready and stepped into the hall, noticing Howard as he passed the bedroom. The face on the quilt looked red and puffy, like an infant's who'd gone to bed squalling. George fastened the door to the attic, sealing out the cold, and headed downstairs.

"I suppose pencil and paper are out of the question . . . "

"Well, sure, I mean what do you expect? Give him a free hand and he'll go for them bandages. Give him a pencil and he'll poke his own eyes out. I don't put nothing past these people, not after what I seen."

The doctor sighed. "It's rather frustrating, you must admit. Suicidal, ripe for therapy, and he's incapable of speech." He stared at the man on the cot; the man on the cot stared back. "Perhaps when his throat heals, if we keep him in restraint . . . "

"Sometimes he'll talk to me."

"Pardon? You say he speaks—"

"Well, no, not exactly. What I mean is, he taps his foot against the wall, see? Like when he wants me to turn him over."

The other shook his head. "I'm afraid that hardly takes the place of real communication. A yes-or-no response, perhaps, but quite useless for our needs. No, I think we'll simply have to wait a month or two, and then—"

"Oh, he don't just say yes or no. He taps out whole words. See, we got this code." He drew from his pocket a frayed scrap of paper. "A is one, B is two; it goes like that."

"And to say a word like 'zoo' would take all night. No thanks." The doctor looked at his watch. "For the time being, some medication—"

"No, you don't understand. You see, Z is two taps and then six. Twenty-six, get it? And O would be"—he studied the paper—"one and then five. Pretty smart, huh?"

"It would still take all night, and I have thirty other patients to worry about." He looked again at his watch. *"And rounds to make before bed-time. No, I think we'll keep him on the Thorazine, and I'll prescribe twenty-five milligrams of Tofranil. We can try that for a while . . . "* He walked down the hall, scribbling in his notebook.

The orderly remained in the doorway of the room, staring at the man on the cot. The man on the cot stared back.

In the living room, Herb Wagner was trying to organize a game. Faces turned as George entered.

"We missed you, George. Thought you'd fallen in!"

George grinned sheepishly and moved toward the bar, both flattered and annoyed that his absence had been noted. Couldn't these people fend for themselves? It wasn't as if they were all strangers to one another.

"Herb here thought you'd been eaten by a bear!"

"That's what I told 'em, George."

George shrugged. "No such luck. I think it was what *I* ate!"

Amid their laughter Phyllis called, "Now don't put ideas in their heads, or nobody'll finish the quiche. I spent all day making it." She pointed to the plates of hors d'oeuvres by the bar. "And you people aren't eating the sausages," she chided. "They'll just lie there in the refrigerator if no one eats them."

A few guests shuffled toward the food. Cissy called to him from across the room. "We're going to tell our fortunes, George. You're just in time. Herb has a pack of cards."

"A Tarot deck," said Herb, pronouncing the final *t*. "I found it up in your attic, in one of the trunks." He held forth a small green cardboard box decorated with line drawings and the words *Grand Etteilla.* Cellophane still clung to the sides. "I wanted to see what they looked like," he explained. "Hope you don't mind. I don't think the pack's ever been opened before."

"Do you know how to use them?"

"There's an instruction booklet inside. Only trouble is, it's in French."

"I'm a little rusty myself," George was saying, but Lenny interrupted.

"Ellie's a whiz at French. Christ, you should've seen her over there last summer. They thought she was a native." He snatched the booklet from Herb's hand and gave it to his wife. "Go ahead, what's it say?"

"Oh, this is easy," she said. *"Maniere de Tirer le Grand Etteilla ou Tarots Egyptiens, Composé de Soixante-dix-huit Cartes Illustrées.'* Well, you can pick that up, can't you?"

"Something about Egyptian cards," said Florence.

"Does it say how to lay them out?" asked Herb.

Ellie flipped through the pages. "Hmm, there aren't any diagrams. Not very helpful. There's something in the front, though. 'To use the cards, it is necessary first to strike the game by the person who . . . '" She paused in her reading. "Oh, I see. The person whose fortune's being told has to hit the cards with his left hand."

"Whose fortune's being told?" asked George, feigning interest. Anything to amuse the guests . . .

Herb shrugged. "We can try Tammie's, if she wants. Does it say how to arrange them?"

"I wish I could remember how Joan Blondell did them in *Nightmare Alley,*" said Ellie. "All I remember is, she kept turning up the death card for Tyrone Power."

"The Hanged Man," said Cissy, with a nervous little laugh.

"Mmm, that's right. Well, let's see." Ellie squinted at the booklet. "Oh boy, this is so complicated . . . I don't know if it's worth it. It'll take half an hour to set up."

"Aw, forget it then," said Herb, already casting about for new games to play.

Tammie put her arm around him. "From now on we'll stick to fortune cookies."

George watched the group falling away around him, dissolving into small clots of conversation, but Phyllis picked up her cue. "Why don't we do it the fast way? We'll all just pick a card, and that'll be our fortune. Here, give me, I'll shuffle."

For tradition's sake she rapped once on the box, and the cards were duly passed among the guests until each held one. "I feel as though we're about to play bingo!" said Fred Weingast, puzzling over his card. "What is this, anyway? It's the Three of something, I can tell, but what are they? Dinner plates?"

Milt peered over his shoulder. "That's it—the Three of Dinner Plates!"

"They look like coins to me," said Weingast's wife.

Ellie was leafing through the booklet. "No," she said, "they're pentacles. See? A five-pointed star inside each circle."

"What's it supposed to mean?"

"Let's see. Okay, here we go." She looked up at Weingast and smiled mysteriously, then turned to the text. "'A person noble and distinguished—'"

"Hey, that's me to a T!" exclaimed Weingast.

Ellie waited for the laughter to subside, then continued. "Sorry, people, but you've got it wrong. Listen. 'A person noble and distinguished has need of silver—uh, money—and you should lend it to him.'"

Milt, predictably, scurried over and slapped him on the back. "Fred, old pal, how about it?"

There were several paragraphs of text still to read, but the gag had run its course. Ellie turned to the rest. "Okay, kids, who's next?" Ignoring the drunken cries of "Me-me-me-me," she reached for Florence's card. In smeary lithograph it depicted a small blond boy holding a gold chalice; the background was pastoral, with dark green hills and a waterfall. "Oh, a picture card," she said. "Maybe that means it's important." She squinted down at the text. "Apparently he's the Page of Cups. Sort of like the Jack of Diamonds, I guess. 'Have confidence absolute,' it says—absolute confidence—'in the young man blond that you offers . . . that offers you his services.' Gee, Florie, who do you know who's blond?"

Milt answered for her. "Damn, I'll bet it's that delivery boy!" Everyone but Florence laughed.

"Do Phyllis next," suggested someone.

"Yeah, come on, do Phyllis." The others took up the chant.

Phyllis squirmed like a little girl asked to make a birthday speech.

"No," she said, smiling nervously, "really, I don't want to hear mine. I always believe in fortunes, and they're always bad." She hid the card behind her back. "Do George's first."

Ellie shrugged. "Okay, then, let me see it." She held out her hand.

"But I haven't got a card," said George.

"Too busy playing host," said Lenny. He picked up the pile of cards. "Come on, there's more than half the pack left. Take one."

"Close your eyes first," added Herb.

George sighed. "Okay, okay. But I'm telling you, the host's supposed to come last." He took the cards from Lenny and shuffled through them, eyes shut. He lifted one from the middle of the deck and looked down at it. "Good God!" He slipped it back in the deck and continued to shuffle.

"Hey," cried Ellie, "I saw that. No fair. You cheated!"

"He's entitled," said Lenny. "I mean, it's his house, right?"

The other guests had lost interest in all fortunes but their own; some had wandered over to the bar. Ellie, however, wasn't mollified. "I'll bet he had The Hanged Man. Isn't that right, George? Just like in the movie?"

"Just like in the movie," said George, his eyes shut. "Here, give me a reading on this one." He drew forth a card and handed it to her.

"The Eight of Wands," she said. "'Learning a trade or a profession. Employment or commission to come. Skill in affairs—in material affairs.' Hmm, I'm afraid that's a pretty dull one."

"Well, it's not so far off," said Lenny. "George is skilled in material affairs."

Herb shrugged. "Yeah, but so are we all. I mean, this kind of stuff could apply to anyone here. It's really no better than that column in the *Post*. You know, 'The Stargazer's Prophecy,' something like that. My secretary lives by it."

George had moved away from them. He stood by one of the windows, staring out at the night, trying to disguise the pain that had reclaimed his stomach. Because of the light inside it was impossible to see well, but he could hear the tapping of dead leaves against the glass. He heard, too, a few of the women squealing over Phyllis's card, The Lovers, and he thought of the one he had drawn forth and had returned to the deck so hurriedly after the briefest glimpse—an amorphous mass of grey, like the back of some huge animal, illuminated as if by moonlight. It had seemed disturbingly familiar. Amid the babble of voices the memory was already beginning to fade, but not the uneasiness it had aroused, the vague, half-buried apprehension . . . With a start he noticed his own reflection in the window and saw the savage twist of his mouth. He smoothed back his hair, smiled, and turned back to the company.

Entropy had set in. All but a few had tired of the game and had once again broken into smaller groups, those most bored drifting toward the bar, others, with thoughts of departure, to the large coffee pot now in the dining room. Ben Millhauser was holding forth to Dennis and Myra Stanley—the fall of the dollar, or perhaps the rise of crime—and Phyllis was trying to get Michael Cooper to talk to poor Cissy Feinstock. Milt Lazarus was making himself another drink. Over by the corner Herb and Lenny sat on the couch, probably comparing the achievements of their children. Others had wandered off to the kitchen and library. For the time being they all seemed occupied; George passed among them unnoticed, on his way back to the bathroom.

"I've never seen him like this," Herb was saying. "He's been so evasive. Usually he'll brag about a smart deal till you're sick of listening, but this time he played modest with me. I could tell something was funny the minute I came in."

"You mean that bit about how he was 'just lucky'? Jesus, wasn't that something!" Lenny shook his head.

"Yeah, all he'd say was the guy went a little gaga and sold him this place for a song."

"Is that what he told you?"

"That was it. But I get the impression you know a bit more about what really went on."

Lenny stared down into his glass, watching the ice cubes shrink and change shape. "Well, I don't know all that much."

"Aw, come on. I hear you've been riding him about it all night."

"Maybe I've sobered up a little since then."

"Aw, hell, you know I'll keep this to myself."

He studied Herb's face and saw the endless cocktails at expense-account lunches, the daily betrayals disguised as good fellowship. Herb would make a good story out of this.

"How about it?"

"Well . . . " Lenny watched George sidle through the room and head upstairs. "Okay, why not?"

In the room upstairs, Howard slept fitfully. A floorboard groaned outside the door—George on his way up the hall—and was echoed by the huge limb of a black oak beyond the window. Howard turned heavily onto his side, buried his face in the pillow, and slept on, one hand twisting a wrinkle of quilt as if clenched upon a steering wheel.

The women on the couch had begun talking about food costs, and Tammie was bored. It took parties like this to remind her that she preferred the company of men. "I'm sure they *are* better for you," Laura Weingast was saying, "but what they charge in those health food stores is outrageous." Tammie looked around for her husband; he was in the corner by the window, talking with Lenny Bregman. Pretty soon they'd be swapping dirty jokes.

A bridge table had been set up near the bar, piled high with paper plates and plastic forks. Roy Bullard was bent over it, showing something to his fiancée—what was her name? Gail.

He smiled as Tammie strolled over; Gail regarded her coldly. "Want your fortune done?" he asked. "According to this, I'm gonna have five kids, but Gail's only gonna have two!" Laughing, he pointed to an open page in the booklet, but Tammie couldn't read a word of French. "Still got your card?"

The green cardboard box lay next to an empty hors d'oeuvres platter, Tarot cards piled haphazardly beside it where guests had left them. The top card showed a stone tower crumbling as a bolt of lightning hit it. In the background the sea raged furiously.

"No, I put mine back in the box. There were just too many people ahead of me. But let's see, I think I can find it again." She began sorting through the deck, aware that Roy's eyes were on her; he was probably trying to decide if she was wearing a bra. "Hey, look at this," she said, producing the picture of a regal woman. "I like this one better than my own card! What's it mean?"

"The Queen of Swords," said Gail. "You're not allowed to choose, you know. You can't just pick the prettiest card and say you want it." She eyed her fiancé.

He was already flipping through the booklet. "Queen of Swords, huh? Sounds dangerous." He stopped and read to himself, lips moving. "Something about old age, I think." Tammie stiffened. "Isn't *vielle* the word for old?" He saw she wasn't grinning, and his own grin faded. "But apparently it means one thing if you hold it one way and something else if it's upside down."

"It was right side up, wasn't it?" said Gail.

"The other way," he went on, "it means the woman tyrannizes her husband. Hmm, poor old Herb! And I always thought *he* wore the pants."

Tammie forced a laugh. "Oh, I just let him think so, that's all!" She looked over at her husband, still deep in conversation with Lenny. "Now I want to find the card I really picked."

She scanned the pack. Most of the cards were bare but for groups of symbols—seven cups, four pentagrams, a series of sticklike objects—reminding her of the canasta deck at home. But some of them bore full-color illustrations, archetypes even she could respond to. "This is nice. A chariot, I guess. Ugh! Here's Death." The skeleton leaned casually on his scythe. "I thought The Hanged Man was supposed to be the death card."

"Not really," said Gail. "See? Here it is." She turned the card upside down, so that the figure stared at them. "And see, he's smiling."

"What's this one?" asked Roy. "Looks like a phallic symbol, doesn't it!" He glanced at Tammie. The card showed an enormous hand emerging godlike from the clouds, clasping an upright stick.

"That's the Ace of Wands," said Gail. As if needing to explain, she added: "I've got a paperback at home. I haven't bought the cards yet, though. I've seen much prettier decks than this. Remember, Roy? That shop in the Village? But it seemed like a waste of money."

"Mmm." He turned over some cards that had been left face down. "Maybe I'll buy you a pack. For slow parties." He laughed guiltily. "What do you think this one's supposed to be?"

Gail took it from him and stared at it. It was a night scene, with a partial moon and a few stars low in the background. At the center was a grey liver-shaped thing; animal, apparently, though the head was turned away. "Gee, I don't think I've ever seen this kind before." She handed it back to him, not looking at it. "Of course, every set is different. I like the modern ones best. Like the deck we saw that time in the Village."

Tammie studied the card for a moment, then gave a tentative smile. "Reminds me of veal cutlet!" A moment later she joined Roy's laughter, laying the card face down on the table. "Do you think there are any of those cute little sausages left?"

"Well, the platter's gone, but I'll have a look in the fridge." He put his hand on Gail's shoulder. "Be back in a second, honey."

The foot tapped against the wall, paused, then tapped eight times in succession. Seated beside him in the little room, the orderly looked down at the paper.

"Eighteen, that's . . . R."

The foot tapped twice, then once. U. Once, then four times.

"I got the story from Bart Cipriano," Lenny was saying. "He works in Commissioner Buchalter's office at the capitol, and he's buddy-buddy with George. So's Buchalter. At first I was surprised they weren't here tonight, but then I realized they'd already been to this house—and often, I'll bet. Besides, George may be just a little ashamed of them."

"Why? Who's this Buchalter?"

"He's with the state highway commission."

"Oh yeah, I remember hearing George had a bit of clout in that department. Not bad for a guy with an office in New York."

"But don't forget, he's lived in Connecticut all his life. And until a few months ago he was living right down the block from Buchalter. Big poker players, both of them." He looked for signs of interest in the other's face. Herb's gaze never wavered. "Anyway, according to Cipriano, the state had been planning a new highway up here, to replace 501—"

"About time! The roads are so dark I damned near had an accident getting here."

"—and it was supposed to cut right through this property." He made a slicing motion. "Yep, that's right—all this land, this house, even, was right in the path of the highway. So some people were going to have to get out of the way. Not that many, of course. It's pretty underpopulated around here. Tobacco country, mainly, and a few small farms. I guess that's why they picked this place to run the road through."

"Jesus, you mean they're gonna demolish this place?"

Lenny shook his head. "Not so fast. The notices were sent out—you know, 'Dear Sir, you've got six months to find another house,' that sort of thing—"

"Sure, eminent domain."

Lenny nodded. "But then, get this, the crooks in the governor's office cut back funds and the whole plan was canceled. No road after all. And thanks to the usual red tape—you know how these state governments are—they decided the cutback wouldn't be official till the end of the fiscal year. Which means that, all this time, Buchalter had a letter sitting on his desk junking the project, except that he wasn't supposed to tell anyone." He paused for effect. "Well, guess who he told."

"George?"

"Your friend and mine. I guess he knew that George was looking for a bigger place, and who knows, maybe he owed him a favor. Let's not be naive—this sort of thing goes on all the time. And maybe George had something on him, I don't know. Anyway, he gave George the go-ahead—said, in effect, 'Pick yourself whatever house you like from Beth Head on up to Tylersville, and we'll help you get it.'" He took a sip of his drink. "I expect a little money may have changed hands."

"I don't understand. You mean he had virtually free choice? Any place he wanted?"

"That's right. And he wanted this." He shrugged. "Who wouldn't? Just look around. I doubt George had ever seen the inside of this place, though, till he watched the state marshals break down the door. You see, the guy in here wouldn't get out. A nut case, they say."

"And once George was in, you mean—"

"Exactly. They announced the highway wouldn't go through after all. And by then it was too late."

"But how about the guy they'd kicked out? Couldn't he sue, for Chrissake? I mean, what a scandal! Hell, he could take 'em all to court for a stunt like that."

"Nope, not where he is now. I told you he was a loony, didn't I?"

"You mean—"

"Uh-huh. They had him put away." Lenny grinned. "Oh, that part was all above board, nothing funny about that. From what I hear, he was a real straitjacket case. Kicked like a wild man when they took him away, biting and spitting . . . And calling for his son. 'Petey,' he kept screaming, 'Petey, Petey . . . ' Or so I was told. I guess he thought the kid would come save him. Only—"

"Only what?"

"Only he didn't have a kid."

"Tsk tsk tsk. Poor guy."

"Yeah, well, that's what I thought. But Cipriano says he wasn't too charming a character. He says the marshals had to literally hold their noses when they broke down the door, that's how bad it was. Like the lion house at the zoo, he said. Maybe the guy'd had pets and never cleaned up after them. Cost George a fortune to have the place fixed up." He stared into his drink; the ice had shrunk and lost its shape, floating on the surface like a jellyfish, evolution in reverse. "Still, he made a killing on this deal. He bought the house from the state and got it for next to nothing."

"How about the other locals they moved out? They put up a stink, too?"

"That supposed to be a pun?"

Herb guffawed. "Now that you mention it!"

"You don't understand—they never *had* to move anyone else. They just held off till George was home free, and then Buchalter announced the cutback. The notices were rescinded, and everybody was happy."

"Oh, I get it." Herb looked disappointed. "So it's too late now, huh?"

"Too late for what?"

"To pick up a place like this for myself."

"R.U.N. Run?"

The man on the cot nodded. His foot tapped once, twice, and three times; once, twice, and five times.

"Run away."

The man on the cot nodded faster.

Irene Crystal put her hand on Phyllis's. "Excuse me," she whispered, "we're going now. I just wanted to say goodbye."

Phyllis left Cissy to fend for herself. "Oh, what a shame!" she cried automatically. "Can't you stay just a little longer? It's so early yet."

"I'd love to, dear, believe me. But Jeff's folks are coming over tomorrow morning, and if I know them"—she rolled her eyes comically—"they'll be ringing the bell at nine."

Phyllis kept Irene talking while ushering her toward the coat closet, anxious lest the sight of one early departure produce a mass exodus among the others. "Well, I certainly do hope you'll find the time to come out again real soon. It's not as far as it looks, really, once you know the way."

"Oh, no, honestly, it wasn't a bad trip at all." Jeff was already standing by the coat closet. Phyllis looked nervously at the other guests. "It's just that his folks are coming down," said Irene, "otherwise we'd never think of leaving so soon."

Jeff leaned toward her. "I wanted to thank George," he said solemnly, a small boy remembering his manners, "but he was in the bathroom. You will thank him for me, won't you?"

"God, is he in there *again?*" Phyllis grimaced. "Yes, of course I will."

"Tell him we think the place is fantastic. The find of a lifetime."

A few of the people at the bar noticed them. Phyllis saw Fred Weingast glance at his watch. "Yes, of course I will." She wished the two would hurry up and leave quietly.

"I'm still amazed about what you said upstairs."

"Pardon me?"

"Upstairs," Irene went on. "In your bedroom. About the man before you, living here all alone."

Phyllis watched Weingast out of the corner of her eye. "Quite a character, wasn't he?"

"But why a nursery?"

"What? Oh, the nursery! Well, we tried to keep things the way we found them. It was like that when we came. We're thinking of turning it into another guest room." She flashed a big grin at the Crystals. "That way you'll be able to come more often, without—"

"No," Irene persisted, "I mean, it was already here when you moved in, right? But you said the man had no children."

Damn it! Now Artie Faschman was looking at his watch. "I'm sure I don't know," she said hurriedly. "I guess it was here when *he* moved in."

"With all those toys? A lot of them looked used."

"Maybe he played with them himself. I told you he was crazy."

"Honey, we're going to have a long drive as it is," said Jeff. "I don't want to get back too late." He moved into the front hall, buttoning his overcoat.

Phyllis held the door open for them. "Whew! These nights are freezing out here! It's the open fields, George says—no wind resistance." She backed away from the blast of cold air. Then, as if by rote: "Just make sure you drive carefully and get home safe."

Irene smiled. "I only allowed him two drinks all night." She kissed Phyllis on the cheek. "Bye-bye, dear, and thanks."

"Be sure to thank George for us," said Jeff as the door was closing.

———

"So you think you're gonna run away, huh?" The man on the cot shook his head. *"No, sir! You ain't going nowhere, buster. Last time an inmate got out, we caught up with him in less than twelve hours, and that was even before we installed the new alarm system. Uh-uh, no way!"*

The other shook his head, more violently this time. His mouth twisted into a snarl.

"Oh, I get it, you want me to run away?"

More violently still. Then, quickly: eight, two and one, one and four . . .

H. U. N. G. R. Y.

The voices from the living room were lost in the twistings of the corridor, and the library stood dark and deserted. The door had been left open, and Ellie lingered in the hall, reluctant to enter. Running her hand along the inside of the doorway and finding no switch, she inched toward one of the heavy floor lamps that stood beside a desk, the two forms outlined by moonlight. The rug felt thick and silent beneath her feet, like animal fur. There was something about the room that made one tiptoe, lest some presence be disturbed.

The lamp's sudden glare dazzled her, and in the instant before blindness she saw something rise from the desktop. A cry came from them both, but the other was first to speak.

"Who . . . ? Uh-oh, what time is it?"

"Doris! *God,* you gave me a fright! Who were you hiding from?"

"Sorry, I must have been asleep. I was in the middle of this story"—she indicated the book that lay open on the desk—"and I thought I'd take a quick nap. It's such a long trip home, and if I know Sid he'll be in no condition to drive." She rubbed her eyes. "Has he been looking for me?"

"I'm sorry to say you haven't even been missed."

"Why, what time is it?"

"Not yet ten, I think."

"Well, *that's* a relief. Still early, then. Sorry I scared you. I probably shouldn't have turned off the light."

"What were you reading?"

She slid the book toward her. "It's a translation of one in the living room. A children's book, really. I can't imagine why he'd buy two copies."

"Looks like you were using it as a pillow."

Doris smiled. "Yes, I—Oh my gosh, did I get print all over my cheek?" She tilted her face in the light for the other's inspection. "This makeup picks up more dirt and soot, especially in the city . . . "

"You're okay. You may have smeared that picture a bit, though." She pointed to a small woodcut in the center of the left-hand page. "God, what is it?"

"Isn't he cute? He's called the Little Devil." She flipped back toward the beginning of the story. "See, the farmer plants this bean, and then he waters it every day"—she pointed to the illustrations— "and when autumn comes, and harvest time, there he is, growing right out of the ground."

Ellie wrinkled up her nose. "Precious."

George snapped off the bathroom light and walked down the hall to the wooden door at the end. When he opened it, a rush of chill air settled around him. Climbing the steep uncarpeted steps, he made a mental note, for the dozenth time, to see about having the attic insulated. Otherwise they'd simply have to keep the door locked all winter.

Upstairs his breath turned to mist, but the cold sobered him; it came in pleasant contrast to the stuffy air below. Anyway, he'd only stay up here for a minute or two, just long enough to see if the memories matched.

He picked his way through the piles of magazines, some neatly bound with twine, the result of their housecleaning, others strewn about the floor. The junk had accumulated here at the top of the house like debris left after a flood. A shape in the corner caught his eye, something pink and vulnerable—the mannequin, with its ravaged head, lying pressed into the crevice where sloping roof met floorboards. Turning away toward the metal cabinets against the far wall, he felt uneasy knowing it was behind him. Someone—Herb or one of the others—had removed the old blanket he'd thrown over it. He thought briefly of searching for another cloth, perhaps some dusty tarpaulin, but the cold had seeped through his thin cotton shirt and added to his growing sense of urgency. Outside a wind stirred the roof beams.

His way to the cabinets was blocked by the dilapidated wreck of a bureau and, propped against it, the shell of a medicine chest, its door sagging open, the mirror somehow intact. He avoided looking at his image as he stepped past it: an old fear, resurrected in the faint attic light, of seeing some other face stare back at him. Straining, he shoved the bureau aside and pulled on the door nearest him. It yielded grudgingly, metal grating on metal. Within, a rack was hung with children's clothes; others lay crumpled on the metal floor, gathering dust. All were wrinkled, as if stored here after having been soiled, and like a gym locker the cabinet reeked of old sweat. He let the door hang open.

The next was lined with deep shelves, empty but for a few rusted tools that had rolled backward into the darkness, and the door to the third had been torn from its hinges; bent double, it was shoved lengthwise into the cabinet, leaving one jagged end that stuck out. The door of the last one swung open more easily but stopped part way, blocked by the bureau; he tugged, jostling the cabinet slightly, but it held fast. He stepped around the bureau and peered inside.

It was as he remembered it. The jars rattled against the metal as if responding to the chill, their liquid insides sloshing rhythmically. In the front row small wrinkled things floated serenely in formaldehyde, fetuses of dog and pig and man, their bulbous eyes closed as if in reverie, with only the labels to tell them apart. He shoved his hip against the bureau; the door opened a few inches more and the slash of light grew wider.

Reaching into the darkness, he succeeded in shoving one of the jars to the side. Below an adhesive labeled *Pig* a huddled figure bobbed up and down. The opening was still too narrow, the jar too big to remove, but in the space behind it he could make out a second row of jars. Pulling one to the front, into a stray beam of light from a crack in the door, he wiped away the thin film of dust that obscured its contents. The tape read *PD #14* in black ballpoint; someday, he told himself, he'd have to figure out what those letters stood for. Carefully he peeled the tape aside to get a closer look.

Yes, the memories matched. It was just like the thing on the card. But the decomposition was worse than he'd remembered, worse than in the other specimens, as if the thing had shrunk and lost shape. Half buried in sediment, the small grey lump rested on the bottom, turning lazily in the cloudy liquid. Once, on his first time here, he'd been tempted to scrape aside the wax that sealed the top, to unscrew the lid and pour the contents down the toilet like a piece of bad meat. But tonight he understood, if only from the faint odor that hung about the shelves, how easily the smell would sicken him. He slid it back into place, between jars labeled *PD #13* and *PD #15*, where it clinked against a third row—and there was still another row behind that. The shelves were deep. There were twenty-two jars in all, he knew, and the specimens seemed to grow progressively larger with each number; he remembered one jar on the bottom, hidden way in the back, nearly filled with something whose rotting flesh hung off it in ribbons. It had been too unpleasant to look at closely.

He shut the cabinet and picked his way back to the stairs, stumbling once on the tiny arm or leg of some long-discarded doll. Descending the steps, he wondered how much it would cost to have the whole place cleaned out. In some ways this house had proved more expensive than he'd bargained for.

The iron railing felt thin and cold in his grip, and gave slightly when he leaned on it; a strong man might easily have yanked it free. The repairs an old house required . . . He wished he were handier at such tasks. Once, long ago, he'd had the necessary skills and had enjoyed working with his hands. He'd been a schoolboy then; the world had contained fewer secrets. Biology had been a source of fascination; he'd even had, briefly, thoughts of medical school. How much he'd forgotten since then, and how mystifying the world had become.

Perhaps he could find a doctor in the area, some country GP he could trust. He'd have a lot of questions for him: about things that

floated silently in jars, and what they fed upon. And how big they
could grow.

"Oh, El, you're just an old fogey. Don't you like fairy tales?" Doris
pointed to the woodcut. "See? The farmer dresses him up in a little
suit and tucks him in at night, and he has himself a little friend."

"I don't think I'd want that thing for a friend."

"Well, that's the whole point. That's why he's called the Little
Devil. He's supposed to help the farmer tend the garden and clean
the house, but he just causes mischief and eats up whatever's lying
around. Including a few of the neighbors."

Ellie grimaced. "I'm afraid I don't approve of fairy tales, at least
not for very young children—they can be quite frightening. And
if you ask me, a lot are excessively violent. Our two grew up quite
nicely without them, thank God." She thought a moment. "Not that
a steady diet of Hardy Boys and Nancy Drew is so much better, of
course."

"Oh, these stories wouldn't frighten anyone. They're all told with
tongue in cheek. Typically French."

"French, huh? That reminds me—that's what I came in for, something French. What's this book called?" She turned to the title page.
"Folk Tales from Provence. Hmm, no author listed, I see. How about
for the story?"

"None there either. All I know is, it's called 'The Little Devil.' I
don't know what it is in French."

She closed the book with a thump. The sound seemed excessively
loud in so silent a room.

The attic door slammed loudly; he hadn't counted on the wind
pulling it closed. Bathed in the warmth of the hall, he turned the
corner, and froze involuntarily at the figure in the doorway—though
his brain had long since identified it.

"Sorry, Howard. I wake you?"

Howard stumbled back to the bed, his eyes puffy and half shut.

Creases from the quilt were etched into the side of his face. "Jesus," he muttered, a slackness still about his lips, "it's a good thing you did. I was having one hell of a nightmare."

George followed him into the room and stood awkwardly by the bed; he wished that Howard had picked somewhere else to sleep. He had left a sour, liquory smell in the room.

"Boy, it'll take me a while to get over this one. It seemed so goddamned *real.*"

George smiled. "They all do, Howard. That's the point."

The other was not comforted. "I can still picture the whole thing. It was night, I remember—"

"Are you sure you want to talk about it? Better to put it out of your mind." Nothing bored him more than other people's dreams.

"No, man, you've got it backwards. You're *supposed* to talk about your nightmares. Helps you get rid of 'em." Howard shook his head and eased himself back on the quilt, the bedsprings twanging with each shift of his body. "It was just after the sun had gone down— don't ask me how I know—and I was driving home. The countryside was exactly like it is around here."

"You mean this part of the state?"

"Yeah. Only it was around seven at night, a few hours ago, and Joyce wasn't with me. I was alone in the car, and I wanted to get home. And somehow—you know how it is in dreams—I knew I'd lost my way. All the roads began looking the same, and I remember being very conscious of the fact that it was getting darker and darker all the time, and that if it got too dark I'd never make it. I was driving on this road that led through a tobacco field, just like the one we passed tonight—"

"Right, it's a big crop around here. We've got plantations just down the road."

"Yeah, crazy-looking things, laid out so flat and regular . . . But I could barely see the land. It was dark, except for a little glow in the sky, and I was driving very, very slowly, trying to find my way. You know, kind of following the beams of my headlights . . . And then way off in the field I noticed a farmer or someone, one of the hired hands, out there in the tobacco, so I pulled over to the side of the road and leaned across the front seat, you know, to ask directions . . . And I'd unrolled the window and was yelling to him when the man turned and made this odd movement with his head, kind of nodding at me, only I couldn't see the face, and then he came toward the car and bent down—and I could see that it wasn't a man."

He fell silent until George grew impatient. "So what was it, then?"

Howard rubbed his eyes. "Oh, something pale, puffy, not completely formed . . . I don't know, it was only a dream."

"But God damn it, you were just saying how realistic it was!" He found himself glancing toward the window, listening for sounds, and was suddenly angry.

"Well," Howard was saying, "you know how quickly you forget dreams, once you tell 'em . . . I don't know, I don't want to think about it anymore. Let's go downstairs. I need some coffee."

George followed him down, the old ache building once again in his stomach, feeling betrayed by both the world and his own body.

"Something French, huh? Were you looking for anything in particular?" asked Doris. She slipped the storybook back onto the shelf.

Ellie grinned at her. "You sound like you own the place."

"Well . . . I like books. Unlike my husband."

"I'll tell you, then—" Ellie surveyed the room, hands on hips. "I'm really just looking for a French dictionary. Is there any order to this place? Anything approximating a reference section?"

"Right this way, madam."

While the books in the living room had been bound almost exclusively in leather, clearly chosen for their decorative quality, the collection in the library was strictly functional. Glossy paperbacks stood pressed against ragged quartos whose titles had long since rotted away. A pocket-sized *Field Guide to the Mammals* was lost in the shadow of an Audubon portfolio, and odd sets of do-it-yourself magazines leaned against a fat home-brewery manual. A worn-looking volume with *Husbandrie* on its spine caught Ellie's eye. Curious, she took it down, but it turned out to be not a quaint archaic marital guide but a treatise on animal breeding.

The reference section was relatively small, as if the more con-
ventional sources of knowledge had held little appeal. There was,
though, a French dictionary on the bottom shelf, side by side with a
battered *Brand's Antiquities*.

"I just wanted to look up a word from that stupid little pamphlet,"
Ellie explained, flipping through the pages. "The one that came with
those cards."

Doris watched her friend read. "Found it?"

"Yes, *ecartée*. It means isolated, alienated."

"Was that from your card?"

She nodded. "That's me, I guess. The original alienated woman."
She gave a short laugh. "Hey, look at this! Speak of the devil!" She
pointed to the shelf a little above eye level, where a trio of books on
the Tarot stood huddled between a history of superstition and an
almanac. "I'll bring all three in," she said; two were cheap paperbacks, the third a scholarly-looking little volume with a brown paper
cover. "Len's probably dying to leave, but first I'd like to give somebody a proper reading."

"Hungry! Aw, for Chrissake, not that again. I tell you I'm sick of that
shit, I really am. You was just fed, not more than—"

The man on the cot shook his head.

"Oh, so all of a sudden you're not hungry, huh? You'd damn well better
not be, because I'm leaving in just one second, I mean it. I don't have
to stick around and listen to this shit." He paused and made a show of
looking at his watch. "Okay, you're not hungry."

A nod.

"Someone else is hungry?"

Another nod, more emphatic.

"Well, who the hell gives a—Oh, all right, go ahead." The foot was
tapping another word. One, then six. P. Five. E. Two, and then a noise-
less tap. Twenty. T.

"All right, that's it." The orderly rose; the tapping continued, but he
stuffed the paper into his pocket. "That's it, buster. I've wasted enough

time on you as it is. You can knock the goddamn wall down for all I
care!" He turned and strode down the hall, muttering to himself. "God-
damn animal lover . . . "

There was a Pyramid Spread and a Magic Seven Spread and a Wish
Spread and a Life Spread and a Horoscope Spread and, according
to one of the paperbacks, something called a Sephiroth Spread, as
well as a Kabala Spread and a Cross Spread—"covering," as Lenny
suggested, "damn near all the religions except a Star of David
spread"—but the Bregmans were in a hurry to leave soon, others
having left already, and Lenny had passed them all up for a simple
Yes or No Spread that used only five cards.

"The two on the right are your past, the two on the left are your
future, and the one in the middle is you now. We turn that over
first." Ellie read from one of the paperbacks; the scholarly volume
had proved a disappointment, its author dampening their spirits at
the outset by informing readers that the Tarot had been invented by
charlatans and that all its supposed fortune-telling properties were
strictly illusory. She had looked up from reading aloud from one of
the paperbacks to find that her audience had dwindled from more
than a dozen to her husband, the Silbers, and Michael Cooper. They
were gathered around a bridge table set up near the front hallway.

"So you've had domestic illusions," Ellie was saying, "but now
you've seen through them—"

"What the hell are 'domestic illusions'?" asked Mike.

"—and you've set your sights higher, on philosophical aspira-
tions." She had both paperbacks propped open before her and—like
the medieval's unquestioning faith in both Christian and Classical
cosmologies—was studiously ignoring the discrepancies in the two
sets of predictions, at odds though they often were.

Lenny's supportive smile had never wavered throughout her performance. "So much for my past," he said. "Now for the present."
He turned over the center card. "This is me now."

Sidney Silber chuckled. "Looks like you're a girl, Len!" Indeed, the card was the Queen of Pentacles. Surrounded as she was by foliage, sitting in a meadow beneath a rosy trellis, she seemed the most feminine of all the queens.

Lenny forced a laugh. "And they say these things never lie!" He reached for the first of the cards depicting his future.

"No, wait," said his wife. "I'm sure there's a reading for you in this. Remember, it's only a symbol." She looked from book to book. "See? Just listen. It's a symbol of fertility—" Lenny's eyebrows rose. "—and charity. It says you're of Libra temperament, whatever that is—"

"Oh, God," said Mike, "not astrology too!"

"—and therefore have a deep love of justice." She looked up; her eyes met Lenny's. "That part's true, anyway."

"Yes."

"And now the future," said Silber. "Come on, Lenny." The other reached for the card.

"Now hold on a second," said Ellie. "Remember, boys, this one's the near future, because it's next to the center . . . And the last is the distant future."

"Understood." He turned over the first card.

"You've got it upside down," said Doris. "Here, let me—"

"No, leave it be," Ellie ordered. "The meaning changes if it's that way." She scanned the illustrations in the guidebook, then shrugged. "Nothing like that in here. This book's no damned good." She looked in the other one, explaining, "All decks follow the basic pattern, but the actual pictures can differ. Like chess sets, it says here. Sometimes a queen is a beautiful young woman, other times she's shown as an Egyptian goddess, or a nun, or a naked girl." Her eyes kept scanning the pages. "But I really don't see anything like this card. And no reference number on the bottom; that makes it harder to identify. What's it look like to you?"

"Like something hanging from a tree," said Doris. "A bat or a sloth. You know, those things that get fungus on them . . . " She turned the card around. "And right side up it looks like—" She frowned.

"A sloth on the ground," said Lenny. "Seen from the rear."

"Like those prehistoric things," added Mike. "Giant ground

sloths." There was, in fact, something ancient in the squat grey form, crawling along a road beneath a starry sky, its half-turned head no more than a bulge in the background.

"Is there a table of contents?" asked Lenny. His wife nodded. "Look up The Sloth. Or better yet, The Beast."

"It reminds me of that Maine folk tale," said Silber. "The one about the hunter who shot the bear and skinned it and went off with the hide, leaving his own coat behind . . . He turns around and he sees the bear following him, wearing his coat. That's what it is, it's a skinned bear."

"Could it be the card for Death?" asked his wife. "That's what it looks like to me."

Silber searched through the pack. "Afraid not, Dorie. This one's old Mr. Death, see?" The skull's eyes stared sightlessly.

"I've looked all through these"—Ellie laid aside the paperbacks— "and there's nothing like it." She began leafing through the third book. "Maybe it's from a different deck."

Lenny turned it over. Its back bore the same design as the other cards.

Ellie sighed. "This book's no good either. I may have to do this by process of elimination." Mike glanced surreptitiously at his watch. "I'll figure it out," she said. "Don't worry."

"I'm not worrying," said Lenny.

"Looks like I'm gonna have to leave," said Mike. "Tell me how it all comes out." He looked around for the host and hostess.

"I'm sure it isn't a number card or a royal card," said Ellie, "so that means it has to be one of the Major Arcana."

"Ah, I've got it," said Lenny. "Satan."

"But it hardly looks like—"

"It must be. I've looked through the whole pack, and there's no Satan card."

"Well . . . " She looked down at the card in question. "Yes, maybe there is the hint of a horn, around the other side . . . but would Satan really be facing away?"

"Maybe displaying his rump for us to kiss," said Doris. She blushed.

"Last call for quiche," yelled Phyllis from across the room. "Get it while it's hot!"

The Goodhues and the Fitzgeralds had left, having spent the evening in conversation with no one but themselves, and Michael was putting on his coat. He paused for one final mouthful of quiche.

The Silbers drifted toward the dining table, more out of obligation than hunger. After making sure his wife was "absolutely stuffed," Lenny joined them, leaving Ellie alone with the cards.

Yes, the grey shape probably represented Satan; the mystery was solved. Still, it was all rather exasperating, for Satan in one book was a Mosaic-looking deity with a flowing beard; in another, a black magician; and in the third, a sullen, goatlike figure officiating at the unholy matrimony of two disciples. The thing that crept across the card resembled none of them; it was simply, as her husband had said, The Beast.

She was thinking of the Little Devil of the storybook—*le Petit Diable,* she supposed it must be called—when her hand, straying to the remaining card in Lenny's spread, unthinkingly turned it face up, revealing Satan upon his throne, the two naked mortals joined in wedlock before him.

The Lazaruses had just left, Milt assuring everyone he was in perfect shape to drive, and Myra Stanley backed away from the cold blast of air that dropped toward her legs as the front door swung shut. Her husband helped her with her coat while Roy Bullard searched in the closet for his fiancée's gloves; like the Lazaruses, they had decided, after furtive discussion, not to spend the night. Headlights were picking out slices of driveway, lawn, and trees as cars moved slowly away in the darkness. Art Faschman stood by the window with Herb, watching the exodus.

"Getting late," said Herb.

Faschman looked at his watch. "Wow, I'll say! Hey, Judy," he called, "do you have any idea what time it is?"

"After eleven. So what?"

"So I've gotta drive Melissa down to rehearsal tomorrow morning, that's what. Unless you want to do it." He turned back to Herb. "Listen to her. Last of the swingers. You ought to hear her the morning after. Better yet, you ought to *see* her!" He looked at his watch, more nervously this time. "Hey, how is it outside? Not raining or anything, I hope . . . " He peered out the window.

"It's cold out there," said Lenny. "George said it may even snow. El and I were all set to go, but now we're thinking of staying over."

"I must say, he's carrying that gentleman farmer charade a bit too far," said Faschman. "I mean, just look. Isn't that a scarecrow out there?"

"Where?" Lenny rubbed his fist against the pane. In the strong light of the living room, he could see little more than his own reflection. "Where, in the yard?"

"No, way the hell out there, over on the other side of the field." Faschman tapped on the glass; it was smeared with condensation. "See? Ah, too late, the moon's behind a cloud. You'll pass it when you leave. You really going to stay the night?"

"Why not? Free breakfast."

"Sure," said Judy Faschman, coming up behind them, "if you don't mind leftover quiche."

Carefully Ellie laid out the cards. The Sun, The Moon, The Star . . . Judgment, Temperance, and Justice . . . She'd been standing here nearly half an hour, checking, and they were all there. The Emperor, The Hermit, The Hierophant . . . Strength, The World, and The Wheel of Fortune. All twenty-two of them, the Major Arcana, each with its message. Satan, and Death, and The Hanged Man . . . and even The Fool. (Why did she associate that with poor George? He'd been so out of sorts tonight.)

All had been accounted for, including the fifty-six playing cards, the Minor Arcana; she'd matched them all with the illustrations in the book. What, then, was this additional card? The box promised "78 cartes." That, and the brand name, *Grand Etteilla*—derived, the book had said, from Alliette, the unsavory magician who'd introduced them to the French court—and below it the seal of the printer,

B. P. Grimaud of Marseilles. Nothing about an extra card, a spare, a joker . . .

She studied it again. She hadn't noticed before, but in places the picture was rather disturbingly detailed. She could make out the bulletlike contours of a head just about to turn in her direction, and an upraised front claw, shadowy against the night. The moon in the background, nearly full, reminded her of the sky outside the windows.

Hastily she placed the cards back in the box, slipping the grey hunched thing well into the middle of the pack, as if to cage it.

"And here I thought you were going to stay over," said Phyllis.

"Oh, Phyl, come on. Admit it, you're relieved to get us out of the way. One less bed to make in the morning." Lenny leaned forward and kissed her on the cheek. "Ellie says she's tired, and when Ellie says she's tired that means it's home for us." The excuse sounded lame; his wife's sudden decision to leave, without even an offer to help clean up, had been rude.

"You sure you don't want a small nip before you go?" asked George. (Where had he come from?) He jiggled his drink invitingly, but it looked like the one he'd been nursing all night. "Or another cup of coffee?"

Lenny shook his head, smiling sheepishly. "Honest, kids, I just want to say, before I hit the road, that if I got a little out of hand tonight—you know, if I said anything I shouldn't have—well, I never was much good at holding my liquor, and—"

"It was a pleasure, old buddy, honest." George slapped him on the arm; he seemed to be rallying. "If you said anything nasty, I sure didn't hear it."

Relief showed in Lenny's face. "Yeah, well, thanks a lot. I mean it. I love this place and I had a great time tonight." He reached for George's hand. "And I just hope you and Phyl are—"

"Honey!" Ellie's voice came from the driveway. "I'm standing out here in the cold, and you've got the car keys."

"Christ, yeah, gotta run." He looked over his shoulder. "Sorry that

El's a little cranky, but you know these women. Can't keep 'em up past midnight!" Pulling up his collar, he flashed Phyllis a big grin. "She really had a great time, and you can bet that—"

"Honey!"

Lenny shrugged. "Bye now." He leaned into the hall. "G'night, everybody. See you soon." Then, stepping outside: "Whoops, get away from the door, Phyl, you'll catch cold." His footsteps crunched on the gravel.

Silence lay on the room; conversation had sputtered and died. The remaining men had taken George's yawn as a signal to depart, but they waited for their wives to finish helping Phyllis clean up, reluctant to acknowledge the lateness of the hour. Alan Mendelson sat smoking disconsolately on the couch, watching Cissy Feinstock fuss over the few remaining platters of canapés and fruit. As the only remaining bachelor, with Mike Cooper having made his exit, he was expected to drive Cissy home. He glanced toward Joyce Stillman, who marched toward the kitchen carrying two bowls of clam dip and the remains of a cheesecake. She was certainly more attractive than Cissy. Howard, her husband, lay sprawled in the big armchair, his face red from drink and fatigue; he had slept through most of the party. "Come on, baby, please hurry it up," he called. Baby. The others in the room were silently amused by that. There seemed in it, somehow, a note of touching self-deception.

When Cissy offered to scrub the kitchen floor, Phyllis had to dissuade her. "Or I can help dry dishes," the girl pleaded.

"Honestly, Cis, you've been a terrific help all evening and there's nothing left to do." She was busy loading the dishwasher. "Now go back in there and relax, and we'll make sure you have a ride home."

Relieved, Cissy returned to the living room, only to face the sullen stares of the men. Awkwardly she moved to the bridge table and began tidying up—then, to busy herself, opened the green cardboard box. The Six of Swords was on top, followed by The Tower.

She would put them in order, she decided, just as, in her apartment, she'd spend hours arranging and rearranging her books. Swords in this pile, Cups in that, picture cards over there . . .

The picture cards were prettiest, but she wasn't sure how to arrange them until she saw the tiny numerals at the bottom. Judgment, number 20, the naked people sprouting from their graves like corn—why, you could see the woman's nipples. And number 7, The Chariot, would come before it, a black sphinx and a white sphinx roped together. And then 10, The Wheel of Fortune, with another white sphinx perched on top, and 12, The Hanged Man, with his knowing smirk, and then The Fool, inexplicably numbered with a zero—perhaps that was a mistake, and she put it aside—and 17, The Star, illuminating a more brazenly naked girl; and then, fortuitously, The Moon, 18, shedding its light onto the open field, dogs howling below it, and then a huge grey animal, head in profile, staring malevolently at something beyond the edge of the card—they'd left off the number and she put it aside with The Fool—and then Temperance, number 14, which made her smile because her grandmother had been in the WCTU. Wondering if, to some people, her own beliefs appeared as ridiculous, she continued counting: The World, The Lovers, and Death . . . When would he ask her if she needed a ride?

Alan had made the mistake of watching her, and when she looked up his eyes met hers. As if on cue, he stubbed out his cigarette and got to his feet. "Uh, Cissy, do you need a lift home?"

When George came into the kitchen, his wife whispered, "So are they planning to stay all night?"

He shrugged. "You know Herb—last to come, last to leave. He has that look on him, too, that philosophical-discussion look." Phyllis sighed. "But you know, I wouldn't mind him staying a while. I'm not really tired."

"Well, Tammie is, and so am I. If you two want to talk all night, that's up to you. I'll put out some things in the guest room for them, but after that I'm going straight to bed." She eyed him accusingly.

"Of course you're not tired, you haven't been running around all day. You spent half the party hiding in the bathroom."

Back in the living room Herb greeted him with unexpected late-night enthusiasm. "You know, George, what this place needs is a nice little fire. That really would have made the evening, to have a fire going."

"Yes, but they're a lot of bother." For a minute he'd thought Herb had suggested burning the house down.

"But what's a fireplace for if you don't build a fire on a cold night?"

"To tell you the truth, I'm not sure how well this chimney works. I ought to get somebody in to check the flue." The bare fireplace looked like an empty stage, the performer still waiting in the wings. "Besides, Phyllis threw out all the firewood, and if you want any more you've got to walk a good hundred yards to the woodshed"— he gestured toward a window—"all the way around back."

Herb stood. "I'm game," he said. "Just tell me where it is."

Tammie came out of the downstairs bathroom, her hair patted back into shape, the tiredness around her eyes concealed. "And where do you think you're going?" she said.

"To get some firewood," said Herb. "Build us a fire."

"Herb here's trying to prove he's an outdoorsman," explained George. "I made fun of him earlier tonight—I mean, about getting lost on the way here—so now he's out to show me up."

Tammie pouted. "Really, honey, you shouldn't have had that coffee. Everyone's tired and ready for bed . . . And all of a sudden you have to build a fire?"

"*I'm* not tired," Herb maintained. "Anyway, a stack of lumber by the andirons would brighten up the living room. Add some atmosphere."

"Fine," said George, in no mood to argue. "You're hired. You're our new interior decorator. Phyl's in the kitchen, she'll give you a flashlight. Go out the door to the greenhouse, but before you reach it, turn right, go down the steps, and you'll see a path around the back of the house. Follow that and you'll see the woodshed, out near the hedges. I'm pretty sure it's unlocked."

"Better put a coat on, honey."

"I don't need it." Herb strode toward the kitchen.

"How'd you like Roy's fiancée?" asked Tammie, when they were alone. She reached for a cigarette. "Think she's right for him?"

"Oh, I'd met her before. She's okay. It was Ellie who introduced them, you know."

"No kidding! Where, at the beach last summer?"

"Yeah."

"And what did you think of *her* tonight, lecturing out of that book?"

"Oh, she just gets a little carried away with the sound of her own voice, that's all." He noticed the books she'd left on the bridge table and went to get them. They belonged in the library; only leather-bound volumes for the living room. "Ellie's a strong-minded woman."

"I'll say. Did you see how she bosses Len around? When she decided it was time to leave, that was it, he had to go. Just like—" She looked toward the window. "Well, here comes Herb with the firewood."

"What, already? No, he must have gotten lost. Wonder why he's coming round the front." Taking a deep breath, he opened the green box. The cards spilled out onto the table.

Phyllis entered the room, wiping her hands on a dish towel.

He turned over several minor arcana, then a picture card, The Tower. Lightning flashed, stone walls crumbled, and beyond them raged the sea. He pushed it to one side. Somehow he wished that Herb had not gone out. "Hey honey, did you lock the back door?"

"Not yet. Why?" She went to the front window and drew the curtains. "Anybody ready for bed? I'll get some clean linen out."

"Now you're sure it's no bother?" asked Tammie. She stood. "Herb and I can make do with these couches, you know." They heard the crunch of gravel outside.

"Nonsense! We'll go upstairs and get the room ready, and by the time we come down the men'll have a fire going." George didn't look up; he was absorbed in sorting through the cards, searching for one card in particular. "And we'll have some hot chocolate. Won't that be nice?"

From outside came a high-pitched whistling; something thudded against the door. Tammie, who was closest, walked into the front hall. As her hand fastened on the doorknob, George gave a little gasp; he staggered back, dropping the card and what glared from it, and as she swung open the door he screamed, "No, Tammie, no!" But it was already too late; a grey shape filled the doorway, blotting out the night—and now, just as in the card, it turned to face him.

BLACK MAN
WITH A HORN

The black [words obscured by postmark] was fascinating—I must get a snap shot of him.

    —H. P. Lovecraft, postcard to E. Hoffmann Price, July 23, 1934

There is something inherently comforting about the first-person past tense. It conjures up visions of some deskbound narrator puffing contemplatively upon a pipe amid the safety of his study, lost in tranquil recollection, seasoned but essentially unscathed by whatever experience he's about to relate. It's a tense that says, "I am here to tell the tale. I lived through it."

The description, in my own case, is perfectly accurate—as far as it goes. I am indeed seated in a kind of study: a small den, actually, but lined with bookshelves on one side, below a view of Manhattan painted many years ago, from memory, by my sister. My desk is a folding bridge table that once belonged to her. Before me the electric typewriter, though somewhat precariously supported, hums soothingly, and from the window behind me comes the familiar drone of the old air conditioner, waging its lonely battle against the tropic night. Beyond it, in the darkness outside, the small night noises are doubtless just as reassuring: wind in the palm trees, the mindless chant of crickets, the muffled chatter of a neighbor's TV, an occasional car bound for the highway, shifting gears as it speeds past the house . . .

House, in truth, may be too grand a word; the place is a green stucco bungalow just a single story tall, third in a row of nine set several hundred yards from the highway. Its only distinguishing features are the sundial in front, brought here from my sister's former home, and the narrow slate path, now rather overgrown with weeds.

It's hardly the most romantic of settings, but under normal circumstances it might make an adequate background for meditations in the past tense. "I'm still here," the writer says, adjusting to the tone. (I've even stuck the requisite pipe in my mouth, stuffed with a plug of Latakia.) "It's over now," he says. "I've lived through it."

A comforting premise, perhaps. Only, in this case, it doesn't happen to be true. Whether the experience is really "over now" no one can say; and if, as I suspect, the final chapter has yet to be enacted, then the notion of my living through it will seem a pathetic conceit.

Yet I can't say I find the thought of my own death particularly disturbing. I get so tired, sometimes, of this little room, with its cheap wicker furniture, the dull outdated books, the night pressing in from outside . . . And of that sundial out there in the yard, with its idiotic message. *"Grow old along with me . . . "*

I have done so, and my life seems hardly to have mattered in the scheme of things. Surely its end cannot matter much either.

Ah, Howard, you would have understood.

> That, boy, was what I call a travel-experience!
> —Lovecraft, March 12, 1930

If, while I'm setting it down, this tale acquires an ending, it promises to be an unhappy one. But the beginning is nothing of the kind; you may find it rather humorous, in fact—full of comic pratfalls, wet trouser cuffs, and a dropped vomit bag.

"I steeled myself to *endure* it," the old lady to my right was saying. "I don't mind telling you, I was exceedingly frightened. I held on to the arms of the seat and just *gritted my teeth.* And then, you know, right after the captain warned us about that turbulence, when the tail lifted and fell, flip-flop, flip-flop, *well—*" She flashed her dentures at me and patted my wrist. "—I don't mind telling you, there was simply nothing for it but to *heave.*"

Where had the old girl picked up such expressions? And was she trying to pick me up as well? Her hand clamped wetly round my wrist. "I *do* hope you'll let me pay for the dry cleaning."

"Madam," I said, "think nothing of it. The suit was already stained."

"Such a nice man!" She cocked her head coyly at me, still gripping my wrist. Though their whites had long since turned the color of old piano keys, her eyes were not unattractive. But I was afraid of her breath. Slipping my paperback into a pocket, I rang for the stewardess.

The earlier mishap had occurred several hours before. In clambering aboard the plane at Heathrow, surrounded by what appeared to be an aboriginal rugby club (all dressed alike, navy blazers with bone buttons), I'd been shoved from behind and had stumbled against a black cardboard hatbox in which some Chinaman was storing his dinner; it was jutting into the aisle near the first-class seats. Something inside sloshed over my ankles—duck sauce, soup perhaps—and left a sticky yellow puddle on the floor. I turned in time to see a tall, beefy Caucasian with an Air Malay bag and a beard so thick and black he looked like some heavy from the silent era. His manner was equally suited to the role, for after shouldering me aside (with shoulders broad as my valises), he pushed his way down the crowded passage, head bobbing near the ceiling like a gas balloon, and suddenly disappeared from sight at the rear of the plane. In his wake I caught the smell of treacle, and was instantly reminded of my childhood: birthday hats, Callard & Bowser gift packs, and after-dinner bellyaches.

"So very sorry." A bloated little Charlie Chan looked fearfully at this departing apparition, then doubled over to scoop his dinner beneath the seat, fiddling with the ribbon.

"Think nothing of it," I said.

I was feeling kindly toward everyone that day. Flying was still a novelty. My friend Howard, of course (as I'd reminded audiences earlier in the week), used to say he'd "hate to see aëroplanes come into common commercial use, since they merely add to the goddam useless speeding up of an already over-speeded life." He had dismissed them as "devices for the amusement of a gentleman"—but then, he'd only been up once, in the '20s, a brief $3.50 flight above Buzzard's Bay. What could he have known of whistling engines, the wicked joys of dining at thirty thousand feet, the chance to look out a window and find that the earth is, after all, quite round? All this he had missed; he was dead and therefore to be pitied.

Yet even in death he had triumphed over me . . .

It gave me something to think about as the stewardess helped me to my feet, clucking in professional concern at the mess on my lap—though more likely she was thinking of the wiping up that awaited her once I'd vacated the seat. "Why do they make those bags so *slippery?*" my elderly neighbor asked plaintively. "And all over this nice man's suit. You really should do something about it." The plane dropped and settled; she rolled her yellowing eyes. "It could happen again."

The stewardess steered me down the aisle toward a restroom at the middle of the plane. To my left a cadaverous young woman wrinkled her nose and smiled at the man next to her. I attempted to disguise my defeat by looking bitter, as if to say, "Someone else has done this deed!"—but doubt I succeeded. The stewardess's arm supporting mine was superfluous but comfortable; I leaned on her more heavily with each step. There are, as I'd long suspected, precious few advantages in being seventy-six and looking it—yet among them is this: though one is excused from the frustration of flirting with a stewardess, one gets to lean on her arm. I turned toward her to say something funny, but paused; her face was blank as a clock's.

"I'll wait out here for you," she said, and pulled open the smooth white door.

"That will hardly be necessary." I straightened up. "But could you—do you think you might find me another seat? I have nothing against that lady, you understand, but I don't want to see any more of her lunch."

Inside the restroom the whine of the engines seemed louder, as if the pink plastic walls were all that separated me from the jet stream and its arctic winds. Occasionally the air we passed through must have grown choppy, for the plane rattled and heaved like a sled over rough ice. If I opened the john I half expected to see the earth miles below us, a frozen grey Atlantic fanged with icebergs. England was already a thousand miles away.

Holding the edge of the tiny sink for support, I grabbed a handful of foil envelopes and used the perfumed paper towels inside to wipe off my trousers, then stuffed several more into my pocket. My cuffs still bore a residue of Chinese goo. This, it seemed, was the source of the treacle smell; I dabbed ineffectually at it. Surveying myself in the mirror—a bald, harmless-looking old baggage with stooped shoulders and a damp suit (so different from the self-confident young fellow in the photo captioned *"HPL and friend"*)—I slid open the bolt and emerged, a medley of scents. The stewardess had found an empty seat for me toward the rear of the plane.

It was only as I made to sit down that I noticed who occupied the adjoining seat: he was leaning away from me, asleep with his head resting against the window, but I recognized the beard.

"Uh, stewardess—?" I turned, but saw only her uniformed back retreating up the aisle. After a moment's uncertainty I inched myself into the seat, making as little noise as possible. I had, I reminded myself, every right to be here.

Adjusting the recliner position (to the annoyance of the aborigine behind me), I settled back and reached for the paperback in my pocket. They'd finally gotten around to reprinting one of my earlier tales, and already I'd found four typos. But then, what could one expect? The anthology's front cover, with its crude cartoon skull, said it all: *Goosepimples: Thirteen Cosmic Chillers in the Lovecraft Tradition.* On the back, listed among a dozen other writers whose names I barely recognized, I was described as "a disciple."

So this was what I'd been reduced to—a lifetime's work shrugged off by some blurb-writer as "worthy of the Master himself," the creations of my brain dismissed as mere pastiche. My meticulously wrought fiction, once singled out for such elaborate praise, was now simply—as if this were commendation enough—"Lovecraftian." Ah, Howard, your triumph was complete the moment your name became an adjective.

I'd suspected it for years, of course, but only with the past week's conference had I been forced to acknowledge the fact that what mattered to the present generation was not my own body of work, but rather my association with Lovecraft. And even this was demeaned: after years of friendship and support, to be labeled—simply because I'd been younger—a mere disciple. It seemed too cruel a joke.

Every joke must have a punch line. This one's was still in my pocket, printed in italics on the folded yellow conference schedule. I didn't need to look at it again: there I was, characterized for all time as "a member of the Lovecraft circle, New York educator, and author of the celebrated collection *Beyond the Garve.*"

That was it, the crowning indignity: to be immortalized by a misprint! You'd have appreciated this, Howard. I can almost hear you chuckling from—where else?—*beyond the garve* . . .

Meanwhile, from the seat next to me came the rasping sounds of a constricted throat; my neighbor must have been caught in a dream. I put down my book and studied him. He looked older than he had at first—perhaps sixty or more. His hands were roughened, powerful looking; on one of them was a ring with a curious silver cross. The glistening black beard that covered the lower half of his face was so thick as to be nearly opaque; its very darkness seemed unnatural, for above it his hair was streaked with grey.

I looked more closely, to where beard joined face. Was that a bit of gauze I saw, below the hair? My heart gave a little jump. Leaning forward for a closer look, I peered at the skin to the side of his nose. Though burned from long exposure to the sun, it had an odd pallor. My gaze continued upward, along the weathered cheeks toward the dark hollows of his eyes.

They opened.

For a moment they stared into mine without apparent comprehension, glassy and bloodshot. In the next instant they were bulging from his head and quivering like hooked fish. His lips opened, and a tiny voice croaked, "Not here."

We sat in silence, neither of us moving. I was too surprised, too embarrassed, to answer. In the window beyond his head the sky looked bright and clear, but I could feel the plane buffeted by unseen blasts, its wingtips bouncing furiously.

"Don't do it to me here," he whispered at last, shrinking back into his seat.

Was the man a lunatic? Dangerous, perhaps? Somewhere in my future I saw spinning headlines: "Jetliner Terrorized . . . Retired NYC Teacher Victim." My uncertainty must have shown, for I saw him lick his lips and glance past my head. Hope, and a trace of cunning, swept his face. He grinned up at me. "Sorry, nothing to worry about. Whew! Must have been having a nightmare." Like an athlete after a particularly tough race, he shook his massive head, already regaining command of the situation. His voice had a hint of Tennessee drawl. "Boy"—he gave what should have been a hearty laugh—"I'd better lay off the Kickapoo juice!"

I smiled to put him at his ease, though there was nothing about him to suggest he'd been drinking. "That's an expression I haven't heard in years."

"Oh yeah?" he said, with little interest. "Well, I've been away." His fingers drummed nervously—impatiently?—on the arm of his chair.

"Malaya?"

He sat up, and the color left his face. "How did you know?"

I nodded toward the green flight bag at his feet. "I saw you carrying that when you came aboard. You, uh—you seemed to be in a little bit of a hurry, to say the least. In fact, I'm afraid you almost knocked me down."

"Aw, heck! Really?" His voice was controlled now, his gaze level and assured. "Hey, friend, I'm truly sorry about that. The fact is, I thought someone might be following me."

Oddly enough, I believed him; he looked sincere—or as sincere as anyone can be behind phony black whiskers. "You're in disguise, aren't you?" I asked.

"You mean the beard? That's just something I picked up in Singapore. Heck, I knew it wouldn't fool anyone for long, at least not a friend. But an enemy, well . . . maybe." He made no move to take it off.

"You're—let me guess—you're in the service, right?" The foreign service, I meant; frankly, I took him for an aging spy.

"In the service?" He looked significantly to the left and right, then dropped his voice. "Well, yeah, you might say that. In *His* service." He pointed toward the roof of the plane.

"You mean—?"

He nodded. "I'm a missionary. Or was until yesterday."

Missionaries are infernal nuisances who ought to be kept at home.
          —Lovecraft, September 12, 1925

Have you ever seen a man in fear of his life? I had, though not since my early twenties. After a summer of idleness I'd at last found temporary employment in the office of what turned out to be a rather shady businessman—I suppose today you'd call him a small-time racketeer—who, having somehow offended "the mob," was convinced he'd be dead by Christmas. He had been wrong, though; he'd been able to enjoy that and many other Christmases with his family, and it wasn't till years later that he was found in his bathtub, face down in six inches of water. I don't remember much about him, except how hard it had been to engage him in conversation; he never seemed to be listening.

Yet talking with the man who sat next to me on the plane was all too easy; he had nothing of the other's distracted air, the vague replies and preoccupied gaze. On the contrary, he was alert and seemed highly interested in all that was said to him. Except for his initial panic, in fact, there was little to suggest he was a hunted man.

Yet so he claimed to be. Later events would, of course, settle all such questions, but at the time I had no way to judge if he was telling the truth or if his story was as phony as his beard.

If I believed him, it was almost entirely due to his manner, not the substance of what he said. No, he didn't claim to have made off with the Eye of Klesh; he was more original than that. Nor had he violated some witch doctor's only daughter. But some of the things he told me about the region in which he'd worked—a state called Negri Sembilan, south of Kuala Lumpur—seemed frankly incredible: houses invaded by trees, government-built roads that simply disappeared, a nearby colleague returning from a ten-day vacation to find his lawn overgrown with ropy things they'd had to burn twice to destroy. He claimed there were tiny red spiders that jumped as high as a man's shoulder—"there was a girl in the village gone half deaf because one of the nasty little things crawled in her ear and swelled so big it plugged up the hole"—and places where mosquitoes were so thick they suffocated cattle. He described a land of steaming mangrove swamps and rubber plantations as large as feudal kingdoms, a land so humid that wallpaper bubbled on the hot nights and Bibles sprouted mildew.

As we sat together on the plane, sealed within an air-cooled world of plastic and pastel, none of these things seemed possible; with the frozen blue of the sky just beyond my reach, the stewardesses walking briskly past me in their blue-and-gold uniforms, the passengers to my left sipping Cokes or sleeping or leafing through *In-Flite,* I found myself believing less than half of what he said, attributing the rest to sheer exaggeration and a Southern penchant for tall tales. Only when I'd been home a week and paid a visit to my niece in Brooklyn did I revise my estimate upward, for glancing through her son's geography text I came upon this passage: "Along the [Malayan] peninsula, insects swarm in abundance; probably more varieties exist here than anywhere else on earth. There is good hardwood timber, and camphor and ebony trees are found in profusion. Many orchid varieties thrive, some of extraordinary size." The book alluded to the area's "rich mixture of races and languages," its "extreme humidity" and "colorful native fauna," and added: "Its jungles are so impenetrable that even the wild beasts must keep to well-worn paths."

But perhaps the strangest aspect of this region was that, despite its dangers and discomforts, my companion claimed to have loved it. "They've got a mountain in the center of the peninsula—" He mentioned an unpronounceable name and shook his head. "Most beautiful thing you ever saw. And there's some really pretty country down along the coast, you'd swear it was some kind of South Sea paradise. Comfortable, too. Oh, it's damp all right, especially in the interior, where the new mission was supposed to be—but the temperature never even hits a hundred. Try saying that for New York City."

I nodded. "Remarkable."

"And the *people,*" he went on, "why, I believe they're just the friendliest people on earth. You know, I'd heard a lot of bad things about the Moslems—that's what most of them are, part of the Sunni sect— but I'm telling you, they treated us with real neighborliness . . . just so long as we made the teachings *available,* so to speak, and didn't interfere with their affairs. And we didn't. We didn't have to. What we provided, you see, was a hospital—well, a clinic, at least, two RNs and a doctor who came twice a month—and a small library with books and films. And not just theology, either. All subjects. We were right outside the village, they'd have to pass us on their way to the river, and when they thought none of the *lontoks* were looking, they'd just come in and look around."

"None of the what?"

"Priests, sort of. There were a lot of them. But they didn't interfere with us, we didn't interfere with them. I don't know as we made all that many converts, actually, but I've got nothing bad to say about those people."

He paused, rubbing his eyes; he suddenly looked his age. "Things were going fine," he said. "And then they told me to establish a second mission, further in the interior."

He stopped once more, as if weighing whether to continue. A squat little Chinese woman was plodding slowly up the aisle, holding on to the seats on each side for balance. I felt her hand brush past my ear as she went by. My companion watched her with a certain unease, waiting till she'd passed. When he spoke again, his voice had thickened noticeably.

"I've been all over the world—a lot of places Americans can't even go to these days—and I've always felt that wherever I was, God was surely watching. But once I started getting up into those hills, well . . . " He shook his head. "I was pretty much on my own, you see. They were going to send most of the staff out later, after I'd got set up. All I had with me was one of our groundskeepers, two bearers, and a guide who doubled as interpreter. Locals, all of them." He frowned. "The groundskeeper, at least, was a Christian."

"You needed an interpreter?"

The question seemed to distract him. "For the new mission, yes. My Malay stood me well enough in the lowlands, but in the interior they used dozens of local dialects. I would have been lost up there. Where I was going they spoke something which our people back in the village called *agon di-gatuan*—'the Old Language.' I never really got to understand much of it." He stared down at his hands. "I wasn't there long enough."

"Trouble with the natives, I suppose."

He didn't answer right away. Finally he nodded. "I truly believe they must be the nastiest people who ever lived," he said with great deliberation. "I sometimes wonder how God could have created them." He stared out the window, at the hills of cloud below us. "They called themselves the Chauchas, near as I could make out. Some French colonial influence, maybe, but they looked Asiatic to me, with just a touch of black. Little people. Harmless looking." He gave a small shudder. "But they were nothing like what they seemed. You couldn't get to the bottom of them. They'd been living way up in those hills I don't know how many centuries, and whatever it is they were doing, they weren't going to let a stranger in on it. They called themselves Moslems, just like the lowlanders, but I'm sure there must have been a few bush gods mixed in. I thought they were primitive, at first. I mean, some of their rituals—you wouldn't believe it. But now I think they weren't primitive at all. They just kept those rituals because they enjoyed them!" He tried to smile; it merely accentuated the lines in his face.

"Oh, they seemed friendly enough in the beginning," he went on. "You could approach them, do a bit of trading, watch them breed their animals; they were good at that. You could even talk to them about salvation. And they'd just keep smiling, smiling all the time. As if they really *liked* you."

I could hear the disappointment in his voice, and something else.

"You know," he confided, suddenly leaning closer, "down in the lowlands, in the pastures, there's an animal, a kind of snail the Malays kill on sight. A little yellow thing, but it scares them silly: they believe that if it passes over the shadow of their cattle, it'll suck out the cattle's life-force. They used to call it a 'Chaucha snail.' Now I know why."

"Why?" I asked.

He looked around the plane and seemed to sigh. "You understand, at this stage we were still living in tents. We had yet to build anything. Well, the weather got bad, the mosquitoes got worse, and

after the groundskeeper disappeared the others took off. I think the
guide persuaded them to go. Of course, this left me—"

"Wait. You say the man disappeared?"

"Before the first week was out. It was late afternoon. We'd been
pacing out one of the fields less than a hundred yards from the tents,
and I was pushing through the long grass thinking he was behind
me, and I turned around and he wasn't."

He was speaking all in a rush now. I had visions out of 1940s
movies, frightened natives sneaking off with the supplies, and I wondered how much of this was true.

"So with the others gone, too," he said, "I had no way of com-
municating with the Chauchas except through a kind of pidgin
language, a mixture of Malay and their tongue. But I knew what
was going on. All that week they kept laughing about something.
Openly. And I got the impression that they were somehow responsible. I mean, for the man's disappearance. You understand? He'd
been the one I trusted." His expression was pained. "A week later,
when they showed him to me, he was still alive. But he couldn't
speak. I think they wanted it that way. You see, they'd—they'd *grown*
something in him." He shuddered.

Just at that moment, from directly behind us came an inhumanly
high-pitched caterwauling that pierced the air like a siren, rising
above the whine of the engines. It came with heart-stopping sud-
denness, and we both went rigid. I saw my companion's mouth gape
as if to echo the scream. So much for the past; we'd become two old
men gone all white and clutching at themselves. It was really quite
comical. A full minute must have passed before I could bring myself
to turn around.

By this time the stewardess had arrived and was dabbing at the
place where the man behind me, dozing, had dropped his cigarette
on his lap. The surrounding passengers, whites especially, were
casting angry glances at him, and I thought I smelled burnt flesh. He
was at last helped to his feet by the stewardess and one of his team-
mates, the latter chuckling uneasily.

Minor as it was, the accident had derailed our conversation and
unnerved my companion; it was as if he'd retreated into his beard.

He would talk no further, except to ask me ordinary and rather trivial questions about food prices and accommodations. He said he was bound for Florida, looking forward to a summer of, as he put it, "R and R," apparently financed by his sect. I asked him, a bit forlornly, what had happened in the end to the groundskeeper; he said that he had died. Drinks were served; the North American continent swung toward us from the south, first a finger of ice, soon a jagged line of green. I found myself giving the man my sister's address—Indian Creek was just outside Miami, where he'd be staying—and immediately regretted doing so. What did I know of him, after all? He told me his name was Ambrose Mortimer. "It means 'Dead Sea,'" he said. "From the Crusades."

When I persisted in bringing up the subject of the mission, he waved me off. "I can't call myself a missionary anymore," he said. "Yesterday, when I left the country, I gave up that calling." He attempted a smile. "Honest, I'm just a civilian now."

"What makes you think they're after you?" I asked.

The smile vanished. "I'm not so sure they are," he said, not very convincingly. "I may just be spooking myself. But I could swear that in New Delhi, and again at Heathrow, I heard someone singing— singing a certain song. Once it was in the men's room, on the other side of a partition; once it was behind me in line. And it was a song I recognized. It's in the Old Language." He shrugged. "I don't even know what the words mean."

"Why would anyone be singing? I mean, if they were following you?"

"That's just it. I don't know." He shook his head. "But I think—I think it's part of the ritual."

"What sort of ritual?"

"I don't know," he said again. He looked quite pained, and I resolved to bring this inquisition to an end. The ventilators had not yet dissipated the smell of charred cloth and flesh.

"But you'd heard the song before," I said. "You told me you recognized it."

"Yeah." He turned away and stared at the approaching clouds. We had already passed over Maine. Suddenly the earth seemed a very small place. "I'd heard some of the Chaucha women singing it," he said at last. "It was a sort of farming song. It's supposed to make things grow."

Ahead of us loomed the saffron yellow smog that covers Manhattan like a dome. The NO SMOKING light winked silently on the console above us.

"I was hoping I wouldn't have to change planes," my companion said presently. "But the Miami flight doesn't leave for an hour and a half. I guess I'll get off and walk around a bit, stretch my legs. I wonder how long customs'll take." He seemed to be talking more to himself than to me. Once more I regretted my impulsiveness in giving him Maude's address. I was half tempted to make up some contagious disease for her, or a jealous husband. But then, quite likely he'd never call on her anyway; he hadn't even bothered to write down her name. And if he did pay a call—well, I told myself, perhaps he'd unwind when he realized he was safe among friends. He might even turn out to be good company; after all, he probably wasn't that much younger than my sister.

As the plane gave up the struggle and sank deeper into the warm encircling air, passengers shut books and magazines, organized their belongings, and made last hurried forays to the bathroom. I wiped my spectacles and smoothed back what remained of my hair. My companion was staring out the window, the green Air Malay bag in his lap, his hands folded on it as if in prayer. We were already becoming strangers.

"Please return seat backs to the upright position," ordered a disembodied voice. Out beyond the window, past the head now turned completely away from me, the ground rose to meet us and we bumped along the pavement, jets roaring in reverse. Already stewardesses were rushing up and down the aisles pulling coats and jackets from the overhead bins; executive types, ignoring instructions, were scrambling to their feet and thrashing into raincoats. Outside I could see uniformed figures moving back and forth in what promised to be a warm grey drizzle.

"Well," I said lamely, "we made it." I got to my feet.

He turned and flashed me a sickly grin. "Goodbye," he said. "This really has been a pleasure." He reached for my hand.

"And do try to relax and enjoy yourself in Miami," I said, looking for a break in the parade of passengers that shuffled past me down the aisle. "That's the important thing—just to relax."

"I know that." He nodded gravely. "God bless you."

I found my slot and slipped into line. From behind me he added, "And I won't forget to look up your sister." My heart sank, but as I moved toward the door I turned to shout a last farewell. The old lady with the eyes was two people in front of me, but she didn't so much as smile.

One trouble with last farewells is that they occasionally prove redundant. Some forty minutes later, having passed like a morsel of food through a series of white plastic tubes, corridors, and customs lines, I found myself in one of the airport gift shops, whiling away the hour till my niece came to collect me; and there, once again, I saw the missionary.

He did not see me. He was standing before one of the racks of paperbacks—the so-called "Classics" section, haunt of the public domain—and with a preoccupied air he was glancing up and down the rows, barely pausing long enough to read the titles. Like me, he was obviously just killing time.

For some reason—call it embarrassment, a certain reluctance to spoil what had been a successful goodbye—I refrained from hailing him. Instead, stepping back into the rear aisle, I took refuge behind a rack of gothics, which I pretended to study while in fact studying him.

Moments later he looked up from the books and ambled over to a bin of cellophane-wrapped records, idly pressing the whiskers back into place below his right sideburn. Without warning he turned and surveyed the store; I ducked my head toward the gothics and enjoyed a vision normally reserved for the multifaceted eyes of an insect: women, dozens of them, fleeing an equal number of tiny mansions.

At last, with a shrug of his huge shoulders, he began flipping through the albums in the bin, snapping each one forward in an impatient staccato. Soon, the assortment scanned, he moved to the bin on the left and started on that.

Suddenly he gave a little cry, and I saw him shrink back. He stood immobile for a moment, staring down at something in the bin. Then he whirled and walked quickly from the store, pushing past a family about to enter.

"Late for his plane," I said to the astonished salesgirl, and strolled over to the albums. One of them lay face up in the pile—a jazz record featuring John Coltrane on saxophone. Puzzled, I turned to look for my erstwhile companion, but he had vanished in the crowd hurrying past the doorway.

Something about the album had apparently set him off; I studied it more carefully. Coltrane stood silhouetted against a tropical sunset, his features obscured, head tilted back, saxophone blaring silently beneath the crimson sky. The pose was dramatic but trite, and I could see in it no special significance. It looked like any other black man with a horn.

New York eclipses all other cities in the spontaneous cordiality
and generosity of its inhabitants—at least, such inhabitants as
I have encountered.
          —Lovecraft, September 29, 1922

How quickly you changed your mind! You arrived to find a gold Dunsanian city of arches and domes and fantastic spires . . . or so you told us. Yet when you fled two years later, you could see only "alien hordes."

What was it that so spoiled the dream? Was it that impossible marriage? Those foreign faces on the subway? Or was it merely the theft of your new summer suit? I believed then, Howard, and I believe it still, that the nightmare was of your own making; though you returned to New England like a man re-emerging into sunlight, there was, I assure you, a very good life to be found amid the shade. I remained—and survived.

I almost wish I were back there now, instead of in this ugly little bungalow, with its air conditioner and its fraying wicker furniture and the humid night dripping down its windows. I almost wish I were back on the steps of the Natural History Museum where, that momentous August afternoon, I stood perspiring in the shadow of Teddy Roosevelt's horse, watching matrons stroll past Central Park with dogs or children in tow and fanning myself ineffectually with the postcard I'd just received from Maude. I was waiting for my niece to drive by and leave off her son, whom I planned to take round the museum; he'd wanted to see the life-size mockup of the blue whale and, just upstairs, the dinosaurs.

I remember waiting half an hour for Ellen and her boy. I remember too, Howard, that I was thinking of you that afternoon, and with some amusement; much as you disliked New York in the '20s, you'd have reeled in horror at what it's become today. Even from the steps of the museum, I could see a curb piled high with refuse and a park whose length you might have walked without once hearing English spoken. Dark skins crowded out the white, and salsa music echoed from across the street.

I remember all these things because, as it turned out, this was a special day: the day I saw, for the second time, the black man and his baleful horn.

My niece arrived late, as usual, with the usual apologies about the crosstown traffic and, for me, the usual argument. "How can you still live over here?" she asked, rolling down the car window as Terry climbed out. "I mean, just look at those people." She nodded toward a rowdy group of half-naked teenagers who were loitering by the entrance to the park.

"Brooklyn is so much better?" I countered, as tradition dictated.

"Of course," she said. "In the Heights, anyway. I don't understand it—why this pathological hatred of moving? You might at least try the East Side. You can certainly afford it." Terry watched us impassively, lounging against the fender of the car. I think he sided with me over his mother but was too wise to show it.

"Believe me, Ellen," I said, "the West Side's changing. It's on the way up again."

She made a face. "Not up where you live."

"Sooner or later that'll change as well," I said. "Besides, I'm just too old to start hanging around East Side singles bars. Over there they read nothing but bestsellers, and they hate anyone past sixty. I'm better off where I grew up—at least I know where the cheap restaurants are." It was, in fact, a thorny problem: forced to choose between people I despised and darker folk I feared, I somehow preferred the fear.

Before we parted, I passed along to Ellen her mother's postcard. It was the pre-stamped kind that bore no picture. *"I'm still getting used to the cane,"* Maude had written, her penmanship as flawless as when she'd won the school medallion. *"Livia has gone back to Vermont for the summer, so the card games are suspended & I'm hard into Pearl Buck. Your friend Rev. Mortimer dropped by & we had a nice chat. What amusing stories! Thanks again for the subscription to the Geographic—I'll send Ellen my old copies. Look forward to seeing you all after the hurricane season."*

Terry was eager to confront the dinosaurs; he was, in fact, getting a little old for me to superintend, and was halfway up the steps before I'd arranged with Ellen where to meet us afterward. With school out the museum was almost as crowded as on weekends, the halls' echo turning shouts and laughter into animal cries. We oriented ourselves using the floor plan in the main lobby—YOU ARE HERE read a large green dot, below which someone had scrawled *Too bad for you*—and trooped toward the Hall of Reptiles, Terry impatiently leading the way. "I saw that in school." He pointed toward a redwood diorama. "That too"—the Grand Canyon. He was, I believe, about to enter seventh grade, and until now had been little given to talk; he looked younger than the other children.

We passed toucans and marmosets and the new Urban Ecology wing ("concrete and cockroaches," sneered Terry) and dutifully stood

before the brontosaurus, something of a disappointment: "I forgot it
was just the skeleton," he said. Beside us a sleepy-looking black girl
with a baby in her arms and two preschoolers in tow tried ineffectually to keep one of the children from climbing on the guard rail. The
baby set up an angry howl. I hurried my nephew past the assembled
bones and through the most crowded doorway, dedicated, ironically,
to Man in Africa. "This is the boring part," said Terry, unmoved by
masks and spears. The pace was beginning to tire me. We passed
through another doorway—Man in Asia—and moved quickly past
the Chinese statuary. "I saw that in school." He nodded at a stumpy
figure in a glass case, wrapped in ceremonial robes. Something
about it was familiar to me as well; I paused to stare at it. The outer
robe, slightly tattered, was spun of some shiny green material and
displayed tall, twisted-looking trees on one side, a kind of stylized
river on the other. Across the front ran five yellow-brown figures in
loincloth and headdress, presumably fleeing toward the robe's frayed
edges; behind them stood a larger shape, all black. In its mouth was
a pendulous horn. The figure was crudely woven—little more than a
stick figure, in fact—but it bore an unsettling resemblance, in both
pose and proportion, to the one on the album cover.

Terry returned to my side, curious to see what I'd found. "'Tribal
garment,'" he read, peering at the white plastic notice below the
case. "'Malay Peninsula, Federation of Malaysia, early nineteenth
century.'" He fell silent.

"Is that all it says?"

"Yep. They don't even have which tribe it's from." He reflected a
moment. "Not that I really care."

"Well, I do," I said. "I wonder who'd know."

Obviously I'd have to seek advice at the information counter in
the main lobby downstairs. Terry ran on ahead, while I followed
even more slowly than before; the thought of a mystery evidently
appealed to him, even one as tenuous and unexciting as this.

A harried-looking young college girl listened to the beginning of
my query and handed me a pamphlet from below the counter. "You
can't see anyone till September," she said, already beginning to turn
away. "They're all on vacation."

I squinted at the tiny print on the first page: "Asia, our largest continent, has justly been called the cradle of civilization, but it may also be a birthplace of man himself." Obviously the pamphlet had been written before the current campaigns against sexism. I checked the date on the back: "Winter 1958." This would be of no help. Yet on page four my eye fell on the reference I sought:

> ... The model next to it wears a green silk ceremonial robe from Negri Sembilan, most rugged of the Malayan provinces. Note central motif of native man blowing ceremonial horn and the graceful curve of his instrument; the figure is believed to be a representation of "Death's Herald," possibly warning villagers of approaching calamity. Gift of an anonymous donor, the robe is probably Tcho-tcho in origin and dates from the early 19th century.

"What's the matter, Uncle? Are you sick?" Terry gripped my shoulder and stared up at me, looking worried; my behavior had obviously confirmed his worst fears about old people. "What's it say in there?"

I gave him the pamphlet and staggered to a bench near the wall. I wanted time to think. The Tcho-Tcho people, I knew, had figured in a number of tales by Lovecraft and his circle—Howard himself had referred to them as "the wholly abominable Tcho-Tchos"—but I couldn't remember much about them except that they were said to worship one of his imaginary deities. I had always assumed that he'd taken the name from Robert W. Chambers' novel *The Slayer of Souls*, which mentions an Asian tribe called "the Tchortchas" and their "ancient air, 'The Thirty Thousand Calamities.'"

But whatever their attributes, I'd been certain of one thing: the Tcho-Tchos were completely fictitious.

Obviously I'd been wrong. Barring the unlikely possibility that the pamphlet itself was a hoax, I was forced to conclude that the malign beings of the stories were in fact based upon an actual race inhabiting the Southeast Asian subcontinent—a race whose name my missionary friend had mistranslated as "the Chauchas."

It was a rather troubling discovery. I had hoped to turn some of Mortimer's recollections, authentic or not, into fiction; he'd unwittingly given me the material for two or three good plots. Yet I'd now discovered that my friend Howard had beaten me to it, and that I'd been put in the uncomfortable position of living out another man's horror stories.

> Epistolary expression is with me largely replacing conversation.
> —Lovecraft, December 23, 1917

I hadn't expected my second encounter with the black horn-player. A month later I got an even bigger surprise: I saw the missionary again.

Or at any rate, his picture. It was in a clipping my sister had sent me from the *Miami Herald,* over which she had written in ballpoint pen, *"Just saw this in the paper—how awful!!"*

I didn't recognize the face; the photo was obviously an old one, the reproduction poor, and the man was clean-shaven. But the words below it told me it was him.

CLERGYMAN MISSING IN STORM

(Wed.) The Rev. Ambrose B. Mortimer, 58, a lay pastor of the Church of Christ, Knoxville, Tenn., has been reported missing in the wake of Monday's hurricane. Spokesmen for the order say Mortimer had recently retired after serving 19 years as a missionary, most recently in Malaysia. After moving to Miami in July, he had been a resident of 311 Pompano Canal Road.

Here the piece ended, with an abruptness that seemed all too appropriate to its subject. Whether Ambrose Mortimer still lived I didn't know, but I felt certain now that, having fled one peninsula, he had strayed onto another just as dangerous, a finger thrust into the void. And the void had swallowed him up.

So, anyway, ran my thoughts. I have often been prey to depressions of a similar nature, and subscribe to a fatalistic philosophy I'd shared with my friend Howard: a philosophy one of his less sympathetic biographers has dubbed "futilitarianism."

Yet pessimistic as I was, I was not about to let the matter rest. Mortimer may well have been lost in the storm; he may even have set off somewhere on his own. But if, in fact, some lunatic religious sect had done away with him for having pried too closely into its affairs, there were things I could do about it. I wrote to the Miami police that very day.

"Gentlemen," I began, "Having learned of the recent disappearance of the Reverend Ambrose Mortimer, I think I can provide information which may prove of use to investigators."

There is no need to quote the rest of the letter here. Suffice it to say that I recounted my conversation with the missing man, emphasizing the fears he'd expressed for his life: pursuit and "ritual murder" at the hands of a Malayan tribe called the Tcho-Tcho. The letter was, in short, a rather elaborate way of crying "foul play." I sent it care of my sister, asking that she forward it to the correct address.

The police department's reply came with unexpected speed. As with all such correspondence, it was more curt than courteous. "Dear Sir," wrote a Detective Sergeant A. Linahan, "In the matter of Rev. Mortimer we had already been apprised of the threats on his life. To date a preliminary search of the Pompano Canal has produced no findings, but dredging operations are expected to continue as part of our routine investigation. Thanking you for your concern—"

Below his signature, however, the sergeant had added a short postscript in his own hand. Its tone was somewhat more personal; perhaps typewriters intimidated him. "You may be interested to know," it said, "that we've recently learned a man carrying a Malaysian passport occupied rooms at a North Miami hotel for most of the summer but checked out two weeks before your friend disappeared. I'm not at liberty to say more, however please be assured we are tracking down several leads at the moment. Our department is giving this matter the highest priority and we hope to bring it to a speedy conclusion."

Linahan's letter arrived on September twenty-first. Before the week was out I had one from my sister, along with another clipping from the *Herald;* and since, like some staid Victorian novel, this chapter seems to have taken an epistolary form, I will end it with extracts from these two items.

The newspaper story was headed WANTED FOR QUES-TIONING. Like the Mortimer piece, it was little more than a photo with an extended caption:

(Thurs.) A Malaysian citizen is being sought for questioning in connection with the disappearance of an American clergyman, Miami police say. Records indicate that the Malaysian, Mr. D. A. Djaktu-tchow, had occupied furnished rooms at the Barkleigh Hotella, 2401 Culebra Ave., possibly with an unnamed companion. He is believed still in the greater Miami area, but since August 22 his movements cannot be traced. State Dept. officials report Djaktu-tchow's visa expired August 31; charges are pending.

The clergyman, Rev. Ambrose B. Mortimer, has been missing since September 6.

The photo above the article was evidently a recent one, no doubt reproduced from the visa in question. I recognized the smiling moon-wide face, although it took me a moment to place him as the man whose dinner I'd stumbled over on the plane. Without the moustache, he looked less like Charlie Chan.

The accompanying letter filled in a few details. "I called up the *Herald,*" my sister wrote, "but they couldn't tell me any more than was in the article. Just the same, finding that out took me half an hour, since the stupid woman at the switchboard kept putting me through to the wrong person. I guess you're right—anything that prints color pictures on page one shouldn't call itself a newspaper.

"This afternoon I called up the police precinct, but they weren't very helpful either. I suppose you just can't expect to find out much over the phone, though I still rely on it. Finally I got an Officer Linahan, who told me he'd just replied to that letter of yours. Have you heard from him yet? The man was very evasive. He was trying to be nice, but I could tell he was impatient to get off. He did give me the full name of the man they're looking for—Djaktu Abdul Djaktu-tchow, isn't that marvelous?—and he told me they have some more material on him which they can't release right now. I argued and pleaded (you know how persuasive I can be!) and finally, because I claimed I'd been a close friend of Rev. Mortimer's, I wheedled some-thing out of him which he swore he'd deny if I told anyone but you. Apparently the poor man must have been deathly ill, maybe even tubercular—I intend to get a patch test next week, just to play safe, and I recommend that you get one too—because it seems that, in the reverend's bedroom, they found something *very* odd. They said it was pieces of lung tissue."

I, too, was a detective in youth.
—Lovecraft, February 17, 1931

Do amateur detectives still exist? I mean, outside the pages of books? Who, after all, has the time for such games today? Not I, unfortu-nately. Though for more than a decade I'd been nominally retired, my days were quite full with the unromantic activities that occupy people my age: letters, luncheon dates, visits to my niece and to my doctor; books (not enough) and television (too much) and perhaps a Golden Agers' matinee (though I have largely stopped going to films, finding myself increasingly out of sympathy with their heroes). I also spent Halloween week on the Jersey shore, and most of another attempting to interest a rather patronizing young publisher in reprinting some of my early work.

All this, of course, is intended as a sort of apologia for my having put off further inquiries into poor Mortimer's case till mid-November. The truth is, the matter almost slipped my mind; only in novels do people not have better things to do.

It was Maude who reawakened my interest. She had been avidly scanning the papers—in vain—for further reports on the man's disappearance; I believe she had even phoned Sergeant Linahan a second time but had learned nothing new. Now she wrote me with a tiny fragment of information, heard at third hand: one of her bridge partners had had it on the authority of "a friend in the police force" that the search for Mr. Djaktu was being widened to include his presumed companion—"a Negro child," or so my sister reported. Although there was every possibility that this information was false or that it concerned an entirely different case, I could tell she regarded it all as rather sinister.

Perhaps that was why the following afternoon found me struggling once more up the steps of the Natural History Museum—as much to satisfy Maude as myself. Her allusion to a Negro, coming after the curious discovery in Mortimer's bedroom, had recalled to mind the figure on the Malayan robe, and I had been troubled all night by the fantasy of a black man—a man much like the beggar I'd just seen huddled against Roosevelt's statue—coughing his lungs out into a sort of twisted horn.

I had encountered few other people on the streets that afternoon, as it was unseasonably chilly for a city that's often mild till January; I wore a muffler, and my grey tweed overcoat flapped round my heels. Inside, however, the place, like all American buildings, was overheated; I was soon the same as I made my way up the demoralizingly long staircase to the second floor.

The corridors were silent and empty, but for the morose figure of a guard seated before one of the alcoves, head down as if in mourning, and, from above me, the hiss of the steam radiators near the marble ceiling. Slowly, and rather enjoying the sense of privilege that comes from having a museum almost to oneself, I retraced my earlier route past the immense skeletons of dinosaurs ("These great creatures once trod the earth where you now walk") and down to the Hall of Primitive Man, where two Puerto Rican youths, obviously playing hooky, stood by the African wing gazing worshipfully at a Masai warrior in full battle gear. In the section devoted to Asia, I paused to get my bearings, looking in vain for the squat figure in the robe. The glass case was empty. Over its plaque was taped a printed notice: *Temporarily removed for restoration.*

This was no doubt the first time in forty years that the display had been taken down, and of course I'd picked just this occasion to look for it. So much for luck. I headed for the nearest staircase, at the far

end of the wing. From behind me the clank of metal echoed down
the hall, followed by the angry voice of the guard. Perhaps that Masai
spear had proved too great a temptation.

In the main lobby I was issued a written pass to enter the north
wing, where the staff offices were located. "You want the workrooms
on basement level," said the woman at the information counter; the
summer's harried coed had become a friendly old lady who eyed me
with some interest. "Just ask the guard at the bottom of the stairs,
past the cafeteria. I do hope you find what you're looking for."

Carefully keeping the pink slip she'd handed me visible for anyone
who might demand it, I descended. As I turned onto the stairwell, I
was confronted with a kind of vision: a blond, Scandinavian-looking
family were coming up the stairs toward me, the four upturned faces
almost interchangeable, parents and two little girls with the pursed
lips and timidly hopeful eyes of the tourist, while just behind them,
like a shadow, apparently unheard, capered a grinning black youth,
practically walking on the father's heels. In my present state of mind
the scene appeared particularly disturbing—the boy's expression was
certainly one of mockery—and I wondered if the guard who stood
before the cafeteria had noticed. If he had, however, he gave no sign;
he glanced without curiosity at my pass and pointed toward a fire
door at the end of the hall.

The offices in the lower level were surprisingly shabby—the walls
here were not marble but faded green plaster—and the entire corridor felt somehow buried, no doubt because the only outside light
came from ground-level window gratings high overhead. I had been
told to ask for one of the research associates, a Mr. Richmond. His
office was part of a suite broken up by pegboard dividers.

The door was open, and he got up from his desk as soon as I
entered; I suspect that, in view of my age and grey tweed overcoat,
he may have taken me for someone important. A plump young man
with sandy-colored beard, he looked like an out-of-shape surfer, but
his sunniness dissolved when I mentioned my interest in the green
silk robe. "And I suppose you're the man who complained about it
upstairs, am I right?"

I assured him I was not.

"Well, someone sure did," he said, still eyeing me resentfully; on the wall behind him an Indian war mask did the same. "Someone with too much time on his hands, maybe, in town for a day and out to make trouble. Threatened to call the Malaysian embassy. If you put up a fuss, those people upstairs get scared it'll wind up in the *Times*."

I understood his allusion; in previous years the museum had gained considerable notoriety for having conducted some really appalling—and, to my mind, quite pointless—experiments on cats. Most of the public had, until then, been unaware that the building housed several working laboratories.

"Anyway," he continued, "the robe's down in the shop, and we're stuck with patching up the damn thing. It'll probably be down there for the next six months before we get to it. We're so understaffed right now it isn't funny." He glanced at his watch. "Come on, I'll show you. Then I've got to go upstairs."

I followed him down a narrow corridor that branched off to either side. At one point he said, "On your right, the infamous zoology lab." I kept my eyes straight ahead. As we passed the next doorway, I smelled a familiar odor.

"It makes me think of treacle," I said.

"You're not so far wrong." He spoke without looking back. "The stuff's mostly molasses. Pure nutrient. They use it for growing microorganisms."

I hurried to keep up with him. "And for other things?"

He shrugged. "I wouldn't know. It's not my field."

We came to a door barred by a black wire grille. "Here's one of the shops," he said, fitting a key into the lock. The door swung open on a long unlit room smelling of wood shavings and glue. "Have a seat in here," he said, leading me to a small anteroom and switching on the light. "I'll be back in a second." I stared at the object closest to me, a large ebony chest, ornately carved. Its hinges had been removed. Richmond returned with the robe draped over his arm. "See?" he said, dangling it before me. "It's really not in such bad condition, is it?" I realized he still thought of me as the man who'd complained.

On the field of rippling green fled the small brown figures, still pursued by some unseen doom. In the center stood the black man, black horn to his lips, man and horn a single line of unbroken blackness.

"Are the Tcho-Tchos a superstitious people?" I asked.

"They *were*," he said pointedly. "Superstitious and not very agreeable. They're extinct as dinosaurs now. Supposedly wiped out by the Japanese or something."

"That's rather odd," I said. "A friend of mine claims to have met up with them earlier this year."

Richmond was smoothing out the robe; the branches of the snake trees snapped futilely at the brown shapes. "I suppose it's possible," he said, after a pause. "But I haven't read anything about them since grad school. They're certainly not listed in the textbooks anymore. I've looked—there's nothing on them. This robe's over a hundred years old."

I pointed to the figure in the center. "What can you tell me about this fellow?"

"Death's Herald," he said, as if it were a quiz. "At least that's what the literature says. Supposed to warn of some approaching calamity."

I nodded without looking up; he was merely repeating what I'd read in the pamphlet. "But isn't it strange," I said, "that these others are in such a panic? See? They aren't even waiting around to listen."

"Would you?" He snorted impatiently.

"But if the black one's just a messenger of some sort, why's he so much *bigger* than the others?"

Richmond began folding the cloth. "Well," he said, "I don't pretend to be an expert on every tribe in Asia. But if a character's important, they'd sometimes make him larger. Anyway, that's what the Mayans did. Listen, I've really got to get this put away now. I've got a meeting to go to."

After he had gone, I sat thinking about what I'd just seen. The small brown figures, crude as they were, had expressed a terror no mere messenger could inspire. And that great black shape standing triumphant in the center, horn twisting from its mouth—that was no messenger either, I was sure of it. That was no Death's Herald. That was Death itself.

I returned to my apartment just in time to hear the telephone ringing, but by the time I'd let myself in, it had stopped. I sat down in the living room with a mug of coffee and a book which had lain untouched on the shelf for the last thirty years: *Jungle Ways,* by that old humbug William Seabrook. I'd met him back in the '20s and had found him likable enough, if rather untrustworthy. His book described dozens of unlikely characters, including "a cannibal chief who had got himself jailed and famous because he had eaten his young wife, a handsome, lazy wench called Blito, along with a dozen of her girlfriends." But I discovered no mention of a black horn-player.

I had just finished my coffee when the phone rang again. It was my sister.

"I just wanted to let you know that there's another man missing," she said breathlessly. I couldn't tell if she was frightened or merely excited. "A busboy at the San Marino. Remember? I took you there."

The San Marino was an inexpensive little luncheonette on Indian Creek, several blocks from my sister's house. She and her friends ate there several times a week.

"It happened last night," she went on. "I just heard about it at my card game. They say he went outside with a bucket of fish heads to dump in the creek and he never came back."

"That's very interesting, but . . ." I thought for a moment; it was highly unusual for her to call me like this. "But really, Maude, couldn't he have simply run off? I mean, what makes you think there's any connection—"

"Because I took Ambrose there, too!" she cried. "Three or four times. That was where we used to meet."

Apparently Maude had been considerably better acquainted with the Reverend Mortimer than her letters had let on. But I wasn't interested in pursuing that line right now.

"This busboy," I asked, "was he someone you knew?"

"Of course," she said. "I know everyone in the place. His name was Carlos. A quiet boy, very courteous. I'm sure he must have waited on us dozens of times."

I had seldom heard my sister so upset, but for the present there seemed no way of calming her fears. Before hanging up, she made me promise to move up the month's visit I'd expected to pay her over Christmas. I assured her I would try to make it down for Thanksgiving, then only a week away, if I could find a flight that wasn't filled.

"Do try," she said—and were this a tale from the old pulps, she would have added: "If anyone can get to the bottom of this, you can." In truth, however, both Maude and I were aware that I had just celebrated my seventy-seventh birthday and that, of the two of us, I was by far the more timid; so that what she actually said was, "Looking after you will help take my mind off things."

> I couldn't live a week without a private library.
> —Lovecraft, February 25, 1929

That's what I thought, too, until recently. After a lifetime of collecting, I'd acquired thousands upon thousands of volumes, never parting with a one. It was this cumbersome private library, in fact, that kept me anchored to the same West Side apartment for nearly half a century.

Yet here I sit, with no company save a few tropical gardening manuals and a shelf of antiquated bestsellers—nothing to dream on, nothing I'd want to hold in my hand. Still, I've survived here a week, a month, almost a season. The truth is, Howard, you'd be surprised what you can live without. As for the books I've left in Manhattan, I just hope someone appreciates them when I'm gone.

But I was by no means so resigned that November when, having successfully reserved a seat on a pre-holiday flight, I found myself with less than a week in New York. I spent all my remaining time in the library—the public one on Forty-Second Street, with the lions in front and no book of mine on its shelves. Its two reading rooms were the haunt of men my age and older, retired men with days to fill, poor men just warming their bones; some leafed through newspapers, others dozed in their seats. None of them, I'm sure, shared my sense of urgency. There were things I hoped to find out before I left, things for which Miami would be useless.

I was no stranger to this building. Long ago, during one of Howard's visits, I had undertaken some genealogical researches here in the hope of finding ancestors more impressive than his, and as a young man I had occasionally attempted to support myself, like the denizens of Gissing's *New Grub Street,* by writing articles compiled from the work of others. But by now I was out of practice. How, after all, does one find references to an obscure Southeast Asian tribal myth without reading everything published on that part of the world?

Initially that's exactly what I tried; I looked through every book I came across with "Malaya" in its title. I read about rainbow gods and phallic altars and something called "the *tatai,*" a sort of unwanted companion; I came across wedding rites and the Death of Thorns and a certain cave inhabited by millions of snails. But I found no mention of the Tcho-Tcho, and nothing on their gods.

This in itself was surprising. We are living in a day when there are no more secrets, when my twelve-year-old nephew can buy his own *grimoire,* and books with titles like *The Encyclopaedia of Ancient and Forbidden Knowledge* are remaindered at every discount store. Though my friends from the '20s would have hated to admit it, the notion of stumbling across some moldering old "black book" in the attic of a deserted house—some compendium of spells and chants and hidden lore—is merely a quaint fantasy. If the *Necronomicon* actually existed, it would be out in paperback with a preface by Colin Wilson.

It's appropriate, then, that when I finally came upon a reference to what I sought, it was in that most unromantic of forms, a mimeographed film script.

"Transcript" would perhaps be closer to the truth, for it was the written record of a film shot in 1937 that was now presumably crumbling in some forgotten storehouse. I discovered the item inside one of those brown cardboard packets, tied with a cord, that libraries use to protect books whose bindings have worn away. The book itself, *Malay Memories,* by a Reverend Morton, had proved a disappointment despite the author's initially suggestive name. The transcript lay beneath it, apparently slipped there by mistake, but though it appeared unpromising—only sixty-six pages long, badly typed, and held together by a single rusty staple—it more than repaid the reading. There was no title page, nor do I think there'd ever been one; the first page simply identified the film as *Documentary—Malaya Today* and noted that it had been financed, in part, by a U.S. government grant. The filmmaker or makers were not listed.

I soon saw why the government may have been willing to lend the venture some support, for there were a great many scenes in which the proprietors of rubber plantations expressed the sort of opinions Americans might want to hear. To an unidentified interviewer's query, "What other signs of prosperity do you see around you?" a planter named Mr. Pierce had obligingly replied, "Why, look at the living standard—better schools for the natives and a new lorry for me. It's from Detroit, you know. May even have my own rubber in it."

> INT: And how about the Japanese? Are they one of today's better markets?
> PIERCE: Oh, see, they buy our crop all right, but we don't really trust 'em, understand? (Smiles) We don't like 'em half so much as the Yanks.

The final section of the transcript was considerably more interesting, however. It recorded a number of brief scenes that must never have appeared in the finished film. I quote one of them in its entirety:

PLAYROOM, CHURCH SCHOOL
—LATE AFTERNOON. (DELETED)

> INT: This Malay youth has sketched a picture of a demon he calls Shoo Goron. (To Boy) I wonder if you can tell me something about the instrument he's blowing out of. It looks like the Jewish shofar, or ram's horn. (Again to Boy) That's all right. No need to be frightened.
> BOY: He no blow out. Blow in.

INT: I see—he draws air in through the horn, is that right?
BOY: No horn. Is no horn. (Weeps) Is him.

Miami did not produce much of an impression . . .
　　—Lovecraft, July 19, 1931

Waiting in the airport lounge with Ellen and her boy, my bags already checked and my seat number assigned, I fell prey to the sort of anxiety that had made me miserable in youth; it was a sense that time was running out. What caused it now, I think, was the hour that remained before my flight was due to leave. It was too long a time to sit making small talk with Terry, whose mind was patently on other things; yet it was too short to accomplish the task which I'd suddenly realized had been left undone.

But perhaps my nephew would serve. "Terry," I said, "how'd you like to do me a favor?" He looked up eagerly; I suppose children his age love to be of use. "Remember the building we passed on the way here? The International Arrivals building?"

"Sure," he said. "Right next door."

"Yes, but it's a lot farther away than it looks. Do you think you'd be able to get there and back in the next hour and find something out for me?"

"Sure." He was already out of his seat.

"It just occurs to me that there's an Air Malay reservations desk in that building, and I wonder if you could ask someone there—"

My niece interrupted me. "Oh, no, he won't," she said firmly. "First of all, I won't have him running across that highway on some silly errand—" She ignored her son's protests. "—and secondly, I don't want him involved in this game you've got going with Mother."

The upshot of it was that Ellen went herself, leaving Terry and me to our small talk. She took with her a slip of paper upon which I'd written *Shoo Goron,* a name she regarded with sour skepticism. I wasn't sure she would return before my departure (Terry, I could see, was growing increasingly uneasy), but she was back before the second boarding call.

"She says you spelled it wrong," Ellen announced.

"Who's she?"

"Just one of the flight attendants," said Ellen. "A young girl, in her early twenties. None of the others were Malayan. At first she didn't recognize the name, until she read it out loud a few times. Apparently it's some kind of fish, am I right? Like a suckerfish, only bigger. Anyway, that's what she said. Her mother used to scare her with it when she was bad."

Obviously Ellen—or, more likely, the other woman—had mis-understood. "Sort of a bogeyman figure?" I asked. "Well, I suppose that's possible. But a fish, you say?"

Ellen nodded. "I don't think she knew that much about it, though. She acted a little embarrassed, in fact. Like I'd asked her something dirty." From across the room a loudspeaker issued the final call for passengers. Ellen helped me to my feet, still talking. "She said she was just a Malay, from somewhere on the coast—Malacca? I forget—and that it's a shame I didn't drop by three or four months ago, because her summer replacement was part Chocha—Chocho?—something like that."

The line was growing shorter now. I wished the two of them a safe Thanksgiving and shuffled toward the plane.

Below me the clouds had formed a landscape of rolling hills. I could see every ridge, every washed-out shrub, and in the darker places, the eyes of animals.

Some of the valleys were split by jagged black lines that looked like rivers seen on a map. The water, at least, was real enough: here the cloud bank had cracked and parted, revealing the dark sea beneath.

Throughout the ride I'd been conscious of lost opportunity, a sense that my destination offered a kind of final chance. With Howard gone these forty years I still lived out my life in his shadow; certainly his tales had overshadowed my own. Now I found myself trapped within one of them. Here, miles above the earth, I felt great gods warring; below, the war was already lost.

The very passengers around me seemed participants in a masque:

the oily little steward who smelled of something odd; the child who stared and wouldn't look away; the man asleep beside me, mouth slack, who'd chuckled and handed me a page ripped from his in-flight magazine: NOVEMBER PUZZLE PAGE, with a cartoon eye staring in astonishment from a swarm of dots. "Connect the dots and see what you'll be least thankful for this Thanksgiving!" Below it, half buried amid *"B'nai B'rith to Host Song Fest"* and advertisements for beach clubs, a bit of local color found me in a susceptible mood:

HAVE FINS, WILL TRAVEL

(Courtesy *Miami Herald*) If your hubby comes home and swears he's just seen a school of fish walk across the yard, don't sniff his breath for booze. He may be telling the truth! According to U. of Miami zoologists, catfish will be migrating in record numbers this fall and South Florida residents can expect to see hundreds of the whiskered critters crawling overland, miles from water. Though usually no bigger than your pussycat, most breeds can survive without

Here the piece came to a ragged end where my companion had torn it from the magazine. He stirred in his sleep, lips moving. I turned and put my head against the window, where the limb of Florida was swinging into view, veined with dozens of canals. The plane shuddered and slid toward it.

Maude was already at the gate, a black porter towering beside her with an empty cart. While we waited by a hatchway in the basement for my luggage to be disgorged, she told me the sequel to the San Marino incident: the boy's body found washed up on a distant beach, lungs in mouth and throat. "Inside out," she said. "Can you imagine? It's been on the radio all morning. With tapes of some ghastly doctor talking about smoker's cough and the way people drown. I couldn't even listen after a while." The porter heaved my bags onto the cart and we followed him to the taxi stand, Maude

using her cane to gesticulate. If I hadn't seen how aged she'd become,
I'd have thought the excitement was agreeing with her.

We had the driver make a detour westward along Pompano Canal
Road, where we paused at number 311, one of six shabby yellow cabins
that formed a court round a small and very dirty wading pool. In a
cement pot beside the pool drooped a solitary half-dead palm, like
some travesty of an oasis. This, then, had been Ambrose Mortimer's
final home. My sister was unusually silent, and I believed her when
she said she'd never been here before. Across the street glistened the
oily waters of the canal.

The taxi turned east. We passed interminable rows of hotels,
motels, condominiums, shopping centers as big as Central Park,
souvenir shops with billboards bigger than themselves, baskets of seashells and wriggly plastic auto toys out front. Men and women our
age and younger sat on canvas beach chairs in their yards, blinking
at the traffic. The sexes had merged; some of the older women were
nearly as bald as I was, and men wore clothes the color of coral,
lime, and peach. They walked very slowly as they crossed the street
or moved along the sidewalk; cars moved almost as slowly, and it
was forty minutes before we reached Maude's house, with its pastel
orange shutters and the retired druggist and his wife living upstairs.
Here, too, a kind of languor was upon the block, one into which I
knew, with just a memory of regret, I would soon be settling. Life
was slowing to a halt, and once the taxi had roared away the only
things that stirred were the geraniums in Maude's window box,
trembling slightly in a breeze I couldn't even feel.

A dry spell. Mornings in my sister's air-conditioned parlor, luncheons
with her friends in air-conditioned coffee shops. Inadvertent afternoon naps, from which I'd awaken with headaches. Evening walks
to watch the sunsets, the fireflies, the TV screens flashing behind
neighbors' blinds. By night, a few faint cloudy stars; by day, tiny lizards skittering over the hot pavement or boldly sunning themselves
on the flagstones. The smell of oil paints in my sister's closet, and
the insistent buzz of mosquitoes in her garden. Her sundial, a gift

from Ellen, with Terry's message painted on the rim. Lunch at the San Marino and a brief, half-hearted look at the dock in back, now something of a tourist attraction. An afternoon at a branch library in Hialeah, searching through its shelves of travel books, an old man dozing at the table across from me, a child laboriously copying her school report from the encyclopedia. Thanksgiving dinner, with its half hour's phone call to Ellen and the boy, and the prospect of turkey for the rest of the week. More friends to visit, and another day at the library.

Later, driven by boredom and the ghost of an impulse, I phoned the Barkleigh Hotella in North Miami and booked a room there for two nights. I don't remember the days I settled for, because that sort of thing no longer had much meaning, but I know it was for midweek. "We're deep in the season," the proprietress informed me, and the hotel would be filled each weekend till long past New Year's.

My sister refused to accompany me out to Culebra Avenue; she saw no attraction in visiting the place once occupied by a fugitive Malaysian, nor did she share my pulp-novel fantasy that by actually living there myself, I might uncover some clue unknown to police. ("Thanks to the celebrated author of *Beyond the Garve* . . . ") I went alone, by cab, taking with me half a dozen volumes from the branch library. Beyond the reading, I had no other plans.

The Barkleigh was a pink adobe building just two stories tall, surmounted by an ancient neon sign on which the dust lay thick in the early afternoon sunlight. Similar establishments lined the block on both sides, each more depressing than the last. There was no elevator here and, as I learned to my disappointment, no rooms available on the first floor; the staircase looked like it was going to be an effort.

In the office downstairs I inquired, as casually as I could, which room the notorious Mr. Djaktu had occupied; I'd hoped, in fact, to be assigned it, or one nearby. But I was doomed to disappointment. The preoccupied little Cuban behind the counter had been hired only six weeks before and claimed to know nothing of the matter; in halting English he explained that the proprietress, a Mrs. Zimmerman, had just left for New Jersey to visit relatives and would not be back till Christmas. Obviously I could forget about gossip.

By this point I was half tempted to cancel my visit, and I confess that what kept me there was not so much a sense of honor as the desire for two days' separation from Maude, who, having been on her own for nearly a decade, was not so easy to live with.

I followed the Cuban upstairs, watching my suitcase bump rhythmically against his legs, and was led down the hall to a room facing the rear. The place smelled vaguely of salt air and hair oil; the sagging bed had served many a desperate holiday. A small cement terrace overlooked the yard and a vacant lot behind it, the latter so overgrown with weeds and the grass in the yard so long unmown that it was difficult to tell where one began and the other ended. A clump of palms rose somewhere in the middle of this no-man's-land, impossibly tall and thin, with only a few stiffened leaves to grace the tops. On the ground below lay several rotting coconuts.

This was my view the first night when I returned after dining at a nearby restaurant. I felt unusually tired and soon went inside to sleep. The night being cool, there was no need for the air conditioner; as I lay in the huge bed I could hear people stirring in the adjoining room, the hiss of a bus moving down the avenue, and the rustle of palm leaves in the wind.

I spent part of the next morning composing a letter to Mrs. Zimmerman, to be held for her return. After the long walk to a coffee shop for lunch, I napped. After dinner I did the same. With the TV turned on for company, a garrulous blur at the other side of the room, I went through the pile of library books on my night table, final cullings from the bottom of the travel shelf; most of them hadn't been taken out since the '30s. I found nothing of interest in any of them, at least upon first inspection, but before turning out the light I noticed that one, the reminiscences of a Colonel E. G. Paterson, was provided with an index. Though I looked in vain for the demon Shoo Goron, I found reference to it under a variant spelling.

The author, no doubt long deceased, had spent most of his life in the Orient. His interest in Southeast Asia was slight, and the passage in question consequently brief:

. . . Despite the richness and variety of their folklore, however, they have nothing akin to the Malay 'shugoran,' a kind of bogey used to frighten naughty children. The traveller hears many conflicting descriptions of it, some bordering on the obscene. ('Oran,' of course, is Malay for man, while 'shug,' which here connotes sniffing or questing, means literally 'elephant's trunk.') I well recall the hide which hung over the bar at the Traders' Club in Singapore, and which, according to tradition, represented the infant of this fabulous creature; its wings were black, like the skin of a Hottentot. Shortly after the War a regimental surgeon was passing through on his way back to Gibraltar and, after due examination, pronounced it the dried-out skin of a rather large catfish. He was never asked back.

I kept my light on until I was ready to fall asleep, listening to the wind rattle the palm leaves and whine up and down the row of terraces. As I switched off the light, I half expected to see a shadowy shape at the window; but I saw, as the poet says, nothing but the night.

The next morning I packed my bag and left, aware that my stay in the hotel had proved fruitless. I returned to my sister's house to find her in agitated conversation with the druggist from upstairs; she was in a terrible state and said she'd been trying to reach me all morning. She had awakened to find the flower box by her bedroom window overturned and the shrubbery beneath it trampled. Down the side of the house ran two immense slash marks several yards apart, starting at the roof and continuing straight to the ground.

My gawd, how the years fly. Stolidly middle-aged—when only yesterday I was young and eager and awed by the mystery of an unfolding world.

    —Lovecraft, August 20, 1926

There is little more to report. Here the tale degenerates into an unsifted collection of items which may or may not be related: pieces of a puzzle for those who fancy themselves puzzle fans, a random swarm of dots and, in the center, a wide unwinking eye.

Of course, my sister left the house on Indian Creek that very day and took rooms for herself in a downtown Miami hotel. Subsequently she moved inland to live with a friend in a green stucco bungalow several miles from the Everglades, third in a row of nine just off the main highway. I am seated in its den as I write this. After the friend died my sister lived on here alone, making the forty-mile bus trip to Miami only on special occasions: theater with a group of friends, one or two shopping trips a year. She had everything else she needed right here.

I returned to New York, caught a chill, and finished out the winter in a hospital bed, visited rather less often than I might have wished by my niece and her boy. Of course, the drive in from Brooklyn is nothing to scoff at.

One recovers far more slowly when one has reached my age; it's a painful truth we all learn if we live long enough. Howard's life was short, but in the end I think he understood. At thirty-five he could deride as madness a friend's "hankering after youth," yet ten years later he'd learned to mourn the loss of his own. "The years tell on one!" he'd written. "You young fellows don't know how lucky you are!"

Age is indeed the great mystery. How else could Terry have emblazoned his grandmother's sundial with that saccharine nonsense?

Grow old along with me;
The best is yet to be.

True, the motto is traditional to sundials—but that young fool hadn't even kept to the rhyme. With diabolical imprecision he had actually written, *"The best is yet to come."* It's enough to make me gnash what's left of my teeth.

I spent most of the spring indoors, cooking myself wretched little meals and working ineffectually on a literary project that had occupied my thoughts. It was discouraging to find that I wrote so slowly now and crossed out so much. My sister only reinforced the mood when, sending me a rather salacious story she'd found in the *Enquirer*—about the "thing like a vacuum cleaner" that snaked through a Swedish sailor's porthole and "made his face all purple"— she wrote at the top, *"See? Right out of Lovecraft."*

It was not long after this that I received, to my surprise, a letter from Mrs. Zimmerman, bearing profuse apologies for having mis-placed my inquiry until it turned up again during "spring cleaning." (It is hard to imagine any sort of cleaning at the Barkleigh Hotella, spring or otherwise, but even this late reply was welcome.) "I am sorry that the minister who disappeared was a friend of yours," she wrote. "I'm sure he must have been a fine gentleman."

"You asked me for 'the particulars,' but from your note you seem to know the whole story. There is really nothing I can tell you that I did not tell the police, though I do not think they ever released all of it to the papers. Our records show that our guest Mr. Djaktu arrived here nearly a year ago, at the end of June, and left the last week of August owing me a week's rent plus various damages which I no longer have much hope of recovering, though I have written the Malaysian Embassy about it.

"In other respects he was a proper boarder, paid regularly, and in fact hardly ever left his room except to walk in the backyard from time to time or stop at the grocer's. (We have found it impossible to discourage eating in rooms.) My only complaint is that in the middle of the summer he may have had a small colored child living with him without our knowledge, until one of the maids heard him singing to it as she passed his room. She did not recognize the language but said she thought it might be Hebrew. (The poor woman, now sadly taken from us, was barely able to read.) When she next made up the room, she told me that Mr. Djaktu claimed the child was 'his,' and that she left when she caught a glimpse of it watching her from the bathroom. She said it was naked. I did not speak of this at the time, as I do not feel it is my place to pass judgment on the morals of my guests. Anyway we never saw the child again, and we made sure the room was completely sanitary for our next guests. Believe me, we have received nothing but good comments on our facilities. We think they are excellent and hope you agree, and I also hope you will be our guest again on your next visit to the Sunshine State."

Unfortunately, my next visit was for my sister's funeral late that winter. I know now, as I did not know then, that she had been in ill health for most of the previous year, but I cannot help thinking that the so-called "incidents"—the senseless acts of vandalism directed against lone women in the inland South Florida area, culminating in several reported attacks by an unidentified prowler—may have hastened her death.

When I arrived here with Ellen to take care of my sister's affairs and arrange for the funeral, I intended to remain a week or two at most, seeing to the transfer of the property. Yet somehow I lingered, long after Ellen had gone. Perhaps it was the thought of that New York winter, grown harsher with each passing year; I just couldn't find the strength to go back. Nor, in the end, could I bring myself to sell this house. If I am trapped here, it's a trap I'm resigned to. Besides, moving has never much agreed with me; when I grow tired of this little room—and I do—I can think of nowhere else to go. I've seen all the world I want to see. This simple place is now my home, and I feel certain it will be my last. The calendar on the wall tells me it's been almost three months since I moved in. Somewhere in its remaining pages you will likely find the date of my death.

The past week has seen a new outbreak of the "incidents." Last night's was the most dramatic by far. I can recite it almost word for word from the morning news. Shortly before midnight Mrs. Florence Cavanaugh, a housewife living at 24 Alyssum Terrace, Cutter's Grove, was about to close the curtains in her front room when she saw, peering through the window at her, what she described as "a large Negro man wearing a gas mask or scuba outfit." Mrs. Cavanaugh, who was dressed only in her nightgown, fell back from the window and screamed for her husband, asleep in the next room, but by the time he arrived the intruder had made good his escape.

Local police favor the "scuba" theory, since near the window they've discovered footprints that may have been made by a heavy man in swim fins. But they haven't been able to explain why anyone would wear underwater gear so many miles from water.

The report usually concludes with the news that "Mr. and Mrs. Cavanaugh could not be reached for comment."

The reason I have taken such an interest in the case—sufficient, anyway, to memorize the above details—is that I know the Cavanaughs rather well. They are my next-door neighbors.

Call it an aging writer's ego, if you like, but somehow I can't help thinking that last evening's visit was meant for me. Aside from the sundial, these little green bungalows all look alike in the dark.

Well, there's still a little night left outside—time enough to rectify the error. I'm not going anywhere.

I think, in fact, it will be a rather appropriate end for a man of my pursuits—to be absorbed into the denouement of another man's tale.

Grow old along with me;
The best is yet to come.

Tell me, Howard: how long before it's my turn to see the black face pressed to my window?

NADELMAN'S GOD

Nadelman would never forget the first witch he'd ever met.

It had been on a drizzly Thursday evening in November in the early 1970s, in an S&M club called the Château 21. The club was in the basement of a brownstone on West Twenty-First Street, just below one of the Chelsea area's oldest occult bookshops. Upstairs you could buy paperbacks by people with names like Dion Fortune and Ashtoreth Grove, along with crystal-ball key chains, Tarot decks, knives with hairy goat's-foot handles, and little wax figurines in the shape of satyrs. Downstairs had been turned into a barroom, complete with black velvet drapes, wrought-iron candle sconces, and a wall mural depicting a lushly bosomed blonde stretched over an altar. On weekends the place doubled as a classroom for self-hypnosis seminars and aura readings, and on Mondays a group from New Jersey held séances there.

Nadelman and the woman who would later become his wife had taken the subway in from Brooklyn that night in the spirit of adventure, Nadelman dressed in a leather bomber jacket he hadn't worn since college, Rhoda wearing the uncomfortable-looking black leather pants that had caught his eye the day she'd first shown up in them at the ad agency. Normally the Château was closed to non-members, but Thursday night, they'd read in the *Voice,* was open house, when outsiders were welcome to check out the goings-on. Admission was twelve dollars for men, free for women.

Even at that disparate rate, nearly all the customers were men. Most of them appeared to be out-of-town businessmen in search of pickups or simply someone to talk to, or perhaps just a good story to bring back to St. Paul. In the dim light they looked lost and faintly embarrassed. There were only half a dozen women in the room, including a homely girl with a flat pockmarked face who strolled among the drinkers in nothing but black panties, a somewhat dazed smile, and a pair of heavy chains fastened in an X across her sad, sagging little breasts. Imprinted on her left cheek was an upside-down five-pointed star, dark as if freshly branded, though Nadelman was sure it was just Magic Marker.

The room itself reminded him of someone's furnished basement. There was nothing to eat but pretzel nuggets in little tin bowls on the bar, and nothing to drink but cans of beer which the bartender fished from a grey plastic garbage can full of ice chunks swimming in dirty water. Several feet away a plump middle-aged man draped himself clumsily over a bar stool, dropped his pants, and was spanked by a negress as large as a linebacker. The businessmen averted their eyes and looked preoccupied, but the sound of the slaps remained audible throughout the room, even above the heavy-metal music that blared from a speaker in the corner.

The witch was standing by the opposite wall, Budweiser in hand, beside a pile of crumpled empties on the floor. With a beer belly bulging over faded jeans, a T-shirt with the picture of a leering skull beneath the words KILL 'EM ALL—LET GOD SORT 'EM OUT!, and a day's growth of beard darkening into a hairy chest, he didn't look at all like a witch. In fact, he looked more like a Hell's Angel. He was talking animatedly to a small, stocky red-haired woman, jerking his head up and down to emphasize a point, and even from across the room Nadelman could see something glinting in the lobe of his left ear. The '70s were still young and Nadelman not widely traveled; this was the first man he'd ever seen wearing an earring, outside of a pirate movie.

As Nadelman watched, the man downed the last of his beer, crushed the can with a casual squeeze of his hand, and dropped it into the pile at his feet with the absent-minded propriety of a diner tossing down a crumpled napkin. Encircling the redhead's waist, he began walking with her toward the bar, pushing one of the businessmen out of the way with a hard shove of his shoulder. Moments later Nadelman saw them pause and greet the girl with the chains across her chest. She nodded to them familiarly, breasts thrust out for their inspection, a celebrity acknowledging her peers. As she strutted off, the man turned to his woman and shouted something in her ear. Both grinned, the woman with evident distaste, and then they were lost amid the crowd of drinkers.

Nadelman leaned his body against the beer-stained wood of the bar and wondered if it was time to leave. Though he was pleased with himself for having actually ventured into an honest-to-god S&M club, the place saddened and depressed him. Rhoda, seated beside him—as the best-looking woman there she had managed to secure one of the few bar stools—looked up from her drink. "Do you think it gets any livelier than this?"

"Yeah, at the end of the evening they squirt seltzer at us."

"I wouldn't mind if they did. These pants are hot."

"Hiya, hotpants!" said a boozy voice. Nadelman felt himself jostled from behind and turned to see the slob in the T-shirt grinning at Rhoda, his arm still wrapped around the redhead's waist.

Nadelman leaned toward him, feeling his own quota of beers pumping fizzily through his head. "I'm afraid I didn't catch your name."

"Manny," said the other. He stuck out a hand, which Nadelman reached for until he saw that it was still clutching a Bud. "I was just admiring your lady's outfit there." He gestured with the beer toward Rhoda's legs.

Nadelman forced a smile. "And I was just admiring your earring," he said, nodding toward the bit of silver that gleamed in the other's left ear. It was a tiny version of the shape he'd seen earlier, a five-pointed star turned upside-down. The redhead, he saw now, was wearing a duplicate of it. "Nice," he added. "Awfully nice workmanship."

"It fuckin' well oughta be," Manny said, with grumpy pride. "There's only nine like it in the entire world. Me and Tina here know the artist who made 'em." He reached up and touched the earring in a curiously girlish gesture. Nadelman noticed that the back of his hand bore a tattoo of a similar design.

"Does that star have some special significance?"

The man's brows lowered menacingly. "Some special *what?*"

"I mean, is it some kind of symbol?"

Tina gave her companion a questioning glance, while he in turn eyed Nadelman and his girlfriend up and down, as if deciding whether they could be trusted. "Yeah," he said at last, "it's a symbol all right—the symbol of our coven. You know what a coven is, pal?"

"Sure," said Nadelman, on firm ground. Years before, in his sophomore year at college, he had gone on an occult kick, reading everything from John Dee to von Däniken. "It's like a congregation of witches, right?"

"Not bad," said Manny. Tina nodded approvingly.

"And that's what me and Manny are," she said.

"You're witches?" Nadelman tried to keep a straight face. Beside him he heard Rhoda giggle.

"You got it, pal," said Manny. He scratched his belly as Tina draped an arm around his thick shoulders. "It ain't like you're prob- ably thinking, though. I mean, we're not into sacrificing babies and shit like that."

Tina chuckled. "We just do our thing, you know? Live and let live, that's our motto."

"Oh, of *course.*" Nadelman nodded strenuously, the way he always did when he was around crazy, possibly dangerous people bigger than himself. Manny looked well-muscled, the kind of guy who lifted weights in his basement or hefted a lot of tire irons as he worked on his car; or maybe he was just the sort of lower-class type who seems born with muscular, hairy arms, the way smart people are born with bad eyesight.

Rhoda spoke up, a little more emphatically than usual thanks to the drinks in her. "*She's* the witch, right?" She nodded at Tina. "But you yourself would be—what? A warlock? A wizard?"

Manny shook his head. "Uh-uh," he said, "that's just a lot of bullshit people believe. A witch can be a man *or* a woman. War- locks—" He made a face. "That's a whole 'nother bag. Those dudes are into black magic. We're into Wicca, the white stuff . . . unless somebody gets us really, really pissed off!" He laughed, blowing gusts of beer breath into Nadelman's face. "Then boy oh boy, they better watch out!"

"And does it actually work?" said Rhoda.

"Fuckin' A!"

They waited for him to elaborate, but Manny was gazing around the bar, as if looking for friends. Finally Nadelman said, "What's magic done for you two?"

Tina giggled and nudged Manny with her hip. "Helped our sex life, hasn't it?"

He grinned. "Lemme tell you," he said, little eyes darting back and forth between his two listeners, "our sex life don't need no help. My old lady here's a fuckin' sex machine!"

Nadelman stole a glance at Tina, who was smiling as if she agreed. He found himself envisioning steamy occult-type sex with her; there was something arousing about the way the guy could brag about their sex life right in front of her like that. Tina had a solid little figure and looked up for anything, the kind who wouldn't say no to an orgy with a bunch of witches or bikers or whatever, though the notion of all those hairy limbs, beer bellies, and tattoos was something of a turn-off.

"It's hard to put your finger on exactly," Manny was saying, eyes still on Rhoda's pants. "Like, one guy in our coven went out and got himself a better-paying gig, just like that. And another couple was looking all over for an apartment, and like out of the blue, they found one."

"With just an incredible rent, too," added Tina.

Nadelman nodded, disappointed. "That's something, all right."

"But it's more than that," said Manny. "It's also a religion, you know?—like any other religion. We have our worship, our ceremonies, our beliefs . . . " He shrugged; he might just as easily have been talking about his bowling league. "Only we try to get back to the source, you dig? The life-force. Before the Church and all that other shit came along."

"I understand," said Nadelman. "A kind of pre-Christian religion, right? Like paganism?"

"Hey, you seem to know a bit," said Manny, eyeing Nadelman guardedly. "You wouldn't happen to be an initiate yourself, by any chance?"

Nadelman was flattered. "Well, I've done a bit of reading in my time." He searched his memory for names. "Like Aleister Crowley, for instance."

"I know who you mean," said Tina. "The bald guy. They sell his books upstairs in the shop."

"And that fellow Huysmans," said Nadelman, "the one who wrote *La-Bas*." Two blank stares. "And Montague Summers . . . "

"Oh, yeah, I know him," said Manny. "We got some books of his at home. Lots of pages in Latin and German."

"Right, with no translations. I also used to read a lot of super-natural fiction. Lovecraft, that sort of thing."

"Hey, that stuff's not fiction!" said the witch. "No way! That dude was into some heavy shit. Believe me, pal, I know. You better learn how to read between the lines. It's all there—those gods of his, and those demons; the whole Dagon myth . . . " He pronounced it *dog-gone*. "I'm telling you, that guy knew a lot more than he was letting on. You just gotta know what to look for—like I do."

Years later, when the letters began arriving from Huntoon, Nadelman would remember what had so frightened him about the witch: the man's boastfulness, his certainty that knowledge was concealed to all but him, and his earnest faith in the pleasures of revenge.

Boy oh boy, they better watch out . . .

There was a lesson to be drawn from those people in the bar, and Nadelman had not been slow to learn it. The world, he had dis-covered, was full of sad, lonely, pathetic people. They were basically good people, most of them, deserving of sympathy; worthy, even, of respect. But many of them—especially the sort who laid claim to celestial wisdom, preternatural power, magical loopholes in the laws of the universe—were not the sort of people he would care to have as friends. They were too disposed to fantasy, play-acting, and delusion: whatever would lend their dreary lives a bit of spurious drama. For too many of them, the occult was just a bridge between cosmology and kinky sex. They were, in a word, creeps.

In later days he'd met their counterparts in other walks of life. There were the military creeps—Nam-droppers, he called them—with their contempt for civilians and penchant for macho-sounding jargon, and the technocreeps, their conversation larded with intimidating scientific terms. There were religious creeps who'd found Jesus or Jehovah and wanted everyone to know, and survival creeps who'd lectured him on the joys of butchering game. He'd met wine creeps and fashion creeps who worshiped labels, literary creeps who read only experimental novels by foreign authors, and consumer creeps who boasted of bargains no one else had heard about. He'd endured harangues from unsmiling left-wing creeps with schemes to promote a workers' revolution, and from right-wing creeps with stockpiles of weapons in their basements. Genealogical creeps had bragged about their illustrious ancestors, Mensa creeps about their IQs. Astrology nuts at the office had given him worthless tips on the market. Fruitarians at the gym had warned him that everything he ate was poison, even most vegetables. Cabdrivers had assured him that national elections were fixed and that they alone knew who was behind it. Their one common denominator, the single sure mark of the creep, was that they were, every one of them, In The Know, privy to information denied to other mortals or that others were simply too stupid to see.

Believe me, pal, I know . . .

They had banished the questions from their lives, these people; they knew all the answers. But in fact, Nadelman had long ago concluded, they knew nothing, and less than nothing.

Over the years, the witch with the hairy chest had become, in Nadelman's mind, a composite of them all, their elected representative in Congress. Credit the creep with one thing, at least: if Nadelman had had any last flickering vestige of an adolescent interest in the outré, the witch had effectively extinguished it, his grubby fingers snuffing out that final mystic candle. No longer would Nadelman waste time over cabalism, holistic healing, the Thirty-Nine Steps to Power, and the Wisdom of the East; they were merely the banners to which losers flocked. Henceforth the daily battleground of the ad agency would be challenge enough for him, and its year-end raises and midyear bonuses enough of a reward. The woods were full of crackpots armed with mantras and mandalas, volumes of occult knowledge, pipelines to divinity, but he doubted that they dressed as well as he did, or smelled as good, or drove as big a car. Everybody died, after all, holy men as easily as ad men.

This robust philosophy had sustained him over the succeeding decade far more efficiently than art or religion ever had. Once he and Rhoda had lived in Cobble Hill, in a drafty fourth-floor walkup where their bookshelves were of bricks and planks, and roaches ruled the kitchen. Now they lived on the rich side of the river, in a two-bedroom co-op with a $240-a-month parking space in the basement garage. He no longer jogged round the little park near the waterfront each morning, or scribbled strange, desperate poems at bedtime in an old spiral notebook; he belonged to a health club near his office now, where he sweated away the extra pounds on steel-and-leather Nautilus machines, and the last thing he'd written that rhymed had been a jingle for Jergen's Lotion. He had a wife who'd just gone back to work for a computer graphics firm, a son in third grade at a special school for dyslexics, a $220,000 mortgage, and a dachshund. On Fridays after work he had guilty athletic sex in a Village apartment with a Yugoslavian divorcée from the health club. He still had roaches, but then, everybody did.

Huntoon's letter, which arrived midway through the second week of October, came as a minor intrusion. When Nadelman got home from work that night, it was waiting for him, laid out alongside the *New Yorker* renewal notice, American Express bill, and annual Cancer Care appeal that had come in that day's mail. He frowned when he saw it, and, as he read it through, he shook his head and muttered "God!" and "Such a creepy kid!"—though other men in his position might actually have been flattered.

The letter was, at least in part, a fan letter; and as Nadelman immediately realized, it had come to him as the indirect result of a poem he had written twenty years ago in college, during his sophomore-year flirtation with the occult.

The poem, grandiosely titled "Advent of the Prometheans: A Cantata," was one of several that Nadelman had published in the Union

College literary magazine, the *Unicorn*. He had written it as a protest against the compulsory Sunday chapel service that Union, as a Baptist institution, had in those days imposed upon all undergraduates, Christian, Jew, and atheist alike. The poem had been, as he saw it, a kind of metaphoric rock hurled at the ancient chapel's ugly stained-glass windows, with their pious flock of prophets, saints, and Savior.

A more compelling motive, though, had been one of simple imitation: having spent half the year reading books on black magic, followed by a dalliance with Swinburne, Huysmans, Villiers de L'Isle-Adam, and the rest of their decadent crew, from the exquisite, blood-drenched torments of Lautréamont to the batrachian-faced horrors of Lovecraft—in short, all the dark and sinister exotics to which adolescents are drawn—he had set out to write the same kind of thing himself. The resulting work, a paean to some imaginary "leprous-featured rival of the Lord," had had ten distinct sections, each with its own peculiar meter, including a gaudily ornate "Invocation" near the end. It had been the longest poem, and by far the most ambitious, that Nadelman had ever attempted, or ever would again.

No one at Union had been as scandalized by the poem as Nadelman had hoped, since no one at Union actually read the *Unicorn,* save for those few souls whose names appeared regularly on its contents page. (It was popularly known around campus as "the *Eunuch.*") Nadelman's epic would have shared the same fate as the rest of that magazine's offerings—to molder away, forgotten, on some dusty library shelf, or, in the case of Nadelman's own copy, stuffed into an old suitcase in the hall closet amid a jumble of papers, school reports, and tattered notebooks from his youth—if it hadn't been for Nicky Sondheim.

Sondheim, two years Nadelman's senior, had been editor of the *Unicorn* in those days, an intense, fast-talking character with a subversive grin. He'd been the first person Nadelman knew who smoked marijuana; he'd lived off-campus, played folk guitar, and was known to have slept with a professor's wife. Nadelman had revered him as an aesthete and visionary, but had lost touch with him in the years following graduation. Sondheim, he'd heard, had gone on to become a not-too-successful songwriter and, later, a highly successful record producer. Today, in fact, Sondheim was an executive at Warner with several up-and-coming young rock groups in his stable, among them one from Astoria, Queens, that—after calling itself Rumpelstiltskin, the Fireflies, and a succession of similarly uninspired names—was now known to the world as Jizzmo.

Like AC/DC, Iron Maiden, Twisted Sister, and a host of lesser-known bands, Jizzmo specialized in purveying a kind of loud satanic rock that appealed mainly to prepubescent boys. Nadelman's cantata, with its lines about "poison'd kisses," "the lord of dark corruption," and "the hunger of the worm that gnaws," would be just their meat. When, a year ago, it had come time for the group to cut its fourth album, *Walpurgis Night,* Sondheim had gone rummaging through his collection of old *Unicorns* and had seen to it that the group's lead singer, Ray Minor, who wrote most of their songs, got a look at Nadelman's poem. It lent itself perfectly to the type of florid, somewhat convoluted scoring for which Minor was famous. Nicky had also gotten Reinhold Schramm, the grave-looking lab-coated actor on the Phiso-Derm acne cream commercials, to narrate the Invocation; he'd described him to Nadelman, with a laugh, as "the poor man's Vincent Price." After a bit of prudent surgery here and there and the excision of some stanzas on divine retribution, Nadelman's poem had found its way onto the album's second side, where it appeared, retitled, as "New God on the Block," just between "Darn Tootin'" and "Devil of a Time."

Nadelman hadn't even heard of Jizzmo until last winter, when Sondheim had telephoned him, quite out of the blue, to tell him that they were interested in his poem. Since, the way the group sang it, you could barely make out the words unless you strained to hear, and since the money he'd eventually received—twelve hundred and change, plus a point or two if the song ever went single and another if the album went gold—wasn't half as much as he'd initially expected, he had greeted the album's release last spring with little enthusiasm. Nicky had invited him to a party marking the event at Tavern on the Green, where Nadelman and his wife, nibbling on caviar-coated squares of pastry, had been introduced to the various members of the band. Despite their shaggy appearance and the air of sneering menace that their public image demanded, they had struck Nadelman as an ordinary bunch of high school dropouts, good-natured, rather giggly, and no more satanic than the boys in the office mailroom. He had nothing in common with any of them; he could barely remember their names.

Besides, he had better things to do. He was now, at forty-two, one of the best-paid group heads at Sheridan-Sussman, creator, almost single-handed, of the highly successful Nobanana campaign that had taken a nine percent share of the fruit-flavored soft drink market away from Sprite and Seven-Up. (The soda was said to contain the combined flavors of eight healthful fruits, bananas not among them—hence the product's name and also its popular jingle, "Yes, we have Nobanana.") Nadelman had no illusions about the actual social value of his work, but he took a certain pride in doing it cleverly.

It was hard to be proud, though, of being immortalized on a rock-and-roll album—especially in light of the other songs on it, most of them written by Minor, all of them juvenile and silly. Even his own words sounded silly, at least the ones he was able to make out.

The patience of the glacier,
The comfort of a shriek,
The cruelty of the razor
As it slices through your cheek—

Whatever had he been thinking?

He kept a dozen or so copies of the album in his record collection, intending to give them away as joke gifts someday, or maybe sell if they ever became valuable. Nicky had assured him that they might; there was, he said, "an excellent market for out-of-print LPs."

"What an odd phrase for record albums," was all Nadelman had said. "Out-of-print!"

Two of the songs from *Walpurgis Night* had already gone single: "Darn Tootin'" and "Mercy Fuck" (under the abbreviated title "Mercy!"). Thanks to the notoriety of its lyrics, a cleaned-up version of the latter had even made the Top 40—not that that particular

honor was one to which Nadelman had ever aspired; the phrase itself
merely reminded him of middle age.

Unlike the two hits, "New God on the Block" had never become
particularly famous. As the longest song on the album, it had been
considered too unwieldy for a single. Friends occasionally informed
him that they'd heard it played in its entirety—or in a slightly cut
version with the instrumental section in the middle removed—on
certain FM progressive-rock stations, the sort that didn't confine
themselves to singles; but Nadelman seldom listened to the radio,
except to find out how the market was doing, and he'd never once
heard it on the air.

The only mention he'd ever seen of his song had been in a West
Coast magazine called *Hippodrome,* which was dedicated to hard
rock and heavy-metal music and featured earnest articles with titles
like "Freak League Hits the Comeback Trail" and "Mötley Crüe's
Grossest Gig Ever." This year's June issue had had a think-piece by
one Jordan Steinbaum entitled "Satan Calls the Tune?" (Nadelman
suspected that the question mark had been an afterthought inserted
by the magazine's lawyers.) It analyzed each of the songs on *Walpurgis Night* in reverent detail and concluded that the album's central
message was essentially one of "guarded nihilism."

Nadelman would not normally have come across it—he'd never
even heard of the magazine—but Sondheim had mailed him a copy
with a note paperclipped to it that read, "You're famous, kid! See
page 31."

The article had devoted far more space to Minor's song "One
Virgin Too Many" and to a ditty called "Blasted" by the group's
notorious drummer, "Rocco" Roskone. Nadelman's contribution
had been the subject of a single meaty paragraph:

> But for sheer metaphysical chutzpah, Roskone's pagan battle
> cry is the merest whimper compared to the LP's longest cut,
> "New God on the Block," in which Minor's bravura tune-
> smithery and club-honed guitar pyrotechnics provide a solid
> heavy-metal underpinning to the arcane maledictions of a
> non-Jizzmo lyricist, the mysterious "I. Nadelman," described

by Warner publicity only as "a decadent poet and surrealist currently residing in a bohemian section of Manhattan." The song's arrangement, complete with a spoken narration, is a bafflingly complex one, and so are the lyrics themselves, hinting at the emergence of some sinister "rival" deity responsible for all the world's ills—

> *The idol of the abattoir,*
> *The god of cancer, insanity, and pain—*

and, unless these pointed ears deceive me, providing listeners with a list of ingredients, a kind of allegorical recipe, for the construction of a servant in this new god's image, presumably to do it some form of infernal worship. Heady stuff for a sub-teen-oriented group like Jizzmo, and perhaps signaling the direction the band will be taking in the years ahead.

Nadelman had been amused to learn that his East Seventy-Sixth Street neighborhood was a stronghold of bohemianism. Presumably Sondheim had had a hand in that. He didn't know Nicky well enough anymore to guess whether the line had been an ironic joke or merely nostalgia.

Apparently it was the article that had led Nadelman's correspondent to him. A little white gummed label, pasted slightly askew on the corner of the envelope, bore the return address—Mrs. Linia Huntoon, 1152 Locust Court, Long Beach, Long Island, NY—and the silhouette of a tiny red lobster. The *s* in *Mrs.* and the first name had been crossed out by the same heavy childish hand that had written the letter, in a thick black ballpoint pen on pages torn from a spiral notebook, leaving ragged perforations at the edge like a line of broken battlements.

Dear sir,
Your the only I. Nadelman in Manhattan so I sure hope this

letter gets to you. If it falls into the wrong hands I bet we would realy be In For It—right? I figured you were one of those West Coast writers & never thought you could actualy be living so close by to me!!! Well sir enough of that. Your probably a busy man & I dont want to waste your time. I realy have got to take my hat off to you though. You do know what your talking about thats for sure. Ive tried the charts in the Crowley books but they don't work worth sh–t & I used to practice the Bledsoe Color Method & belong to the Astar Society & the E.O.D. but frankly the States Ive gotten into are not all that powerful. And I tried playing that new Judas Priest album backward (you know the cut I mean) on a device I personaly invented but though I heard some hints at Who was up there calling the shots (I dont have to tell YOU—right?) & the last cut on the album has a line I distincly heard about "He waits" & "watch us over" or "watch us suffer" or some such—the rest was not too clear.

Got sick of following Priest after there Jersey City gig. Well sir you cant blame me—right? But Ive been a Jizzmo fan since that dynamite Out/Rage/Jizz album. (By the way are you friends with Rocco Roskone? Whats he like?) The main reason Im writing is I was realy excited by your song. The way you come right out & give those Instructions & all for making that Creature to serve the God. Thats just got to get the others scared shitless dont you think!! I think your really brave for letting out the Process like that—I have been building one of these Creatures on my roof in the Gods image just like you say. It will sure as Hell scare the Bejeesus out of those little pests that keep leaving there sh–t up there & disturbing Mama—so she is all for it!

I have all the necessary Ingredients right here on the beach & will follow all your Instructions. Well sir I know you are a very busy man but theres just one thing I want to ask you—How do I give it the face thats in the song? ("Licorice" is it? Its hard to make it out with all those guitar riffs.) I cant carve a rock like

the song says—there arent even any around here big enough
anyways & the melons I try keep coming out a mess.

    Please write back real fast!!!

Faithful
Your / Follower,
Arlen Huntoon

No doubt the boy had meant this as a fan letter, but Nadelman
found it disturbing. It reminded him of the strangers' letters that
occasionally found their way into the agency, full of rambling com-
plaints about a faulty product, sometimes in tones of deference
bordering on obsequiousness, sometimes making veiled threats or
hinting at a payoff, often veering from sentence to sentence between
these two postures. He usually read them over with a mixture of
pity and revulsion, mentally adding *sic* every few lines. Huntoon's
letter aroused the same reaction; he was sorry that the young creep
had found out his address. At least, though, he didn't live nearby;
Long Beach was nearly an hour away on the Long Island Railroad.
Nadelman himself had spent most of his childhood in Woodland
Park, only two stops earlier on the same line.

The average Jizzmo fan was all of twelve, but this one sounded
older. At any rate, he still lived with his mother, and apparently he
cared enough about her to erect some kind of scarecrow on the roof,
a scarecrow built to Nadelman's design. *"It will sure as Hell scare the
Bejeesus out of those little pests . . . "* Nadelman remembered how, back
in Brooklyn, he'd had to keep scaring away the pigeons that would
try to roost on the ledge of the window by the baby's bed, lest his son
get one of those pigeon-shit diseases Rhoda was always reading about
in the *Times*. Out in Long Beach it was probably seagulls.

"Daddy?" Michael trotted into the kitchen, where Nadelman
had been reading the mail. He was now a few months short of
eight and seldom content just to walk anymore. "See? Look what
I did." Nadelman put down the letter and looked at what his son
was holding out. It was an ordinary wooden pencil with a thin wire
staple protruding from the middle, like a tiny croquet wicket.

"And what might that be?"

"It's a pencil with a handle, so you can carry it with you. I invented it."

"Ah-hah. And very useful, too!" He gave the boy a kiss on his curly hair, remembering how Huntoon had alluded to *"a device I personaly invented."* Perhaps all men were inventors; hadn't he himself invented a god? Nadelman had no clear mental image of Huntoon, but for a moment he pictured him as a shabbier, more distant version of his son, wonder-struck with the awesome possibilities of bending things, fastening things, wiring together the myriad contents of this world.

"I certainly hope you're going to write the child back," said Rhoda at dinner that night.

"Well, I'm not sure that's such a good idea," Nadelman said carefully. "Better not to start with him. Let him think I'm not the Nadelman he wants."

"Aww . . . " Rhoda made a concerned face, the kind that, when she'd made it years ago, at bag ladies and bums, had forced him to realize that she was more than just a sexpot. In some ways he still preferred the sexpot. "Honey, that isn't very nice," she said. "I'll bet it's the first fan letter you've ever gotten."

"And probably the last," said Nadelman, "unless I decide to turn rock star."

"Well, I just think you owe him a reply."

"Yes, yes, I guess so," he said, to avert the chance of any more concerned faces, but swayed as well by the image of a forlorn teenaged version of his son waiting somewhere out in Long Beach for a friendly word.

He carried the boy's letter with him to the office the next day and showed it, chuckling but secretly proud, to two of his colleagues. Then he typed a short reply—one that, by carefully raising no questions, would discourage further communication.

Dear Mr. Huntoon:

Many thanks for your kind letter. It's good to know there's someone out there who enjoys my work. No, I'm sorry to say I don't know Mr. Roskone or any other members of the band. In fact, I don't as a rule follow rock music. As for the question of what sort of face to give your creation, I'm afraid I may have been a bit impractical in having my hero carve "a leprous*-featured visage, hewn from solid rock." Probably the easiest way to make an effective face for the figure would be to buy a rubber Halloween mask and simply put it over one of those melons of yours. Good luck, and hope it accomplishes its purpose!

* not "licorice"

He dropped it in the out bin on his desk and turned, pleased with his efficiency, to other work—a sheaf of glossy product specs for a new frozen dessert with which he had to familiarize himself for tomorrow's meeting, some copy to approve *("I cannot tell a lie. The flavor of Holiday Farm Cherry Treets comes right off the Cherry Tree!")*, a phone call to his broker. Midway through the call, while the broker, never more than a voice on the phone, left to verify the day's prices, a nagging thought assailed Nadelman—*Don't start with these people!*—but he was soon distracted by the man's return and a litany of figures that could spell the difference between a vacation in Dubrovnik or one in Vermont. When he thought of the letter again, his out bin had already been emptied.

There was no one else at the office he could think of to show Huntoon's letter, no one else who'd be anything but contemptuous. Fan letters from semiliterates were, at best, a dubious honor, and though most of his associates were aware that an old college poem of Nadelman's had lately been turned into a rock song, he wasn't sure it was politically wise to remind them of it. They were all failed writers here, after all, and not inclined to look kindly on a fellow employee who dabbled, however humbly, in the arts.

He slipped Huntoon's letter into his shirt pocket, and that

night, after dinner, while his wife and son were in the living room silently absorbed in *All Creatures Great and Small,* he swung open the hall closet and from its depths, smelling of galoshes and ice skates, dragged out the battered suitcase that contained all that was left of his college work. There seemed no more appropriate place to file Huntoon's letter. It would never have occurred to him to throw it away; someday it might provide solace, like an old love letter.

The suitcase, inherited from Rhoda's father, had been elegant once and probably expensive, but now the leather bore a zigzag of scratches, as from a mad scribbler, and the pair of brass clamps that held the two sides closed were stiff with age. As he pried them loose, the suitcase fell open like a book, and a cascade of papers spilled out onto the rug. At his feet he recognized the faded pastel covers of the college literary magazine, several legal pads containing early attempts at composition, and a stack of ancient notebooks filled with lecture notes and doodles. Here, in fact, lying amid the pile, was the very issue of the *Unicorn* in which his poem had first appeared.

Seating himself cross-legged on the rug, he flipped through the magazine's yellowed pages, shaking his head at the thick institutional-looking type (how the crew in the Sheridan-Sussman art department would wince), the uneven leading and margins, the self-important revolutionary rhetoric, and the pretentious "Aesthetick Manifesto" (God, had they really spelled it with a *k*?) with which his friend Nicky had prefaced the issue. ("We seek no wide audience for the expressions herein contained, but rather the informed understanding of a small band of like-minded amateurs of the written word . . . " Christ, could he ever blackmail Sondheim with this stuff now!) The issue's lead story was a thinly fictionalized sketch by some coed from Connecticut about losing her virginity. Nadelman recalled that both he and Nicky had had the hots for her; that intense, fragile quality of hers had had him drooling in those days, but today he'd probably find it exasperating. Strange, to think that she'd be forty now.

Ah, here was his opus—"Advent of the Prometheans: A Cantata." How in the world had he ever arrived at so pompous a title? He didn't even know what the hell it meant anymore, though he recalled laboring over the phrase for hours one night in his dorm room. The "Cantata" part, at least, he dimly remembered; it was taken from some poem he'd had to read for one of his courses—"The Beggars' Cantata," something like that. He suspected that his use of the term was technically, at least, incorrect, but no doubt in those days it had struck him as *le mot juste*.

The poem itself was not entirely pleasant to come back to after all these years; it hardly seemed his own work at all, but rather that of a naive, headstrong young son, tied to him by blood but something of an embarrassment to his old man. He knew that Jizzmo had deleted several portions of the poem from the band's musical version, but he'd never been interested enough to compare the two.

He scanned it now with some trepidation, wincing as his first glance discovered a typo in the opening section's title: "The Divine Impresonation." Jesus, no wonder he'd gone into advertising! There were ten such sections in all, each with its own lofty title preceded by a Roman numeral. How ambitious he'd been then. To think that he'd set out to bring down God!

Indeed, Part One read like a prosecutor's brief against the Lord:

> *A god who stinks*
> *of carrion because*
> *Our blood He drinks*
> *and on our flesh He gnaws.*

He'd had it both ways in those days: capitalizing the pronouns for mystical effect, yet—just for the *frisson*—lower-casing "god" throughout, like one who deliberately mispronounces an enemy's name.

His enemy, of course, hadn't really been God; it had mainly been those damned chapel windows every Sunday, with their saccharine visions of heaven. (He had long ago decided that anyone who could believe in such an afterlife deserved to be sent there forthwith.) His primary interest in writing the poem, in fact, had been a simple and earnest desire to blaspheme. In his own adolescent way, Nadelman had been trying to live up to his name: he'd set out to needle God.

He hadn't needed a reason; young men liked to blaspheme, just as young boys liked to play at being good.

Ironically, for all the passion of his jeremiads, he'd been something of a skeptic even then. Far from actually believing in the cruel new "rival god" described later in the poem, he'd even had his doubts about the old one.

The Lord, in fact, had long since vanished from his life in the same manner as the three gods of his childhood—Santa, the Tooth Fairy, and the Easter Bunny. Even as a schoolboy, despite the rabbi's tedious sermons and the wonders described in his Hebrew texts, there'd seemed no reason to believe in this one god any more than in the others; all were merely amiable supernatural fictions designed to comfort childish minds. Later, in high school, when he'd read Freud's "The Future of an Illusion," he had found it old hat.

He had moral doubts about the Lord, as well. He'd been raised not only on Santa Claus but also on fairy tales, fables, and nursery stories: colorful fantasies in which goodness was invariably rewarded in the end, and evil punished. As a child, he'd believed such things were true. He had also believed—thanks to his childhood picture books, the ones filled with fuzzy felt animals—that the only proper response to something furry was to reach out and pet it.

The world, in return, had proved a bitter disappointment, punctuated here and there by nasty surprises. At age three he had reached out in the garden to pet the enticing yellow fur of a passing bumblebee, and had been rewarded with a wicked sting on the palm of his hand that left it swollen twice its size. At school he'd discovered that there were no heroes: that the weakest lived in terror of the strong, and that God favored the bullies.

Not that he himself had much to complain of; save for the inevitable pains of growing up in this world, his own life had always been comfortable enough. But the lives of others, the ones he saw depicted on the TV news and in the magazines, seemed overwhelmingly tragic. It was hard to have faith in the justice of things when all around him people were dying in curious and terrible ways.

Sometimes, admittedly, the deaths of his fellow men had been easy to accept, merely demonstrating the good sense of the universe. As a boy, he'd heard about an overeager deer hunter who had stumbled over a root and had blown the top of his head off; the tale had merely confirmed the rightness of things. Years later he would hear reports about revolutionaries of one stripe or another who blew themselves to bits while building homemade bombs; he found such stories quite cheering. The cosmos was just, after all.

By the time he'd reached high school, he'd discovered that, with a little intellectual effort, he could justify damned near anything—and it certainly helped stave off despair. Innocent people, it turned out, were in no real danger; it was only the guilty who died. Did cigarette smokers cough their lives away? They'd clearly brought it on them-selves. Did some alcoholic poet drink himself to death? It served him right. When a planeload of nuns went down over the Andes, he told himself that this was what happened to people who tried to jam their religion down other people's throats. Pious do-gooders!

With a few small logical contortions, you could take the game still further. Was a socialite found stabbed to death in her apartment? The empty-headed parasite, she'd probably deserved it. Was a lawyer mugged? We've got more than enough greedy lawyers, thank you. Did a doctor wreck his private plane? Think of all the money that jerk was making! Another OD'ed rock star? How trite! A father of twelve killed by a hit-and-run driver? The thoughtless bastard, who told him to foist all those children on the planet? A family in Utah slain by a tornado? Only schmucks lived out there anyhow.

Sometimes the game became difficult—but doggedly he kept right on playing, if only to preserve his peace of mind. Did old men and women suffer strokes? Maybe they should have exercised more. Were people dying right and left of heart attacks and cancer? Well, he'd make damned sure to watch what he ate.

Then one day, disconcertingly, he'd read about a young Columbia student killed by "youths" in the subway while going to the aid of a stranger. The guy had been the same age as Nadelman, from almost the same background, at the top of his class. They'd even had the same major.

Nadelman, at that point, gave up the game.

Not everyone would have done so, even then. A Job might have convinced himself that all human beings were guilty, he as well as the rest; that all were living here on borrowed time; and that the Lord was therefore perfectly justified in killing anyone He damned well chose. But then, Nadelman had always regarded Job as a hopeless fanatic.

He himself had reached a somewhat more reasonable conclusion: rather than worshiping God as a divine and highly arbitrary executioner, it made more sense to see the position as vacant. There was no one in control up there. The office was empty. Nobody home.

Or maybe (and here was the germ of his poem) there was simply another god in charge, deranged and malign, delighting in cruelty and mischief. How else to explain the things he read about in the *Post*?

For Nadelman, the *Post* was a guilty pleasure. He didn't read it regularly—it was far too downmarket—nor did he ever deign to buy it, but he seldom passed up a chance, when the opportunity arose, to riffle through a copy on the newsstand or on a colleague's desk at the office, or to peer at the headlines over someone's shoulder on the subway. Most issues contained at least one story that, however shocking or appalling, served as a useful reminder of what the universe was capable of dishing out: the couple in their nineties who had taken their own lives when a new landlord evicted them from their apartment, claiming he needed it for relatives (the law, and God, had done nothing); the high school honor student, returning from her after-school job, who'd been accidentally killed by a stray police bullet (the cop had been firing at a mugger, whom the Lord had helped to escape); the social worker who, on her way home from tutoring the blind, had been murdered by a cleaver-wielding psycho (still at large); the little girl who'd died because her fundamentalist parents refused her the medicine that might have saved her life. (The parents had claimed religious freedom, and saw evidence of "divine justice" at work.)

Today, Nadelman knew, the morons who'd shelled out five hundred bucks for a couple of weekends at *est*—there were several of them at the office, each creepier than the last—would probably assure him that we are all responsible for everything that happens to us, even tumors or cellulite deposits, even a loose brick tumbling onto our heads as we stroll down the sidewalk. But it had seemed much more satisfying to Nadelman, as a college sophomore, to blame it all on God—even one he didn't believe in.

The one freshman-level religious studies course he'd been pressured into taking at Union had failed to change his mind (and had also given him his only D). The God whose praises were sung in the Bible simply didn't seem to square with the reality Nadelman saw all around him. The fellow in the Bible could be cruel, vindictive, and jealous—a mean SOB, in fact, especially in the Old Testament—but at least He was, in some harsh, authoritarian way, a just God. Yet despite the propaganda the students were fed each Sunday, Nadelman had seen evidence that another god was at the wheel—"a furtive god," the poem had said, "a greedy god":

> *We struggle for an answer, but no kindly god is there—*
> *Just the deity of cancer, of anguish and despair.*

He frowned now as he read over the verses. They seemed the merest doggerel, like lines from a bad translation. Back in those days he'd apparently thought it cool to stick "ravaged" on the same line as "ravished," and to put *accents graves* over the last syllable of words like "punished," so they'd sound more poetic. And to use, heaven help him, words like "foam-fleck'd" and "slime-drench'd." (Had he really gone in for the apostrophes? He checked the magazine and winced. He had.) A lot of the poem, he knew, recorded nothing more meaningful than some youthful experiments with a rhyming dictionary. He remembered the dictionary itself, a bar mitzvah present from Aunt Lotte, along with an expensive leather notebook whose corner he saw now, peeking from the bottom of the pile.

Nadelman had had enough theology for one night. Getting to his feet, he stuffed the papers back into the suitcase, slipped Huntoon's letter inside, and snapped the bag closed. Shoving it to the back of the closet, he went into the living room to catch the end of *Creatures*. By bedtime the letter was forgotten.

———————

On Thursday of the following week, however, the mail, like a sea forever demanding offerings and casting up unexpected new objects in return, brought a second letter from Huntoon. It was shorter than the first, but considerably more unnerving—in part, no doubt, because of the photograph.

Dear Mr. Nadelman,

　Thank you for writing back to me so fast. Mama says shes going to frame your letter. Weve never had the autograph of an actual author before though I have shaken hands with Joe Elliott of Def Leppard on several occasions & have a signed photo in the dinette of Eddie Van Halen. The mask is a great idea & looks just fine. Itll scare the living sh–t out of those Bravermans!!! (They wont be so "Braverman" then—right?) I couldn't find anything that looked right at the 5 & dime, its all Star Wars crap & Gremlins these days, but I bought a big birds head sort of like a rooster head because of that line in the song about how the Creature "comes before cock crow" & I turned it inside out. It looks damn good that way. You can see it in the picture Mama took. I keep the thing on my roof where the sun can get at it & maybe the god will consent to give it life.

The photograph showed what appeared to be a mass of rotting garbage, the sort that Nadelman had seen washed up by the tide, glistening with grease and reeking of dead fish, when, as a boy, he'd walked the Long Beach shoreline in winter. It lay piled in a roughly manlike shape, arms outspread, like those false aircraft images that New Guineans built out of underbrush to attract passing planes. The figure was lying on the tarry black surface of an apartment rooftop; in the distance Nadelman could see the flat top of a similar building and the peaked roofs of neighboring houses. Jagged things that looked like shards of glass, perhaps from broken windows, gleamed amid its body, especially at the hands. A used toilet-paper roll and gobs of crumpled Kleenex, the former sticking upright like a phallus, showed where Huntoon had dumped the contents of a bathroom wastebasket onto the roof.

It was strange to see a creature from the back room of his imagina-tion—something he'd conjured up in a few scribbled lines conceived in the loneliness of his dorm—take hideous concrete form in the photograph. Looking at it embodied there on the roof made him feel vaguely godlike—but an imperfect, irresponsible god who let others do his dirty work, and who had no real hint of what he had created until he saw it face to face. It was a little like the shock he'd felt the previous year, working on the campaign for a new vitamin-enriched peanut-butter-like spread called Qiffle, when one of his illustrators had first unveiled the strange peanut-shaped creature he'd drawn to go with Nadelman's tag line ("What in the world is a Qiffle!"); or like the feeling he'd had, the uncertain pride and disbelief, when a beaming nurse had first shown him his son. Only this thing was something he'd prefer to disown.

He wondered, briefly, who the Bravermans were, and why it was important they be scared.

At the top of the photo was the thing's head, presumably a melon, though the fruit was concealed beneath a grotesque-looking full-face rubber mask turned inside out. Instead of a bird, it looked like some travesty of a sea creature, an immense, smooth, pink-skinned shrimp, dragged from the depths with mouth sealed over and eye sockets vacant.

Crouched at the head, cradling it like a trophy, was a grinning hatchet-faced man with a black moustache, sideburns, and a long, wolfish-looking jaw. He was dressed as if for winter—it was cold near the water, Nadelman remembered—in heavy gloves and a shapeless green overcoat with a pair of brownish stains down the front. He was holding the thing's head up to the camera like some exultant lawman posed beside the corpse of John Dillinger, or like the sol-diers propping up the head of Che Guevara. The man was easily in his thirties and looked rough, broad-shouldered, and beefy, the sort who wouldn't go out of his way to avoid a brawl. And something

malicious in his smile reminded Nadelman of the witch he'd met
that night in the bar down in Chelsea.

The letter continued:

> Thats me there on the roof with it. No cracks please about
> my ugly mug! Im raring to go & there are certain people wholl
> be sorry they ever chose to cross me. Now all I have to do is
> invoke the god & get it moving.
>
> A.F.A. (A Friend Always)
Arlen

> P.S. Would you mind if I called you up some time? Theres a lot
> you & me should discuss. I know your a busy man & promise
> I will not abuse the privilege.

Nadelman's heart beat faster. So this was his supposed teenaged
fan, the one he'd felt so sorry for. (Or rather, the one Rhoda had felt
so sorry for; another mark against her.) His instincts had been right:
he should never have written back to the fellow. He should have
sensed that wolfish face even in Huntoon's first letter, peering at him
just behind the paper's ragged edges, whispering to him from the
smeared black ink.

And to think that the dumb bastard took Jizzmo's song seriously;
he actually believed that the words Nadelman had cribbed from
a rhyming dictionary and a bunch of college library books were a
magical spell, and was now waiting patiently for the Holy Ghost to
come and animate his garbage pile. Nadelman remembered something Rhoda's analyst had told her: "Reality is never enough for some
people."

He resolved that tomorrow, immediately upon getting up, he
would attend to something he'd been meaning to do for years, what
with clients who felt free to bother him at any hour here at home:
he would get himself an unlisted phone number and keep the creeps
at bay.

The night was chillier than any so far that fall, a preview of November just ten days away, while December, the real thing, lurked just beyond the horizon. Three floors down, among the dim shapes of cars parked on Seventy-Sixth Street, an automobile alarm went off with an insistent animal yowl, no doubt from the mere touch of another car's bumper. Nadelman lay unmoving with his head on the pillow, conscious of the other hundreds of people in the neighborhood who must be waiting, as he was, for the siren to stop. An hour after midnight he heard distant thunder, strange on so cold a night, and probably the last he'd hear till spring. Whipped by the wind, rain slapped against the windows like something solid and alive. He thought of the same rain soaking the thing that lay out there on the roof in Long Beach. Was it no more now than a sodden mass of garbage? Or did it lie there like a corpse?

Rolling out of bed so as not to waken Rhoda, who, over the years of their marriage, had become more and more unmovable in sleep, even as his own became increasingly uncertain, he tiptoed out to the hall in his underwear, closing the bedroom door behind him. In the kitchen he poured a finger of cognac into the "World's Greatest Dad" mug Michael had given him last Father's Day, but after taking a sip he decided it would give him heartburn. Anyway, this stuff didn't do his body any good; he had to stay in shape for his weekly session downtown tomorrow with Cele. Carefully he poured the dark liquid back into the bottle.

From the living room came the sound of rain beating urgently against the windows. He rose and went toward them. From the end-table beside the couch, where remnants of the day's mail were still gathered, he withdrew the snapshot from Huntoon's most recent letter. Studying the blind, smooth-faced thing that lay on the roof, he smiled, remembering a comic-book character from his childhood: "Heap," it had been called, a slithering mass of living garbage, complete with flies and wavy odor-lines. And suddenly he remembered how he'd arrived at the name of his poem. The creature mentioned in its closing stanzas, the servant of the nameless god, had been a monster he'd made up of equal parts Heap, the Golem, and a third figure, one that had given him his unlikely title, "Advent of the Prometheans." He had taken it from "The Modern Prometheus," the subtitle of Mary Shelley's *Frankenstein.*

Like a child frightened of a face staring from the cover of a monster magazine, and who, even in a darkened room, must turn the picture over before he dares give himself to sleep, Nadelman felt an urge to hide the letter and photo in the same place he'd filed the previous one. Opening the closet in the hall, he dragged out the old suitcase again. But once he'd gotten the catch unfastened, instead of slipping the envelope inside, he reached in and drew forth the *Unicorn,* which he opened back to his poem.

Maybe it wasn't quite so bad after all. Maybe he'd had some talent then. The second section, severely truncated in Jizzmo's version, was entitled "A Vision of Decay." It advanced an explanation of the Lord's apparent callousness and neglect. Perhaps, it said, He had simply grown old, senile, weak:

> *A dull grey god of fizzle, fail, and blunder,*
> *Who speaks to us in drizzle, not in thunder.*

In the third section, "Recognition," the poem's narrator decided that the sheer sadism of the god he'd been observing was far too energetic, and too fiendishly ingenious, to be the work of an old, sick, burnt-out god. All the evidence bespoke a new god, a blood-thirsty young upstart, "not mild, / but savage, wild"—"A hyperactive god, too viciously inventive to be sane." Nadelman's intention, at the time, had been to compare the position of the human race to that of beleaguered medieval peasants, hapless pawns in an incomprehensible war between two uncaring lords. As the battle raged this way and that, they suffered the agonies of both sides.

Part IV, "Retribution," had been cut altogether by the band—perhaps properly so, since it amounted to something of a false lead. In it the narrator tried to imagine where this upstart god had come from. Perhaps the old God had created him ("'I'll create Me a Creator,' He would say") in order to punish mankind for its polluted civilization and warlike ways, which spelled ruin for all life on earth. (Nadelman shook his head as he scanned the ringing phrases, remembering the certainties of the early '60s.)

The next section, "Hymn to Corruption," half Swinburne, half Pete Seeger, had been left intact. It wondered if there might be "pollution in heaven, just as here on earth," and if this new god might be some sort of mutation—in short, a true adversary. Such a hypothesis struck the narrator as correct, for the new god appeared to be, in terms of pure hellishness, as powerful as the old: "A rival god who sides with the bullies, the landlords, and the bees."

"Honey, come to bed." It was Rhoda, passing through the hall on her way to the bathroom. He rubbed his eyes and stood, just as glad to put away the poem; but before he closed the suitcase, he took the magazine out and hid it in the end-table drawer.

As he lay in bed, waiting for sleep more resignedly now, he wondered whether he should answer Huntoon's new letter; perhaps it would be wiser to ignore it. He forced the thought away, listening instead to the more soothing voice of the rain. At last, as the rain stopped, he slept, but dreamed that something hovered at his window, a great angelic thing with the face of a bumblebee.

His concern over what to do about Huntoon's letter proved academic, because Friday of the following week brought a postcard from him. The picture on the front showed the deserted dining room of the Sea Glades Manor, "On the Boardwalk at Long Beach, L.I. Providing world-famous cuisine and unparalleled service for over 40 years."

I tried calling you but they said its not a working number. You never wrote back how I could reach you or maybe your letter was lost in the mail but thats OK because by following your Instructions I am now in communication with your God & Hes everything you said. Thanks again for your courage & guidance. Dont worry no ones going to get punished except the ones who deserve it.

Nadelman felt himself sliding further down the feathery slope to the land of unreason. First the creep believed the Rival God was actually real; now he claimed he'd talked to him. Earlier that week one of the ad industry trade magazines had recounted the story— with unalloyed approval—of an Englishman who, writing a history of UFOs, had playfully invented a supposed sighting over Oxford, and of how amused he'd been when, for years afterward, the incident was cited as authenticated fact by dozens of other saucer books. The lie had become real. And a certain Welsh writer named Machen, the article went on to say, had written a story during World War I about the so-called "Angels of Mons," ghostly Saxon bowmen who'd come to the aid of embattled British troops. The story had become a full-fledged legend, with war veterans claiming in later years that they themselves had actually seen these spirits. "All of us in the communications industry can learn something useful from this," the article had concluded.

Nadelman spent that weekend preparing for a presentation on the Holiday Farm account, and on Sunday he took Rhoda and Michael for a drive to a seafood restaurant on the Jersey shore. The next day at the agency, while in the middle of a meeting with one of the creative directors, he was buzzed by the secretary who worked in the corridor outside his office and whose services he shared with his neighbor.

"Mr. Huntoon for you," she said.

Nadelman, his hands full of sketches from the art department, froze.

"He's here?"

"Uh-uh," she said. "Call for you. Shall I put him through?"

"No!" His voice was loud enough to bring conversation in his office to a temporary halt. Dropping a sheaf of cartoons of the boy George Washington wolfing down frozen desserts, he hurried out to the secretary's desk. "Listen," he whispered, "just take a message. I'm not in, and you don't know when I'm coming in. I'm *never* in for that guy, understand?"

The girl nodded as if chastened. Nadelman waited by her desk as she told Huntoon he was out, cursing himself for having blown his cover by writing to the guy on company stationery. He watched her begin to jot down the message on a pink slip, then stop when it became clear she'd be able to remember it all.

"Uh-huh, okay, I'll tell him," she said. "Yes, I will . . . I will . . . Yes, yes, I promise." She hung up and looked at Nadelman. "What a weird guy," she said. "It was hard to hear him. He sounded like he was calling from a bar."

"What was the message?"

She gave a half shrug. "He says to tell you, 'I've got it up and dancing.'"

The meeting did not end until long after five, when the city outside his window had already begun to grow dark. Emboldened by the trappings of his office—the bright fluorescent lights, the serene curve of his steel IBM, the plush burgundy carpet, and the view of the East Side of Manhattan, a world so much higher, and consequently safer, than that of his apartment—with the spires of Pan Am and Chrysler looming beside him like guardians, Nadelman wrote back:

Dear Mr. Huntoon:

You may indeed, as you say, be "in communication" with a god, but I have to inform you that it isn't *my* god. Mine does not exist! It was merely something I made up years ago for a college poem, long before the members of Jizzmo and the rest of those groups were even out of kindergarten. Please understand that I don't mean to disparage your religious beliefs; I'm someone who respects all people's rights to worship whatever gods they choose in whatever manner they choose. That's one of the things that makes this country great. But the particular god you claim you've contacted is just a work of *fiction,* and it disturbs me to see you taking it so literally.

Also, I must ask you to please refrain from trying to call me here in the office. As you noted, I'm terribly busy and cannot allow myself the luxury of personal conversations. My home phone number is unlisted because of the medical problems of someone in my family, and, as I'm sure you understand, I cannot give it out. Whatever you want to do with the scarecrow or whatever it is you've constructed is fine with me, but I have absolutely no interest in the matter and really don't care to be involved. I wish you the very best of luck and suggest that you do not try to contact me again.

He prayed that this would do the trick. Later that evening, as he walked home from the office, he felt dimly oppressed by some menace the streets held tonight, and was sure he'd glimpsed a cloaked, dwarfish creature scurry into a building half a block ahead. He attributed it to his state of mind, until, entering his apartment, he was greeted by the tiny shrieking figure of his son, pirouetting before him in one of Rhoda's old black raincoats, with blood-red makeup on his face and deep black rings beneath his eyes. Behind the boy, smiling, stood his wife, a damp washcloth in her hand. Nadelman realized, with relief, that he had missed another Halloween.

His letter must have crossed Huntoon's in the mail, because on Wednesday of the same week—another stormy evening with echoes of unseasonable thunder, just as if they'd never passed through summer—there was a third envelope waiting for him, weighing slightly more than the earlier ones. It contained a packet of snapshots.

Dear Mr. Nadelman,
    Tried you yesterday at work but they said you were out. Thats like the dispatcher at Val-U-Rite who has no time for me now that Im laid off but Im not saying your in the same boat he is. Did they give you my message?
    These are for you, I think your the one who realy deserves them. Im sure youll recognize Whos in these pictures. I took them on the roof last night but I wasnt sure how to use the flash attachment & it didnt work on all of them. It should be better when the moonlight gets stronger.

There were six photos in all, and they were ludicrous. They looked like the sort of crazy, slightly skewed shots people brought back from fraternity initiations, hunting trips, or Halloween parties, despite the fact that they showed only a single figure—clearly that of Huntoon himself, the over-the-head pink mask concealing his face, dancing on the rooftop in the darkness. His arms were thrust grotesquely in the air, like a broken doll's, and in one shot his right arm was bent behind him in an angle that looked almost painful. In several of the pictures one of his legs was raised like that of a dog about to urinate, revealing a dull brown military boot, the laces loose. He was wearing thick grey gloves that made his hands look comically oversized, except in one shot where they were raised to the sky as if in supplication. Nadelman recognized Huntoon's baggy pants and stained green overcoat from the earlier photo. Despite the man's assertion in the letter, the photos had presumably been taken by his mother—though an old lady (perhaps the mother's friend?) appeared in the background of one of them, solid and kerchiefed like an East European peasant, the flashbulb's glare making her stand out against the blackness behind her as she gazed solemnly at the proceedings. Her face was lined and glowing, her eyes and the eyes of the masked dancing thing flashing weirdly in the light.

Nadelman was momentarily unnerved to discover that across the back of the last photo, Huntoon had written: *Mama.*

Well then, some friend had taken the photos. Even people like Huntoon had friends. Didn't they?

Nadelman kept returning surreptitiously to the pictures all evening—after dinner, between *Taxi* and the news, just before bedtime—as if to a cache of pornographic photos. And his thoughts kept returning to the letter he had sent Huntoon earlier that week. He wondered if the man had received it yet, and if so, whether he'd been hurt by it; and, if he were, what that hurt might portend for himself.

Meanwhile, Nadelman peered out the window of his bedroom as the rain pelted the few remaining pedestrians making their way down Seventy-Sixth Street and the crash of far-off thunder echoed up and down the block. Somewhere great wheels were rolling through the ocean, plunging down some secret track, making their way ever closer to the mainland; he could almost hear them. He got up, stared once more at the face of the thing in the photos on the living room table, and slid the poem from the drawer.

"With lidless eyes and lipless mouth"—that phrase, so annoyingly apt, came from "The Lineaments of Despair," the sixth section of the poem, in which the narrator attempted to imagine what the savage new god must look like. This part Nadelman remembered well. Judging by its handiwork, the god was not a thing of beauty, but must indeed be "a leprous thing." The narrator described it as monstrous, a travesty of other deities, and referred to it throughout the section as "Spider Eyes," "the Mosquito God," and "the Bee." In further defiance of logic, but perhaps in misplaced homage to William Golding, the god was also referred to as "Lord of the Roaches."

The poem's seventh section, "A Celebration," threw in the towel, philosophically speaking, declaring, in effect, You can't fight this new god, or at least you can't defeat him. The narrator instead preferred to celebrate him by building a creature in his image—"A thing to walk among us, and carry on His work":

> I'll set it free to murder and maraud,
> To serve the dictates of this nameless god.

The eighth section was the so-called "Chant of the Fabricant," the part the rock critic had likened to a recipe, in which the narrator, in the tones of an occult Julia Child, exhorted the reader to "Gather garbage, offal, and pollution / From the waste places of the world . . . / From the dumps, the cities' sewers, the dry deserts, / From the refuse of the shore." (Perhaps, mused Nadelman, this was why the song had so excited Huntoon out in Long Beach.) The result was to be mixed together, with a boulder for the head, and shaped into "a semblance of the monster in ourselves."

At last it was time to give the creature life, to release the thing to wander the world and teach humanity the truth. The ninth section had therefore been titled "Prolegomenon to the Creature." Seated in his living room, Nadelman scowled as he must have scowled twenty years before to notice that the section contained another unfortunate typo, perhaps even a malicious one: "a message from beyond the veil of night" had become "a massage." He wondered if anyone else had noticed.

The section also contained the Invocation that the old kraut actor had narrated.

The hunger of the worms that feast
On sacrificial goat.
The yammers of the pious priest
That echo till my song has ceased—
Till he's devoured by a beast
Who tears away his throat!

The god was invited to please breathe life into "my humble creature builded in Your image." Begged the narrator: "Make him truly Your son."

In the final section, "The Creation," the creature rose. It was described: it had its parent's "lidless eyes and lipless mouth" and "poison in its glance, and in its touch"; it was a thing "that fastens with its claws and won't let go."

With a single mad gesture the narrator commanded it—"Rise, thou, and do thy Father's bidding. Teach us to fear."

Here the poem ended. As if to prevent any reader from lingering too long under the spell of its gloomy last lines, it was followed, on the same page, by a breezy drawing of a group of Union students sunning themselves on the lawn beside the college chapel.

If Nadelman thought for a moment that he was out of the woods— and for brief periods at the office on Thursday, he did—he was quickly set straight, for on Friday he returned shampooed and showered from his lunchtime workout at the gym to find a phone message from Huntoon waiting for him:

Went upstairs this morning & the only thing I found was its gloves.

"He said you'd know what he meant," the secretary said, with a tiny lift of her tweezed eyebrows to signal commiseration.

Nadelman nodded. "Yeah, I do. It's good news, in fact." Even as he said it, he wasn't sure, but he forced himself to smile as he rounded her desk and continued into his office, telling himself that it *was* good news. Maybe the thing had been eaten by the birds. Didn't seagulls live on garbage?

That night he stayed out past twelve, ostensibly from having bar-hopped with two old Union alums just in from the Coast, but in fact from having spent a celebratory evening with Cele in her rent-controlled apartment on Ninth Street. Waiting for him on the kitchen table, alongside a tuition bill from Michael's school and an L.L.Bean catalogue, was another postcard from Huntoon, this one a black-and-white view of the Long Beach boardwalk at mid-season—a view that stirred memories of his childhood, even as he read the postmark and realized that the card had obviously been mailed several days before, in response to Nadelman's include-me-out letter. He studied the picture for almost a minute in an effort to put off reading Huntoon's message, searching the boardwalk and beach for a small, skinny boy in the photo that could have been himself.

Giving up, he swallowed and read the card.

I dont see how you can deny the God. He says He knows *you*. He did breathe life into His servant just like in the song & He's everything you said He was. Well you did get one thing wrong, He does have a name. He's called The Hungerer.

Rhoda had, touchingly, been waiting up for him, lying propped up in bed immersed in last month's *Commentary*—something he would never have found Cele doing—or at least pretending to be immersed in it so as to make a pretty picture when he came into the room. Maybe half-consciously she suspected what was going on, harmless though Nadelman swore to himself it was. Either way, he felt guilty.

Or maybe it was Huntoon's little kiss-off that bothered him, that bit about "The Hungerer." Nadelman sensed a wolfish smirk in it, like a tiny twisted vein of poison. It gnawed at him, that phrase. And he knew why, too.

"This sounds absolutely crazy," he told Rhoda, as he sat on the bed after recounting—in just enough detail, he hoped—his evening's adventures at a trio of Yorkville bars. "The guy's really got me spooked. It's like he's reading my mind. I'm sure I've seen that name somewhere before."

"In the rock song?" There was impatience in her voice. He knew she wanted him under the sheets with her.

"No, that's just it. It doesn't appear in the song, I'm sure of that. And it's not in the *Unicorn,* either. But somehow I still associate it with the goddamn poem."

She looked blank, unwilling to be drawn into the game. "So?" she said at last. "Where's it from?"

He shrugged. "I just don't know. It could be in my original typescript."

"But you would have handed that in to the magazine."

"True, but I may still have the carbon."

Until uttering those words, he hadn't decided on what he would do. But now he realized that he couldn't go to bed without assuring himself that Huntoon was mistaken. Guiltily he stood, promising his wife he'd be back in a few minutes, but knowing she would probably be asleep by the time he returned. It was just as well; he doubted he could summon up much passion for her tonight anyway.

"Close the door when you go out," she said tonelessly. Before he had shut it behind him, she had already snapped off the light.

He had no trouble finding the carbon of the poem; right below the stack of old *Unicorn*s he saw it, a sheaf of onionskins fastened with a rusted staple. One seldom came across such things anymore in these days of the Xerox machine. He recognized, in the smeared black ink, the slightly uneven letters of his old second-hand Royal portable.

He scanned the poem quickly, though carefully enough to see that it was the same as the published version. There was nothing in it, not a single line, about the Rival God's having a name. The discovery came as a relief: Huntoon stood revealed as just another madman, not even in touch with reality, much less with a god.

He was about to put away the suitcase once again, but the thought of rejoining his wife, of tiptoeing back to that darkened room and sliding sheepishly into the bed where she lay angry and unfulfilled, made him pause; or perhaps it was simply that he knew he'd blame himself if he gave up the search so soon. He would have to go all the way back to his original draft. It was worth the extra effort to make absolutely sure Huntoon was wrong.

Below the carbon typescript—bless his retentive nature!—was a yellow legal-sized pad containing the handwritten draft of the original manuscript. He could see, even at the top, that he'd tried out several different titles: "Return of the Master." "Advent of the Master." "The Post-Modern Prometheus." "The Eighth Day of Creation." How solemn he had been in those days!

The long yellow sheets were a rat's nest of scribblings and cross-outs. Why, he wondered, had he bothered to save such stuff, this evidence of an inconstant purpose, of a disordered mind? Probably out of the same sense of self-importance that had led him to write the poem in the first place. He'd believed—hoped, at least—that someday someone would want to retrace step by step, phrase by phrase, his proudest act of creation. But he'd never expected that the someone would be him, and with so insane a purpose.

How obsessively he had fussed with the wording. Almost every line in the poem had undergone minor variations and alterations. "The idol of the abattoir" had started out life sans alliteration as "the idol of the slaughterhouse." The "god who stinks of carrion" had debuted more crudely as "a god who reeks of rotting meat"; no doubt he'd found "carrion" more poetic and hadn't been able to come up with a suitable midline rhyme for "reeks." (Listed in the margin beside it, shamelessly, were *beaks, cheeks, leaks, peaks, speaks, shrieks,* each one neatly crossed out.)

Funny, the things that had concerned him as a young man. There'd been lots of shuffling between "a god that" and "a god who," as if it were a matter of great moment. Curiously, one of the lines describing the creature—"That fastens with its claws and won't let go"—had originally been "that fastens with its claws and *can't* let go." The latter image was curiously disturbing; he wondered how he'd ever come up with it.

He was about to put the yellow sheets away when he came across a discarded line from the bottom of the seventh section. Above the couplet that, in the final draft, he'd settled on—

> *I'll set it free to murder and maraud,*
> *To serve the dictates of the nameless god.*

—he saw an alternate line that he'd rejected, perhaps for want of a proper rhyme. There it was, right beside the newer version, carefully crossed out with three blue lines through it—his original thought:

> *To serve the dictates of The Hungerer.*

For a moment, his eyes refused to focus on it; the pages seemed heavy in his hand. He remembered something Nicky had once told him back in college, about how you could disprove thousands upon thousands of phony haunted-house stories, reports of apparitions, UFO sightings, claims made by psychics and charlatans—but if even a single ghost or spell or saucer could truly be proved to exist, that one example would change everything forever. Grant the reality of a single spirit and you found yourself faced with an entire cosmos of them. And it dawned on him, suddenly, that this was what had happened—that, in an instant, everything had changed: those two small words that stared at him from the page, eleven scribbled letters barely an inch long, had punched a single tiny hole in his universe, like the hole at the bottom of a bucket. He sat there, staring dumbly, as all his certainties leaked out.

Just as quickly, he reached for explanations. These pages he'd been studying—might Huntoon, somehow, have seen them too? But where? Not even the editors of the *Unicorn* had seen this early draft. Nadelman himself had forgotten what was in it, much less that he'd ever penned that phrase.

The Hungerer . . .

What was it Huntoon had claimed? "He knows you."

Impossible, he told himself. *Impossible!* He just plain wasn't going to admit it into his world. He felt a sudden affection for the yokel in the old joke, the one who, visiting the zoo, gazes wide-eyed at the giraffe towering above him, higher and stranger than anything in creation has a right to be, and declares, "There ain't no such animal."

From outside came a low metallic scraping, followed by a clatter. It sounded as if it had come from just beyond his window, but he knew how sound carried in the city; three floors up was just like being on the sidewalk. He stood and peered down from the hall window. A trash can was lying on its side in the street, its lid beside it, like a mugged man whose hat had been knocked off. Vandalism, and for no reason except that the kids knew they got away with it these days; last week they'd painted swastikas on the old grey temple two blocks to the west and had smashed one of its rosy stained-glass windows. Well, he'd felt like smashing windows himself once. Above the street the narrow strip of sky was overcast, with no light but a cloudy yellow smudge that might have been the moon.

Warily he turned back to his problem, as if to an opponent who, while he'd lingered at the windowsill, had been standing behind him, waiting patiently. The possibility that Huntoon was right—that there *was* a being out there, that it had spoken to him, that all the words of Jizzmo's song were true—was just too preposterous to consider. After all, dammit, hadn't he himself made the whole thing up? He even remembered the circumstances of the writing: his dorm room, his desk shoved up against the wall at one end and his roommate's at the other, each with its own depressing little gooseneck lamp; the dreary winter afternoons, coming back from the library with an armload of poetry anthologies to inspire him, volumes he'd be bringing back the following day; the snow against the window as he typed the final draft, painstakingly whiting out his mistakes, as if the snow were covering his tracks. He'd been touched by no divine inspiration; the poem had been a thing of lowly choices, word after word. The influences on it were easy enough to trace; he could point to the origin of virtually every line.

The reference to the Fabricant's "living up an alley / in a house with poisoned glass" had been based on a boyhood superstition in his town, something about an old abandoned house near the ocean reputed to have "poison windows" it was dangerous to break. (The tale had probably been started by some real estate agent.) The creature with "its arms stuck from its head" had been a family joke—a bedraggled old stuffed seal that Nadelman had owned as a child, and which had been repaired this way after most of its stuffing had been lost. The monster's "lidless eyes and lipless mouth" had been inspired by one of the corny horror movies they'd shown at Union on Friday nights, probably the one about the Black Lagoon. The line about "The god of Mars, of battles lost and won, / Who gives us stars but takes away the sun"—that had been lifted from Swinburne. He was certain of this because next to it he'd written *Swinburne, p. 59.*

The page number, he knew, referred to the old leather-bound notebook, his aunt's bar mitzvah gift. He retrieved it from the pile. Originally it had come equipped with one of those slim silver Mark Cross pens that were so uncomfortable to hold, but now the loop was empty. So were half the pages of the notebook; years ago he had turned to other projects and never gone back to it. On page 59 appeared the lines

> *The lord of love and loathing and of strife*
> *Who gives a star and takes a sun away*

from Swinburne's "Atalanta in Calydon."

Idly he flipped through the earlier sections of the book, marveling at how little his handwriting had changed over the years. He was still the same boy who'd written, "Wonder if the high school yearbook is the only thing I'll ever get to autograph," and "If God's so great, how come Rabbi Rosen smells like old potatoes?" There were dozens of fantasies about girls—"Linda all the more naked because of her freckles," "Margie D., nipples like a baby's thumbs"—and quotations from whatever he'd been reading, from *Kidnapped* to *The Catcher in the Rye.*

He had gone through the notebook while composing his poem, ransacking it for images and ideas, much as Coleridge had done before he fell asleep and dreamed up "Kubla Khan." And obviously the book had proved a treasure trove. Here, on page 46, was the story about the brain's resemblance to a Portuguese man-o'-war, which he'd used in the Chant of the Fabricant. Earlier, on page 40, was the note about man-eating plants "that slide up travellers' nostrils whilst they sleep"; it had appeared in his Hymn to Corruption. The references to "the Insect God" in the same section of the poem had come from an anecdote on page 33, which he'd written on a mosquito-plagued camping trip in Maine.

On the page just before it was a Mencken quotation that had obviously influenced him—it spoke of "a Creator whose love for His creatures takes the form of torturing them"—and beneath it lay the lines from *Melmoth the Wanderer* that had given him the "Who goes there?" passage in Part III:

> Who is among us?—who?—I cannot utter a blessing while he is here. I cannot feel one. Where he treads, the earth is parched!— where he breathes, the air is fire!—where he feeds, the food is poison!—where he turns, his glance is lightning!—*Who is among us?—Who?*

From the street came a squeal of brakes and, with it, the blare of a horn. He got to the window in time to see a car's retreating taillights as it sped toward Second Avenue. The early-morning clouds had parted, and a chilly moon a few days short of full hung just above the tenements at the poorer end of the block. The street in both directions was deserted, save for movement directly below him as a lone figure hurried past his building, so close to its base that Nadelman could barely see more than a flash of green coat and a gleaming pink bald skull. Something shiny in the figure's hand caught the light as he rounded the corner of the building, heading toward the line of stores, parked cars, and pay phones on the avenue.

Frowning, Nadelman returned to the notebook, wondering about that large pink skull. Surely Halloween was over.

Studiously keeping the night's unanswerable questions sealed off from the rest of his thoughts, as if in a tiny water-tight bag, he plunged back into his literary excavations, moving further into the past. On page 27, in the midst of some passages of nature description, he was struck by a pair of lines whose diction seemed to foreshadow that of the poem.

> *With enemies who tremble at His glance,*
> *And followers who shamble at His feet.*

He hadn't realized that his ideas had been germinating for so long; he couldn't have been more than sixteen when he'd written that entry. Three pages before it, he found the same thought in a slightly different form:

> *He cometh. The ground doth shake. His enemies fly before Him.*
> *His followers shamble in His wake.*

A similar reference, expressed somewhat more primitively, appeared on page 22:

> *He wakens. Come He will:*
> *A rival god who means us ill.*

And even earlier, on page 19:

> *There's something up there who means to do us harm.*

It was on page 11 that he saw it—two simple words on a line all their own, written without explanation:

> *The Hungerer.*

He sat there dumbfounded, the words burning themselves into his brain like a squiggle of hot wire.

Suddenly the cheap plastic one-piece telephone hanging from the kitchen wall gave a single startled chirp, echoed immediately by a ringing from the bedroom.

Nadelman was on his feet and dashing toward the kitchen before it rang again, hoping it hadn't awakened Rhoda and fearful that it might, just might, be Cele, reaching out to him in the grip of some post-coital passion. He yanked the thing from its plastic cradle.

"Hello?" His voice was louder than he'd intended, and the silence afterward stretched on too long. "Hello?"

There was no voice in reply, just the sound of wind, a hint of far-off traffic.

He was about to whisper Cele's name, when it occurred to him that it couldn't be her on the line; he intentionally hadn't given her his new unlisted number. Softly he replaced the receiver.

This is crazy, he told himself. He'd had the number changed less than two weeks ago and was already getting crank calls.

Perhaps it was the thought of cranks that triggered it—the sudden suspicion of who the caller had been.

Huntoon, of course; who else? The unlisted number was clearly no hurdle; if the man was able to divine what lay buried in Nadelman's old notebooks and to fathom a god's secret name, he could certainly figure out a phone number. Maybe, in some mysterious but no doubt perfectly logical way that would someday be explained by science, he'd contrived to read Nadelman's mind.

Unless, perhaps, he had somehow managed to gain entry into the apartment . . .

Nadelman's eyes strayed to the window, but he was thinking again of the phone call. What he'd heard in the background had been traffic, he was sure of it. On impulse he returned to the kitchen and peered through its grimy side window overlooking the corner and, across Second Avenue, a lonely pair of pay phones. Squinting, he moved closer. At first it looked as if there were a body curled at the foot of one of them, but the headlights of a passing car revealed that it was only a sack of garbage someone had left piled there.

He was tempted to call Huntoon back and talk to him—there were so many things he needed to ask—but it was far too late at night, especially with the guy's old mother probably asleep hours ago. He contented himself with muttering *"Creep!"* for the dozenth time that night and resolved to phone Huntoon in the morning.

He returned one more time to the notebook, wondering what in the world had possessed him to write that stark, disturbing name in the middle of page 11. One thing he noticed, as he studied the pages that preceded and followed the entry, was that this particular section was filled with childhood dreams. Maybe he had recently read a paperback on the subject, or maybe it was the influence of some friend at school; in any case, he appeared to have been much taken with his dreams in those days, faithfully recording them each morning in all their perplexing detail.

He read through a few such entries. *"In a meadow, like the one at camp, only there's a city at the edge of it . . . " "In study hall, it's really hot, and then this girl comes in . . . "* He soon gave up. They were alien, boring, like the dreams of another person. They meant nothing to him.

He forced himself to read a few more. Despite the subtlety and detail with which his daytime fantasies were composed, most of his dreams tended to be trite, childish affairs, the crudest of melodramas, like fleeing from a lion, or holding a bear at bay on the other side of a door. The most common of all, whose meaning needed no explanation, involved wandering through the corridors of a large institutional building searching vainly for a bathroom.

He envied those whose dream worlds were built on a grander scale, opulent and colorful as a Hollywood epic—like Lovecraft's, which provided the plots of his stories, and Fuseli's, which were so vivid the artist would eat red meat before going to bed in the hope of inducing them. Kubla Khan's Xanadu, the subject of Coleridge's grand dream, had itself been inspired by another dream half a millennium before, the Emperor having conceived its design in his sleep, complete with stately pleasure dome.

Maybe, in the same way, he himself had conceived of "The Hungerer." Perhaps those very words had been the product of a dream. Was that why he'd committed them to his notebook? Now that he thought about it, he did seem dimly to remember waking up one morning and jotting the phrase down, just as he'd done with other dreams.

Or was this simply his imagination? Why, after all, would he have scribbled two mysterious words and stopped right there?

Behind him, in the kitchen, the telephone emitted another chirp. He jumped to his feet and answered it.

"Hello?" His voice, this time, was guarded.

No answer. Again the whisper of traffic, then a closer, more intimate sound, like the soft, deliberate, liquid stir of mud—mud opening its jaws, yearning to speak words. A tiny click now, and someone breathed directly in his ear. "Hello?" It was his wife's voice, hoarse from sleep. He heard the shift of sheets.

"It's okay, honey. Just a crank. Go back to sleep."

He heard a muffled crackling, as of crumpled paper pressed against the speaker of the phone. He doubted it came from the bedroom.

"Hang up, honey. It's okay."

He waited until she got off the line, then gave vent to his fury. "Listen," he said, trying to keep from shouting, "I know it's you, Huntoon, and it isn't goddamn funny. You want to talk? Okay, good—let's talk!"

He waited. There was no sound.

"Okay, schmuck, have it your way! I'm just going to call you back, and I don't give a shit if I wake up your mother."

Trembling, he hung up, then picked up the phone again and dialed 516 information.

There was an unexpected delay in finding the number. "No," the operator said at last, "we have no one by that name in Long Beach. Are you sure that's the right spelling?"

Then Nadelman remembered: there'd been no return number on either of Huntoon's two phone messages. In fact, the secretary had said something about his sounding "like he's calling from a bar." Maybe the guy had no phone. Maybe he always called from phone booths . . .

Nadelman hurried back to the window. There was no one standing at the pay phones on the corner. Even the bag of garbage that had been lying there was gone.

The kitchen suddenly felt very cold. All he wanted now was to slide into his cozy, wife-warmed bed. Wearily he scooped up his college papers, like a child putting away toys, and dumped them back in the suitcase. He stared at the notebook for a moment, knowing he didn't dare reopen it, then laid it on top of the magazines.

He flipped one last time through the scribbled yellow manuscript of the poem. Here, in this hodge-podge of handwriting, cross-outs, and arrows, was the jungle where the monster lurked.

On the next-to-final page, right after the Invocation, another crossed-out passage caught his eye—not just a line, this time, and not merely rearranged wording, but an entire four-line rhyme; imprisoned on the page behind a row of heavy X's, it had never made it into the typed version. Aside from the god's name, it appeared to be the only element in the poem that had been totally altered. The substituted passage, printed neatly beside it, was much easier to read—"Success at last! / Across the miles of space / Appear the vast / proportions of His face"—but Nadelman could just make out, through the latticework of X's, the original lines:

The ritual works!
  The god at last breaks through—
A god who smirks
  and says, "The joke's on you!"

Saturday, drizzly as somehow it had to be, he slept late, as if unwilling to leave the world of dreams, however shabby they might be compared to Kubla Khan's. He lay in bed long after Rhoda had gotten dressed and gone off to her indoor tennis lesson, then spent the afternoon with Michael, whom he'd promised to take to Macy's for new boots and another in a long line of pocket video games. All day, so much that even the boy noticed, he remained grave and uncommunicative, weighing how he was going to deal with the new facts in his life, like one who's just received bad news from the doctor.

On Sunday, a day set aside for visiting Rhoda's parents in New Rochelle, Nadelman bowed out of the expedition.

"I've got to confront this Huntoon character," he said over

breakfast. "The creep's driving me crazy. He's a terrible pest, and he could mean real trouble someday."

"I'm worried about you going out there all alone," said Rhoda, solicitous in a way she hadn't been in years. "How do you know he's not dangerous?"

"Well, he seems to take awfully good care of his mother."

"Sure," she said, "and good care of his record collection. That doesn't mean anything. I just don't think it's a smart idea to go challenging people like that. You don't know what he might be capable of. I've read those letters."

"Look, I'm not going to challenge the guy," said Nadelman. "I'm going to be very, very nice to him. You know how nice I can be, once I get going."

"I'd almost forgotten." She gave him a worried smile. "What bothers me is the thought of him getting you inside his house. Why don't you just meet him at some coffee shop somewhere? Wouldn't that be safer?"

"I keep telling you, honey, he doesn't have a phone. I have to go inside just to talk to him."

"Well, if you still insist on schlepping all the way out there, at least don't stay long. Just poke your head in and tell him to come for a walk or something. I don't like the idea of you going inside that house. God knows what he's got in there."

"What's he got in his house, Mommy?" asked Michael. He waited in vain for an answer. "What's he got in his house, Daddy?"

"I've heard he's got all the handkerchiefs you keep losing," Nadelman said, pushing himself back from the table. "And all the gloves."

Michael gave a shout of laughter until Rhoda hushed him. "Sweetie, go inside and get your shoes on. We don't want to be late to Grandpa's." Once he'd left the room, the worry returned to her face. "Honey, I mean it. Promise me you'll speak to him outside. And don't let him take you on that roof."

"I promise," he lied.

———

He drove the two of them to Penn Station, then kissed them both goodbye as he slid from the car and left the wheel to Rhoda. Watching them drive away, he felt a quickening sense of excitement, as if he were a boy setting off alone on an adventure, in pursuit of some unknown he would have to face squarely, eyeball to eyeball, the way Davy Crockett had grinned down bears. His train, waiting noisily for him in the depths of the station, was a great silver tube that would carry him to the sea—and to knowledge. As he found his seat and heard the doors slide irrevocably shut, he felt his heart beat faster, and reminded himself that he was merely going to see a man who had somehow managed to read his mind. It had to be a trick—and one he had to learn.

He settled back in his seat with *Advertising Age* and *The New Yorker,* and only when the conductor came to take his fare did he notice the woman seated across the aisle from him, idly picking her nose as she sat immersed in a paperback. On her left cheek, jagged and obscene-looking, was an upside-down five-pointed star. Life had clearly taken its meat cleaver to her—her face was lined, the skin sagging and roughened—but he recognized her, after a moment, as the homely, pockmarked girl he'd seen ten years before in the S&M bar in Chelsea. Only then she had been naked from the waist up and had worn a pair of chains across her chest. Now she sat bundled up like a child in a light blue quilted ski jacket. The design on her cheek now looked old and pale instead of dark, like the scar from a bygone operation. Wrinkles had formed amid the lines of the star, like vines growing over a trellis.

Jesus, he told himself, it really *had* been a brand! These people were for real. He was intrigued to see her in mufti, looking so ordinary, and to think that he alone knew her secret. Unattractive as she was, he found himself aroused by the memory of those small naked breasts. How bizarre she had looked, there in the crowd; how brazenly she'd marched from man to man! Was there anything a woman like this wouldn't do?

Leaning in her direction, he attracted her attention by waving the magazines. "Excuse me," he called, "didn't I once see you in a bar on Twenty-First Street?"

She glanced up with none of the suspicion a normal woman might have displayed. "You mean the Château?"

"That's right."

She grinned, showing her gums. It was not a pretty grin; her teeth were long and yellow. "Yeah, that was me," she said, her face a mixture of embarrassment and pride. She'd been sitting next to the window, but now she slid into the aisle seat. "Wow, I'm so amazed you recognized me." She pronounced it *reckinized;* there was more than a hint of Brooklyn in her voice.

"Well, you made a pretty strong impression," he said, reluctant to tell her he had merely recognized the brand.

"I don't think I recall you," she said. "Were you a member?"

He shook his head. "No, in fact I only went once."

"I went every Thursday night," she said proudly. "I never missed a single open house, as long as the club lasted."

"It closed down?"

"Oh yeah, years ago."

He nodded politely, wondering who else in the car might be listening to their conversation. "I'm sorry to hear that."

"I'm not," she said. "I haven't been part of that scene in years. I'm miles beyond that now."

He stared at her. "You mean, even rougher stuff?"

"No, I'm trying to channel more energy into the spiritual side of my nature. That other bullshit, it was like eating junk food, you know? What I'm doing now is getting integrated with who I once was."

"Ah." Nervously he clutched his *Ad Age*.

"I found out that I used to be a sorceress in a tribe of Celts."

Nadelman nodded, smiling, but he was already depressed.

"And before that I was a sibyl in a pharaoh's court."

"Amazing!" It was invariably the celebrities these people claimed to have been—never the commoners, the peasants, or the slaves. "And where are you off to now?" he asked. "Some kind of meeting?"

"Oh, no," she said, giggling, "I'm seeing my girlfrin' Linda." The phrase came out like a single ceremonial title. "She used to work in my department at Loeser's, but she got a job with the phone company and I haven't seen her since summer. I get off at Kew Gardens, she's only four blocks from the station." She paused, twirling a strand of hair around her fingers. "Where you going?"

"Out to Long Beach," he said.

"That's a long way's away." She thought a moment. "My friend's grandmother got put in one of those nursing homes out there. You from there?"

He shook his head. "I haven't seen the place since I was around ten. I had an aunt who rented a house near the boardwalk, and my family used to visit in the summer. We lived a couple of towns over, in Woodland Park."

"Oh, sure," she said. "I know where that is." She picked at something on her nose. "You stopping there, too?"

Nadelman shrugged. "I hadn't planned on it."

"You should. Believe me, it's no good to lose contact with the past—bad things can happen. You get cut off from things."

Her stop had come. Standing, she smiled her toothy smile and patted the book she'd been reading so that Nadelman could see the title: *Discover Your Past Lives*.

He hadn't been back to Woodland Park in—how many years had it been? His family had moved to Rye in the late 1950s—around two years after his bar mitzvah, he recalled—and just before his mother had retired to Florida in '77 she'd made a trip back there on her own. She had wanted him to accompany her, but there'd been some kind of crisis at the office and he'd been unable to get away. That's right, the Ocean Spray account, which had later fallen through. So how long had it been? . . . God! Nearly thirty years.

The train reached Woodland Park shortly after one. The first thing Nadelman noticed was that they had modernized the station. Stepping from the train, he wondered if anything from his childhood would be left. He had checked the timetable and knew he'd have nearly an hour and a half to walk around. Whistling tunelessly, he buttoned up his coat, dug his hands in his pockets, and headed toward the main street of the town.

Two blocks from the station, he passed his old brick grammar school; it was still standing, like some huge empty monument to his childhood. The building looked the same as he remembered it, but a decade ago, with the post–Baby Boom shortage of children in the area, it had been turned into an administrative center; the playground, he could see, was now a parking lot, inhabited only by ghosts. Its high metal fences, today guarding nothing but a Mercator-like grid of white lines, had once enclosed a microcosm of humanity: lovers, adventurers, bullies and their victims, team players, compromisers, and, somewhere, the misfits. Nadelman walked on, not caring to look back; thank heaven Michael went to a small school.

The village looked much the same too, though once again it was only the buildings themselves that stood unchanged; the individual signs they bore were new. The bright front windows of a computer store and a shop that sold nothing but jogging shoes made a strange contrast to the old brick buildings that housed them, like modern pictures set in ancient frames, but it was the frames that interested him more. He saw, above one window, a plaque that said "1943," and his heart beat faster. That woman on the train had been right; he was glad he'd come. He had made a great unexpected loop in time, returning himself to the center of things.

Still whistling, he left the village behind and strolled past blocks of suburban homes that looked cozy and secure against the grey November sky. The front yards stood empty today, except for a teenager in one of the driveways, waxing his Toyota. The rest were probably inside watching football. Recognizing the outlines of a wide Queen Anne–type house that stood on the corner, Nadelman turned down the curving little lane where he had lived, forcing himself not to break into a run as he passed two more large homes, a smaller red Cape Cod, a row of evergreens; he was trying to prolong the anticipation.

But as he came to his own block, he saw at once, with a pang, that all the homes along one side—his house and three neighboring ones—had been replaced by a line of new split-levels, their lawns quite bare of trees. He walked for several blocks more, then doubled back, searching like a lost dog for the scent of home. But there was no getting around it: the old house was gone, and with it a large chunk of his past. Memories had been lost that could never be reclaimed.

And yet the past was here, all around him now; he could feel it, he could smell it in the faint scent of the ocean. As he walked tiredly back toward the station, already thinking of the water that lay miles ahead, he told himself that he was traveling toward the one dependable element from his boyhood, the one thing history couldn't change.

Long Beach was just over the bridge, on an eight-mile-long sand bar running parallel to the mainland. The railroad station stood near the center of the main commercial avenue, lined with banks, shopping plazas, and synagogues. Nothing looked familiar.

It was after three by the time he located Huntoon's street, as far inland as one could get on that narrow strip of oceanfront suburbia, several blocks up from the old wooden boardwalk that connected the town's residential hotels and nursing homes. Locust Court was a dowdy little pocket of garden apartments and multifamily houses, a world of privet hedges, peeling paint, and narrow, broken sidewalks. Even on this cold November afternoon, the air held a hint of sour cooking smells, like the hallway of a tenement. The street was deserted except for a wrinkled old man in a ski jacket and felt hat with earflaps, his breath visible as he bent to gather the dead leaves and trash that had accumulated beneath the sagging green wire fence bordering one of the private homes. From somewhere behind him came the faint sounds of a playground, though Nadelman didn't remember passing any children. In the distance he thought he heard the pounding of the surf, but maybe it was only the wind. He was all turned around here, in this landlocked little enclave, though he was fairly certain that beyond the furthest row of rooftops, the ocean began.

Number 1152, the shabbiest house on the block, was a half-timbered stucco building that stood flush with the sidewalk. Two cars were parked in the driveway, its sparse gravel overgrown with weeds, and another two were visible in the open garage in the rear. He wondered if one of them was Huntoon's.

That name appeared at the top of a column of doorbells, like the grand prize question in a quiz show. Nadelman pressed the bell, noticing, as he did so, the name immediately below it—Braverman. Those must be the people Huntoon was so eager to throw a scare into. Neighbors.

He was just about to ring again when the door gave a loud, unsteady buzz and admitted him. The front hall, masked by shadows, looked badly used, like a child's playroom. Someone had crayoned a crude design on the wall, the image of a dog defecating. As he climbed the narrow stairs he heard, four flights above him, the sound of a door being opened.

"Arly?" It was an old woman's voice, but it still had muscles in it. "You forgot the key?"

He paused on the stairs. "Mrs. Huntoon? I'm the guy Arlen's been writing to. The one who wrote that song."

"You're Nadelman?"

"That's right. May I come up?" Without waiting for a reply he continued climbing, fueled by the nervousness he'd been feeling all weekend.

"Arly's out," she was saying, as he rounded the final flight. There was the trace of an accent in her voice, but he couldn't place it. By the time he reached her front door, panting despite his workouts at the gym, she had the chain on the door.

"I ain't so sure I ought to let you in."

He saw a pale slice of her head, wavering back and forth in the opening, as if to give him the fullest view possible. Her mouth was grim.

"Jesus, Mrs. Huntoon," he said, catching his breath. "I came an awfully long way to see you two." He'd be damned if he'd go trotting back down those stairs.

"Well, I guess he's due home soon." The door closed, and he heard a scrabbling against the wood; then it opened to admit him. "This place ain't fit to be seen. We don't get many visitors." She was still shaking her head over some private worry. He recognized her from the photograph, a small, stout, grey-haired woman with a face like a Cabbage Patch doll. She had not, then, been the one who took the pictures.

"I would have called first," he said, "but you don't seem to have a phone."

The woman frowned, still distracted. "No, they came and took it." She looked around, scratching at the creases in her forehead. The house dress she wore was wrinkled and not very clean, as if she'd been asleep in it. "Arly's going to be here soon enough, I guess. He'll be surprised we got a visitor."

Clearly visitors were rare. The front room, with a threadbare rug and one small window to let in the light, was a jumble of cushions, old clothes, and magazines. Three broken-backed chairs were grouped like old-age pensioners around a large television with flares of aluminum foil attached with tape to its antenna. The room obviously saw a lot of use; there were dirty cups and dishes on the little table in front of the TV, and the air smelled faintly of garbage. Dog-eared issues of *Prevention, Fate,* and *TV Guide* lay strewn about the furniture, cookie crumbs sprinkled on their covers. Lying on one of the chairs, spine cracked, was a paperback: *Stranger Than Science—73 Fully Documented Case Histories That Science Is Powerless to Explain.*

"This place has gone to pot ever since Arly got laid off," said the woman, settling herself in the chair by the window. Nadelman sat tentatively beside her.

"How long ago was that?"

"Just after Labor Day. All they said was they didn't want him to drive for them anymore. He had a perfect safety record."

"Who'd he work for?"

"A firm in Valley Stream. They deliver to stores—albums and things. Green Acres, Gimbels, other places. That's how he got interested in that music." She pursed her lips. "They said he was stealing, but you and I both know he wasn't. He was just listening to the songs."

Nadelman nodded. "That's a shame. I'm glad, at least, that my song was one of them."

"Oh, he's a fan of yours. He loves your work, Arly does."

From outside came the crunch of gravel in the driveway. They heard a car motor stop, followed by the slamming of a door. Mrs. Huntoon inclined her face slightly toward the window, her eyes narrowing. "It's him now. He's going to get a surprise, seeing you here." She looked worried.

"One reason I came," said Nadelman, seizing what time was left to speak to the woman alone, "was to see your son's handiwork—the thing he based on my song. Is it still up there on the roof?"

She shook her head, the loose flesh below her chin wobbling back and forth for emphasis. "No, no, that's all gone. It was just up there for a couple of nights. Arly only meant it as a joke."

Nadelman smiled. "Yes, I thought so."

Downstairs a door slammed; they heard heavy footsteps on the stairs. "That'll be Arly," she said. Struggling to her feet, she went to the door and opened it. "Arly," she shouted, "guess who decided to pay us a visit." A grunt sounded amid the footsteps from the stairwell. "It's the one who wrote that song."

"Holy shit!" Moments later a large, hatchet-faced man burst into the apartment, looking more surprised than pleased. He was dressed like a redneck, in boots, sideburns, and a battered leather jacket. In his arms was an assortment of lumber with rusty nails protruding from it. "So you're Mr. Nadelman," he said.

Nadelman stood. "I wanted to call first," he said quickly, "but you don't have a phone."

Huntoon regarded him skeptically, then nodded. "Well, you're here now, so make yourself at home." From beneath the lumber he stuck out a huge hand. "I just got back from the dump over in Oceanside," he said, holding out the wood as if in evidence. "Had to get rid of some trash." He gave Nadelman a meaningful look, hinting at complicity. Nadelman pictured the creature from the photograph being summarily dumped into a garbage bin. "And look what I found there!" he said, leaning the wood in the corner. "This is all stuff I can use."

Nadelman eyed the rows of rusty nails. "You really like to build things, don't you?"

The other rubbed his hands and nodded. "Got me a real genius for it. Just like you've got one for magic." With a sudden look of guilt, his glance darted to the wall behind Nadelman's head. "You know, I really did mean to frame your letter," he said. "I just haven't gotten around to it."

"Oh, I don't care about that," said Nadelman. "What I came out for was to talk."

Huntoon grinned. "Yeah, I kind of thought you'd want to talk to me sooner or later." He seated himself in the largest chair and kicked off his boots, propping his feet on the table. "I had a premonition you'd be coming to me."

Nadelman sat down across from him, trying not to breathe too much of Huntoon's socks. "I haven't been avoiding you," he said. "I'd have contacted you before, if there'd been any way of reaching you."

"Oh, there are ways," said Huntoon. "There are ways of reaching anyone. I should think you'd know one or two yourself." Beside him his mother nodded solemnly.

"I'm afraid I depend on the telephone."

"Yeah?" Huntoon sounded annoyed. "What you want one of them things for? They just waste your money, and people talk nothing but nonsense and gossip about you behind your back."

"That's true," said Nadelman, like a nervous courtier. "Some people can be pretty malicious. Is that one of your, um . . . problems? I mean, with the Bravermans?"

Huntoon shook his head. "I don't have any problems with the Bravermans."

"They're away," the old woman added. "I heard Mrs. Braverman say they were going away. Florida, I think. Somewhere like that."

"Who are these people, anyway?" asked Nadelman. He decided to pursue this line until he met some resistance; then he'd back off.

"They're our neighbors." Huntoon smiled. "If you want to call 'em that."

"Yes, I saw the name," said Nadelman. "They live downstairs."

Huntoon's eyes narrowed; his smile grew wolfish. "Maybe they do and maybe they don't."

"They went away," said Mrs. Huntoon.

"I get the impression," said Nadelman, "that there's no love lost between you."

Huntoon shrugged. "Let's just say we had some differences of opinion about a few things."

"Like what?"

"Like where you walk a dog, and about leaving dog shit all over a roof when there are people living down here who happen to want to walk up there."

So that was it, Nadelman thought. Now he understood. It didn't seem like much to him, but it obviously bothered the hell out of Huntoon. "In that case," he said, "I don't blame you for wanting to throw a good scare into them."

Huntoon snickered. "We threw a scare into them, all right! Didn't we, Mama?"

Mrs. Huntoon nodded. "And they won't be coming back too soon."

"I'll bet!" said Nadelman. He tried to imagine what the effigy on the roof must have looked like to someone walking up there in the dark. Or worse, Huntoon himself, dressed up as he had been in the photo. For all he knew, the poor bastards had fled the state, they'd been so scared. "Well, I guess things'll be cleaner up there for a while," he said. "Any chance I could go up and walk around?" He was looking for a way to get the other alone, where it would be easier to talk.

Huntoon shrugged. "Suit yourself. There's nothing up there now. But we'll go, if you want."

The old woman reached for his arm. "Arly, you don't want to take him on the roof."

"Is there a problem?" asked Nadelman, already standing but ready to sit down again. The worry in the woman's voice made him think of Rhoda's words this morning, and he had a sudden vision of the burly Huntoon heaving him over the edge.

"No," said Huntoon, "no problem. No problem at all." He reached for his boots. "Come on, we'll take a look around."

The roof was one remaining flight up the stairs in the hall. At the top stood a dented iron door, partially ajar and letting in cold air. Huntoon pushed through it, bright grey sky filling the doorway. From the distance came the sound of children's voices.

"See? Nothing here. Just like I told you." He gestured around.

Nadelman followed the sweep of his hand, not seeing anything he remembered from the photographs. The flat rooftop reminded him of an arena. He took deep gulps of the untainted air and gazed at the line of hotels in the distance, like monstrous spectators.

"You're right," he said. "Of course, I've known that since Friday. Your message said the thing had disappeared."

The other cocked his head, suddenly coy. "Yeah, that's right—it did."

"Where is it now?" asked Nadelman, already suspecting the answer. "At the dump?" If Huntoon had hauled the thing out there today, he'd probably had a good reason. Perhaps it had scared the Bravermans so badly that he'd thought it best to get rid of it.

Huntoon crossed his arms. "Maybe it's at the dump, and maybe it isn't. Maybe it came back last night—and maybe it didn't. I'm not saying anything without a lawyer."

"Why in the world would you need a lawyer?" asked Nadelman. Huntoon reminded him of a child who has a secret and wants everyone in the world to know it.

"Maybe I do and maybe I don't. That's for you and the rest of them to find out."

His mixture of bravado and evasiveness made Nadelman uncomfortable. Huntoon was big, and the roof was very high. "Well, it's none of my business anyway," he said. "I'm just glad I could help solve your little problem." He looked around. "At least I don't see any dog shit."

"You won't," Huntoon said bitterly. "I cleaned it up last night. Took me nearly two hours." He examined the roof with a critical eye. "But now that it's light, I see I missed a thing or two." He stooped down and picked up something that gleamed in the waning sunlight.

"What's that?" asked Nadelman.

"Hold out your hand," said Huntoon, coming toward him. Nadelman backed away, the smaller boy on the playground. "Come on, hold out your hand. I'm not gonna hurt you." He dropped the thing into Nadelman's upturned palm.

Nadelman examined it. It was a jagged splinter of glass nearly two inches long and red as a ruby. He handed it back to Huntoon, remembering with distaste the shards of glass he'd seen in the early photograph, where the thing's hands should have been.

"Is this from where I think it's from?" he asked. "From your, uh, servant?"

Huntoon gave him a guarded look. "He's your servant just as much as mine. Seems to me, in fact, that he'd rather take his orders from you."

The man's use of the present tense unnerved him. "Well, at least you've finally solved the servant problem!"

Huntoon didn't smile. "Maybe so."

"And was this glass part of him?"

For a moment the other looked pleased. "Sure is," he said. "I threw in a couple of busted windows."

"Windows?" The thing had been bright red. "You mean, from a church?"

Huntoon shrugged. "A church, a temple—who gives a shit?" With a casual swipe of his arm he tossed it over the edge of the roof. "Come on, let's get out of here. I'm frozen."

Perhaps it was the power of suggestion, but Nadelman was shivering by the time they got back to the apartment.

After being out on the roof, he found the air inside even more sour; he could almost taste it. If he lingered here, it was possible that he could draw something more out of Huntoon, some hint as to the sources of his power, but he doubted he could stand being around the man much longer.

"I'm going to have to be leaving soon," he announced, as they sat facing one another across the little Formica table in the kitchen. They had moved here not because Huntoon had offered him anything to eat, but because the old woman was watching a game show on TV in the living room. "It's getting late, and there are only two trains left today." He would never be home before dark.

"Naw, it ain't late," said Huntoon, suddenly affable. He shoved his wrist toward Nadelman's face, like a feinted punch. Strapped to his wrist was a black plastic digital watch. "See? Just after three."

"You're kidding." Nadelman checked his Tourneau. It was already past four. "I hate to tell you, Arlen, but that watch of yours must be broken." He smiled cautiously. "Unless you operate on a different time from the rest of us."

Huntoon burst into laughter, echoing the TV in the next room. "*I* knew you were too smart to fall for it!" He tapped the face of his watch. "I keep this sucker set seventy minutes behind."

"Why?"

He flashed an extravagant grin. "To fuck people up. I hate it when people peek at my watch, you know? Let 'em buy one of their own."

Nadelman nodded. "Interesting." He had to get out of this place. Rhoda had been more right than she knew. "And now, I think I'm going to have to head back to the city."

Huntoon seemed to digest this, disappointment warring with relief. "Well, just hold on a second. There's something I want to show you." He leaned across the table, which bore a tiny plastic salt and pepper set in the shape of lobsters. "You gotta see my invention first. For playing albums backwards."

"Oh, right, right." Huntoon had written him about this. "I remember. Where is it?"

The other jerked his head toward the doorway. "In my room."

Huntoon's bedroom was the sort that would have intrigued Nadelman in the days of his boyhood two towns away, but now it looked like nothing but a junk shop, a particularly unsavory one. The shelves that filled one wall were laden with objects—souvenirs, talismans, a plastic crystal ball—that, standing alone, might have preserved a certain integrity; but piled atop one another, they resembled a gallery of fetishes. A tiny octopus floated like an extracted organ in a jar of preservative. A smooth white shard of what looked like broken china was in fact, Nadelman later realized, a section of skull, not necessarily human. He recognized the thin aluminum rod leaning in the corner by the window as a mail-order blowgun; he might have mistaken it for a fishing pole, had not his own son once tried to order one from a catalogue. There were other weapons, too—a machete dangling from the knob on the closet door, and, along the bottom shelf, bayonets and sheath knives and a set of tiny silver throwing stars. Piles of paperbacks rested here and there against the walls, worming their way ceilingward like stalagmites. On the bookshelves *Slaves of the Gestapo* rubbed shoulders with *Psychic Self-Defense. Your Sexual Key to the Tarot* lay open on the nightstand, resting on a copy of *Symphony of the Lash.* Opposite the window hung a large color poster of Jizzmo—Rocco at the drums, mouth open wide in a silent scream; Ray clutching a mike, eyes glaring like a maniac's—and another of a group called Death Orchid. Taped above the unmade bed was a large pastel mandala, 1960s-style, with a familiar-looking upside-down star crayoned over it: the creep world's version of the have-a-nice-day smiley face. Their trademark popped up everywhere.

"Mama never comes in here," Huntoon said off-handedly, fiddling with a turntable on the floor by the bed. "I don't allow her to. She'd just mess everything up."

"Are these things safe?" asked Nadelman, nervously examining a knife whose handle was a set of brass knuckles.

"Oh, yeah. You just have to know how to use 'em."

"Are they actually, um, legal?"

"Hell, yes!" said Huntoon, suddenly angry. "That's another thing about old man Braverman. He damn near got me in trouble with the law."

"What do you need all these weapons for anyway?" asked Nadelman. He had taken a position near the doorway.

"I've got to protect my mother, don't I? I mean, Mama's housebound. She don't go out anymore."

The logic seemed twisted, but Nadelman didn't pursue it, for by this time Huntoon had dragged forth his invention. It looked straightforward enough, a turntable mounted on a wooden base with an overturned motor to drive it in reverse via a short rubber belt. Eyes glistening with excitement, Huntoon played two cuts backward from a Judas Priest album, but Nadelman was unable to make out the references to Satan that the other assured him were there.

Huntoon then did the same with Jizzmo's *Walpurgis Night.* "It's even harder to pick up on this one," he explained, playing a section of "New God on the Block" and nodding in time to the music. "You really gotta know what you're listening for." But all Nadelman could hear was an alien wail that rose and fell endlessly, close enough to human to be frightening.

He studied the Jizzmo poster on the opposite wall. "Did you perform the Invocation in here?"

Huntoon looked up, startled. "No," he said. "On the roof. Don't you remember? You gotta do it underneath the stars—'beneath the void of space.'"

"Oh, yeah, that's right," said Nadelman, abashed to have forgotten his own poem. He felt more than ever like an imposter. "Speaking of that god of mine, there's something I've been meaning to ask you. How'd you know I called the thing 'The Hungerer'? Even *I* didn't remember that."

"I told you in the letter—He spoke to me."

"But how did he . . . communicate?"

"You know," said Huntoon. "The way a god's supposed to talk to you."

"You mean, like, with a Ouija board?" Even as he said it, he knew that it wasn't the right answer.

Huntoon eyed him suspiciously, as if the other were putting him on. "Come off it, that stuff's for old ladies."

"Did a voice speak inside your mind, like the born-agains claim?"

Huntoon shook his head. "No, sir, I heard Him just as plain as I hear you. Just the other night, too. It's like the song says. I heard Him in the thunder."

Nadelman almost gasped. "And that's when he told you his name?"

The other nodded.

"Well—" Nadelman chose his words carefully—"it certainly came as news to me."

Huntoon's wolfish features widened in a grin. "Oh, come on, pal. You knew! Maybe it was even you that named Him."

Later, pondering Huntoon's words as he descended the stairs to the front entrance, Nadelman recalled the unpleasant odor of garbage in the man's apartment, and realized that the smell had been the strongest in Huntoon's bedroom.

Hurrying away from that house and eager to escape from the Huntoons' squalid little neighborhood, he took deep breaths of the chilly air. It tasted good to him. But now he was hungry; Huntoon, that *goyische* jackass, had never thought to offer him so much as a glass of water. He knew he'd probably be able to find a candy bar at the station, but he yielded instead to the demands of his empty stomach and to the rush of nostalgia that had gripped him earlier that afternoon. He would make a brief pilgrimage to one more childhood haunt, the boardwalk several blocks away.

He knew it wouldn't be the same; it couldn't be. In those days, when he'd spent whole week-long stretches of his summers with his mother's brother's family at their rented yellow bungalow on Michigan Street, the street names had been a way of learning the states, the skies had been much bluer, the boardwalk down the block a place of fun and danger, of Ski-Ball coupons you collected for a prize, jelly apples that got you sticky, and dizzying Tilt-a-Whirl rides that rivaled Coney Island's. The town's commercial district, in his memory, was a frontier outpost to which one made forays, accompanied always by grownups, to stock up on comic books and candy, and to thumb endless stacks of pennies into the charm machines at the supermarket. The bland suburban landscape he found himself in now, on this grey November afternoon, was like waking up after a dream.

Checking the time once more before the last train, he strode past a succession of nearly deserted streets that led down to the boardwalk, hidden in places by the shabby residential hotels that crowded up to it like great beasts before a wooden trough. Just off the main thoroughfare he found a brightly lit coffee shop at the end of a row of darkened stores; it was one of the few places he'd seen that still looked open.

There were only four people inside. The quiet fit his mood. An elderly man down the counter to his right was holding a newspaper up to his face, peering at the classifieds with the intensity of a lost motorist studying a map. It was Saturday's *Post*, already limp and tattered, grown old along with yesterday's news. Periodically the man would tap the ash from his cigarette into his empty coffee cup.

Nadelman, ordering a cheeseburger and a Coke, found his gaze drawn, as it inevitably was, to the headline: SAMARITAN CRUSHED RETURNING 50¢. Another poor slob who had fallen victim to some god or other. When his burger arrived, he stared at the greasy reddish liquid oozing from it onto his plate and, momentarily sickened, thought of a slaughter-house floor. Pushing the plate away, he ordered a melted cheese and tomato on toast.

What he really needed was to think. Reviewing the events of the afternoon, he realized what inflated expectations he'd come with; he had arrived at Huntoon's half convinced, or at least hoping, that the man would prove to be a kind of home-grown sorcerer, wise and benign, the suburban version of some character out of Castaneda. He would reveal how he'd magically read Nadelman's mind or, with equal magic, gained entrance into Nadelman's private files. Anything to affirm that the god they had talked of so familiarly was merely a shared fiction.

But Huntoon had affirmed nothing. Indeed, judging from the stench in his room, he already had the makings of another creature hidden in his closet. And he'd refused to explain away The Hungerer.

Worse, in their final conversation Huntoon had all but suggested not only that the god was a reality, but that Nadelman himself was responsible for its existence.

Nadelman swirled the watery amber of his Coke and wondered if it could be true. *"Maybe,"* Huntoon had said, *"it was even you that named Him"*—as if, on that forgotten day thirty years ago when he'd first inscribed "The Hungerer" in his crisp new leather notebook, he had introduced something new into the universe, something conjured up within his brain, a being that had sprung into existence with the mere stroke of his pen. Unless, of course, he had dreamed it into existence, his notebook entry a mere record of the fact, a kind of birth certificate. Who could say where it had actually begun?

Was it possible?—that in some latter-day Naming of Names, he had given the god life in the very act of naming it, and given it substance with every new line of his poem?

How weird that would be: the notion that the universe might in fact be listening to him, waiting upon his decisions, his carefully chosen words, responding to his commands. How had that line from the poem gone? *"'I'll create Me a Creator,' He would say"*—a god made to order!

But what a dreadful responsibility to contemplate! For it meant that he might in some way be the original cause of the very things that had always horrified and appalled him, all the work of the dark god he'd invented: the fathers stabbed, the mothers raped, the children left to starve.

To his right the old man stood and, before leaving, pointedly slid the paper toward him, proffering another cause for guilt, another death for which he was responsible: that hapless fifty-cent Samaritan.

The pages of the newspaper were greasy, but he couldn't resist reading the story. The night clerk of a small midtown hotel had stepped out for his usual evening's sandwich. Upon returning to his post, he'd discovered that the cashier in the all-night deli had given him half a dollar's extra change; and, being an honest man and a good Christian, he'd informed his superior that he was going back to return it. Halfway there, he'd been killed by a heavy chunk of cornice that had broken off the ledge of a building.

It was too perfect. The god had shown His hand too clearly. Dumb! Why, they'd be onto Him any day now.

He forced himself to scan the other stories, toying with the possibility that he was responsible for each of them as well. A Jersey mother and four kids had been killed when a drunk teenaged driver veered from his lane and plowed head-on into her car. (The teenager was in serious condition in a Passaic hospital, but Nadelman presumed he'd pull through.) Five members of a family in the Bronx, four of them children, had died in a fire that night. Arson was suspected. (And surely in the background there lurked a spurned husband, jealous lover, or unscrupulous landlord; and behind him, a god.) Police were still searching for the head of the dispatcher employed by a local trucking firm, whose mutilated body had been found earlier that week in the company's Long Island warehouse. The article hinted at Mafia connections. (Nadelman suspected that the hit man would never be caught.)

Could something he'd created be responsible for such carnage? It was inconceivable.

Nadelman paid and, pocketing his change, crossed the empty street and strolled the three blocks to the boardwalk. The beach beyond looked grey and ragged, littered near the water's edge with mounds of wood and garbage that had been washed up by the tide and would have to be removed before summer. Two old women in black overcoats were picking their way carefully over the sand, their backs bowed with age or concentration. Seagulls screamed overhead. Beyond the tide marks the ocean plunged and retreated, hungry and disconsolate, spilling its power across a narrow barrier of sand.

Prey to its mood, he ascended the ramp to the boardwalk. The sun was sinking toward the line of buildings to the west; beyond them, far below the horizon, lay the city. Nadelman turned his back to the blinding glare and walked in the direction of an overturned life-guard's stand, watching his shadow stretch an impossibly long way down the rough wood of the boardwalk.

Aged figures sat unmoving as gargoyles on the benches, many of them in yarmulkes, silently watching the ocean. There was nothing else for them here; everything was boarded up now—the few food stands that had not been torn down, a tiny row of game booths whose corrugated metal gates were covered with graffiti. AMUSE-MENT ARCADE, the sign said, the letters cracked and peeling.

He had known, in some buried memory, that it would be like this; he and his father or friends had often come here in the winter. This time of year had its own austere beauty—cold, lonely, and bracing. But the boardwalk was different today. The once grand hotels, which, even when he'd been a boy, had had a certain faded glamor, were now turned into rest homes and nursing homes, though they had kept their old names—the Paradise, the Palace, the King David Manor—as if in hope of some future resurrection. Elderly faces gazed blankly from their windows. Some of the figures who sat huddled on the benches out front, bundled up like babies, looked more dead than alive. One old bearded man sat folded up like a jackknife, eyes shut. Here and there tall black attendants stood like sentries beside rows of unmoving figures in aluminum wheelchairs, or walked with aching slowness down the boardwalk while their bent and shrunken charges clutched their arms. A bike rider sped by, wheels thrumming on the boards, then a jogger with a Walkman. Several of the younger faces Nadelman passed struck him as crazy: vacant of expression, or with a birdlike glint of lunacy in their eyes. One gaunt man in a rain-coat and scarf was talking angrily to himself, but stopped for several seconds as Nadelman approached, as if still touched by remnants of embarrassment. Nadelman felt sorriest for the ones who stared bleakly at the sea; he wished that he could conjure up a ship for them to watch, or even a small fishing boat. But the ocean, clear to the horizon, was as empty as a desert.

A waning of the light reminded him that it was time to return; the wind was cold, and he had to get back to the city. He turned and retraced his steps, the light no longer blinding now, the sun settled behind further layers of cloud and the distant hotels' ornamented roofs. Ocean and sand seemed bathed in a sad, nostalgic glow, the final scene in some half-remembered travelogue. Ahead of him the brown strip of the boardwalk receded almost to the vanishing point, then curved gently toward the water.

Something in the quality of the light released a few stray child-hood memories, images from an ancient slide show. He remembered walking just this stretch of boardwalk as a boy, staring at that same almost-vanishing point. He'd been happy, he remembered; but of course, it hadn't taken much in those days: a pinwheel, a few unbroken seashells, a mass of cotton candy on a white paper cone, the anticipation of a Cracker Jack prize. Today the world was changed, or rather, it was he who had changed; he felt as if everything he gazed upon—the boardwalk, sea, and sand—were doomed to pass away with the dying light, and that the passing would be bitter.

It occurred to him at that moment that there was a third and more likely explanation for the crabbed words that his boy self had written in the notebook—one that explained, as well, the source of Huntoon's knowledge. It was, quite simply, that he hadn't invented the god after all, hadn't created Him in giving Him a name; imagina-tion had had nothing to do with it. The being that he feared, this force, this plague, *really existed,* and had existed long before he'd ever become aware of it. He'd had only the briefest glimpse of it; that bee sting on the hand had been only a warning. And in recording those two words in his notebook, he had set down its identity as faithfully as any good reporter.

Hadn't there, in fact, been one particular moment of vision, when the glimpse had come? He was sure that there was; it lay just off the edge of his memory—a day long ago, in the faintly lurid world of his childhood, when the god had made His presence known.

The more seriously Nadelman considered the possibility—with each new step westward, back toward the place from which he'd started—the more certain he became. And with the certainty came memories, long-buried snapshots floating lazily to the surface of a pool, soggy but still recognizable after years of lying hidden in the depths.

He remembered—it *felt* like a memory—a certain morning; a haze across the sun; pussy willows in a patch of woods. Spring. He'd been on his way to school, well pleased with the world, a Scout knife in his pocket, or a magazine to sneak into class, or maybe his brand-new leather notebook; school in those days had not yet grown oppressive. He remembered the warmth of the sunlight, the smell of the buds on the trees, like tiny green sprigs of broccoli, the slap of his shoes on the sidewalk, the sound of birds, the unnerving buzz of bees . . .

How strange to think it could have happened then, for morning had represented safety to him in those days, ever since his earliest childhood. Often waking long before dawn, he would greet the morning with a sigh of relief, free at last to lie back and let his guard down, the terrors of the night survived once more, the world returned again to visibility, the noise of traffic, the comforting presence of people on the street, whistlers on the sidewalk, human footsteps, voices. Everything would be all right if only he could hold out till morning.

But this one morning had been different. Something had intruded on the day—a darkness suddenly filling the sky, like the dark before a storm, only much worse: for in this darkness lurked the suggestion of a face . . .

Wait. Was that a real memory, or merely the memory of a dream he'd once had? It was maddeningly hard to be sure.

Or had the vision perhaps come at home? For now another memory had surfaced, of lying alone and ill in bed one afternoon in his old room, where pastel animals smiled from the wallpaper and, through the window by his head, the shingles of a neighboring roof curled brown and familiar through the maples.

Yes, he remembered now. He had lain there staring dazedly at the ceiling, listening to a distant airplane recede in wave upon wave of sound—and suddenly he had heard in it a note of horror, the whisper of a monstrous voice that spoke and sang and threatened.

Unless, of course, that, too, had been a dream. Or a boy's half-delirious fantasy.

But dream or daydream, what was it he had heard at that moment? What secret had he stumbled upon, back there in the hazy light of his childhood, that he'd recorded so cryptically—yet so correctly—in his notebook?

He no longer knew. All mysteries paled beside that of his own vanished past. He walked on, the boardwalk wide and empty before him, but he felt as if he'd come to a dead end. The trail had simply disappeared, like words on a blackboard wiped clean with a swipe of the eraser; like the long-demolished houses on his old block.

And then a gull cried sharply, hungrily, above him, and he remembered.

He hadn't been in bed or on his way to school. It had happened here, on this very stretch of beach, at the height of the summer, with the ocean filled with bathers and the cloudless sky an eggshell blue.

Something had inexplicably felt wrong; a terror had come over his young heart as he walked along the sand. A sudden insight. A vision. For a moment the view overhead had flickered, as from a loose connection—a momentary darkening of the sun—and he'd thought he glimpsed a face that leered across the sky, too wide for him to take it all in: a vast inhuman shape that grinned and mocked, like a figure gazing down into a fishbowl . . .

But might not this, too, be mere fantasy—some infantile memory of a face peering into his crib, but blurred now, dimmed, distorted by the intervening decades until, gigantic and malevolent, it filled the sky?

The boardwalk on which he was retracing his steps appeared to reach to the horizon. He tore his gaze from the vanishing point in the distance, where all lines converged in the furnace of the sun, to stare at the beach beyond the boardwalk's iron railings. And as he did so, the memory leaped into focus.

Something, he remembered, had happened to him there, down on the sand; something had tripped him—a bump, a stone, a piece of driftwood, an uprearing in the earth . . .

No, that wasn't it; he remembered now. Just as the sky darkened, beneath the glare of eyes as big as galaxies, he had felt his foot slide, then sink into a hollow in the sand. And the sand had opened beneath him, then pressed in upon him, clutched him, tried to draw him in. As if the earth were yearning to crush him, smother him, blot out the very memory of him. As if the planet, all nature, all creation, the very fabric of reality, were inimical to beings of his kind.

And hadn't it all happened on this very stretch of beach? Wasn't this the very spot where, on that long-forgotten day, he'd first had an inkling of the truth?

All gods yielded before the implacable demands of habit. Monday saw him back at the office, his schedule unchanged, dutifully laboring on the Holiday Farm account. He put in a full day on it, skipping his session at the gym and working right through lunch, his only departure from routine. It was as if, by sheer industriousness, he could shore up the props of his life that had begun to slip away. Even he was aware of it, at odd points in the day; pinning a selection of cherry-tree sketches to the cork board by his desk, he saw himself, for a moment, as a man frantically papering over the holes in his home, layer upon layer, while around him walls crumbled and fell.

Those same walls trembled and nearly collapsed when, leaving work meticulously at five-thirty, pleased with the thought that, on the way home, he would complete some early Christmas shopping before the stores closed, he rode down in the elevator crowded with

lower-ranking members of the office staff and heard the new receptionist complain to one of the secretaries about the crank calls she'd
been getting all afternoon.

"And when I'd say hello, no one would answer. I don't know who
they thought they were trying to annoy."

He felt more guilty than angry, like the father of a psychopath, a
father who had failed to warn the world. He knew that the calls were
meant for him, that behind them, repulsively, leered Arlen Huntoon,
and that they'd somehow been provoked by his previous day's excur-
sion. *I never should have bothered going out there,* he told himself. *I'll
have that creep pursuing me till the grave.*

At work the next day Nadelman hurried past the receptionist,
avoiding his usual small talk. He felt sure that, face to face with her,
he'd betray his guilty secret, and at the end of the day he refrained
from asking her the question foremost in his mind: whether she'd
received any more mysterious calls.

His question, nonetheless, was answered soon enough, for at
dinner that evening another such call came to Nadelman's home. It
was picked up in the kitchen by Michael, for whom answering the
phone was still more an adventure than a chore.

"Hello?" The boy's voice, as always, was eager, as if a present
awaited him at the other end of the line. Nadelman watched his son's
expression nervously, waiting for the next response. The boy pressed
the phone to his ear, then frowned, confused. "Hello?"

Nadelman was out of his chair and across the room in an instant,
taking the phone from Michael's hands. "Hello!" he said sharply. The
phone might as well have been dead. "Hey, Huntoon," he yelled,
aware that his wife and son were listening, "now you're really getting
me angry! I wish you and your mother would just get the hell out of
my life! I swear to God, you should be locked up!"

He slammed the phone back into its cradle; then, thinking better
of it, he lifted it again and switched off the ringer. "Now at least we'll
get some peace and quiet around here."

And they did. Once more the world was kept at bay—until
Thursday of the same week, when Nadelman's secretary buzzed him

as he sat writing in his office, a DO NOT DISTURB sign on his door, to tell him that a man was waiting to see him in the reception area.

"I don't see any appointments written down," he said crossly, already thinking of Huntoon and wishing there were a back door to his office through which he could sneak out.

"He doesn't have an appointment," said the secretary. Then, puzzled, relaying the message third-hand: "He says he doesn't need one. It's someone named Sergeant Berkey."

Could this be a joke? The only Berkey that Nadelman knew was an account executive at Kone, Ruderman, who'd been in charge of the Life-Saver campaign.

"Find out what he wants."

There was a pause. "Denise says he's a police officer."

Nadelman felt his insides knot. Bodies in the morgue, grainy photos in the *Post*—he could already picture them: Rhoda, Michael, smiling the inane, pathetic smiles of the world's front-page victims. He swallowed, wondering which one it would be.

"Send him in."

He opened his office door, then sat down again to wait, already seeing himself as the father, the husband—the one who is told the terrible news. Sharon was returning, leading a middle-aged man in a blue patrolman's uniform. Nadelman's heart beat faster. She ushered the man into the office and closed the door behind him.

Once he saw the man's distracted smile, Nadelman knew he had nothing to fear. The other stood with cop's hat in hand, gazing out the window past Nadelman s head.

"Nice view," he said with just a touch of envy, sinking heavily into one of the low leather chairs facing the desk. He studied Nadelman's face. "I'm Sergeant Berkey. We tracked you down here from the address on your stationery."

Stationery? How had the police seen his stationery? But the officer was peering at a black leatherette notepad. "The reason I'm here, Mr. Nadelman, is that we've found the bodies of two friends of yours—" He flipped a page. "A Mr. Arlen Huntoon and a Mrs. Linia Huntoon."

"My God!"

So the *Post* had claimed someone after all. Relief flooded through him—relief that, if someone had to die, it had been those two—followed immediately by guilt. That poor old woman!

"When?" he asked. "How?" Hadn't the mother said something about an ex-boss of Arlen's, someone he'd quarreled with? Or had those downstairs neighbors finally come back for revenge? The Huntoons had seemed to have a lot of enemies.

Berkey shook his head. "That's not for me to say, Mr. Nadelman. But I'll tell you this much, the guys out in Long Beach came across the two of 'em by accident, in the course of an entirely separate investigation—or at least they thought it was."

"What sort of investigation?"

The other looked down for a moment, tracing his finger around the sweatband of his hat. "I'm not really at liberty to say. The God's honest truth is, I'm here to see if you could answer a few questions."

"Of course." Nadelman waited, expecting the man to whip out a laminated card and read him his rights, but instead the other merely withdrew a ballpoint pen from his shirt pocket and opened the pad to a fresh page.

"Did you know the deceased?"

"Only slightly." Keeping his voice low, lest his secretary hear, Nadelman recounted some of the events that had led to his visit to their home this past weekend. There was no sense lying about it; hell, if the police already had possession of his letters, they certainly must know the main facts of the story.

"So why exactly was it you went out there?" Berkey sat forward, pen poised.

Nadelman shrugged. "Because I felt I was getting harassed by this guy—" Whoops, that sounded too hostile! "I mean I felt he was a nuisance for my family and me—" He saw the lawman laboriously writing down "nuisance," and felt better. "And since he didn't seem to own a phone, I figured I'd have to go out there and confront—I mean, talk to him. Believe me, it was the one and only time I ever met him."

The officer finished writing—were these guys really dumb, he wondered, or did they just play dumb, like Colombo?—and slipped the pen back in his pocket.

"Don't worry, Mr. Nadelman, you're not on the suspect list. We got a description of the guy, and it's nothing like you. A big galoot, I hear. I'm just checking up on a few facts." He flashed a smile; he had probably had a course or two in human relations. "We gotta do our job, you know? It's what all of us pay taxes for."

Nadelman tried to remember his final goodbye to the Huntoons, his march downstairs, hurrying outside to breathe the good air. He had left them both alive and smiling, unprotected. Had the murderer been watching, even then? Waiting, perhaps, for him to leave?

"As I mentioned," he said, "the last time I spoke to Huntoon, so far as I know, was Tuesday night—even though he didn't speak back. And when were the bodies discovered?"

Berkey scratched his thinning hair. "Wednesday morning, I think."

"So they couldn't have been dead for very long."

"I guess not. Lucky thing the officers out there were in the building, otherwise it could've been weeks. I get the impression those two didn't have many friends."

Nadelman nodded. "I got the same impression myself."

He hadn't been a friend of theirs either—*friends with those creeps? you've got to be kidding*—but for the rest of the day, after Berkey had fortified himself with one more envious glance out the office window and had departed, Nadelman couldn't shake the feeling that he had lost two colorful old comrades: a little eccentric, perhaps, but valued nonetheless. He felt unexpectedly downcast.

At least he did until he got home that night and discovered Huntoon's final message.

Rhoda had taken Michael to a classmate's eighth-birthday party and had left Nadelman some ham and cheese in the refrigerator for his dinner. The day's mail lay in a pile on the kitchen table, a scrap of paper atop it with the message, in Rhoda's jubilant handwriting: *Another one from guess who?* Nadelman immediately recognized the address label and its tiny red lobster.

Though he tried to be conscientious, Nadelman had always had trouble keeping up with the news; leafing through the paper in that Long Beach luncheonette last Sunday had been a rare diversion. Even his reading of the *Times* was, on weekdays, usually confined to the front page (if there were no gigantic headlines, the world was safe for another twenty-four hours), the opinion pages, and the business section for news about the advertising world. And so it wasn't surprising that, until he tore open Huntoon's final envelope, he hadn't seen the item it contained, a clipping cut from Tuesday's *Post* that Huntoon must have mailed the very day he'd been murdered.

L.I. DUMP GRAVE FOR SLAIN COUPLE, it read. A posed photo showed a workman in overalls, his face shadowed by the hardhat he wore, pointing to an equally shadowy depression in the mound of rubbish he was standing upon. "The bodies of an unidentified man and woman were discovered Monday morning by landfill engineers working at the county dump in Oceanside, Long Island," the article said. It noted that the bodies had been described by police as those of "an elderly white couple, apparently in their seventies," and that workmen had also found, lying beside them, "a large dog, probably a terrier."

It was the mention of the dog that did it. Nadelman, sickened, saw how naive he'd been. He remembered the smell from Huntoon's closet, and realized that what Huntoon had left out at the dump that morning had not been the creature at all.

It was them, it had to be. The old couple from downstairs.

He knew now why the police had paid a visit to the Huntoons' apartment yesterday. They'd obviously had time to identify the dead as Mr. and Mrs. Braverman.

Judging by the state of decomposition, the article said, the pair had not been buried long; the deaths were believed to have occurred over the weekend. The bodies had been, in one detective's phrase—which the *Post* repeated as the article's subhead—"slashed to ribbons." Remembering the broken glass on Huntoon's roof, Nadelman shuddered.

Written at the top, in Huntoon's heavy hand—the crazy, boastful creep!—was, *"Dont worry I'd never let it hurt YOU."*

———

Standing beneath a streetlight by a Second Avenue newsstand, his shoulders hunched against the evening's chill, Nadelman peered hurriedly through the two tabloids he'd just bought. He felt like a fugitive, furtively scanning the pages for an affirmation of his crime.

The report in the *News* was restrained, almost disappointingly so.

HUNT FOR MURDER CLUES YIELDS TWO MORE DEATHS
Nassau County police, attempting to identify the elderly man and woman whose bodies were discovered Monday in a dump outside Oceanside, L.I., yesterday stumbled upon two more bodies in the course of the investigation, police spokesmen said. The first victims have been identified as Leo Braverman, 76, and his wife Flora, 73, of Locust Court in Long Beach. The two most recent victims were Linia Huntoon, in her late 70s, and her son Arlen, 33, fellow tenants in the same apartment building.

The *Post* put it more flamboyantly—SOUTH SHORE SLASHER CLAIMS VICTIMS 4 & 5—and it included a photograph of the Bravermans, both of them small, plump, and white-haired, taken on what looked like a Miami Beach vacation. The woman was smiling, though her smile hadn't saved her; the man appeared more grave, as if he'd known where the photo would someday appear. "The bodies of the Long Beach couple, along with their pet dog, were found Monday morning by workers in the Oceanside town dump," the article said.

Nadelman was puzzled by the headline (how had the body count reached five?—were they counting the dog?), until his eye fell on a later paragraph identifying the first victim as "Esteban Farella, 46, chief dispatcher at the Val-U-Rite Delivery Service in Valley Stream, whose headless body was found last week."

Nadelman caught his breath, remembering the story he'd read Sunday. He had failed to make the connection, but obviously the authorities had not—though they were clearly on the wrong track. "Police are still investigating a possible gangland motive," the paper said.

Despite the headline, slasher victims three and four were not pictured, but the story described Huntoon as "a former Val-U-Rite employee laid off last August."

Nadelman did no more than skim the rest, if only for self-protection—"the widowed mother . . . mangled remains . . . work of one man . . . reports of a figure seen leaving the building that night"—but he froze when he came to the story's final line: "Police said the bodies were discovered locked in the younger Huntoon's closet."

He closed the paper with trembling hands. His fingertips felt dirty. What was it Huntoon had said that day on the roof? Something about the servant preferring to take orders from Nadelman himself?

Yes, that's what he'd said. Nadelman remembered well enough. But he didn't remember precisely what he himself had yelled into the phone two nights ago, at what he'd thought was Huntoon—and was just as happy he did not.

The idea that anyone could be afraid of a dachshund was ridiculous, especially one as small as Nadelman's. She was called Brownie—the name, of course, had been given to her by Michael, who as yet had no stake in being clever—and she was a good-humored, comical little creature, trotting briskly up the sidewalk with the complacent smile of a young PTA mother. So it seemed extremely odd to Nadelman that one night during the week of Thanksgiving, as he walked the dog along Seventy-Sixth Street, a clear plastic baggie in hand, he saw two male pedestrians coming his way stop, squint at him, and scatter. One of them crossed to the other side of the street; the other turned and hurried back the way he'd come.

Puzzled, Nadelman wondered if they had been terrified of Brownie . . . or of him. Fancy, grown men so scared of a dachshund! Suddenly a third alternative dawned on him; but when he turned and scanned the sidewalk behind him, there was no one there.

On Wednesday afternoon of that same week—really the mere stump of a week, with only three days of work to endure—Rhoda took the car and drove up to Westchester with Michael and the dog. They would spend the night with her parents; Nadelman would join them on Thanksgiving. He'd claimed he had a Thursday morning meeting with an important soft-drink client who'd be flying into New York for the long weekend and had insisted on squeezing in some business obligations. In truth, he knew that Cele would be available—uniquely so. Because she was a foreigner the holiday meant little to her; she would simply be having dinner at a friend's.

"Some people have such a nerve!" said Rhoda, helping Michael pack on Wednesday morning.

"It'll only be an hour or so," said Nadelman. "Just one of those stuffy breakfast meetings at the Carlyle, with the sixteen-dollar scrambled eggs. I'll take the train up afterward, and you can pick me up at the station."

"Just leave room for the turkey," said Rhoda.

"And just you be sure to call me tonight before bedtime," he said, kissing her fondly on the cheek as he left for work.

He lingered at home that night until ten-thirty, when her call came. After chatting with her about the train schedule, he hung up and, leaving the phone off the hook, took a taxi down to Cele's.

Their night together was not all that Nadelman had hoped. Maybe it was nerves, or simple guilt, as if the unhooked phone back in his apartment were still sounding warning beeps in his ear.

He felt even more disturbed the next morning when, as Cele unlatched the front door and prepared to kiss him goodbye, she suddenly wrinkled up her delicate Slavic nose.

"Ugh, the people in this building, they are so disgusting!"

She pointed to a small irregular puddle in the hall just in front of her door. Nadelman, gingerly stepping over it with his overnight bag in hand, intent on getting to Grand Central in time, smelled a sour, fishy smell and thought for a moment of the house in Locust Court.

But that was an idea he immediately cast back into the pile. In truth, Cele's building *was* a bit shabby.

It was only when he was on the train to New Rochelle and had laid aside his *Advertising Age* and *Fortune* to watch the fleeting scenery that, as if suddenly touched by a trickle of ice water, he was struck by a vision of what might have left the puddle—something, he suspected, that had waited patiently by their door all night. But here on the train, with well-groomed suburban lanes rolling by beyond the window and the smell of the snack bar to whet his hunger, such visions were hard to believe in.

Still, he was glad his own building had a doorman.

One thing, at least, was certain, or so he told himself from time to time over the next few weeks: justice had been done. The creep had reaped exactly what he'd sown. His poem had hit it on the nose:

> *A god who smirks and says, "The joke's on you!"*

And the joke had been on Huntoon.

One later incident, at least, was almost certainly a product of Nadelman's imagination—though it was somewhat unnerving at the time. Alone in the kitchen one weekend afternoon in December, while Rhoda was in the bedroom getting ready to go to the supermarket, Nadelman peered into the refrigerator and yelled, "I need more roast coffee!"—at which point, as if on command, the brown paper trash bag in the corner obligingly collapsed in on itself and tipped over, spilling its contents, including a flood of old coffee grounds, onto the kitchen floor.

He avoided entering the kitchen again until the following week.

He began to mutter at odd times about "the servant problem." One day his secretary discovered a memo pad in his office on which he'd written half-distractedly: "There's a masked figure looking up at my window—I know that when I go out there, it'll be gone—What scares me is, what happens the day I go down & it's *not* gone?"

His final scare came one night just before Christmas, while his arms were laden with last-minute presents.

Most of his friends complained about the holidays—the pressures, the commercialism, the materialism—but Nadelman had always enjoyed them; they were one of the few times he was truly happy being a family man. He wasn't a Christian, but he celebrated Christmas of a sort. As he saw it, material goods gave the holiday its meaning, just as they did in days of old when pagans stuffed their larders with good food and drink. It was the season for shopping, something Nadelman enjoyed, just as he enjoyed, as a professional, the corny seasonal ads—Santa with the perennial Coke in hand, elves telephoning one another long distance to stay in touch.

Walking north on Third Avenue just a block from his home, he headed toward the only place still open on the block, a small neighborhood liquor store where he intended to buy some cognac or, even better, some Armagnac. As he passed the window of a toy shop, he paused out of habit to study it, even though the hour was late and the shop was closed. Suddenly, as if in warning, the shop lights dimmed—and as they did so, he noticed a figure reflected in the window, ghostly in the dim light and juxtaposed against the images of toys, games, and stuffed animals. For one crazy moment he took the reflection for his own, wildly distorted, or that of a fellow shopper wearing a paper bag over his head. Then something gleamed below the apparition's wrist, something small and jagged, and he recognized what was standing behind him.

Those in extreme situations are often known to drop what they're holding and run, but few have just paid $245 for a salmon-colored cashmere sweater and $110 for games and a new joystick for a son's Atari. Holding tight to his gifts, Nadelman took off down the block, legs flying. He didn't care that he almost bumped into the backs of a couple walking ahead of him, nor did he care what they probably

thought of him for shouting, "Leave me the hell alone!" as he ran.
He was far more concerned with whether his servant could hear him,
and whether it was still inclined to honor his commands.

Approaching the liquor store, Nadelman slowed down, preparing
to dash inside, but increased his speed again when he heard a sound
behind him that might have been the echoing tinkle of Christmas
chimes, but which sounded far more like the breaking of glass. He ran
on, footsteps pounding the sidewalk, sensing above him a vast face
that leered down from the cold sky. Ahead, on the corner, loomed
the stony grey mass of a synagogue, looking as solemn and solid as a
fortress. The ancient wooden front door, through which a group of
dark-coated worshippers had just passed, was slowly swinging shut.
Putting on a burst of speed, he hurried up the wide stone steps and
slipped inside.

The synagogue was Orthodox; he'd never set foot in one before.
A large gold menorah stood on a platform at the front, five candles
lit. A skeptical-looking attendant handed him a *yarmulke* as he came
in. Slapping it onto his head, he sat down in one of the rear pews,
brightly colored presents in his lap with pictures of Santa Claus and
reindeer, and gazed, still panting, at the high stone walls, the tapestries, the candles, the grave-looking figures depicted in the windows.
And hours later, when the attendant came to tell him it was time
to leave, he politely but firmly refused. He was willing to explain it
once, he would explain it a dozen times if necessary, and always with
infinite patience: he would not be moved, and he would not look
back, and he didn't intend to go outside until the night was over.
Everything would be all right if only he could make it through till
morning.